William Shaw has been shortlisted for the CWA Historical Dagger, longlisted for the Theakstons Crime Novel of the Year and nominated for a Barry Award. A regular at festivals, he organises panel talks and CWA events across the south east. Shaw is the author of the acclaimed Breen & Tozer crime series: *A Song from Dead Lips*, *A House of Knives*, *A Book of Scars* and *Sympathy for the Devil*; and the standalone bestseller *The Birdwatcher*. He is writing a new crime series starring the character DS Alexandra Cupidi from *The Birdwatcher*, the second of which is *Deadland*. He worked as a journalist for over twenty years and lives in Brighton.

DEADLAND

William Shaw

riverrun

First published in Great Britain in 2019 by riverrun
This paperback edition published in 2020 by

riverrun

An imprint of

Quercus Editions Limited
Carmelite House
50 Victoria Embankment
London EC4Y 0DZ

An Hachette UK company

Copyright © 2019 William Shaw

The moral right of William Shaw to be
identified as the author of this work has been
asserted in accordance with the Copyright,
Designs and Patents Act, 1988.

Lines from *The Wasteland* by T.S. Eliot quoted with permission
from Faber and Faber Ltd.

All rights reserved. No part of this publication
may be reproduced or transmitted in any form
or by any means, electronic or mechanical,
including photocopy, recording, or any
information storage and retrieval system,
without permission in writing from the publisher.

A CIP catalogue record for this book is available
from the British Library.

Paperback 978 1 78648 663 9
Ebook 978 1 78648 662 2

This book is a work of fiction. Names, characters,
businesses, organisations, places and events are
either the product of the author's imagination
or used fictitiously. Any resemblance to
actual persons, living or dead, events or
locales is entirely coincidental.

10 9 8 7 6 5 4 3 2 1

Typeset by CC Book Production
Printed and bound in Great Britain by Clays Ltd, Elcograf S.p.A.

Papers used by Quercus Editions Ltd are from well-managed forests
and other responsible sources.

With much gratitude to Jon and Rose

PART ONE

The Cruellest Month

ONE

The first time they tried stealing a phone, it went arse-tit. The second time, much worse.

It was a Friday. Two boys, both aged seventeen, sitting on a borrowed scooter, one behind the other, helmets on. The first time they waited twenty metres away from the entrance to the town's poshest hotel; not so close that people would notice what they were up to. Amazing how many people walk out of a hotel door with their phones right in their hands for everyone to see.

'What about him?'

'Nope. Shit phone.'

'You can't even see it.'

'I can. iPhone 5. Wouldn't get twenty for it.'

'That one. There.'

'She's got a baby with her, douche.'

'What?' With helmets on, neither could hear much the other said unless they shouted.

'You can't do people if they've got a baby.'

Right. 'Him?'

'Scary-looking one? You mad?'

'We're on a bike. He'll never catch us.'

Enough hesitation for the man to disappear again, out of view, behind a crowd of hen party girls.

Sloth sat at the front of the scooter, Tap on the pillion.

'I'm bored,' said Tap after ten minutes. 'This is pointless.'

'You've got no ambition, bro. No aspiration.'

'Kind of thing your mum says, Sloth.'

'Shut up. Her?' said Sloth. Woman, maybe forty, quite posh in heels and shades, hair still wet from a shower, coming out of the hotel.

'Let's do it.'

'Sure?' They had been sat on the bike outside Snack Box for what felt like ages now, hyped and twitchy. Way too long. Now or never.

'Samsung Galaxy. S9.'

'Reckon?'

'OK. Her.'

Sloth kick-started the engine. 'We doing this?'

'Serious.'

'We sure?'

'Frick sake. Go, you'll miss her,' urged Tap and slapped Sloth's helmet.

Sloth kicked the scooter into gear, releasing the clutch so quickly Tap almost tipped off the back.

''Kin' hell.'

The tiny engine screamed. Way too fast. They were on the woman so soon Tap had no time to think. She was negotiating

4

the brick paving of the pedestrian zone with careful high-heel steps. Tap had just time to glimpse her open mouth as she looked up at the noise of the bike, phone still at her ear as his outstretched arm sped towards her.

But Sloth was riding so hard Tap didn't have a hope of getting his gloved fingers round the phone. Next thing they were past her and, through his visor, Tap could see the shiny device spinning in the air in a long arc.

Never saw where it fell.

Already, Sloth was zig-zagging, avoiding startled pedestrians with buggies and shopping trollies on the narrow street, and Tap was clinging on to his waist again, until they could cut down Market Place and get a bit of real speed up for the getaway.

Sloth wove through cars crazily, leaning this way and that, finally skidding a left into the dead-end lane beside the disused video shop. Engine still puttering, he removed his helmet.

'Get it?'

Heart still thumping from the buzz, he slapped Sloth's bare head. 'That was way too fast. Bloody hell.'

Sloth punched Tap back. 'Oh I can't believe you missed it. You're just too slow, bro.'

They burst out laughing.

'I don't know,' said Tap. 'Maybe we call it a day.'

'Douche.'

'Seriously.'

'You give up way too easy, bro. Too hectic there anyway. That was the issue. I know somewhere good we could try,' said Sloth, putting his helmet back on.

★

Second time was definitely a better location. There was no CCTV on the cut-through from the station down to TK Maxx.

'See?' said Sloth.

He was right. They arrived there as a local train pulled in. Coming off the platform, exactly the same thing, everyone pulling out their phones. 'I'm home, love.' 'Need anything from the shop?' Made it easy.

But by the time they'd figured out the area, everyone from the first train had gone, so they had to wait for the next one from London to pull in. They found a spot to hide this time, tucked out of the way beside the Chinese takeaway.

'Spliff?' said Tap after fifteen minutes.

'Nah.'

'Might slow you down a bit.'

'I don't need slowing down, bruv. Stay woke, not broke.'

'Deep. Just keep it nice and subtle this time. All right?'

'Like a girl asking me not to be rough with her.'

''K off. You wouldn't even know what that's like.'

Neither of them would, as a matter of fact.

A train arrived. Sloth started up the motor again. The first commuters were too tightly packed together to bother with. It was like lions, you had to wait to pick off stragglers.

They both saw him at the same time. Ordinary-looking bloke. Jeans and brown jacket. Balding slightly. Earring. Holdall in his left hand, phone at his right ear. The man's face was red, as if he was flustered. From where they sat, out of view, they couldn't make out what he was saying.

'What's he got?'

'Can't see.'

And then, as if just to oblige them, the man held out his phone, looked at his screen, then returned it to his ear and continued talking.

'iPhone X,' said Tap, quietly. 'Look. For sure. Get a few hundred for that. Easy.'

'Reckon?'

'Got to be. Look at the size.'

The man paused by the gate. They could hear him talking now. It sounded like 'Keep your hair on. You still get to keep your half, I just get all the rest.'

'Come this way, come this way,' whispered Sloth.

Tap was suddenly unsure. There was something odd about this man, the tightly wound way he gripped that bag at his shoulder, the redness of his face. Later he would wonder if he should have said something, told Sloth to leave it, but in front of him on the bike, Sloth seemed so sure.

The man ended the call, reached down, opened the bag, and placed the phone inside.

'See that?' said Sloth.

'Yep.'

This time Sloth did everything right. The moment the man was past them, walking across the expanse of litter-strewn tarmac, Sloth kicked hard on the pedal and launched the bike forward off the stand, out of the darkness at the side of the old takeaway restaurant. The man didn't have a chance. In the second that he heard the sound of the motor coming up behind him and stopped to turn, Sloth braked a touch, slowing the bike just for long enough.

Afterwards, they roared down the ramp onto the pavement,

bumping onto the carriageway, Tap clutching the stolen holdall to his chest and shouting, 'Got it this time, bro.'

And Sloth accelerated round a white BMW 218i Sport, shouting, 'Sweetness.'

The feeling was mad; the fear and thrill like being on the wildest theme park ride, only better.

Uncle Mikey opened the door to his council house, looked at the two grinning teenage boys, one black, one white. An old black moped was parked on its stand, motor still puttering next to his bright red Suzuki GSX.

'Hey, Uncle Mikey,' said the white one.

The other one turned to switch off the engine, not by turning a key, but by plugging in the kill switch, so they'd obviously nicked it.

Mikey shook his head. Benjamin wasn't his real nephew but he had had this on–off thing with his mother for years and liked the lad as if he was his own. Sloth, the black kid, was super-short for his age, only five three. Benjamin was almost a foot taller and milky pale. A right pair.

'Yeah, yeah. What this time?' Mikey, himself six foot tall, an ex-merchant navy man who tapped fags on a packet before he smoked them; still the Paul Weller haircut, though his hair was grey now and thinning at the back.

'iPhone-fuckin'-X. Mint condition.' Sloth held up the holdall like a prize.

Mikey shook his head. 'Oh, boys. Why are you doing this? Get a bloody job.'

'How much?'

8

'Are you addled? Jesus. Not interested. I'm straight these days. Get out of here.'

'Honest to God, Uncle Mikey,' said Tap. 'It's proper.' They'd called Benjamin 'Tap' at school ever since Year 5 when Mr Parker said he must have been tapped on the head too hard as a baby.

'Don't bloody care. Did you switch the phone off?'

Tap and Sloth looked at each other. 'No.'

'Benjamin Brown. You are unbelievably dense. Beep beep beep. Right now that phone is telling people exactly where it is. The feds can be on you in ten minutes. Bet they're on the way now. Get out of here. I don't want them coming to my door causing me aggravation. I've had enough of it.' He paused, looked them up and down. 'How's your mum, by the way, Benji?'

Sloth yanked Tap by the sleeve. 'Let's go somewhere else. He's not bothered.'

'She's using again, I think,' said Tap. 'Drinking, anyway.'

'Very sorry to hear that. I'll come round. See what I can do. OK, mate?'

'Appreciate it.' Though Tap wondered what Mikey ever saw in his mother.

'You've got to look after her, Benji. I know you think she's a pain, with all that. The thing about growing up is learning who you care for. OK, mate?'

Tap nodded.

'Deep,' mocked Sloth.

'Yeah, yeah,' said Mikey. 'True, though. You'll figure that out one day. Took me long enough. You got to learn it, Benji.

Nobody tells you the rules in this game. You got to work them out for yourself.'

'Very, very deep.'

'Get lost.'

'Can't you wipe it? iPhone X. Mint. Worth hundreds,' said Sloth. 'Show him, Tap.'

Tap delved in and pulled out a small black Alcatel.

'You are such failures,' scoffed Mikey. 'That's some cheap pay-as-you-go shitbrick. Is that some kind of attempt at a joke?'

'Yeah,' said Sloth, smiling. He took the phone and put it in his pocket. 'Now show him the other one, Tap.'

Tap pulled out the second device: a brand new iPhone. When they had stopped to examine the bag, there had been two phones in it. One worthless, the other a top-of-the-range device, barely used.

Mikey hesitated, looking at the device, then said, 'Bollocks. I don't want it. Take it away.'

But, as Tap held it, the screen lit up and the phone vibrated. A message appeared on the lock screen. Mikey reached out and took the handset.

Tap leaned forward to read the words '*Pls give what you stole back £5000 reward no questions*', followed by a phone number.

'Christ in a bucket,' Mikey said eventually.

Sloth pushed past and read what was there too.

'Frickin' hell.'

'Is that five grand?'

'Yeah.'

'Five grand? You could get another five frickin' iPhones for that.'

Sloth giggled. 'He's going to pay us five grand?'

'Sure there's nothing else in the bag?' asked Mikey.

Tap shook his head. 'Nothing. Searched it.'

'Must be something extra-bloody-special on the phone.'

Tap held out his hand. 'Give us it back. It's ours.'

'Actually, technically speaking, not,' said Mikey, holding on to the phone.

'It's our phone. It's our money.'

Mikey smiled. 'Yeah? OK. I'll give it back to you.' But he didn't. 'And what if it's a trick? What if the police put the message on there and when you turn up to get your reward –' pronouncing the word 'reward' with heavy irony – 'they're all waiting for you? Bloke knows two lads on a shit moped nicked it from him. I can say I just found it, accidental. They can't prove anything, can they?'

Tap hesitated. 'Five hundred for you. If you go instead of us.'

'Nope. Fifty–fifty.'

'You are joking? Two-and-a-half grand for being a delivery man? We took the risk nicking it.'

'And I'll take the risk taking it back.'

'That's shit,' said Sloth.

'That's business. Don't I always tell you, lads? Think about the weekend you'll have.'

They thought about that for a second. 'What you reckon?' muttered Sloth.

'Five grand, man. We did the work.'

Mikey shrugged. 'Ten minutes ago you'd have been over the moon if I'd given you a hundred for it.'

'True.'

11

'I think it's shit,' Sloth complained.

They stood for another minute on the doorstep, before Mikey called the number on the screen.

'Here's a thing. I found this phone,' he said. 'Apparently there's a reward.'

The voice at the other end of the phone spoke.

'Yeah. I know it. Up by the river.'

Tap looked at Sloth; he had that frown on his face, lips pursed tight, like when he was about to start going off. 'It's OK, bro,' he whispered. 'I trust him.'

'Make it twenty minutes. I'll be there. Yeah . . . and the bag. I'll bring it.'

When he'd ended the call, Mikey said, 'Come back this evening. If he's on the level, I'll give you half.'

'Right,' Tap said. 'Two point five?'

'If that's what I get.'

Sloth rolled his eyes.

Helmets off, they rode a little way to the edge of the estate, then stopped, puttering on the footpath.

'Don't believe him,' said Sloth.

'He's OK. He'll give us the money. I promise.'

'Yeah, but reckon the one we stole it off is going to give him the money for real?'

Tap shrugged. 'I'm over it, anyway.'

'How can you be over it? You just give up so easily. Douche.' He thumped his friend on the arm.

Tap dug in his jacket and pulled out tobacco and some spliff. 'Don't know, mate. Just need weed.'

'We should follow him,' said Sloth. 'See if he gets the money.'

'Give us a break, mate. You're always on it. Just relax. It'll be fine.' It's why they had called him 'Sloth' at school. Because he wasn't one. It was better than the one he had before, which had been 'Donnie Darko', or mostly just 'Darko'.

Sloth revved the throttle in neutral, making the little engine whine. He pushed the scooter back a little, down the alleyway.

'I'm going if you're not.'

'Fuck sake,' said Tap, replacing his weed in his pocket and putting his helmet back on. 'He'll be mad if he sees us spying on him.'

'Won't see us,' said Sloth.

And they waited until the red motorbike roared past them, and then Sloth nudged the scooter back into gear and started to follow it down the A106.

But the 50cc engine was so useless they lost him in five minutes.

TWO

Ross Clough loathed his work at the Turner Contemporary. He should have never taken it in the first place. He had never wanted a job. He was an artist.

You're thirty-one. You need to get out there. You'll meet people. Important people. It's one of the best modern art galleries in the world.

When, on his first day here, he had told the gallery director he was an artist too, he had smiled thinly. 'How nice.'

The conventional art world was a fortress that built clean white walls around itself to protect the favoured few. It was uninterested in people who hadn't come up through the system.

He wasn't even suited to this kind of work. He hated the public, the dull ones who came here and shuffled round the rooms, awed by the art just because they were supposed to be. They bought postcards and canvas bags and believed they had experienced something.

Now one of them stood in front of him, crying.

'I can't find my daughter,' she whispered, the angular old woman in the maroon paisley.

'I beg your pardon?'

'She's . . . gone,' she was saying. 'My daughter.'

Panic rose. 'Where is she?' he blurted.

'I don't know. She's lost.'

He hadn't been trained for missing persons. Shouldn't he have been trained? Or had he forgotten what they had told him? He looked around, but his supervisor was nowhere to be seen. All the other staff members seemed to have disappeared. 'Which room were you in when you last saw her?'

'She went to the toilet. But she's not there.'

'How old is she?'

'Six. No . . . five.'

He left his desk, running towards the security man who was standing just outside the front door. It was April. A cold wind was blowing off the North Sea.

'Missing girl,' he panted.

'What's that?'

Ross repeated what he'd just said as the man spoke into his walkie-talkie.

What if she had been kidnapped? Assaulted? He looked around, hoping that when he pushed open the door and returned to the large reception area he would see mother and daughter reunited and the problem solved. Instead, his line manager, a woman in her thirties, was standing behind the desk giving a visitor directions to the Antony Gormley sculpture. 'I told you, you are not supposed to leave the desk unattended,' she scolded.

'Missing child,' Ross explained. He spotted the mother again, alone by the big window. 'That woman there.'

The manager broke into a smile.

'What?'

'Sorry,' she said, trying to stifle the laughter.

'It's not funny.'

'That's Lucy. She comes in most days and says her daughter's missing. Or that her handbag's been stolen. One time she had everyone looking for a floral bouquet she said she'd put down somewhere. We should have warned you.'

The white room seemed suddenly over-lit by sunshine. Now that he thought about it, the woman who had approached the reception area in tears had been in her seventies, too old to have a daughter of five. 'Stay at the desk. Use the phone. Alert someone. Don't leave your post unless it's an emergency.'

It was pointless to reply that it *had* been an emergency.

Five minutes later it was an elderly man, a European of some sort, complaining of an unusual smell in the main gallery room, demanding he come upstairs to do something about it. 'I am not able to leave the desk,' Ross replied.

The man leaned towards him and said, 'Like old meat. Horrible.'

His wife was thin, with a shock of blonde hair. She peered at Ross through large black spectacles, explaining, 'Oscar is very sensitive. He was a perfumer for over thirty years. He is very aware of aromas.'

'I'll report it, obviously,' he said. He pulled out the incident book, and wrote: *Tuesday. 4.15 p.m. Visitor complained of nasty odour in main gallery.*

★

16

By Thursday there was a regular trickle of visitors coming to the front desk, mentioning the stench. On his break, Ross went up to the large gallery room to experience it for himself. The attendant said someone had just asked whether the smell was an artwork of some sort.

It was like a room full of bad breath; curiously sweet, but fetid. Almost peppery. It pleased Ross. *The art in here stinks.* The room was too hot anyway. A fault with the heating and ventilation, apparently, that couldn't be fixed till Monday.

That afternoon, the Visitor Experience Manager complained to the Gallery Manager. He was supposed to be working from home that day, but he came in and walked around the large white room.

'Oh my God,' he said. 'Disgusting.'

He ordered employees to thoroughly clean the floor overnight, but in the morning, when they opened the doors, it was much worse. They closed the room; staff wandered around sniffing the air.

'What if something's crawled into the heating system and died?' suggested the Operations Manager.

For now, it seemed the most likely explanation. There was talk of vermin. The gallery, designed by a well-known architect, sat on the seafront of the seaside town, on the site of an old boarding house where the artist Turner had stayed when he had come to paint his famous sunsets here. Sometimes you saw rats in the Old Town, scurrying along gutters.

They fixed signs: *We are sorry. This gallery is temporarily closed for maintenance.*

Early on Saturday morning, engineers came to see if there was a problem within the ducting. Non-staff were not supposed to be unsupervised in the gallery, so Ross was ordered to go with them.

He watched the two workers shine torches into the white vents on the angled ceiling and peer inside. If anything, the smell had subsided a little since the day before. Whatever it was had probably done all the rotting it needed to.

Of course, if it was under the floor, that would be a problem. They would have to move the art. You couldn't just lift this stuff up and dump it in the corner.

Ross took the chance to wander round. In the centre of the room was a large-scale sculpture by a British artist whose work had become popular recently. It was made from found materials, sheets of brightly painted wood and rectangles of dull concrete; the piece scared him a little. Its planes seemed to swell as he walked around them, filling the space. Its solidity and confidence were intimidating. His own work was so delicate and flimsy. But he was as good as this, wasn't he? Better, in fact. He deserved to be in this gallery as much as the next artist.

Ross moved on to the next plinth. A pot by a Chinese artist, whose work he loathed on principle because of its obviousness, stood within a perspex cube. Carefully drawn faces were etched into the black glaze; a picture of an *X Factor* contestant, another of Kurt Cobain. Ross found it crass.

He found it amusing that a fly had somehow worked its way into the perspex box. It had assailed the perspex defences of art and insinuated itself into the world of privilege. How had it managed to get in there? Not one, but two flies, he realised.

'Nothing,' said the man, carefully descending the long ladder.

That's when Ross noticed a darker patch, just where the base of the black jar sat on the white paint of the square wooden plinth. The flies buzzed in the perspex box. Three of them now. Bizarre. If art was not about talent, but about context, then these insects were being transformed into art by the very act of being here on a plinth. He stared, fascinated.

The flies somehow had become much more significant than anything in this room, he realised. Art didn't need to be big and overpowering. Scale was such a cheap way to get attention.

He shouldn't be here at all. He should be in his studio.

He put his ear to the perspex and listened to them. The buzzing seemed much louder, as if there were more insects inside the big jar, longing to escape.

THREE

William South was coming home.

Alexandra Cupidi had only heard the previous morning; a brief call from Maghaberry Prison. 'I've been paroled. I'm catching the first plane from Belfast to Gatwick tomorrow.'

'When?'

'Don't know.'

And almost before Cupidi had had time to absorb the news, the call was over. William South, a man who had lived at Dungeness all his adult life, then served two years of a sentence for the manslaughter of his own father, was now coming home to Dungeness where he belonged. Energised, Cupidi rose early Saturday morning, spooned freshly ground coffee into the jug.

'Why don't you make a cake for him?' she suggested to her daughter Zoë. 'A welcome gift.'

A groan. 'Mum.' Zoë; seventeen years old, still wearing Harry Potter pyjamas that she had been given for Christmas when she was thirteen.

'I'm going to go and clean his cottage up a bit. Get the windows open. That place gets damp. Then go into Lydd and get him some milk and bread. Maybe some flowers to brighten it up a little.'

'Listen to yourself, Mum.'

'It's neighbourly.'

'It's 'cause you feel guilty,' said Zoë. 'On account of sending him to prison in the first place.'

'No I don't,' replied Cupidi. 'I don't feel guilty at all.'

'Well you should.'

'No I shouldn't. I was doing my job.'

'Stupid,' muttered Zoë.

One of the first things Detective Sergeant Alexandra Cupidi had done when she had joined the Kent Serious Crime Directorate was uncover a difficult truth about a fellow police officer, William South, a good man, well-liked. At the age of fifteen, South had killed his own father. That his father had been violent and abusive had been taken into account, but South had still lost his job on the Kent police force. The arrest had not made her popular with her colleagues, or her daughter. Arriving here two years ago from London with no friends, young Zoë had worshipped William South, calm and quiet-spoken and so unlike her own mother.

'It wasn't like I wanted to do it. If you're in the police, you don't make the rules. I discovered what he'd done. I couldn't un-know it.'

'Of course you could,' said Zoë. 'Nobody actually cared about what had happened. Nobody apart from you. You could have just pretended.'

'I don't do this job to pretend things haven't happened.'

'Stupid,' muttered Zoë again.

But now William South was coming and everything would be like it was again.

'Get some coconut oil for the cake,' said Zoë. 'And oat milk.'

Cupidi was about to say that William South wasn't a vegan, but stopped herself. She had asked her daughter to make him a cake. Zoë was doing it. That was good enough.

After fetching the ingredients for the cake, Cupidi left Zoë at home, still in her pyjamas.

A clear blue sky. Though the spring wind was chilly, there was some heat in the sun, bringing out fat bees that circled the yellow gorse bushes. Purple orchids pushed through the shingle. It had been a long grey winter. Dungeness was coming alive again.

They lived just three hundred metres away from South's small wooden bungalow. Of all the oddly shaped shacks, cottages, converted railway carriages and caravans that dotted the flat landscape of Dungeness, Arum Cottage was the closest to the nuclear power station that blocked the sea views it must have once had. From the front, as she approached, its symmetrical eaves formed a perfect 'M'-shape. Cupidi let herself in, carried in her bag of shopping and looked around. The shack felt dark and unloved, the timbers damp.

She was hoovering in a half-hearted way when Zoë appeared at the door. Cupidi switched off the vacuum cleaner, and followed her daughter's gaze towards the pot of irises. 'They were all they had.'

'They exploit migrant labour to grow those,' said Zoë.

'I'm a terrible person.'

'Awful.' Her daughter agreed. 'He's probably changed. They treat coppers differently in prison, don't they? Do you think he was picked on?'

'Are you trying to make me feel bad?'

Zoë shrugged. 'If you feel bad, it's all your own doing.' Cupidi switched on the vacuum cleaner again. 'I better go,' said Zoë. 'Cake will be burning.'

Her daughter was not an easy girl. Last Christmas Zoë had announced she was dropping out of sixth form college. Cupidi had tried reasoning with her about the need for qualifications, but Zoë had been scornful. The science courses she had been studying were irrelevant to what was really happening in the world, she said. So Cupidi had hoped her daughter would find a job instead, but she hadn't. Over the last few weeks, Cupidi would see her waiting at the bus stop by the light railway station, hood up, head down. If she offered a lift, Zoë would decline it, saying the bus was fine. When she returned, Cupidi would ask her who she'd been with all day. Zoë would list names Cupidi had never heard of. 'Pinky, Jon and Juliette. You don't know them.'

In March Cupidi had been at work when a call from her mother had come through. 'Don't worry, but Zoë has been arrested in London. She's fine. Everything is OK.'

'Arrested? What the hell was she doing?' Cupidi had demanded.

'Some demonstration outside the High Court. They charged her with a public order offence but they're not going to do anything about it. She'll be fine.' Helen, her mother, had moved back to London, back to her house in Stoke Newington. 'She can stay here overnight, OK? I'll put her on a train in the morning.'

'A demonstration?'

'Anti-fascist, she says. Look on the bright side,' her mother had said. 'You were always wanting her to hang out with people her own age.'

Back at home, she was in the kitchen, the smell of Zoë's cake filling the room with sweet warmth, when Zoë came downstairs. 'I think I saw a taxi.'

It was impossible to see South's house from the ground-floor windows. Their cottages had been built within the banks of an eighteenth-century gun battery, a large circular earthwork that surrounded the buildings.

Cupidi walked out of the front door, out to the lane. She reached the gap in the bank in time to see the taxi driving away.

'Shall we go and say hi?' said Zoë.

Cupidi stood on the track, looking. 'I expect he'll pop up and say hello in a minute. You could ask if he wants to go bird-watching with you.'

'I'm not fifteen any more, Mum.'

They went back inside and waited for a knock on the door. The oven timer pinged. Zoë took the cake out and looked at it, disappointed. 'I thought it would rise more.' The edges were dark; it dipped low in the middle.

It was almost midday when they finally ventured down the road, side by side, Zoë holding the cake carefully as she walked.

'Do you think he's changed?'

'I don't know.'

'I mean, he's lost his job and everything.' Another rebuke.

It was true, though. Twenty years of service and he was out

with no pension. It would be hard for him now. 'I thought you didn't like the police anyway.'

'You knock,' Zoë said, when they reached the door of the cottage. The new woodstain Cupidi had painted onto its timber last spring had already peeled away. Winters here were hard.

Cupidi rapped. There was no answer.

'You sure the taxi came here?'

'Positive,' said Zoë.

Cupidi knocked again. 'Weird. Maybe he's gone out?'

'I can hear him,' whispered Zoë.

Sure enough, from behind the door came the sound of footsteps on the bare boards. The door opened.

That he looked so much older was a shock, but maybe that was because he hadn't shaved in a while. Grey stubble coated much of his face.

Zoë held her cake forward. 'Ta-da!'

'What?' South stood in the doorway, staring at the gift, as if confused by it – and by her. It wasn't just him who had changed. Zoë had been fifteen when he had last seen her, a slight, vulnerable girl. Now her hair was cut within an inch of her scalp and there was a line of rings through the top of her right ear.

'I made you a cake. To say welcome home.'

That was the moment Cupidi's phone started ringing in her jacket pocket.

'I didn't put a file in it or anything,' said Zoë.

'Just a minute.' Cupidi looked at the number on the screen of her phone. 'It's work.'

'Sorry, bad joke.' Zoë held the plate a little further towards

25

William South, who made no move to take it from her. 'I wouldn't have needed to put a file in it, because you're out already.'

'A body part?' Cupidi was saying, into her handset.

She turned away from the cottage, from her daughter and William South, towards the power station. Gulls were rising in the warm air, way above the huge squat concrete block. 'I'm on my way.'

She turned. Zoë was standing alone in front of the door of Arum Cottage which had been closed again. 'What happened?' Cupidi asked.

'Nothing, really. It was a bit weird. He just took the cake and went back inside. I thought he would be more happy to see me.'

'I'm sure he was happy to see you. Of course he was.'

'It was a bit rude, if you ask me.'

Cupidi frowned. 'I expect he just wants some time to himself.'

They walked back, north along the track.

'What kind of body part?' asked Zoë.

'They didn't say.'

'A head? A lung? Or a toenail? I mean, they're all body parts, aren't they?'

When they got home, Zoë went upstairs to her bedroom and closed the door. She was spending so much time on her laptop these days.

FOUR

'Told you. Shouldn't have trusted him,' said Sloth.

'Do you know another song, bro? That one's old.'

Saturday morning was sliding towards afternoon; they were sitting on Sloth's bed, despondent, smoking the last of Tap's weed. 'Watch me. I'll go jihadi on him,' said Sloth.

Tap laughed. 'Mikey? He'd smash you in if you even tried.'

They had waited four hours outside Mikey's house last night, getting cold. The estate had been quiet. Anyone young had gone into town; the old ones stayed in watching TV. The red motorbike never came back.

There was only a sniff of petrol left in the moped's tank. On the way back home they'd run out of fuel and had to push it. After half a mile, exhausted, they had wheeled it off the road into a gap in the hedge and abandoned it there, walking the rest of the way without it.

Friday night, when they should have been out in town attempting fake IDs in the local bars, they had sat playing Spyro on Sloth's PlayStation and working their way through Tap's weed.

In the morning, Sloth's mother came back from her shift at the hospital, picked her way across the room and pulled the curtains back.

'Mum.'

'This room smells disgusting, Joseph. Put your laundry in the bin downstairs at least.' She tugged his window open for him. She turned towards them. 'You two boys happen to know anything about Mr Richardson's motorbike?'

'No.'

'Someone stole it yesterday.' She was looking at them, frowning. 'He says they seen a couple of youngsters taking it.'

Sloth shook his head, cool as anything. 'That's terrible, Mum. Not heard anything. Let you know if I do.'

'You do that, Joseph. And you, Benjamin.'

'Will do, Mrs Watt.'

She paused at the door, looking tired. On nights at the hospital, she was more than ready for her bed now. 'Joseph. I saw they're looking for kitchen staff at the Wetherspoons.'

'Told you, Ma, I'm too young. You got to be eighteen.'

'Not in the kitchen. Mind you go down there today.'

'Right, Mum. Will do.'

When she finally closed her bedroom door, Sloth stood, shut the window again and went downstairs to find the home phone. Back in the room, he threw the handset at Tap. 'Call him again.'

'He doesn't pick up. Ever.'

'Leave him another message then.'

While Sloth fired up the stub of the spliff, Tap dialled the number which went straight to voicemail. 'Uncle Mikey. Hit me back, man. I'm not at home, case you've been trying to reach me there. I'm at Slo's house. It's—'

'Don't tell him my address. I don't want him knowing my address.' Sloth grabbed the handset off him. 'Give us our money, man! You stole it.'

Tap snatched the phone back. 'Don't.' He ended the call.

'He's got our cash. I'm skint.'

'He's not like that, Uncle Mikey.'

'He's full of shit,' said Sloth. 'Like you.'

Sloth lifted his hoodie off the floor and started putting it on. The pay-as-you-go Alcatel from the man's shoulder bag fell out of his pocket. He picked it up. 'How much would we get from this one?'

'What have you got that for?'

'Ain't worth nitch. Thought I put it back in the bag.'

'Anything on it?'

Sloth fingered the keys. 'Nah, man. It's locked.'

They finished the spliff and sat down on the bed. Sloth and Tap had been going round each other's houses since Year 6 at school, staying over, getting up to the same mischief. They usually had Sloth's place to themselves because his mum was out at work or asleep. Tap's mum never worked, but she was out a lot too, or sleeping it off.

'What we going to do?'

'Nothing *to* do.'

Seventeen was a bad age, too old for kids' stuff, too young for anything else. The weekend was worse than the week if you had no money. Without cash, there was nothing to do in this town.

'I could borrow some paper off my mum,' Tap suggested.

'Pff.'

'Don't say that. She might have some.'

'Sure.'

'She's not that bad, these days. Not really.'

'Yeah,' said Sloth, encouragingly. 'Maybe she's getting it together, your mum.'

'Think so. She's making an effort. Just had a little slip, that's all.'

'Good for her, bro.'

Tap nodded. 'Right. So I should go and ask her if she's got any money we can borrow.' He got up and started pulling on his shirt. 'Coming?'

'No. You're all right, bro. I'm not bothered.'

Probably better that way, thought Tap. Because after everything they'd just said, he didn't like his friend to see her if she was a mess.

All their lives they had lived in this scrappy North Kent town where there was never anything to do.

Tap got home just after midday; a 1950s pebble-dashed two-bedroom terrace on West View Road, just east of the town centre. A rusting bicycle frame which Tap had been meaning to fix leaned against the wall by the white uPVC door.

Mum was sitting at the breakfast table with a mug of tea and a cigarette, Heart FM on the radio, dressed in the same clothes Tap had seen her in yesterday, lips still covered in a trace of lipstick, eyeliner spreading into the wrinkles around her eyes. She looked bad.

'Got any money, Mum?'

'Good morning to you too, Benjamin.' There was a pile of washing-up in the sink. 'What have you been up to, Benjamin Brown?'

'What do you mean?' he asked cautiously.

'What I said. What kind of trouble have you been getting yourself into?'

Tap took the sharp knife from the wooden block and opened the bread bin. The loaf inside was spotted with mould. He dropped it into the rubbish, returning the blade to the block. 'You're the one who gets into trouble all the time, Mum.'

She stubbed out her cigarette. 'Don't be cheeky,' she said quietly.

In the cupboard he found a can of beans.

'Annie Lee says there was a man here just now, knocking on doors, looking for you.'

The tin fell out of his hands, onto the floor and rolled across the vinyl.

Annie Lee was an ancient next-door neighbour who had lived round here all his life, had to be in her eighties at least. You had to watch out for her, because she was always putting something into her dustbin in the hope of meeting someone to talk to, and when she started she was impossible to stop.

'Where were you?' Tap asked.

'I was out, wasn't I? Just got back five minutes ago. Was having this cup of tea before going to bed. Annie came rapping at the door, moment I got in.'

Tap bent to pick up the can, dented from the fall. He rolled it between his palms, feeling the unevenness. 'Heard anything from Uncle Mikey?'

His mother frowned. 'Why would I have heard anything from him?'

'This man. What did he look like?'

'So you have been up to something, then?'

'Mum. I was just asking.'

His mother curled her upper lip. 'What have you and Mikey been doing?'

'Nothing. Just wanted to talk to him about stuff.' He dug his finger under the can's ring pull, and paused. 'Did Annie Lee say what he wanted, this man?'

'He wanted to know where you lived. And your mate.'

'He asked for Sloth by name?'

'Just said he was looking for you and a young black lad. What's up, Benji?'

Tap chewed his lip. 'When was this?'

'I don't know. Probably fifteen, twenty minutes ago. Wouldn't surprise me, you being in some trouble.'

'Thanks for all the likes, Mum.'

'Don't be cheeky.' She rubbed her stomach. 'God. My guts ache.'

'Can I borrow your phone?'

'What's wrong with yours?'

'No credit.'

She pulled her handbag onto the table and dug around in it. 'Stick it back in when you're done. I'm knackered. What a night I had. Should have seen me. I was on form.' She stood, put her arms round him, and kissed him on the cheek, leaving him with the smell of cigarettes and make-up.

★

First time he dialled Sloth's house it went to the answering machine so he tried again. Second time Sloth picked up.

'What?'

'It's me. There's a man looking for us,' Tap said, keeping his voice low in case his mum was listening.

'What?'

'He was here, like, twenty minutes ago, before I got in, asking for both of us. Annie Lee talked to him. Probably told him all kinds of stuff about us. Know what she's like.'

'Who is it?'

'Don't know.'

'What about your uncle Mikey?'

'Nothing.'

And then, over the phone, Tap heard the noise of the doorbell at Sloth's house. 'Shit.'

'Don't answer.'

The bell rang a second time.

'They'll wake Mum.'

'Look out the window. Can you see? Who is it?'

'Can't frickin' see. Wait.'

'No, no, no. Don't answer it.'

'Keep your hair on, Tap. I'm only looking through the curtains. It's your uncle Mikey I think. I can see his motorbike parked outside. Think he's got the cash?' Tap heard the sound of Sloth clattering downstairs. 'I'll get back to you.'

For just a second, Tap relaxed. If Mikey had the money, everything would be fine.

A thought struck him.

Mikey had never been to Sloth's house. They hadn't told him

Sloth's address. Tap's scalp started to tingle. Was it just the weed, or was something very wrong? Picking up his mother's handset again, he called Sloth a second time, but the phone rang until voicemail kicked in.

He called it again.

And again.

And again.

FIVE

The way Peter Moon just felt it was all right to walk around her flat naked. Jesus, thought Jill Ferriter.

She had windows, like anyone else. Even if she was on the seventh floor. He was in the living room now, not even under-pants on, lifting up cushions, peering underneath them. From the kitchen area, she watched the muscular curve of his spine as he bent. He had patches of hair on his shoulders that she had noticed before. She shuddered.

'I heard it buzzing,' he said.

He was on his hands and knees now, looking under the sofa. Was she expected to go round looking for his phone too, because he'd put it down somewhere and couldn't remember where?

The kettle clicked off. She poured boiling water into a cup.

'I had it last night. I know I did. I wasn't that drunk.'

She must have been, though. In the Flying Boat for Friday drinks after work. Everyone from Serious Crime there, apart from McAdam. Even Alex Cupidi, though she left after they all

35

said they were going clubbing. In Cameo, afterwards, she and this girl who did the prosecution paperwork started on shots. She took such good care of her diet, avoiding toxins and trans fats, then spent three hours pouring any shit down her throat.

'What's that smell?' he asked.

'Chamomile tea. Do you want one?'

He wrinkled his nose. 'Haven't you got coffee?'

'No.'

He turned to her, full frontal. 'Everybody has coffee.'

She shook her head. 'Not me.'

'Could you phone it?'

She dialled his number. 'Can you hear it?' He was off again, crawling around the floor on all fours, peering under furniture. 'Have you looked in your trousers? Or your jacket?'

'Yes,' he said, irritated.

'Worried your mum is wondering why her baby didn't come home last night?' Jill Ferriter was just a constable, but she had her own flat. In a few days' time she would be twenty-five. A quarter of a century. Peter Moon, detective sergeant, three years older than her, still lived with his mother in a bedroom with his old school books and football trophies.

'I messaged her from the taxi,' he said, missing the dig. 'Will you go and listen in the other room in case I dropped it some-where?'

God. They had caught a taxi. She didn't even remember that. Another lurch in her stomach. She put down her tea, undrunk, and went back to the bedroom.

'Was that the last time you used it?' she called, dialling the number again. 'Bet it's in the cab.'

'No. I heard it buzz just now, I tell you. Listen.'

She listened. He was right. There was a faint buzzing coming from somewhere and it stopped the moment the call went to voicemail. '*Hi. Peter Moon here. I can't get to the phone. Wait for the squeak.*' She spoke into the handset. 'Message for Sergeant Peter Moon. If you want to sit on my sofa, wear bloody trousers.'

'What?' he said from the living room.

She dialled it again. The buzzing was close. She paused, listened, then pulled back the duvet. It was there, tangled in the linen. She picked it up, and was about to say, 'Found it,' when she noticed the details of five missed calls were on the lock screen. The last three were from her just now; but two before that were from the office. There was a text message too:

U havin a good night? ;-) ;-)

Oh God. Everyone knew.

'Where was it?' he asked, when she came into the living room holding the handset out in front of her.

'Get your clothes on,' she said.

'Give us a chance,' complained Peter Moon.

'Who's that texting you?' She put the phone under his nose.

He took the device, looked at the lock screen and had the grace to look embarrassed. 'Oh. Jesus. Sorry.'

'Get dressed, Peter. Go home.'

'Bloody hell.' He stood, bollock naked, examining his call list. 'The job called. Something must be up. I better get in touch.' He started dialling.

'Pity's sake, get some clothes on first.' But the phone was already against his ear.

She shouldn't have got that drunk. Right now she just wanted him out of her flat so she could hoover, change the sheets, stick them in the hottest wash her machine had, and put fresh scent in the dispensers.

'An arm?' Moon was saying. 'What? A human arm? Bloody hell.'

She went back to the bedroom, picked up his clothes from the floor and carried them through to the living room.

'Whose arm is it? Actually I'm not at home.' She was about to drop his shirt and trousers and the rest of it at his feet when she heard him say, 'Who told you? Yeah. Jill's place. I'll get in a taxi and get home, then head straight there.'

'What the actual . . . ?' said Ferriter. 'You just told someone on the job you were at mine?'

'They knew already.' He put his hand over the phone. 'I don't know how they found out. Honest. Swear to God.'

Still holding the clothes, she walked out to the small balcony and looked out over the town. Her flat. It was her own. She had bought it with the money she'd inherited when her mother died. She loved this little outdoor spot, with the metal table and chairs and a string of solar lamps. It was her special place. Some evenings, even in winter, she would sit there, looking out at the lights and listening to the noise below her. She was above it all, untouchable.

She held Peter Moon's clothes over the railing and looked down at the parked cars.

'What are you doing?' he mouthed, ear to his handset.

'Get your bloody things on or I'm dropping them.'

'I have to go home first,' he was saying to whoever he was talking to. 'Have a shave.'

38

She dropped a shoe.

'Fuck,' he said.

The shoe fell between two parked cars, bounced and ended up underneath a Kia.

'What are you doing? You mad cow. Jesus. OK. I'm getting bloody dressed.'

The second one landed sole up on the tarmac just as her own phone started ringing.

SIX

Tap ran the half-mile between his house and Sloth's, taking the shortest way across Central Park, zig-zagging past biddies with shopping trolleys, leaping over dog walkers' leads, swerving off onto the flower beds to avoid toddlers tantruming on the path.

By the time he got to Phoenix Place his lungs were hurting: too much weed. Sloth's street was a cul-de-sac, but you could get to it by a cut-through by the flats. Tap slowed as he rounded the corner, tucked himself behind the front door of the block, chest heaving, and took a quick look down the short road.

Beyond the flats stood a terrace of small houses. It was a nicer neighbourhood than the other side of the park where he and his mum lived; bigger cars, not so much debris on the streets, homes with flower pots hanging outside. Sloth's place was in the middle of the row.

Why was he worried? Maybe Mikey had figured out Sloth's address after all. Maybe he had brought round the money he owed them. He probably didn't want to come round to his house and end up tangling with Tap's mother, specially not when he'd told him his mum was using again. It was just the weed making him paranoid.

Peering round the yellow brick of the flats, he looked towards Sloth's door. As far as he could see, there was no motorbike outside.

An old man emerged from the front door of the block and turned in Tap's direction, hesitated, nervous of the young man in a hoodie.

Old people were so anxious. How could you live your life like that?

'Boo,' whispered Tap, still out of breath from the run.

''K off,' said the old man, turning the other way, deliberately walking the long way round to avoid him. Pathetic, really. These people, they had no idea how scary life really was.

Cautiously Tap walked closer to Sloth's house. Still no sign of Mikey's motorbike.

Sloth's mum's nets were always drawn, her windows always clean. Tap put his face up against the glass and looked in. The front room was dark. On the opposite wall, framed family photos of weddings, birthdays and graduation days stared back at him, but the room was empty.

Sloth's mum would be fast asleep upstairs now. He'd ring the bell but she went nuts if you woke her after a night shift.

There was no point trying to shout up to him either, because Sloth's room was at the rear of the house, so he walked back towards the flats, then round the end of the terrace and back down the next road, to Sloth's small garden.

41

The back gate was always locked. He hauled himself up over the fence and dropped onto the path.

First thing he noticed: the kitchen door was open, which was unusual.

Tap stuck his head into the small kitchen. A hint of last night's food hung in the air. 'Slo?'

No answer.

A little louder, but not too loud. 'Sloth. You there?'

He went through into the hallway and peered up the stairs. Everything seemed quiet.

He knocked on Sloth's door – 'Mate?' – then opened it to the thick, familiar waft of trainers and weed, but the room was empty, looking just as it had been three-quarters of an hour earlier, except without his friend on the bed.

So where the hell was he?

Maybe Sloth had gone to find him and they'd missed each other, crossing town? Maybe he'd got the money after all. But why had he left the back door open, then? Sloth hadn't been that stoned.

He was still standing in the doorway to Sloth's room when a hand touched his shoulder.

He jumped, spun round, and there was Sloth's mother, in a large white nightie.

'Christ. What you doing, creeping up?'

'What's wrong with you, Benjamin?'

'I thought—'

'You thought what?'

'Nothin'.'

She looked at him disapprovingly, arms crossed in front of her chest. 'Where's Sloth?'

'His name is Joseph.' He stared at a small glob of moisturiser on her forehead that she had missed before going to bed.

'Where is he?'

'How did you get in here, anyway. He give you a key? I told him you're not allowed a key.'

'He's not in his room. Where's he gone?'

'How would I know?' Her Guyanese accent was always stronger when she was angry. 'I'm just trying to get some sleep without you banging on my front door and ringing the bell. Go away. You're not welcome here.'

Tap blinked. 'I didn't ring the bell.'

'Don't you lie to me, boy. You woke me up, ringing it.'

'Wasn't me. Swear to God, Mrs Watt.'

She shrugged, disbelieving, and retreated to her bedroom, padding back across the laminate floor. Her door had a sign hanging on it: *My worries are few because my blessings are many*. Before she closed it behind her, she said, 'Let me sleep, Benjamin, please.'

Downstairs, he locked the kitchen door, then left by the front, looking both ways before stepping out onto the path. Out in the open, he felt anxious now, just like that old man. He broke into a run again, this time heading up Lowfield Street, and into town.

Ten minutes later, he was pushing his nose up against the glass of the KFC, but Sloth wasn't in there. He looked up the High Street and saw some lads who had been in his year at school standing outside Primark, sharing a cigarette. They gazed at him with contempt as he approached them. 'Hey. Any of you seen Sloth?'

'Joseph? No, mate.' The tallest of them shook his head. 'That black lad you mean? Your boyfriend? You still hanging round with him?' A snigger.

'Can I borrow your phone to call him?'

'Give me a fag and you can.'

'Haven't got any.'

''K off then, scrounger.' He turned his back on Tap. It was like being back at school again with them. He'd hated them then, too.

This place where he had lived all his life: he loathed everything about it. Pathetic people who would live and die here. Sloth and him had never been in the in-crowd.

He was about to walk away when a fat lad named Dennis, who always wore khaki like he was a commando, called, 'Oi, Tap. What about Mikey Dillman?'

Tap's head snapped round to look the boy in the eye. 'What about him?'

'What happened to him? What's the story?' Dennis was close enough that Tap could smell his breath.

Tap looked at him, frowning. 'What do you mean, what happened?'

'Who do you think shot him?' Dennis asked.

Shot him? Tap wasn't sure he'd heard properly. 'What?'

'Shot him.'

Tap felt an unexpected prick of tears at the corners of his eyes, a brittleness in his chest.

The other lads looked round, interested now.

'On the radio this morning,' Dennis said. 'My mum knew him.'

'Dennis, your mum probably shagged him.'

'Shut up,' shouted Tap. 'Shut up, shut up. What did they say?'

44

'Somebody shot him,' said Dennis. 'Honest to God. Gangland assassination, they said. Found his body at a scrap metal yard out towards Crayford Ness. He'd been shot, like, a million times.'

Tap tried not to let the shock show on his face.

'Had it coming,' said one of the boys. 'Bad lad.'

''K off. He's dead?'

'Your mum used to muck about with him too, didn't she, Tap?'

Tap nodded cautiously. 'While back, yeah.'

A man on a maroon mobility scooter honked at them, even though there was plenty of space for him to go round. Tap stepped back, away from the group of lads, to let the man pass, trying to let nothing show on his face, and all the time thinking, what the hell was happening? And if Mikey was dead, who was that on his motorbike, ringing Sloth's doorbell? Though he already had a pretty good idea.

SEVEN

'You were having some fun last night,' Cupidi said, as she approached Ferriter.

'Don't. You should have stopped me.'

'I know better than that, Jill.' It was hardly a surprise, being called in to work on a Saturday. The spring had brought a reprise of the norovirus with it, thinning a team that had already cut back to achieve efficiency savings. After declining for years, robbery, rape and violent crime stats were all up.

Six days ago a student had been killed in a drunken fight on the University of Kent campus in Canterbury. It was not a question of trying to find who was guilty – both the fatal blow and the face of the killer were clear in a CCTV recording taken from behind the bar – but every violent death made a mountain of work.

More draining, resource-wise, was yesterday's body, found last night in a scrap metal yard just outside Erith. A man shot twice, once in the chest, a second bullet in the side of the head.

Michael 'Mikey' Dillman was a local hoodlum, known to police. The man's wallet and phone were on him, so it wasn't likely to be a robbery.

'I feel like hell. OK if I drive?'

'Sure you're up to it?'

Hungover or not, Ferriter still looked annoyingly well-kempt. Called in at short notice, Cupidi was in jeans and an un-ironed white T-shirt. As she got into the passenger seat, Ferriter started the engine of the unmarked Sierra. 'Aren't we supposed to be waiting for Sergeant Moon?' Cupidi asked.

'Can't he find his own bloody way?'

'Give him another five minutes.'

'First hour of an investigation,' Ferriter said. The first hour was the most important, supposedly.

Cupidi was keen to get under way too, but she looked at her watch. 'It's been sitting in a ceramic jar for a week at least, they said. It can wait a little longer.'

Reluctantly Ferriter turned off the engine. 'Weird one, eh?'

'They're all weird.'

An arm had been found inside a jar, an artwork by an artist Cupidi had never heard of.

'Bet it's worth an extra million or two now.'

'Is that supposed to be a motive?'

'Got to admit, it's a possibility, isn't it?' Ferriter sat, hands on the steering wheel. 'I don't think Moonie's coming. Let's just go, can't we?'

'One more minute.'

And then Peter Moon was there, loping around the corner at Bank Street, running his hand through his short hair, unusually dapper in a slim-fit suit. For a copper he was stupidly good-looking. Cupidi would look twice as dowdy standing next to these two.

'Hello again,' he said as he pulled open the back door. 'Didn't realise you were being called in too.'

'Again?' Cupidi said.

'You took your time,' complained Ferriter, starting the engine. 'Could be halfway there by now.'

'Had to go back to my mum's first, didn't I? Get a change of clothes. Freshen up.'

'Were you a dirty stop-out last night, Peter Moon?' asked Cupidi.

Moon didn't answer. Cupidi could almost feel the heat from Jill Ferriter's red face from where she was sitting. 'Oh,' she said as the penny dropped.

'Thanks a fucking bunch, Peter Moon,' muttered Ferriter as she pulled out into traffic and headed out of town onto the Canterbury Road, heading up to the M2. 'Arsehole.'

'Weird though, isn't it?' Moon continued blithely. 'An arm is what I heard. What's that about? How come nobody noticed it? Probably thought it was by Picasso or something.'

'What you on about?' Ferriter said, irritated.

'Picasso.'

They crossed the M20 on a flyover, lorries roaring beneath them. 'Bet you never even been to the Turner, have you?'

'No.'

'Didn't think so.'

'I mean, Jill, I like good art, obviously, but that contemporary stuff . . . They're taking the mickey, aren't they?'

48

When they pulled over to fill up with petrol, Moon went out to get them some bottled water and crisps.

'The morning after the night before,' said Cupidi.

'It's not like I believe in regretting mistakes.' Ferriter watched Moon in the shop. 'I don't. Except last night's.'

'I thought you liked him.'

Ferriter said nothing.

'Going to be a long day,' said Cupidi.

'And how. You won't tell anyone, will you, boss?'

'It's him you should be saying that to.'

Ferriter looked away. 'Don't I know it.'

'Are you going to be OK?'

But Moon was making his way back to the car with a plastic bag full of snacks for him and Cupidi; Ferriter didn't answer. 'They didn't have Chilli so I got you Caramelised Onion and Balsamic Vinegar.'

Ferriter made a face; she disapproved of crisps. She drove on the dull road north towards the other coast.

'Wonder where the rest of him is.' Moon popped open one of the packets. 'Not being funny, but I don't suppose they've checked the other sculptures and stuff for him yet.'

'If it's a him. Could be a her,' suggested Ferriter.

'It's an arm. He or she might not even be dead,' said Cupidi.

'Oh,' said Moon. 'Shit.'

They knew nothing yet. Apart from the fact that there was an arm. Out of nowhere, a gust of rain splattered against the windscreen.

EIGHT

This place could be freezing when the rain came down.

Tap had hung about in Silverland Arcade for an hour, wiping his eyes with the sleeve of his jacket, until the cashier had said, for the third time, with more menace, 'If you're not playing the slots, get out.'

So he dodged the April showers and made it to County Square shopping centre, which was warm, at least. He sat on a bench, head in his hands, trying to think.

Mikey was dead. God, he had looked up to Mikey. The only decent man his mother had ever hung around with, his own dad included. Wanted to be like him, with a place of his own, playing his own music, loud as he liked, putting whatever he wanted on the walls. All that stuff.

The thing about growing up is learning who you care for.

What if Sloth was dead too? This was all his fault.

It couldn't be happening. This was nuts. This town was too

50

boring for anything like this. Yet Dennis had told him. Mikey had been shot.

A mum came out of the Muffin Break Bakery and Cafe opposite and parked her pushchair in front of the bench, sitting down next to Tap. Pulling a Danish pastry out of a paper bag, she broke off a bit and gave it to the small boy in the buggy. The toddler gobbled it down, then reached out a pudgy fist for more.

Tap realised how hungry he was too. He had eaten nothing all day, but he didn't even have fifty pence on him.

The small boy giggled. 'Don't be greedy,' said his mum, and popped a bit into her own mouth. 'Ooh,' cooed his mother. 'Don't cry.' And she held out a second piece for him, then hesitated. 'Shouldn't really,' she said. 'Not good for him, all that sugar.'

'Ah, he's OK,' said Tap. 'Go on.'

The mum, who was probably only a couple of years older than Tap, smiled and gave the baby the piece. The little boy popped it into his mouth and grinned at Tap, flakes falling from his lips onto his Babygro.

Out of the corner of his eye, Tap spotted a security man approaching. He shunted an inch closer to the mother, leaned forward towards the baby, so they could look like a family: him, the baby and the young mum. 'Sweet one, isn't he?'

The mother laughed. 'Only sometimes. You should hear him when he's going at it.'

'Pair of lungs on him?'

'Takes after his dad,' said the woman.

The boy's eyes darted from one face to the other, smiling.

The security guard passed on. 'Great little lad,' said Tap.

'I know,' she said. 'I'm lucky.'

'Look after him,' said Tap as she wrapped the rest of the pastry up in the paper and threw it into the bin at the end of the bench, then stood.

'Nice talking to you,' she said, and wheeled the pushchair away.

Tap contemplated digging out the empty fag packet in his pocket and throwing it away so he could then dig in the rubbish to fetch the rest of the pastry back; he'd seen homeless guys doing that and it always looked pathetic.

There would be food at home, though. He would risk it. Just once. He would get some stuff and leave. Hide out somewhere for a few days. No idea where though.

He lingered in the alleyway at the north end of West View Road. Nothing looked unusual. There was no sign of the man, or of Mikey's red Suzuki.

Before emerging onto the street, he put his hood up. One last glance up and down the road, then he loped out, walking towards his house, half expecting to hear the roar of a motorbike behind him.

But there was nothing, just a radio playing Ed Sheeran. Annie Lee was out as usual, sweeping the pathway, though it looked clean enough. 'I told your ma there was a man looking for you, Benjamin. And your friend, Joseph.'

'What you go telling him where Joseph lived for, Annie?'

'The man was civil to me. Not like some people.'

'You seen him again?'

'No. He went.' She pushed the broom across her pathway.

'What did he look like?'

'Don't really remember. Like nothing much. He had a little earring. I don't like that in a man.'

How had the man found out where he lived? Had Mikey told him? Walking on, he slotted his key into the door, opened it, looked around one last time, then slipped inside. 'Mum?'

No answer. The radio was still playing Heart FM. She would be fast asleep, anyway. The house looked normal, familiar.

'Mum? Got some bad news. About Mikey.'

In the kitchen he looked around for anything to eat. The can of beans he had pulled out of the cupboard was there on the table, slightly misshapen from where he had dropped it. Taking a spoon from the drawer, he tugged the ring pull on the top and started eating the contents cold, stuffing them into his mouth, barely chewing. He noticed his hand shaking as he lifted the beans to his lips.

The plastic wrapper for a fresh pair of washing-up gloves lay on the floor, which was odd. Had his mum decided to do some cleaning? When she was drunk, though, who knew what went through her head?

In the cupboard under the stairs he found his old school *Star Wars* backpack, returned to the kitchen and, between mouthfuls of beans, started adding whatever he could find to it, but there wasn't much: two cans of rice pudding, another of mandarins, a half-eaten jar of peanut butter and a Pot Noodle. He opened the freezer and saw a packet of fishfingers, but ice had built up around it. He turned and looked for the sharp knife that his mother kept in the wooden block. It wasn't there. Funny. Hadn't he put it back there this morning? He peered into the sink, but it wasn't there either.

Instead he found an ordinary table knife and dug away at the ice with it until his fingers hurt from the cold. When he tried pulling the pack out, it ripped, spilling fishfingers onto the floor. Stupid. He picked them up and dropped them, loose, into the side pocket of the backpack. Finishing the beans, he put the empty can back down on the kitchen table, then moved to the front room, where he peered through the curtains, looking up and down the road. All clear. Upstairs, he paused outside his mother's half-open door. She would be fast asleep. These days, like Sloth's mum, she slept through most of the day. Sometimes, after a heavy night out, she snored, but today she was quiet.

In his bedroom he pulled a waterproof out from under his bed and added that to the bag, along with a pair of pants, some socks and a couple of T-shirts.

He was just scrabbling through his bedside drawer to see if there was any change in there when he heard an engine outside.

Definitely a bike; the motor stopped. Frickin' frick!

He moved to the bedroom window.

When he was about twelve his mother had brought home some dinosaur curtains that she'd bought in a bring-and-buy sale. He had been too old for them then. Now he stood behind them listening to the bike's engine, afraid to even twitch them in case he gave himself away.

He took a breath. Pulling back the material just a fraction of an inch, he peeked down. Breathed again.

Just a Deliveroo driver, with one of those big stupid blue boxes on the back of his bike, dropping off a Chinese or something across the road to the house by the garages.

Calm down, Tap. Calm down.

He closed the curtain, tucked the few coins he'd retrieved into his trousers and found a biro. On the back of a Pizza Hut flier, he wrote: *MUM GOT TO GO SOMEWHERE URGENT WILL BE IN TOUCH IN A FEW DAYS*. He wondered if he should tell her about Mikey, too, on the note. She would be upset. Really upset. Whatever she said about Mikey, she had really loved him. The pen hovered above the paper. In the end, he just added: *LUV U BENJAMIN XX*. He picked up the note, intending to leave it downstairs on the kitchen table, put the pack on his back, and stepped back out to the landing, but stopped the moment he was out of his own doorway.

His mother's door was no longer half open. There was just a crack now, between the door and the frame.

The note fluttered onto the carpet. He must have dropped it.

The door had moved, he was sure of it. Hadn't he just looked in there?

Perhaps she had got up and pushed the door to herself because of the racket he had been making? He hadn't heard her complaining, though, and she would have. Had she left a window open? Could a breeze have caught the door?

He listened.

No noise. Nothing.

What if somebody had gone into his mother's room?

He stepped forward onto the dirty pink carpet that covered the landing. A floorboard creaked loudly beneath his foot.

'Mum?' he half whispered.

No answer.

He was calculating how fast he could run down the stairs and out of the front door.

Backing into his room again, he jerked his head around,

looking for a weapon of some sort. All he could spot was an empty beer bottle; picking it up he returned to the landing.

Nothing.

Inching towards his mother's door, bottle in hand, he put his foot against it, then pushed. It swung open.

The room was dark. As his eyes grew accustomed to the light, he saw his mother on her back, mouth wide, one arm drooping off the far side of the bed.

Dead to the world, immobile. Almost as if she wasn't even breathing.

No one else in the room at all. Behind the curtain the window was open. The cloth billowed out in a breeze. It must have been the wind.

He breathed again.

Standing in the doorway, he watched her, lying so still. She had gone to bed half clothed, shirt off, tights still on. He thought about the mum in the shopping centre and wondered if his own mother had ever been like that. If she looked after herself a bit more, she could be pretty. She still was some days.

He should not spend any more time here. The man, whoever he was, knew where he lived. Mikey was dead, Sloth had disappeared. He should get out of here.

He turned, stepped onto the landing and stopped. From downstairs, the unmistakable creak of a door.

He listened again. Nothing, save the sound of the radio. But he could swear he could feel the presence now.

There it was again. Definitely this time. His hands were shaking again, like crazy this time.

Someone else was in the house besides himself and his mother.

NINE

Stark and white against the grey sky, the gallery made Cupidi think of a cathedral built by missionaries.

Margate had once been a grand place, an elegant curve of Georgian houses facing a bay with sand the colour of honey. The town had been sliding downhill for decades. The tourists who had come here to scream on the wooden roller coaster now went abroad. The boarding houses and bed-and-breakfasts had become migrant hostels and bedsits for London's poor.

A decade ago they had built this great gallery in an attempt to save the place. And it was working, insofar as artists and artisans were re-opening the empty shops around the Old Town and a richer class of Londoners was buying property, renovating the crumbling houses. Money was finally coming back to the place. But the poverty had just retreated a few hundred metres. It still encircled the older buildings, waiting for gentrification to falter.

Ferriter parked the car on the Harbour Arm, a solid sweep of pale stone that curved out to create a sheltered bay in front of

57

the Old Town. The tide was out. On the land end of the stone jetty, a small Victorian customs house had been adorned with the words *I Never Stopped Loving You*, glowing in pink neon; the pink of sticks of rock. Cupidi stared at it for a while. An artwork by Tracey Emin, a sign explained. Was it about this place, or a person? Both, probably.

'Sarge?' said Ferriter. She was nodding towards the gallery on the other side of the customs house.

The three of them approached the big glass door. A sign, taped to the inside, read: *The gallery has been closed due to an incident. We apologise for any disappointment.*

A young man led them up the stairs to a large, bright room where a CSI stood outside the door with the boxes of protective gear.

Inside, the scene of crime team were photographing the black pot, still on its plinth, lid on the floor; white figures in a white room.

Outside the door, Cupidi introduced herself to the art gallery's director, a businesslike man with neat, shoulder-length hair who stood, arms crossed and tight-lipped, observing the scene. 'We've contacted the artist, of course,' he said.

Dark clouds hung over the Channel, lending the spring light on the horizon a bright intensity. Alex Cupidi looked through the north-facing glass out to sea.

'You won't find anything,' called the director through the door as they dusted the pot for fingerprints. 'We take particular care to keep the exhibits as clean as possible.' They moved inside, standing at the edge of the room, outside a ring of queue tapes someone had set up around the plinth.

In a place like this, the normally confident crime scene investigator seemed hesitant. 'Can we lift it down, then?'

'As long as you don't break it,' said the director, arching his eyebrows. 'If you like, one of our people can do it.'

'No, no. It has to be us.'

The jar was about 60 or 70 centimetres tall. Two people from the forensics team positioned themselves on either side and cautiously lifted the pot off the plinth. There was a small gasp from the director and a colleague standing near her. A dark round 'C'-shape, like a coffee stain, remained on the white paint, where liquefying flesh had seeped through the unglazed base.

Carefully, they placed the artwork on the floor and the lead forensics woman peered into the opening. 'Photograph,' she said.

The cameraman approached again, laid a scale alongside the pot. The black of the jar had been covered with beautifully detailed drawings of dragons, birds and gods next to modern young couples kissing and holding hands. On the lid were carefully etched pictures of celebrities, each named in small scrolls.

Ferriter, in white, pointed, and said, 'That's Jade Goody.'

'What do you reckon?' asked Sergeant Moon.

'I like it,' announced Ferriter.

'No . . . I mean, why did someone put an arm in there?'

'I wouldn't know yet, would I? That's what we're here to find out, isn't it?' Constable Ferriter could be tetchy to work with at the best of times; today she seemed particularly moody.

Suited up in white, Cupidi stepped inside the tape and read the label on the plinth:

Funerary Urn (2010). Dead celebrities such as Kurt Cobain and Heath Ledger take the place of household deities, while the decorative work below contains depictions of gods and auspicious animals, elements inspired by an early Buddhist funerary urn in the British Museum.

'When exactly would the arm have been put in there?' Constable Ferriter asked out loud, to no one in particular.

'Good question,' said Cupidi, turning to the director.

'I wasn't here when they installed the artwork,' he said.

'Installed it? It's not part of the permanent collection?'

'It's on loan for the current exhibition, "In Memoriam". It opened last week.'

When the photographer stepped back, Cupidi took his place and peered into the jar.

'So it might have been in the jar when it arrived?'

For the first time she saw the arm. The stump lay at the bottom; close to the rim, four pale fingers were curled into a loose fist. Drained of blood, the knuckles looked like milky knots.

Cupidi pulled out her phone, turned on the torch and shone it down into the ceramic jar.

Ferriter joined her, peering into the dark interior. 'What's that moving?'

'Maggots,' said Cupidi.

'Oh shit.' Ferriter held her hand in front of her mouth.

The crime scene team were whispering notes and instructions to each other as if they were in a cathedral. Even their cloth-clad footsteps sounded respectful.

'We'll need the date and time the pot arrived here, the details of who brought it, who packed it, unpacked it, and whoever was in charge of it . . .'

The director nodded; the silent man next to him made a few more notes.

Cupidi spotted a pile of shredded cardboard lying on the floor next to the plinth. 'What's that?'

'That was on top of the arm when we opened it. It was stuffed into the jar, like packing. I'd assume that whoever installed it may not have even noticed there was anything underneath it.'

Squatting down, Cupidi photographed it on her phone. 'Could it mean anything? Someone putting an arm into this particular work of art?'

The director looked uncomfortable. 'Yes. Of course it could. Inevitably. This is an art gallery. Things acquire meaning simply because they are here.'

Cupidi thought about that for a second.

'An intentional meaning?'

'What?' The director seemed amused by something now. 'It's something we struggle with, the intentionality of an artwork.'

Cupidi stared at the director until the smile disappeared from his face, then said, 'We don't struggle with that so much on Serious Crime. Mostly it's pretty intentional when you remove someone's arm.'

'Sorry. It's just . . . we're all a little shocked. This kind of thing hasn't happened here before. Obviously.'

'Someone leaves a body part in a very public place. It's not a very successful way of hiding it, is it?'

'Clearly not, no.'

'So they weren't hiding it. Then, what were they trying to

communicate by leaving it here? Is there anything about this particular artwork which we should be thinking about?'

'I see,' said the director, straightening a little. 'The work is by an artist of Chinese origin who is asking questions about our relationship with the dead, how it compares with her own culture and with the ancient Buddhist culture of her ancestors. In some ways, it's as much a piece about immigration and globalisation as it is about death.' He spoke as a curator, referencing some artists Cupidi had heard of, many she had not. 'It's a work about death, but is as much about the way that our British culture delegitimises the way in which others think about death.'

Cupidi wrote a few notes, then turned to leave the gallery. 'Ironically,' the director added, 'the artist herself died shortly after finishing the work. A great loss.' As he removed his mask at the door, he asked, 'Would you like coffee? I sent most of the staff home, but I've kept the public cafeteria open.'

Ferriter and Cupidi sat at a table, while Moon went to the office to record details of when the artwork had arrived. Cupidi ordered an Americano with two shots, Ferriter went for a mug of hot water.

'*It's something we struggle with, the intentionality of an artwork,*' muttered Ferriter. 'Jesus.'

Cupidi said nothing.

'Notice that, though? It's like he was saying the arm was art or something.'

Cupidi looked up from her coffee. 'Yes. He was, wasn't he?'

Murder investigations started with a body. This one was already different. How much would a pathologist be able to tell them from just a limb? How had it got there? Had it been in the jar when it had been delivered to the gallery, or had it been concealed there more recently? The crime scene itself was a challenge. It was too clean.

Turning a page in her notebook, she became conscious of being watched. Looking up, she saw a young man ten metres away on the other side of the glass, looking at her. He was dressed in black, pale-faced, with a sweep of dark hair running across his forehead.

'Who is that?'

'Jesus,' said Ferriter. 'He's staring at us. That's kind of creepy.'

Cupidi looked back at the young man, but he didn't seem at all discomfited by her gaze. Instead he reached into the pocket of his black raincoat, pulled out a small leather notebook and wrote something in it.

'Weirdo,' muttered Ferriter. 'Reckon he's a reporter, or just a gawper?'

Cupidi went back to her work. She and Moon would have to present a strategy tomorrow morning for how they would advise the senior investigating officer to tackle this case.

Was this even a murder investigation? A few years ago, members of the public had discovered three separate human feet in a park in Bristol. They had launched a murder inquiry, but in the end, after an operation that had cost tens of thousands, if not hundreds, no culprit had been found. They concluded that the feet had been simply discarded medical exhibits. Worse, it could turn out to be someone's attempt at guerrilla art. A Banksy? Or somebody who envied that kind of notoriety. She could imagine someone stepping forward to claim credit for it. A genuine human arm was presumably not easy to source, but not impossible either. The pot was a kind of funerary urn. Whether it was a prank or not, it had to mean something, the act of placing an arm in there. And it was someone's arm.

Cupidi looked up, sucking at the end of her pen.

The director returned. The lad was still watching them.

'Who is that?' Cupidi pointed at the man. He seemed to smile back.

'He's one of ours. I don't remember his name. Started a few weeks ago.'

A gust of wind caught the man's black mac and it blew upwards, exposing an old maroon lining.

'A bit strange, that one, to be honest. It's his probationary period,' said the director. 'I'm not sure if we're going to keep him on.'

The figure had turned now and was walking away towards the old customs house and its pink neon sign. Cupidi made a note to find out his name; she should remember to talk to him, she decided.

TEN

Tap shut himself in his bedroom, heart thumping.

He tried to believe he had just imagined the noise, until it came again. The squeak of a floorboard this time. The sound of someone moving slowly.

Could he run down the stairs and make it out of the front door?

'Mum,' he hissed.

No answer.

And it dawned on him again that the sharp knife he had been looking for was missing from the block. In the same second he also remembered how his mum had not moved when he had looked in on her earlier, not even snored. She had lain there still, silhouetted in the darkness.

Oh Christ. The washing-up gloves too. It had not been her who had taken them out of the packet.

He leaned back against the closed bedroom door. His eyes filled; he wiped them with his sleeve.

'Hello,' he said, loud, heart galloping. 'I know you're there.'

Nothing, just another stupid pop song chattering away somewhere.

Thing is, he and Sloth always acted hard, like all the boys did, but everyone knew they weren't. It had always been like that. Sloth and Tap, black kid and loser, bunking off school to avoid another day of being bullied. Amongst the other boys, they were a joke.

Still grasping the beer bottle, he took the backpack off to hold it in front of him as he ran – thinking that if someone was coming at him with a knife, he would have something to protect himself with. But he didn't seem to be able to move. He was too scared.

If he knew where the man was hiding, it would be better, maybe.

'What do you want from us?' He tried to sound confident, but his voice came out high and thin.

Nothing.

He took a deep breath and blew it out slowly. Drugs made you paranoid, he knew that. They made you think people were waiting round corners. All he had heard was a creak of some kind. It could have come from outside, or from the neighbours. The walls of these houses were thin.

But Mikey was dead. Someone had killed him. And someone had been ringing Sloth's doorbell.

Count to ten, then run.

He breathed again. One . . .

But before he made it to two he heard another noise. At the bottom of the stairs, between the last step and the front doormat, was a single loose floorboard. It was a particular sound: half

66

groan, half squeak. Beneath it was the cold-water pipe that led to the street outside, and an ancient tap. When you trod on it, it rocked, gently, rubbing up against the joists below.

That noise. Wood against wood. The man was at the bottom of the stairs, waiting for Tap to show himself.

'I can see you,' lied Tap. 'I know you're there.'

Still nothing.

'What are you after? I'll give it you if you tell me.'

Dropping the backpack and the bottle, he brushed a pile of comics off the seat of the chair that sat by his bed and wedged it under the door handle, then laid his ear against the door listening. All he could hear was the thump of blood in his own head.

He sat on the bed, put his head in his hands, tried to think.

And then the door handle twisted, and the door nudged open a crack, just as far as the chair would allow it.

Jesus.

There was a thump. The man must have laid a shoulder into the door – or a boot – and as he did so, the whole thing seemed to bend on its hinge over the top of the chair.

Oh shit.

Scrabbling through the debris of empty cans, discarded clothes and makeshift ashtrays, he made it to the window and yanked the curtain back. Brightness filled the room. He looked back. The chair hadn't fallen yet, but it was a cheap thing, made from plywood. One big shove and it would splinter, or its feet would skid on the carpet it was wedged on.

He fumbled with the casement, fingers suddenly weak. Most of the time he kept it closed because Annie Lee and the other neighbours complained about the noise of his music.

The third thump was accompanied by the crack of wood, just as the window finally swung open. Tap pushed himself up onto the sill, perched for a second, squatting on the frame.

The area in front of the house was concrete. If he jumped from here he would break a leg.

He turned in the window frame, so that he was facing the bedroom again, just as the whole door frame began to finally splinter. Letting his legs drop, he caught the sill just for a second to slow his fall, then uncurled his fingers and plummeted.

He was up again before the man had even made it to the window.

Tap knew he only had a few seconds' advantage. The man would be down the stairs soon, and out of the front door, after him. Tap knew every little alleyway and dark corner, but he was limping as he ran from the way he'd jolted his leg as he landed. It wouldn't anyway take long to catch up with him. He picked the routes towards the centre of the town, heading to the thin passageway that led down to the park.

It was a cut-through only locals knew, hedge on one side, fence on the other. When he reached it, it was empty. Looking over his shoulder as he ran, he almost slammed straight into the pushbike coming the other way as it braked and spun sideways in front of him.

'Out me flippin' way.'

'Oi. Quick. Get on,' shouted a voice.

Tap looked up. Wearing a pair of girl's dark glasses, hood up, and standing on one pedal of a BMX was Sloth.

Tap grinned. Beautiful Sloth looking like a total mug with stupid shades, on a kid's BMX.

'Go on. What you waitin' for?'

Tap ran to the back of the bike. Hands on Sloth's shoulders, he climbed onto the rear pegs, feet on either side of the wheel, and as soon as he was on, Sloth stood to put all his weight on the pedals.

Spitting gravel behind him, Sloth pumped his legs as they careered down the path, away from West View Road, and then out onto the wider, scrubby track – one of those streets the council had never bothered with – weaving past the parked cars.

'Bloody hell,' said Tap, looking behind him. There was no sign of the man.

'What the frick is going on?' said Sloth, panting.

'Hear about Mikey?'

'What about him?'

But Tap didn't have a chance to answer.

From behind came the huge roar of a big motorbike engine. He looked round only for long enough to see it was red.

'Shit-shit-shit.'

To their right, another smaller footpath sloped down behind the houses ahead of them. Without waiting to see the bike appear at the junction in front of him, Sloth stood on the pedal again, heading for the path as Tap clung on.

The incline helped, as did the weight of the two boys. The bike freewheeled fast, Tap ducking low branches. On the tarmac, a man with a Yorkshire terrier was coming towards them.

'Get out the way,' screamed Tap.

The man pressed himself into the shrubs, yanking on the small dog's lead.

'Bloody wan—' the man shouted after them.

Sloth didn't stop, not even when they got to the end of the track, where it turned onto Ninety-Nine Steps.

'No,' yelped Tap.

Sloth was not listening. Ninety-Nine Steps was the quick way down; a path down the escarpment to the main road at the bottom.

Sloth turned the BMX right, straight down into the steep incline, front wheel bumping against the first of the stone steps. Tap's legs juddered as the bike gathered speed. Sloth could duck down because he hunched over the handlebars, but Tap was standing on the back, trying to keep a hold on Sloth's shoulders. Branches and brambles slapped him in the face.

They were about two-thirds of the way down when the front wheel slid into the weeds at the side of the path, lifting the rear of the BMX into the air. Tap released his grip on Sloth's back and found himself catapulted over Sloth and the bike that was already slithering sideways now down the remaining steps.

They were going to die.

But he landed on his hands, head down, and bounced across the pavement, hitting the metal barrier at the bottom just before Sloth rolled into him.

There was a moment of stillness, the bike's rear wheel spinning on its ratchet. The front wheel's spokes were wrecked, pointing at all angles.

Without saying anything, they stood and ran, abandoning the BMX, dodging through the moving traffic as horns blared around them.

ELEVEN

It was a hell of a story: Severed Limb Discovered in Art Gallery. Two TV news cameras were setting up on the harbour arm, framing shots of the building.

The gallery director seemed to be remarkably calm about it all. There were things that needed to be done, so he was doing them.

Cupidi had requested the gallery's CCTV footage. They would have weeks of it to look through. Some civilian would be given the job of staring at a screen for hours on end, logging anything interesting. Even if the arm had arrived inside the artwork, whoever had done this might have come to gloat.

'Sergeant?'

Cupidi looked around. The director was standing behind her, his assistant close by.

'Before we give this statement to the press, we're going to need to inform the owners, obviously. I've tried phoning them but have been unable to get through. We don't want them just switching on the TV and finding out about this that way.'

'Who's that? A gallery?'

'The work belongs to a private art fund.'

'Which is?'

'The Evert and Astrid Miller Foundation.'

'I meant, what exactly is a private art fund?'

'It's an organisation set up by people who buy art as an investment. And in this case, they sometimes loan the works out to institutions such as ourselves.'

'Why would they do that?' asked Cupidi.

The director's smile was the thin kind people wear when you've hit some nerve. 'Because . . . because they are art lovers who want the work to be seen.'

It took a second for the penny to drop. 'And investors who want the value of the art to rise, which presumably it does if you show it at a gallery like this?'

'I can assure you that our curators only select work on its merit.' Cupidi supposed it would be awkward for him to admit that a gallery built with millions from the public purse was playing a role in increasing the value of private art. Cupidi was in unknown territory. The art world had rules she didn't understand.

'Would this art fund have been responsible for the artwork before it got here?'

'I'll be honest, I don't know whether it was on display elsewhere or in storage.'

'What's the name again?'

'It's the Evert and Astrid Miller Foundation.'

'I'll need their contact details,' said Cupidi.

The director hesitated. 'I would prefer to speak to them first. We have a duty of care for any artwork loaned to us. That includes any negative publicity that may occur surrounding it. Obviously, they are public figures.'

'And they own the work?'

'Their foundation does, technically.'

'Astrid Miller?' said Ferriter, looking up from her notes.

'Yes.'

Cupidi looked round. 'Who?'

'Astrid Miller,' Ferriter whispered, raising her eyebrows. 'You know. You *must* know.'

Cupidi turned back to the director. 'Call them again.'

'It's a Saturday. I'm not sure anyone's there to pick up.'

'I'm sure there are other ways to contact them if you can't supply the details.'

'I wasn't suggesting for a second that I wouldn't,' the director said curtly. 'Give me a minute. I'll try again.'

When he'd turned his back on them to make another call, Cupidi turned to the constable and mouthed, 'Who?'

'Seriously?' Ferriter's mouth hung open.

'Seriously.'

'You've never heard of her?'

'No.'

'I don't believe you, sometimes. Astrid Theroux. The model. Used to hang around in clubs with Kate Moss and Oasis and all that. No? She was amazing. Then got married to that rich bloke.'

'Model marries rich bloke. Surprise,' said Moon.

The name Astrid Theroux was beginning to ring a vague bell.

'When I was a teenager she was in the papers all the time,' Ferriter told her. 'Then she married that internet entrepreneur. She kind of disappeared . . . Well, not disappeared. She does

73

charity stuff, but she stopped working as a model. I mean, she used to be huge.'

'Brilliant.'

'Yeah, she is,' said Ferriter, missing Cupidi's irony. No officer wanted famous people involved in a case. 'She was just so bloody beautiful and cool. And positive, you know? I loved her.'

'Nobody's picking up still,' said the director. 'I had to leave a message.'

'What are you going to tell that lot, then?' Cupidi nodded towards the press, waiting with their cameras.

'I'd appreciate it if we could keep the name of the artwork itself quiet for now. That's the only thing that connects the Foundation to this. We owe the Millers a duty of care.'

'Our duty of care belongs mainly to the person without the arm.'

The director had the grace to look embarrassed. 'Obviously. Yes. But . . .'

'However,' Cupidi continued, 'there's currently no operational reason why we need to mention publicly which artwork it was found in . . .'

The man looked relieved.

'But we will be contacting them ourselves whenever we have to.'

The director's lips tightened, just a fraction.

'We're investigating what may be a murder. Or not. There's a possibility the victim is still alive.'

'Oh.'

'So you can understand why we would prefer to proceed at our own schedule.'

He nodded. 'I'm not trying to be an arse. It's just we're not used to this kind of thing, and we're used to doing things in our own way.'

'Me too,' said Cupidi and set off back to the car, walking past the reporters.

Cupidi got in the driving seat this time and started the engine. Moon got in beside her. 'We'll need to find what documents they have on where that artwork's been this last two months and who's been in charge of it.'

'Serious? Astrid Miller? Can I do it?' begged Ferriter, in the back.

'I doubt she actually runs it,' said Cupidi.

'Yeah. I know. Just saying.'

'An arm. Crazy.' Moon shook his head. He turned to face Ferriter in the back of the car. 'Fancy a meal later? We could go out somewhere.'

'I don't think so. Got too much work.'

'We could do that together.'

There was a long prickly silence until Ferriter said quietly, 'Take a bloody hint, Peter.'

'Suit yourself.'

Cupidi drove, wondering what exactly had gone on between the pair of them.

TWELVE

They ran across the road, into town, looking over their shoulders, thumping into kids staring at their mobiles, finally ducking into the alleyway by the old video shop. Sloth stood at the corner, scanning the street. 'He was in your house, Tap. I saw him.'

'I know.' Tap had a stitch. He was bent double, gasping. His leg still ached and his arm was bruised from the fall down Ninety-Nine Steps.

'The same guy we robbed. In your bloody house. How did he get in?'

'Don't know,' Tap gasped. 'Was it him round yours too?'

'Yeah. On your uncle Mikey's bike. He must have nicked it. Mikey's a hard nut. His Suzuki. How did he get it? What are we going to do, Tap?'

Tap straightened, clutching his side. 'Mikey's dead.'

'Say that again.'

Tap repeated what Dennis had heard. Sloth's eyes were wide.

'This is some mess, bro. He knows where we both live. What's going on?'

'I don't know. I don't frickin' know.'

'It's the guy whose phone we nicked, right?'

'Think so.'

There was a pile of rubbish at one end of the alley: somebody's half-eaten takeaway dumped on the street, the top of a pineapple, an empty cigarette packet.

'What we going to do, Tap?'

Normally it was Tap who asked questions like that; it was Sloth who came up with all the ideas. Tap just shook his head. 'All it was was a phone. We just filched a stupid phone. I'd give it back to him, only I don't even know where it is now. Mikey had it, didn't he?'

'We should go to the cops. Say we think we know who killed Mikey.'

'We nicked his iPhone, bro.'

Sloth giggled nervily. 'He's going to tell the police that. "Yeah, OK, I murdered this man, but they stole my mobile first." We don't have to tell the feds that, just that he's the one who killed Mikey.'

'We don't know hundred per cent it was him that did Mikey.'

'Listen to yourself. Course it was. Otherwise you wouldn't have run like your arse was alight.'

'Yeah,' Tap said, 'but we don't actually know, do we?'

Sloth went to the end of the alley, looked up and down the street, then retreated towards Tap. 'Any cash?'

'Nope. Skint. About sixty pence.'

'Me too.'

They looked at each other.

'What we going to do?'

'Don't know.'

They stood together, backs against the wall, saying nothing until Sloth returned to his lookout position on the corner. 'He's not here, anyway.'

'Right.'

'Tomorrow. Maybe go to the cops tomorrow. Once we have a chance to think. Get our story straight. OK?'

'Yeah.'

'Come on, then.'

'Where?'

'Anywhere. Stinks here,' said Sloth and he turned right, towards the centre of town. Tap, looking left and right as he stepped into the street again, followed him anxiously.

Saturday evening, and the town centre was emptying out. They approached street corners warily, glanced behind themselves as they walked.

Outside Cash Converters, a man in a dark mac was staring at them, his lips moving. Was he watching them? Or just talking to someone on a mobile? Tap looked around. It seemed like everybody was sneaking looks towards them.

On the High Street, Dennis was still waiting outside Primark, this time on his own. 'Hey, lads,' he called. 'Joseph. Benj. Come 'ere.'

Tap and Sloth looked at each other, nervous about hearing their names shouted in the street.

'Over here.'

'What's going on?' muttered Sloth.

'What's happening?' Dennis hailed them.

'Nitch. Got any ciggies, Den?'

'No.' From the depths of his combat trousers, Dennis dug around, but instead of cigarettes, pulled out his phone and started texting.

'Lend us a fiver,' said Sloth.

'Bog off. Why do you want it?'

''Cause we're starving. Couple of quid?'

'No.'

'Remember that time we went on a school trip and you didn't have anything to eat, and I gave you half my ham sandwich?' said Sloth.

'Nope.'

'Nor me,' Sloth admitted.

'What's so funny?' said Tap. 'I'm hungry. Just wanted to get chips or something.'

Dennis's phone buzzed. He looked at the screen.

'Come on, Slo.' Tap tugged at Sloth's sleeve. 'Keep moving.'

They had only gone about ten metres further when Dennis called, 'What about a burger?'

They stopped. 'What?'

'Buy you a burger.'

'Why?'

''Cause you shared an imaginary sandwich with me. 'Cause I'm nice.'

Tap and Sloth exchanged a glance. 'Serious?'

'Why not?'

Another look passed between them. They were hungry. 'Bloody right. Come on then.' And Tap took Sloth's arm, dragging him back up the street.

'What's he up to?' Sloth was saying.

'Wimpy all right?'

'Suppose.' Right now Tap's stomach actually hurt, he was that hungry.

Dennis thumbed another text, hitched up his khakis, and set off towards the restaurant with the wide-legged gait of a man who had just got off a horse.

'God, I'm starving,' said Tap.

'We sure about this?' asked Sloth, pushing open the door.

Tap was at the counter already. 'Can I have a Halfpounder?'

'Yes.'

'With bacon and cheese?'

Dennis hesitated. 'OK.'

'Me too,' said Sloth. 'And chips. And Coke.'

'Regular or large?' The woman behind the counter was a teenager herself, with heavily pencilled eyebrows and a tattoo on her forearm that said '*Believe*'. Her hand hovered over the till.

Sloth smiled at Dennis and said, 'Large.'

Dennis looked anxious now.

'Same as him,' decided Tap.

'Twenty-one sixty,' said the server.

'How much?' The server repeated the total. 'Jesus,' Dennis mumbled. Tap thought he was going to refuse to pay, but instead, he dug back into his military trousers, pulled out a plastic wallet and removed two ten-pound notes and some change. 'I'll just have a Coke,' he muttered.

'You got a boyfriend?' Sloth asked the server.

The girl smiled back. 'You're way too young for me.'

'That's discrimination,' said Sloth.

The woman handed them three paper cups. 'Go find someone your own age.'

They went to the drinks dispenser to fill them. 'Thanks, Dennis. We'll pay you back.' Tap winked at Sloth.

'I don't get it,' hissed Sloth. 'He was always such a shit to us at school.'

'Everyone was, mind you.'

'True.'

Sloth was about to head for a table near the rear of the restaurant, but Dennis walked in the other direction, towards the window. 'Come on,' he said.

Sloth hesitated, looked at Tap. 'No, we'd prefer it back here.'

'Come on. I paid for it. Least you can do is sit with me.' He picked a four-seat table next to the glass.

Tap's hunger got the better of him. He sighed, scanned the High Street outside for any sign of the man they had robbed, then joined him at the table. Sloth put his hood up so it covered his head, then followed.

'So,' said Dennis. 'What's going on with you two?'

'What do you mean?' asked Sloth.

'Just passing the time. Making conversation. Just bought you dinner. Least you can do is chat.'

'Nothing much. Just hanging around.'

Dennis nodded, looking away.

Outside, street lights flickered on. Tap could hear the sizzle of meat on the hotplate.

'Know what? I need a piss,' said Sloth.

Tap was aware of someone kicking him beneath the table. He looked down. Sloth's trainer was nudging his ankle.

81

'I need to go to the toilet,' Sloth repeated.

'Go on then,' said Dennis.

Sloth was nodding towards the Gents at the back of the room.

'Me too,' added Tap, standing.

'You go together? Like girls?'

Tap ignored him.

'Don't be long. Your food'll be here. Might have to eat it myself.' He took the phone out of his big pocket again and looked at the screen.

Sloth disappeared into the bathroom; Tap followed. 'What?' he demanded.

'Why's he spending, like, twenty quid on us? He'd never do that.'

'We said we'd pay him back.'

Sloth said, 'Yeah, but for starters he knows we couldn't. Plus, you noticed the way he keeps checking his phone and looking out of the window, like he expects someone to arrive?'

'He's dobbing us in.' Tap had been so hungry, he hadn't seen what was happening.

'That's why he bought us the meal. To keep us hanging around until . . .'

Tap opened the door a crack and peered through. The large boy in army gear was scanning the High Street, left and right. 'You're right.'

'I'm always right.'

'What a bastard.'

'C'mon,' said Sloth, pushing past him.

'What are we doing?'

'Getting out of this place.'

At the table, Dennis turned and smiled. 'Have a good time in there, lads?'

'Get up,' ordered Sloth. 'We got to go. Snap, snap.'

Dennis was bewildered. 'But the food isn't here yet.'

'Quick. No time to explain.'

'The food . . .' Dennis said again.

Sloth had decided Dennis was coming with them. Surely, thought Tap, the best thing to do would be to just run for it and dump him here? But Sloth had a plan.

'Come on, mate.' Tap pulled at the sleeve of Dennis's army jacket. If he was trying to turn them in, he would have to come with them, or lose them.

Slowly Dennis stood, looking out the window one last time.

'Hurry up,' hissed Sloth.

Tap looked out into the street, then opened the door, and they stumbled out onto the paving. 'Easy, lads,' said Dennis.

Tap took his left arm; Sloth took his right, grabbing it firmly, and they marched him down the road fast, before he could think about what was happening, until they reached the alley that went to Bull's Head Yard. 'Let go.'

Tap shoved him into the cut-through that led towards the station.

'What's going on, boys?' Dennis sounded scared now.

Tap grabbed the other arm from Sloth and tightened them both behind his back while Sloth dug into the boy's trousers, first one pocket and then the other.

'You're hurting me.'

Sloth pulled out Dennis's phone just as a message lit the home screen: **At Wimpy now. Where are u?**

Sloth held the device up to the boy's face. 'Who's that texting you?'

'No one.'

Sloth looked at the back-lit words. 'How much did he offer you?'

'What?' Dennis wrinkled his brow in an effort to look confused.

'He offered you money, didn't he? You'd never be splashing out twenty quid on burgers for us if you weren't getting something for it.'

'Nothing serious, lads. He said he just wanted to talk.' A gob of spittle hung onto his lips.

'You're such an imbecile, Dennis.'

'What are we going to do now?' asked Tap, his mind still on the Halfpounder with cheese and bacon.

The device buzzed again: **Where?**

Dennis wriggled in Tap's clutches. 'You're hurting me.'

'Let him go,' said Sloth.

Tap released him.

'Give me my phone.'

'You just grassed on us. Lucky we don't properly hurt you. Who is he?'

'I don't know. What's he after you two for?'

Neither answered. Sloth turned and headed north, away from the High Street; Tap followed.

'What about my flippin' phone?'

Again, neither answered.

'Guys?'

Sloth stopped, took the phone off Tap, turned and shouted, 'Catch.'

He threw the phone high. Dennis squinted in the low light,

hands up in the air. The handset sailed past him and smashed down onto the paved walkway.

'Fucking hell.'

'What did you do that for, you idiot?' said Tap. 'You gave it him back.'

'I'm done with nicking phones, mate. 'Sides, we can use yours, can't we?'

'No. Left it at home, bro, when I ran out the place. Haven't got one.'

'You're kidding me? Still got this one though.' He dug in his pocket and pulled out the Alcatel phone from the man's shoulder bag.

Tap stared at it. 'What you got that for?'

'Don't know. It was just in my pocket. Forgot about it.'

'That's his phone. The man's.'

Sloth pressed the keys.

'Don't!' shouted Tap.

'Hello. Anyone there? Is that you, bitch? Well we got away from you, didn't we? Your fat little friend gave you away.'

Tap went to snatch the handset.

Sloth held it up. The screen was blank. He had just been pretending. 'Don't get your bollocks twisted, bro. It's locked, anyway. Thing's useless.'

Down the alley, Dennis was trying to put the back onto his own phone. 'Screen's smashed,' he was shouting. 'I'll make you bloody pay for that.'

But he didn't follow them as they walked north, away from the town centre, with no idea at all where they were going.

THIRTEEN

'What's wrong with you?'

'Don't know what you mean,' Ferriter said, stone-faced. Cupidi had dropped Moon first, at his mother's house. When he had closed the front door behind him, she had turned to the young constable sitting on the back seat.

'Until the name Astrid Miller was mentioned, you have spent the whole day moping round like a teenager.'

'Stupid case.'

'Don't you bloody start. We're going to get enough of that from the others. *An arm. In an art gallery.*'

'Yep. That's going to be a riot, isn't it?'

They sat in the car for a minute.

'It's still somebody's arm,' said Cupidi.

'Sorry,' said Ferriter. 'I'm a bit off.'

'Go and have a drink.'

'I'm never drinking again.'

Cupidi laughed, then said, 'William South came back home today.'

'He's been let out?' Ferriter whistled. 'There goes the property values round your way. Convicted murderer.'

'The crime was over forty years ago. He should be allowed to live in peace.'

Ferriter said, 'Though maybe the poor bastard should never have been prosecuted in the first place.'

Cupidi looked at her. 'Is that a criticism?'

Ferriter got out, but instead of closing the door she leaned inside and said, 'His father deserved it.'

It had all come out at the trial. South's father had been a violent man who had assaulted South's mother and who had killed at least once himself. But that wasn't the point, was it?

Rattled, Cupidi drove off without saying goodbye. The driving was going to kill her. This was a big county. She seemed to spend her whole time travelling from the local nick to County HQ, then to scenes of crime that could still be hours away.

Zoë emerged from her bedroom when she heard the front door. 'Hard day at the office?'

'I've had worse. Strange, though. I was at the Turner in Margate. Someone put a human arm in a jar that's owned by a multi-millionaire.'

'Different,' her daughter said.

She followed her daughter to the kitchen. 'How much do you think it would cost to buy a human arm?'

'About five hundred dollars.'

'How do you know that?'

'I'm guessing. Why would I actually know that fact?'

'I have no idea what you're doing up there in your bedroom these days.'

'I'm trading vital organs, Mum, obviously. You can buy pretty much any body part you want from the Ukraine. They dig up bodies there, from the graveyards.'

'Where do you get this stuff?'

'BuzzFeed. Vice. The news.'

'That's not news,' said her mother.

'What, and the *Daily Mail* is?'

Cupidi looked through the fridge, trying to decide what they could have for supper. Her daughter's veganism proved challenging. Sometimes she longed for a piece of meat. 'What have you been doing all day?'

Zoë shrugged. 'Nothing much.'

When they lived in London, Cupidi had worried about her daughter growing up too fast, hanging out with the wrong crowd. For a while after they had moved here she had gone feral, spending her days out on the nature reserve to the north of their house. It was William South who had taught her the basics of birdwatching, patiently spending time with the girl, tramping around the foreland with her. Zoë had become obsessed. They had been close. Now she was worrying whether Zoë was spending time with the wrong crowd again, during those days when she disappeared on the bus, or upstairs online. When she asked her what she was doing up there, the answer was always jokey or vague. 'Nothing much.'

Cupidi started chopping a cucumber to make a salad. 'The arm was in an artwork that is owned by some millionaire investment fund. Astrid Miller. Have you heard of her?'

'Astrid Miller? Jesus, Mum. Astrid Theroux?'

'I was a working mother bringing up a child, if you remember. I didn't have time to read *Hello!*'

'I ruined your life,' said Zoë, leaning over and taking a slice of cucumber, chewing on it. 'Astrid Theroux. She was pretty amazing . . . and then she sort of disappeared.'

Cupidi reached for a tomato. 'I was wondering, what if it's some attempt to rig the market? The arm. Someone trying to wreck the value of a piece.'

'Wouldn't it actually be much cooler to own a bit of art that had had a dead body in it?'

'Just an arm. Don't get carried away.' Cupidi considered the idea for a second. Her daughter was right. In the art world, notoriety would only increase an item's value. Could that be a motive? 'What about William South?' she asked her daughter. 'Did you see him?'

'It's kind of weird. He's not come out. He's been in there all day.'

'You were watching?'

'Sort of. Do you think he's OK?'

'We should probably let him find his feet a bit, first.'

'Yeah,' Zoë said.

They ate supper in the kitchen. Afterwards, Cupidi said, 'I think I'll go for a walk. Been stuck in the car half the day. Want to come?'

Her daughter shook her head.

'No special birds to see today?'

'Don't know,' she said, and stood.

'You should get out, at least.'

'I'm all right.'

'Seriously? What are you doing up there all day?'

'Internet porn mostly. Mum. That's what us teenagers do. According to the *Daily Mail*.'

Cupidi left the house, heading towards the sea. Saturday night, and she was out here on her own in the growing darkness. The Britannia and the Pilot, the two local pubs, would be full.

She walked past the shacks, down to the water, and walked north towards the darkening sky. At the edge of Dungeness, the huts and wooden houses gave way to more ordinary bungalows; the duller coast. She turned, feet crunching on the stones. Apart from a solitary angler on the beach, sitting in a circle of light from a Tilley lamp, she was alone. The sea was still for once, small waves nibbling at the shingle.

On her way back she approached South's shack again. She considered knocking, inviting him out for a drink, but thought better of it. Maybe in a day or two. As she passed, she saw a solitary bulb lit inside the small house. It made the world around it look darker.

FOURTEEN

It was dark and cold, and they were both so hungry in the way that only teenagers can be. They tramped up the tarmac walkway that ran parallel to the road, past street after street of red brick houses.

'Where are we even going?' demanded Tap, though the answer to that was simple. Out of town. He knew where they lived. 'Why has he even got it in for us?'

''Cause we robbed him, obviously.'

'Like Terminator or something. Jesus. Can I have the phone?'

'Why?'

'Call my mum.'

'It's not working.' Sloth handed over the small handset anyway and Tap punched 0000 on the keys. Then 1111. Neither worked. After 3333 it displayed *1 attempt remaining*, so he punched in four random numbers and then the screen went black. Locked out.

'You OK, bro?'

Tap wiped his eyes with his sleeve. 'Yeah.'

'We find somewhere to sleep for the night, something to eat, we'll be OK. We'll sort this in the morning, right?'

As they approached the Chinese fish and chip shop on the opposite corner, the smell was unbearable. 'What if we just say we're skint?'

'What about the Co-op next door?' asked Sloth.

Tap had been so transfixed by the chip shop, he hadn't noticed the small supermarket, lights still on.

'OK.'

Supermarkets were easy. They had been nicking small stuff from them for as long as they could remember. They put up their hoods. Sloth donned the stupid dark glasses. 'No face, no case.' He grinned.

On the other side of the glass door, a security guard was talking to the woman on the till; an Asian guy whose shirt hung out of the back of his trousers.

Retreating, they sat on the grass verge on the other side of the road, watching for the guard to move away from the front of the shop. Cars drew up outside. Customers came and went.

'I can feel my ribs,' said Sloth.

'Weirder if you couldn't.'

'No. Serious. I'm losing weight, just sitting here.'

The security guard said something to the woman on the till, then disappeared behind a door.

'Quick.' Sloth stood and grabbed Tap's hand to yank him to his feet. The moment they walked into the store, Tap's mouth started watering. With the guard out back, there was only one other person in the shop, a middle-aged woman on the till who watched them, tight-mouthed, as they turned and disappeared down the aisles, scouting.

At the end of each row there was a curved mirror mounted on the ceiling. They walked around again, still obviously being watched by the woman. They would only have a couple of minutes before the guard came back; it would have been easier if there were other people in the shop to distract the woman.

Sloth stopped at the wine aisle and picked up a bottle of red. He marched up to the counter and put it down in front of the woman.

'I'll have that please, and a packet of Marlboro.'

The woman said, 'You're not eighteen.'

'Yeah. I am. Twenty, in fact.'

'Show me your ID then.'

'It's genetic,' said Sloth. 'Makes me look way younger than I am.'

'I'm not selling you anything until I see your ID.'

'It's for my mum. It's her birthday. She likes . . .' He peered at the label. 'Ree-oh-jah.'

'Get out, before I call the police.'

'Sell me the wine and I'll go. Won't tell no one, swear to God.'

'Out.' The woman was pressing the bell below the counter now. The light above her till was flashing red.

'Go,' called Tap, running past him towards the opening door, pausing at the chilled food shelves just long enough to try and pick up some sandwiches, but they spilled onto the floor. No time to retrieve them.

Outside, Tap sprinted across the road. On the far side he stopped to look back.

Sloth was still in there, calmly picking up the packages he had dropped, while, behind him, the door next to the tills opened. One hand holding his trousers, the security guard emerged, looking around.

'Shit.'

Across the street, Tap could see the woman shouting. The door slid back and Sloth shot out, sprinting, a packet of sandwiches in one hand, the bottle of wine still in the other.

The security man was a beat behind him.

Without looking, Sloth headed on, straight across the road. Out of nowhere – a roar, as a white Range Rover sped in from the left, braked, skidded.

Everything seemed to move slowly. Looking on, horrified, Tap could make out every detail of the moment.

He expected his friend to be hit. Instead, the tiniest of swerves and the SUV missed him. Tap could see the shake of Sloth's hoodie as the car gusted past.

And here he was, powering on towards Tap over the road, a big grin on his face.

Noise filled the air. The Range Rover was sounding its horn in a long, angry note, swerving left and right as the driver tried to correct his steering after avoiding the youngster who had just run out in front of him.

And, visible now the Range Rover had passed, the store guard, a shocked expression on his face.

Tap realised that it wasn't just his friend who had escaped being hit. The guard too had been about to dash out into the road after him.

And Sloth, grinning like an idiot, almost at the other side as the guard stepped out into the road after him . . .

. . . And in that instant was slammed into, side on, by a motor-bike travelling in the opposite direction to the Range Rover.

Sloth, all smiles still, oblivious to what had happened, sprinted on. Behind him, the guard tumbled, his head bouncing off the black tarmac.

The bike slewed on down the street, rider tumbling off onto the ground.

The guard lay there, abruptly inert while everything else continued to move around him.

'Run.'

'But—'

'Frickin' run.' Sloth grabbed Tap's arm and dragged him away.

Tap followed, but after what he had just seen, his legs felt like they belonged to another person.

'Come on, bro.'

They scampered up a side street, away from the main road. Something fell behind Tap and he turned his head to see a packet of digestives rolling down the tarmac behind him, disappearing under a parked car.

Ahead, Sloth had tucked himself behind a wooden fence; Tap joined him. They paused, peering back. Nobody was following them. Sloth made to set off again.

'Give us a sec.'

'There'll be a cop car along in a minute. C'mon.'

'Did you see what happened?'

Sloth, grinning still. 'What?'

'To the guard.'

'Too busy running, mate. Come on.' And he ran away up the small suburban street. 'Got away, mate. That's what matters.'

Tap took a lungful or air, started to move again. At the end of the road was a footbridge over the A206. No police car coming this way would be able to follow them over it. They paused halfway across, watching the vehicles speed along the dual carriageway beneath them, gathering breath.

'What did you get?'

'I think the guard's dead,' Tap said.

'What?'

The roar of the traffic was too loud.

'The guard was hit by a bike. Must have been going sixty. Didn't you see?'

Sloth frowned. 'What guard?'

'The one from the shop. The one that was running after you.'

'You're joking? I didn't see anything.'

'No.' Sweating now, Tap unzipped his jacket. Two packets of Jammie Dodgers and a cheese pie fell onto the path.

'You sure?'

'My own eyes.' He could never un-see it: the bounce of the skull, the sudden vacancy of the man's face. 'I never meant for that to happen. I swear.'

Sloth was still clutching the bottle of wine.

'Shit, man. Shit.'

'I know.'

'Shit, man. We better get away from here. They'll be after us. CCTV and everything.'

Again, Tap just nodded, too shocked for any more words.

Hoods up, shoulders down, they walked past building sites and empty new flats.

'This way. Bloody hell, Tap. Is that you? Keep it in, mate.'

The sewerage treatment plant lay between them and the wide reach of the Thames.

'Not funny,' shouted Tap, punching Sloth hard on the arm. 'Not now.'

'No. Sorry. Shit, man.' Sloth rubbed his arm.

Walking a little further, they turned off the road into Dartford Marsh, flat and dark. They sat out of sight beneath brambles.

'We came here from school, didn't we?'

Sloth looked around. 'Yeah. I remember. The workhouse, weren't it?'

It came back to him now. They had come here in minibuses and scuffed around the old foundations of the huge building, long torn down, sneaking cigarettes when teacher wasn't looking. This is where they had once shipped London's old, sick and the unwanted, carrying them down the Thames and dumping them here. After that there had been a firework factory nearby, until that too had been destroyed in an explosion.

'We had to write an essay, remember?'

'You did a drawing. I remember they pinned it up in the classroom till someone drew a dick on it. It was pretty good. You used to be great at drawing, bro.' Sloth looked around

97

him. 'I used to frickin' hate school. Don't seem so bad now, does it?'

'I remember the essay. We had to pretend to be an orphan, caught stealing a loaf of bread, and we'd been sent here as a punishment. I got an A minus.'

'You never got an A minus for anything.'

'Did.'

Nothing remained but the odd derelict outhouse now.

'What are we going to do?' asked Tap, looking around.

'Keep our heads down. Nobody will look for us here. It's a dump.'

Beyond the sewerage plant, the Dartford Crossing rose up over the Thames, a string of red brake lights arcing over the wide river.

The scrub land smelt of foxes and dog shit. It was covered in huge bramble thickets, skirted by muddy paths. Down one of the tracks, they found an old brick shed. There was no door.

'This used to be part of the firework factory, wasn't it?' Tap looked around.

'Don't know.'

'Remember? Everything blew up. My gran told me. She heard it.'

'You're making this up.'

'No. It was massive. Friend of my gran's was having dinner and a head came flying in the window.'

'Bullshit.'

'True. Swear to God. Human head. The glasses were still on and everything. My gran told me.'

Sloth peered in.

Someone had slept in here not so long ago. A few empty tins of cider were stacked next to some sheets of newspaper that some wino must have once used for a bed.

'Here?' questioned Tap.

'I don't know. It's a bit . . .' Sloth made a face.

'Least it'll be dry if it rains.'

Sloth nodded, took the packet of biscuits and fumbled to open it. They sat together on the cold, bare concrete inside the small shed. Sloth was on his fourth biscuit, but Tap struggled to finish his first.

He was thinking of the guard's head. The impact of a skull. The stillness of the body when everything around it was in motion, the bike skidding on past him, the Range Rover roaring on up the road.

'You got to eat something, mate.'

'Really thirsty,' said Tap, starting to shiver.

Sloth stood, gathered up the newspaper, then went outside and returned after two or three minutes with a pile of sticks.

Tap watched him squatting to carefully build the fire, just inside the open door.

He flicked a lighter several times at the damp paper, blowing the flame gently until it lit, filling the small space with white smoke. Once it caught, he disappeared again, returning with more wood, bigger pieces this time. It took a few minutes for the fire to warm the air around it, for the smoke to begin to drift out of the open door and broken windows.

'Better?' Sloth asked.

Tap nodded, holding his hands in front of the flame.

The wine had a cork in it. Sloth looked around for something to open it with. He tried pushing the stopper in with a stick, but the stick broke. Eventually he found an old door knob that was still attached to its spindle. He placed the spindle on top of the bottle and pushed down hard, until the cork gave way, dropping into the neck, spurting wine over Sloth's hands. Face lit by the red of the fire, he handed the open bottle to Tap. 'Go on. Drink.'

Thirsty, his mouth dry from the biscuit, Tap took a gulp and swallowed. 'That's horrible. I think it's off.'

Sloth took the drink off him, sniffed, then took a slug of it himself. 'That's what wine is supposed to taste like. It's delicious, man.'

'It's vile,' Tap announced, but he took another mouthful. The sandwiches were egg and cress. Tap picked them up. ''Kin' hell, man. Couldn't you get chicken?'

For the first time, Sloth laughed. Side by side, they sat, backs against the brick wall, staring at the flames, passing the bottle back and forth.

'You serious, about the guard? Aren't you?'

'Yes,' said Tap. In his stomach, the wine felt better than it tasted. 'He didn't stand a chance, man.'

'His own fault for chasing us.'

'Can't say that, man. It was just his job. It was our fault.'

Sloth's face remained stony. 'Can't go to the feds now, can we?'

'No,' agreed Tap. 'We can't.'

Sloth nodded. They watched the flickering light. 'Bullshit, though. If that head was blown all the way to Dartford, how come his glasses stayed on? That's ridiculous.'

'It's what my gran said,' said Tap.

At some point, Tap must have fallen asleep. He woke to see Sloth feeding the fire with more pieces of timber, sparks flying up, out of the open door, into the black sky.

Maybe they could live out here. Nobody would find them. Not the man who had killed Mikey; not the police. They could be safe here, couldn't they?

FIFTEEN

Michael Dillman had been a smiler. His face was projected from his laptop onto the whiteboard at the far end of the incident room. A middle-aged man, tanned, dark-haired, handsome in a well-used way.

Most people looked resigned in arrest photos, their ears shadowed in flash against a white background, hair unbrushed, maybe a cut on their face from some altercation. A few still looked angry, or affronted. Only a few, like Michael, smiled, as if unable to resist the impulse when faced by a camera.

Semi-circles of chairs were ranged around the board, dotted with officers, some with plastic cups of tea and coffee, notebooks open on their laps, stifling Monday morning yawns. Most had already worked the weekend.

'Had no idea of how the victim got to the scrap yard, so we looked at vehicles registered under his name.' A sergeant was standing by the whiteboard going through briefing notes.

The man in the picture, shot in what looked like a gang-related killing, had been known to the police for a rich variety of offences, including theft, common assault, handling stolen goods and criminal damage. The concern was that if this was a gang assassination, there would be reprisals.

'Turned out he has a BMW and a high-end Suzuki motorbike.'

Cupidi looked around. Sergeant Moon was sat with some of the younger lads, near the back.

'There's a construction company on the Walhouse Road. They've got CCTV facing the street. Fortunately there's not much traffic on that road. At 4.42 p.m. on Friday there's this.'

He clicked the space bar on his laptop. The face on the whiteboard was replaced by a fuzzy black-and-white image of a man hunched over a motorbike.

'We're pretty sure that's the victim, Michael Dillman, on his way to the yard. The make and model of the bike appear to match.'

'That a bag?'

'Yes. He's carrying what we think is a black shoulder bag. There was no sign of that at the crime scene. Nor of this motorbike. We can only assume that whoever killed him took the bag and the bike. It's a valuable machine, worth several grand.'

Cupidi stared. The photograph was fuzzy. Besides, the black visor was already closed on the man's helmet. You couldn't actually see his face. Was it a man who knew he might be heading towards his death, or not?

'So we ran the plates of Michael Dillman's bike on ANPR and look what we found.'

He clicked the space bar on his laptop and a map of North Kent appeared.

'The plate has been recognised in multiple locations around the town of Dartford, all between midday and three p.m. on Saturday. Since then, nothing. We're running CCTV at those locations to see if we can find anything which has the rider on it, but don't expect much.'

'Was Dillman's helmet left behind at the scene?' asked Cupidi. The sergeant shook his head.

'So presumably whoever nicked the bike, took the helmet too. Full face. So he could conceal his identity.'

'Or her identity,' interrupted Ferriter.

'Obviously. His or her face.'

'Why's he hanging around in Dartford?'

'Why would anybody hang around in Dartford?'

'Any phone record?'

'We've looked at all Dillman's calls over the twenty-four hours leading up to the murder. Nothing that looks suspicious. Nothing that indicates any reason why he left to go to meet someone in a scrap yard in the middle of nowhere.'

The sergeant pressed the space bar again. A photo of Michael Dillman, lying between fridges, dishwasher and washing machines, stacked to form a ramshackle street, eyes open still. The exit wound had left what looked like a strange swelling, a bulge of shattered bone beneath the skin.

'Note the ring around the entry point, indicating that the victim was shot by a weapon held directly to his head.'

A click. Another photo, this time a wider angle. Bright green shoots of nettles and grass, caught by the low light, among the discarded metal and mud.

'Any idea what Dillman had his hand in this time?'

'Last December, that's four months ago, he just got out of a four-year stretch for ABH. Dillman was working as muscle for a local loan shark at the time. The assault appears to have been about a debt. Anyone remember it?'

'Yeah. Battered a guy who owed a few grand, didn't he? Broke the guy's arm.'

'We need to see if there's some connection with that. Maybe revenge? We need to know who he might've pissed off over the years. Back in the nineties he was involved in a bit of dealing, a bit of protection. We've been asking all known associates. They all swear on their mothers' graves he was going straight.'

Older officers chuckled knowingly. *Like that would ever happen.*

'There was a lot of indignation we would even be suggesting that Dillman was up to his old tricks. How dare we? But you don't wind up shot in the side of the head unless you're up to some shite, do you?'

The Senior Investigating Officer, a heavyset DI in his fifties called Wray, handed out a few actions to officers, then looked up, checked his watch and said, 'Next. The amazing arm-in-the-jar mystery. I've got, DS . . . Cupidi?' He looked around the room.

Cupidi shuffled her way to the whiteboard, through the chairs. 'You all heard of this one, yes?'

'On the news last night,' said a constable in the front row.

'Yeah. Couldn't miss it.'

'Right arm. Probably male. As you possibly know already, concealed in an artwork, two weeks ago or longer. No idea yet why . . . whether it's some attention-seeking thing, or . . . It's pretty strange.' She looked up.

The mood in the room had changed. Before, when they'd

105

been talking about the supposed gang murder, the faces around her had been grim and serious. Now they were smiling. Already, the case was a joke.

'The arm appears to have been placed in the jar before it was installed at the gallery.'

'What's a jar doing in a gallery?'

'Can I get my laptop up on screen?' asked Cupidi.

'Oh. Right.' The DI stood again, unplugged the other officer's computer. 'Let me show you. That goes in here,' he said, pointing to a port at the side of Cupidi's laptop. 'You need to sync it,' he explained. And it was easier to just let him do it than to tell him that she knew how.

The jar finally illuminated the screen behind her.

'My nan does stuff like that in pottery class. Gives it to us as birthday presents.'

'You're a bunch of philistines,' said Ferriter.

Cupidi raised her voice above the chatter. 'Packing material had been inserted into the jar around the arm, covering it from sight.'

She looked around. The short attention span of the room was already moving on.

'It's a profound comment on the human condition,' someone was saying.

'I don't know much about art, but I know what I like . . .'

'A little bit of *help* here.' Cupidi shouted. 'This is a potential murder investigation . . .'

There was a second's shocked silence. 'Any sign of formaldehyde?' someone suggested.

'You mean, was this a medical specimen?'

106

'Just a thought.'

'And not a bad one,' Cupidi said. 'We're expecting a preliminary forensic report at the end of the day. I'm guessing any trace of preserving fluid would show up early, so that may make things clearer.'

'So is this a murder inquiry or not?'

'Exactly. Two preliminary questions. One, have any other body parts turned up elsewhere in recent months? Peter? You were looking into that.'

Sergeant Moon looked up. 'No.'

'Nothing at all?'

'Nope. Not so far, anyway.'

'OK. Two. Was this someone attempting to conceal a body part, or the exact opposite? Someone who was trying to hide it would not have been happy that it ended up on public display in a gallery. On the other hand, maybe that's the point. To make us notice. Peter? In what you've been doing, have you come across anything else like this? Is there any kind of incident that makes this part of a pattern?'

'Nothing similar I can find.'

She looked around the room. People were starting to look at their phones; never a great sign.

She raised her voice again. 'Constable Ferriter is attempting to establish a timeline for the exhibit – where it was before it was delivered to the gallery. Would you like to update us on that?'

Ferriter stood, held up her notebook and read, 'The jar is owned by the Evert and Astrid Miller Foundation. I have contacted them to discover where it was previously. How it got there.' She looked up. 'Etcetera.'

107

Either because it was a Monday, or because their minds were on the other case still, nobody seemed impressed.

So she said the name again, this time a little louder. 'Astrid Miller. You know. Astrid Theroux as she was.'

For the first time, they had the room's full attention. 'Astrid Theroux? The model?'

'You've been interviewing Astrid Theroux? You jammy arse,' said a young woman, Ferriter's age.

'Not yet.'

'Get me her autograph, will you?'

'I attempted to contact the Foundation's office yesterday and again this morning. So far, nobody picked up.'

'Where are they based?' DI McAdam asked from the back of the room.

Everyone turned to look at him.

'Not sure. Just a phone number and an email.'

'It's probably London. Call the Met. Get someone to go round.'

'Can't I go myself? I don't mind.' Ferriter smiled.

'Call the Met. We're stretched enough as it is.'

'Short-handed,' someone muttered. A snigger.

McAdam ignored it. 'And if that's where the arm came to us from, we'll be able to hand the whole thing back over to the Met.'

Cupidi saw what McAdam was trying to do. In these strait-ened times, managing the caseload was everything. If there was a chance they could pass the arm on to the Met it would be their problem. 'Chances are,' said McAdam, 'the whole thing turns out to be pointless, but the press will be all over it.'

'Already are.' Ferriter grinned. 'BBC were down there again today. Going to be on national news.'

A woman constable said, '*Hand* it over. Just got it.'

There was a big laugh.

'Did that one take you long?' asked Cupidi.

''Armless fun,' said Wray, holding up his hands as if to defend himself.

'Keep them coming.'

'You must be feeling out on a limb on this one.' They laughed louder at the DI's jokes, on account of his rank.

'Pure genius. Finished?'

'Yes. Sorry. Carry on.'

Cupidi stared at him.

'Honestly. Just messing about. Go on.'

'You're all treating this like it's some joke,' Cupidi said, looking around the room. 'What if the person who's arm it is isn't dead?'

A constable spoke first. 'It's not actually likely, though, is it?'

And then everyone was talking again.

'That's not the point, though, is it?' Cupidi raised her voice above the noise. 'You all think this is a laugh, don't you. Yes, Michael Dillman is dead. We know that. But what if this one isn't?'

'Why would someone chop off an arm, then leave it to be found in a gallery?'

'I don't know. What if it's a kidnapping?'

DI Wray leaned back in his chair. 'A finger is the conventional item. Not the whole bloody arm.'

'How much arm is it?'

'It was severed below the elbow. You could survive that. Think about it. What if putting that arm in that particular place was meant to send someone a signal?'

DI Wray gave the smallest of nods. 'Alex is right. Until we know more, we must adopt the precautionary principle. We treat this as a full murder investigation. And hopefully we can load it off onto the Met, as DI McAdam suggests. But try and keep a lid on it until we know what we're dealing with, shall we? Let's not add to the background chatter and speculation. Anything else new?'

McAdam read out from his sheet. 'Security guard killed during a robbery on a Co-op in the Dartford area.'

'Bloody hell. All going on up that way.'

'I haven't seen that on the system yet.'

'When I say "killed", it appears to have been an accident. He ran out into the road after a couple of lads. Got hit by a motorbike. Bike was speeding. Dead at the scene.'

'Not the same motorbike guy . . . ?'

'That would have been too easy. Different motorbike, different rider. This one's in hospital with a fractured femur following the accident. He'll live.'

'Armed robbery?'

'Just a couple of young lads shoplifting. Teenagers. Guard picked his moment to chase them, that's all, poor bastard.' He pulled up a map on the screen. 'Just there.'

Then the meeting was over. People stood, notes in hand, ready to log back on to their computers. The room was throwing everything at the murder of the man whose body had been found near Erith. To them, that looked like a real crime, with real villains. The kind they were used to.

Cupidi pulled up a photograph of the arm, still in the jar. The white flesh. The curled fingers. If this had been someone's idea of a prank, wouldn't they have come forward by now? What was the point of a joke if it had no punchline?

110

SIXTEEN

The first night had been a long one. Though they had huddled together, the floor beneath them had been hard and cold. Tap had turned from one side to the other, thinking about his mum, about the security guard. The second night, he had slept better but woke around four when it was still dark, hearing rustling outside the hut.

'Hear that?' Tap whispered.

Sloth didn't answer. Tap tried to go back to sleep but he couldn't.

A couple of minutes later he kicked Sloth.

'What?'

'Listen.'

But the rustling had stopped now.

There must be ghosts around here. Old people from the Victorian workhouse; all the dead people from the fever hospital. People had come here just to die. He remembered how the schoolteacher had said that there had been a tramline built to take the infected from the ships that ferried them away from the city, to the beds in the hospital, long demolished.

For breakfast the boys ate the last of a tin of warm rice pudding, burning fingers on the can propped on top of the embers. As long as they avoided the walkers and the anglers who sometimes appeared along the bank of the muddy creek to the west of them, they seemed to be OK.

'We could do this place up a bit,' said Sloth. 'Nobody would know we're here. Couple more days, I reckon, we'll be safe. As long as we can find some more food.'

'We're not safe. We'll be on CCTV. They'll know it was us.'

'Didn't mean that. Meant the other one. The phone man.'

'I don't know. Crazy stuff, Slo.'

Sloth nodded.

They stood, stretching, and wandered aimlessly, exploring the derelict land around them.

There was warmth in the spring sunshine. Brambles were sprouting new green shoots, bright lines curving out of the dead wood. They walked through the scrub towards the wide reach of river, smelling the mud before they could see it.

'In't your mum going to worry about where you gone?' asked Tap.

Sloth nodded. 'I'll call her some time, I guess.' He pulled the stolen Alcatel out of his pocket. 'Still one blob of charge on this phone, if we could actually use it.'

'Why do you reckon he had that phone, Slo?'

'I don't know. Some people just got two phones.'

'Drug dealers mostly,' said Tap.

'Reckon that's what he was? Some county lines bigshot?'

'Didn't look like a drug dealer, did he? Just looked like . . . a bloke.'

It was true. The man they had robbed didn't look like a dealer at all.

A dead seagull lay on the ground. Something had tugged at its insides, scattering feathers across the dry mud. Tap picked up a long stick and started poking.

'What about your mum?' said Sloth.

'Dunno.'

'Don't suppose she gives a shit where you are.'

''K' off.'

'Serious. You're lucky, man.'

'Shut up.'

'Wish my mum was a druggie.'

'Shut up.' Tap shouted this time, and as he did so, he dug the stick into the dead bird and flipped it into the air, lifting the heavy carcass off the ground so it swung towards Sloth.

'What the frick? That's disgusting. That thing almost touched me.'

Tap dropped the stick. 'Don't talk about my mum like that.'

'You're the one who always calls her a skank.'

With a wail, Tap launched himself at Sloth, head down, knocking him to the ground.

'Get off!'

They tussled, each trying and failing to land punches on the other.

'You're pushing me into dog shit.' Sloth finally landed a knee into Tap's solar plexus, knocking the air out of him.

He stood, leaving Tap gasping on the dirty ground.

'I mean, Jesus. If your mum means that much, why don't you give her a call?' He threw the useless phone at Tap and turned, heading off in the direction of the shed they'd been sleeping in.

When Tap got his breath back, he stood, picked up the phone and threw it as far as he could, watching it rise up into the air, black against grey sky, then drop somewhere beyond the scrubby trees, where the big river lay.

Tap turned and headed off towards the water. A fence blocked the way, but he found a place where he could climb over it. It took another ten minutes to reach the bank where he found a big old lump of concrete to sit on, a huge lopsided square, spray-painted with somebody's tag.

To the east, the big road bridge stretched across the Thames. Ahead of him, the greeny grey water, tugging everything out to the sea.

Birds pecked at the sand along the river edge. Living in a small town, bounded by small walls and small people, all this looked huge. And sad. Why did it all look sad? Maybe it was just him and what had happened, and his mum and stuff, but it all looked so . . . overwhelming. It was like he was noticing every twig sticking up from the mud, every bubble in the river, every footprint left by the birds. There was a strange kind of ache in his chest. He wished he had some spliff or something. That would sort it. Glue, even.

'What you doing?' Sloth had returned to him. 'Did you get the hump?' Tap didn't answer. Sloth sat down on the concrete next to him. 'Just a frickin' joke.'

'I'm hungry.'

'You're always hungry,' said Sloth, looking at the big bridge, cars and lorries constantly streaming over it. 'We could hitch a ride somewhere far away so he couldn't find us. Get a job or something.'

'Hitch a ride?'

'I've seen people do it. Car dealers going to pick up vehicles. They stand holding up their trade plates by the roundabout by the Holiday Inn and catch the drivers heading over the bridge.' Then, looking downriver: 'Sorry about what I said.'

'OK.'

From the east, a towboat pulling empty barges was chugging leisurely up the river, making slow progress against the outgoing tide.

'We're not car dealers, though, are we?'

'I know, but . . . wait there long enough, bet someone would give us a ride.'

'Maybe,' said Tap. But getting far away from this place sounded good. He slid off the concrete and ambled away, leaving Sloth alone, sitting cross-legged on the big lump.

A huge branch, leafless twigs pointing up out of the water, drifted downriver, dragged by the force of the water. When he turned, Sloth was shouting something, waving his hands. Tap stared, then walked back towards his friend. As he came closer he heard the descending notes of an old-fashioned ringtone.

'Someone's calling the phone.'

'Where is it?' shouted Tap, looking around.

'I don't know. You're the one who bloody flung it.'

It was somewhere close. The phone kept on ringing, the same

115

cheap chirpy notes, going round and round. Whether it was the gentle winds, blowing across the flat shoreline, the noise seemed to move as they approached it.

'There!' shouted Sloth.

Tap ran towards a small clump of pale green grass. The black handset sat right in the middle, like a bird on a nest. But just as he reached out and picked it up, the ringing stopped.

'Shit. Shit. Shit.'

They both stood looking at the phone's screen. '*Missed call.*'

'Reckon it was him?' asked Sloth.

'Don't know.'

'Or maybe one of his gang?'

'How do you even know he's got a gang?'

Out on the river, a tugboat, chugging up the Thames in front of a line of rusty barges, sounded a long, shrill warning note.

'What would we even say if it *was* him?' asked Tap.

Sloth didn't answer. He just stood, frowning at the screen.

SEVENTEEN

Between the power station and the Channel, Cupidi always had the beach to herself at this time of day, after work, when the spring chill was coming off the water. Sometimes a few fishermen hung around the hot water outflow to the nuclear power station, and you might find the occasional birder scanning the horizon, but mostly you could be here on your own in peace and quiet. And then her phone rang.

She swiped her screen. 'What?'

'It's me,' said Jill Ferriter.

'I know it's you.'

'I found out where the offices of the Evert and Astrid Miller Foundation are. Listen. Astrid Miller runs the Foundation from home. Guess where they live.'

'About ten miles outside Canterbury.'

'Oh. How did you know?' The young constable sounded disappointed.

'I looked it up. On the internet.'

'Right. Same.'

'Our millionaires live in Kent. That's why they are benefactors of the Turner Contemporary. They're locals.'

'So you knew that all along?' Ferriter sounded offended.

'If it makes you feel better, I didn't know that that's where the Foundation is based, no. Just that they're based around here.'

'And about their house in Dungeness?'

'Their what?'

'You didn't know that, did you?'

'They have a place here? No.'

'There you go. See? I am useful.'

'Which one?' asked Cupidi. 'Which house do they own?'

'No idea. I don't know if they still got it, actually. I just got home and I was looking through all my old magazines. I used to keep stuff about Astrid Theroux. I properly idolised her. Her dad abused her. She talked about that stuff when no one else did. She'd come from nothing and proved that you could be beautiful and in control. I was having such a shitty time as a teenager . . . you wouldn't believe it.'

'I might,' she said, thinking of Zoë.

'No. Really, I promise. But that's not the point. For me she was like a beacon of hope in a sea of absolute shit. And she was so good. She was in that Franz Ferdinand video, remember?'

'Actually, no,' said Cupidi.

'Once, when she was at the peak-peak-peak of her fame, she did this weird performance at an Alexander McQueen show – or was it Westwood? – where she came onto the catwalk looking really hot in a short dress and asked people why they thought she was so good-looking. Why her and not all the other women

118

in the audience? And there were all these blokes in the audience saying, "Because you got great boobs," and stuff like that. And she just stares them out. You should see it. And the whole place goes quiet. It's amazing. You can find it somewhere on YouTube. And it was cool, because she was accusing all the model agencies and photographers of this abuse but they didn't dare drop her because she was so mega. And then she kind of fell off the radar when she got married. I'll bring the magazines into the station if you like. I have loads. But anyway, there was an article from 2003 in *The Face* magazine when she was going out with this famous photographer who was done for drugs more than once as it happens, and it says they bought one of the shacks down there together. But then he ran off with this American actress and they split up but I think, from what the article said, she kept the place.'

'Did it say if she still had it?'

'No. Maybe they sold it. But they're gazillionaires. If they did own it, they're probably not wanting everyone to know.'

Cupidi turned and looked north, up the long shingle beach. Between where she was standing and the Pilot Inn, the landscape was dotted with dozens of shacks. The rich had been buying them up for years, converting these low ramshackle buildings into discreet hideaways. Fashionable magazines featured glossy photos, namedropping the architects who had remodelled them. There were several that could be the Millers'.

'You know what this means, though, don't you?'

The Channel was still, the air clear and dry. You could see for miles. The dark blue horizon was dotted with lights of ships and fishing boats.

'It means that McAdam can't offload this case as easily as he wanted,' Cupidi said. 'It's not going to be foisted off to some team at the Met.'

'Yes. But what else?'

'Tell me, Jill. Go on.'

'It means we're going to need to talk to Astrid Miller. Face to face. I was thinking of volunteering.'

'Of course you were.'

'Don't be like that. I'm young and keen. I'm the future of modern policing.'

'What does that make me?'

Ferriter didn't answer.

It had been a long winter. This had been Cupidi's second full year out here on the headland; with nothing to stop the wind out there, the cold was harsh, but it made the exhilaration of these spring evenings all the more thrilling.

'OK,' she said. 'We need to get access to their records to find out when the sculpture was tampered with.'

'I could come up to Dungeness now,' Ferriter suggested. 'We could look for Astrid Miller's shack. We could have that drink you talked about, in that horrible pub you have out there, walk around, press our noses against some of the windows and see if we can guess which one is hers?'

'She's probably sold it. Know how much these places go for now?'

'It would be nice anyway, wouldn't it? Hang out like we used to. It's so busy at work we never get the chance to chat about stuff.'

'What do you mean, "like we used to"?'

Afterwards Cupidi wondered if Jill Ferriter had been trying to to talk to her about something else; whether the phone call was about more than just the Millers.

But then Venus appeared low in the western sky, as if somebody had just flicked on a light switch, and the thought was gone.

There was a light on in Arum Cottage. Cupidi paused at the door, unsure if she would be welcome at this hour, but knocked anyway.

William South opened it only a chain's width, peering out.

'Oh,' he said, not removing the lock.

'I've got a question. Do you mind if I come in?'

He hesitated. 'I was going to bed.'

'It will only take a second.'

He looked at her for a second. She was about to turn away when he said, 'What?'

'You used to be the community policeman here.'

'Thank you for reminding me.' He closed the door.

She stood on the frayed black rubber doormat, annoyed at his moodiness.

'I didn't mean to put it like that,' she called out, loud enough for him to hear. Stupid woman, always opening her mouth before she'd thought what she was saying. 'Did you ever hear about a rich couple, the Millers, having a place round here?' she said, raising her voice so he could hear her. 'A model named Astrid Theroux?'

He didn't answer. The light went out in the living room.

Leaning down, she pushed open the letter box and called, 'Don't be childish, Bill. I've just come to ask for your help. Simple question.'

But the light stayed off. She noticed the cardboard box by the door. It was full of empty bottles. And he had had no company either. She knew because she, like her daughter, had been keeping an eye on him.

121

EIGHTEEN

Tap had tried telling Sloth about the ghosts, but Sloth had said he didn't like to talk about that stuff. It freaked him out.

They slept side by side, fully clothed, bodies close to each other for warmth. The April nights were cold. It had happened perfectly naturally, both bodies, curled together on the hard floor. Tap didn't say anything about that either, in case Sloth thought it was weird.

The muttering of ghosts had woken him again; he heard their footsteps now. It didn't scare him at all. What harm could they do? It was the man who was chasing them who was frightening.

Then, in the darkest point of the night, the phone rang again, singing out its chirpy melody into the night.

'Wake up, Slo.' Tap shook his shoulder.

'Wha?'

Sloth was a deep sleeper. Tap pushed inside his friend's jeans pocket.

'What you frickin' doing?'

In his hands, the screen glowed.

'That phone. It's ringing again. Shall I answer it?'

'Is it him?'

'How would I know?'

'Yeah. Go on.'

Tap pressed the green button, held the handset to his ear.

The sound of a man breathing as the glow from the handset lit the small space around them. Then, a guttural voice. 'Where are you?'

'What's he saying?' asked Sloth.

'He wants to know where we are.' Tap spoke into the phone. 'Who are you?'

'That's my phone you're holding. I want it back.'

Tap put his hand over the microphone.

'He says he wants his phone back.'

'We'd have given you it back . . . only you shot the last guy,' said Sloth.

'Don't,' hissed Tap.

'Well, he did, didn't he?'

'I'll find you,' said the voice. 'And when I do, I'll fucking kill you too.'

'Leave us alone,' said Tap.

'Do one thing, and do it right . . . and I'll leave you alone.'

In the darkness Tap looked at Sloth.

'Yeah? What?'

'Unlock the phone.'

'We would do,' said Sloth. 'But we not got the code, arse-hat.'

Tap's mouth was wide. 'Don't.' He shook his head.

'I'll give it you. Then do exactly as I say, right?'

In the darkness, Sloth frowned. 'You'll leave us be?'

'Two, seven, six, seven,' said the man.

'What?'

'Unlock the phone. Do exactly as I say and I won't come after you.' The voice repeated the four digits.

'Why should we?'

'Because if you don't I'll hunt you fucking down.'

A message flashed up onto the screen: *Battery Low.*

'Go on then,' said Sloth. 'Do it.'

Tap entered the numbers. The screen shone more brightly now. 'It's unlocked.'

'I'm going to give you some instructions and I want you to follow them exactly, OK?'

'Right.'

'Press these keys one at a time. Star, five, two. Got that?'

'Star, five, two. Wow.'

'What can you see?'

'Words,' said Tap. The small grey rectangle was suddenly filled with words. Rows of capitals and spaces.

'What does it say?'

'Don't know. Makes no sense.'

The voice attempted calm. 'OK. There should be twelve words there. I want you to read them to me. Slowly and clearly. One by one. Got that?'

'Right.'

'Go on then.'

'What's this about?'

'Just read the words,' the voice snapped. 'OK?'

Tap peered at the screen, trying to figure out what he was seeing.

'Hurry up,' said the voice.

'Keep your hair on,' said Tap. 'And if I read this, you'll definitely leave us alone?'

'Yes.'

'Swear to God?'

'For fuck's sake. Come on.'

'Got your pencil?'

'Read it.'

Tap read. 'SUNRISE. EXCEED. PURPOSE.'

'Wait. Slow down.' The man was writing down the words. 'Yes . . . and?'

'It's just weird shit like that. Pointless.'

'Keep reading.'

'It's just gibberish. SURVIVOR. ANALYST. BATTLE. What is this? A word puzzle or something?'

'Come on,' shouted the man.

'TUMOUR. PARALYSED. POTENTIAL.'

'Is that spelled the American way or the British way?'

'How would I know?' said Tap. Sloth giggled.

'Paralysed. With a *z* or an *s*?'

Tap peered at the word. 'An *s*. Why's it so important?'

'And tumour with a *u*?'

'What does it matter?'

'Just believe me, it matters.'

'Yes. With a *u*.'

'The last three words?'

'And we can keep the phone?'

'Just give me the fucking words.'

'BUTTOCK—'

Sloth burst out laughing in the darkness.

'You having me on?'

'Honest to God. That's what it says. BUTTOCK.' Tap spelled it out.

'I'll fucking kill you if you're lying.'

'I trust you, mate,' said Tap. 'Next word, DEADLY.'

'And?' said the man.

But just as Tap was scrolling down to read the final word, the screen went black. 'Hello?' he said into the darkness, but there was no one there.

The phone had run out of battery. It was dead.

'What was the last word?' asked Sloth.

'Couldn't read it.'

Sloth snatched it off him. 'What was the lock code?'

'I can't remember.'

Sloth hit him. 'What's the code? If we can charge it, we can use it, then at least we got a phone.'

'We should throw it away, mate.'

Sloth hit him again. 'What's the code?'

'Two, seven, six, seven . . .'

Sloth found an old screw on the floor of the shed and spent ten minutes carefully grinding the number into the case.

In the morning, Tap blinked into the sun that lit the land outside the open door. A flock of green parakeets chattered ridiculously in a small tree that grew between where they lay and the creek beyond.

'What the frick was all that about, last night?' said Sloth, lying next to him.

'Some guy wanting the answers to his Sudoku.'

'That's numbers, you prick.'

'Weird, though. *Potential . . . Deadly . . . Buttocks*. Like a code or something.'

Sloth sniggered, sat up, picked up the dead phone. 'Reckon he was a spy?'

'Like it's some *Mission Impossible* shit going down.'

'Not around here. If it was London or Tokyo or something, not here.'

'Got anything to eat?'

'No.'

'Chuck it in the river,' Tap said. 'Far as we can.'

'No. We need it. It's all we have.'

'Hide it then.'

In the end Sloth just scraped a hole in the earth at the back of the shed and dropped it in there. 'Happy now? No one can find it.'

By lunchtime they were restless, hungry and twitchy, the kind of twitchiness you get when you haven't had a smoke in days and the colours are all too bright.

Tap checked the pockets of his trousers, his shirt and his hoodie, just in case he could find a few crumbs of weed. There was a tiny piece of silver paper, and he unwrapped it cautiously, trying to see if there was anything inside, but it turned out just to be a sweet wrapper.

'I'm so bored. Let's go for a walk.'

'No. What if somebody recognises us?'

'I'll go crazy just stuck here. Besides, he said he'd let us go, didn't he, if we read him them words? And we read most of them.'

They walked south of the fence that surrounded the patch they were camped on and found themselves on a new estate, houses dotted on the flatland like Lego, neat and full of promise.

'Imagine living in one of them,' said Tap.

'Yeah. Fancy. I'd go nuts.'

'I don't know. I reckon it'd be pretty cool.'

A black Kia slowed; the man inside was in his forties, wearing a grey suit. He lowered his window, peered at them, then drove on.

'Fuck. He recognised us,' said Tap.

'Why would he recognise us?'

Tap frowned. 'Maybe we were on the news.'

'Don't be daft.' But there was uncertainty in Sloth's voice.

They were at a newly built place called Ruby Tuesday Drive. 'That's a song, isn't it?'

'No, mate.'

'It is. My mum sings it.'

Nearby there was Tumbling Dice Mews, Sympathy Vale, and Lady Jane Place.

'They're all songs. Swear to God. Some group my mum likes.'

'I'm that hungry I would go through their bins.'

'That's disgusting,' said Sloth.

'Bit of pizza or something. I tell you, I wouldn't care if there were teeth marks in it already. I'm going to die.'

The flats had large green bins lined up behind little fences. They both stared at them for a second, then Sloth pulled on Tap's arm, dragging him away.

At the next corner, they watched through a ground-floor

window as a young woman in a silver T-shirt poured water from a kettle into a pan.

'What do you think she's making?'

'Shut up.'

A black car turned off the main drag and drove towards them.

'Is that the same one? The bloke who was looking at us couple of minutes back?'

'You're freaking me out now. Why would it be?'

'It is,' hissed Tap, staring at the pavement as the Kia rolled passed them, round the bend in the road.

'Don't get para, mate.'

'I promise. It's him. C'mon.' He pulled at Sloth, increasing his pace towards the end of the street.

The low hum of the engine returned.

'Don't look. He's behind us. Act casual.'

The bonnet of the Kia nosed ahead of them until the driver was alongside.

They walked deliberately slowly down Ruby Tuesday Drive. On the far side of the junction was the derelict land they were camped on. If they made it to the fence, he wouldn't be able to follow.

The car moved on, but stopped about ten metres in front.

'Keep walking,' muttered Sloth.

They could see the window sliding down as they approached.

'Shit.'

As they reached it, the man in the grey suit leaned across the passenger seat. 'Can I help you, lads?'

'Nah,' said Tap.

'Are you lost? Only, I seen you wandering around here.'

'We're OK. Jog on.'

They walked past the car towards the main road, hesitating at the junction, where the car caught up with them again.

'Thing is, you need to be careful in this area,' the man said. 'We've had a few burglaries. People might get suspicious when they see a couple of young lads nosing around the place.'

'We weren't nosing,' said Tap. 'We were just . . .'

'Looking for a shop,' finished Sloth.

'Yeah,' said the man. 'I know. Nightmare round here, isn't it? Build all these houses and there's nowhere to buy anything. Nearest is the other side of the main road. Get in. I'll give you a ride.' He pushed the side door open.

'You're all right.' Tap looked straight ahead.

'Don't be daft. It'll only take me a minute.'

'My mum says I shouldn't get into any cars with strange old men,' said Sloth.

Tap's snigger turned into a laugh, and though he raised his hand to his mouth to stifle it, he couldn't stop himself.

Sloth started giggling too, with that high-pitched wheeze he made.

But the man was laughing now, hands gripping the steering wheel. 'Your mum was right.'

Tap's stomach hurt from the laughter. All the air was leaving him.

'Go on,' said the man. 'Get in, you daft idiots. What you want? Food? I'll take you to the KFC. Five minutes.'

Sloth stopped laughing. 'KFC?'

'Yes.'

'Try anything and we could have you,' he said.

130

'Well, that's lovely. I'm just trying to be Christian, that's all.'

'OK,' said Sloth slowly. 'Can you get us a meal? Only we got no money.'

'I thought you were going to the shops. What were you going to buy there?'

'Not enough for a burger, anyway.'

The man smiled, leaned over again, and opened the passenger door. 'Get in. You can pay me back.'

Ignoring the door he held for them, Sloth got in the back instead and moved across the seat, making space for Tap.

The man just kept on smiling at them and closed the front door again. 'Buckle up,' he said and the car drove away.

NINETEEN

The pale young man opened the door, eyes wide. 'You!'

Cupidi wasn't used to people grinning at her when she showed them her warrant card. 'Detective Sergeant Cupidi,' she said.

'And you're Ross, aren't you?' added Ferriter. 'Remember us from the gallery? They passed us your address.'

He wore a black T-shirt, black trousers and black trainers. 'You were the one who discovered the arm,' said Ferriter, from behind Cupidi.

'Smelt it.' He looked Ferriter up and down, smiled. A tiny smile. 'That was fast.'

'What was fast?'

'I called that 0800 number just an hour ago – the Crime-stoppers one you put in the newspapers asking for information about . . .'

Cupidi looked enquiringly at Ferriter. The constable shook her head, puzzled. 'No. They didn't contact us . . . We were coming here as a routine enquiry because you work at the gallery. Do you have particular information?'

'Well . . . no. Not exactly particular. I just wanted to find out what was going on.'

'Right,' said Cupidi slowly. 'May we come in?'

'Sorry. Yes. Of course.'

It was a two-bedroom flat on the seventeenth floor of Arlington House, the giant sixties block that rose above Margate's low curve of old seaside buildings. Ugly on the outside, the view from the inside was breathtaking. The living-room window looked across the sweep of honey-coloured sand, up to the angular roofs of the gallery which sat on the headland in front of the harbour arm.

'Whoa,' said Ferriter, looking around.

The apartment was sparse, but full of old sixties furniture, gathered in from junk shops.

'Nice,' said Ferriter.

'Not mine,' said Ross. 'My bloodsucking landlord's. He says he's going to evict me for non-payment of rent.'

'So . . . they told us you're not working at the gallery any more?'

'They let me go,' he said archly, amused by the phrase. 'It was just a probationary period. It wasn't really my thing anyway. And after the incident . . .'

'That doesn't seem fair.'

Ross shook his head. 'It didn't suit me anyway.'

'We came here because we wanted to interview you about finding the remains. It was nothing to do with your phone call.'

He sat down on an ancient leather sofa whose stuffing leaked out of the arm. Cupidi found a plastic dining chair and placed it next to him; Ferriter remained upright, facing the window, looking out.

'Why did you call us this morning?'

'I have been very . . . affected by all this. I wanted to find out whether you had found out anything.'

Ferriter turned, sneaked a glance. Cupidi said, 'People generally call us when they want to give us information, not the other way around.'

'There has been nothing in the papers that makes any sense. It's all just speculation.'

'So you didn't have anything you wanted to tell us?'

'No. Not really.'

'Because on the day we were at the gallery you seemed very interested in the investigation,' said Cupidi. 'We noticed you watching us.'

'Of course.' Ross nodded. 'Yes.'

'Why?'

'Wouldn't you expect me to be interested?'

Cupidi smiled. 'Yes. But most people pretend hard not to be.'

'Do they? Why?'

'Because they're worried people might think them prurient. And because maybe they think it's none of their business.'

'Well, I'm different. Have you found out whose arm it is yet?'

'No.'

Cupidi stared at the young man for a second, then said gently, 'Mr Clough. If you have something to tell us about the arm or who put it there, you know you have to tell us, don't you?'

Ross looked grave.

'Well?'

'I'm not really ready,' he answered.

Ferriter frowned, mouthed, 'What?' at Cupidi.

'If you know someone or something that can help us,' Cupidi repeated, 'you must tell us. Otherwise you may be concealing an arrestable offence. Officially that's called "perverting the course of justice". Do you understand?'

He stood up decisively, but only to say, 'Would you like a coffee?' as if he'd suddenly remembered his manners.

When he was safely in the kitchen, Ferriter whispered, 'He bloody knows something, doesn't he?'

'Do you take sugar?' he called.

'Give him a hand,' said Cupidi.

Ferriter left the room. Cupidi waited until she could hear them both chattering.

Cupidi stood quietly and looked up and down the short hallway. To the right was the main bedroom, the door slightly ajar. Walking towards it, she nudged it with her foot and it swung open.

The room was untidy. A double bed covered in a dirty white duvet. The landlord's room, she guessed.

There were two other doors, both shut. She tried the first; a bathroom. She closed it gently, then turned to the other door. The handle creaked as it moved.

'Hello?' said Ross, head poking out of the kitchen door.

He must have heard her.

'I was just looking for the bathroom.'

He stared at her for a second. 'Other door.'

After a minute, she joined them in the small kitchen. Ross handed Cupidi a cup of black coffee.

135

'You were wanting to tell us something.'

'I know, but it's not ready. I don't know why I made a big thing of it. It's not important really.'

'Tell us.'

'What does an arm in a jar mean to you?'

'You think there's some kind of symbolic meaning to the arm being left at the art gallery?'

'Obviously. An arm in a jar. It's a signifier, isn't it?'

'Of what?' asked Cupidi.

'I've been thinking,' he said. 'When you took out the hand, was it like this –' he held his hand loosely, the fingers loose, then bunched them into a fist – 'or like this?'

'Why would it make a difference?'

'Obviously it would. You're not answering my question. Was there anything else at the bottom of the jar?'

'We don't share details of an investigation. Why do you ask about the hand?'

He grinned. 'The monkey trap,' he said.

'What monkey trap?' said Ferriter.

'Don't tell me this didn't make you think of the monkey trap? You know . . .' He bunched his fist again.

'That's stupid,' said Ferriter.

Ross looked surprised, disappointed by their lack of understanding. 'Come and see, then.'

He opened the door of the room Cupidi had tried to look into and stood behind them.

'I told you it wasn't really ready.'

Pushing it back, the two police officers both peered in. 'Bloody hell,' said Jill Ferriter, looking around the small room.

TWENTY

Tap had a Boneless Banquet, Sloth a Zinger Box Meal. They sat in a booth not far from the door, boys side by side facing the man, who had taken his grey jacket off and laid it on the seat beside him.

'Well, that barely touched the sides,' said the man. 'What's your names?'

Neither of them answered. Tap opened another sachet of ketchup.

'Come on. I bought you a meal. All I'm asking's your names.' He watched them eat, a small, irritating smile always on his face.

Tap wiped sauce from his lips.

The man lowered his voice, leaned forward. 'Don't think I'm stupid. You're running away from something, aren't you, lads?'

Under the table, Sloth nudged Tap with his knee. Tap understood. *Don't answer.* Wouldn't have anyway. They both knew that.

'I'm Frank,' said the man. 'OK.' He held up his palms. 'I'll call you Thelma,' he told Sloth, 'and –' he nodded at Tap – 'you're Louise.'

'You taking the pistachio?'

'They were runaways,' said Frank. 'Like you.'

'Who says we're runaways?'

'Oh come on. *Thelma and Louise*. It was a movie. Not heard of it? Suppose not. You're too young. How old are you, anyway? Fourteen? Fifteen?'

'Fuck off,' snorted Tap.

'Sixteen? Seventeen? What about your family? They know where you are? They're probably worried.'

'I actually doubt that,' said Tap. But he thought about his mother and suddenly felt sad. Maybe this man had a phone on him. He hadn't seen him use one, but he had noticed the way his jacket had hung before he'd taken it off. Side pocket, he guessed.

'Where are you two staying?'

'Nowhere in particular,' said Tap.

'What? In a place called Nowhere in Particular?'

'Can I have another chicken burger?' asked Sloth. Tap wondered how quickly the two of them could run from the restaurant. Would there be time to filch his jacket too?

But Frank looked back at Sloth for a second, then said, 'Sure. What about you, Louise?'

'What did you call me?' demanded Tap.

'Lighten up,' said Frank.

'Yeah. Lighten up.' Sloth grinned.

'You what?' Tap mouthed at his friend as the man called Frank ordered the burger.

'If you want to, you can stay over at my place,' said Frank,

138

putting the fresh tray in front of Sloth. 'I have a spare bedroom. Till you get yourself sorted.'

Neither of the boys answered.

'I expect you'll want to discuss that.' He smiled. 'I'll give you a couple of minutes to talk it over,' he said, standing. With one hand he picked up his jacket, with the other, he retrieved his empty coffee cup. On the way to the toilet, he dropped the cup into the waste bin.

'Reckon he's a bender?' said Sloth.

'Reckon.'

Sloth nodded. 'I'm so full I think my belly button just popped out,' he said, pushing the tray away from him, though there was still food on it.

They sat in the back of Frank's car as he drove them from the KFC to his flat, ten minutes away.

It was a small shared block. He let himself into the front door, picking up mail from the box. Frank's apartment was on the second floor.

'You look done in, lads,' he said. 'Sleep in my spare room.'

He showed them a small room off the hallway. 'There's only a single bed. What do you think we are, Frank?'

'I don't care what you are, mate. One of you can kip on the floor, then. Bathroom's opposite the kitchen.' He opened a small cupboard and sorted through a pile of towels. 'Use these. You need a shower.'

'Trying to say we smell, Frank?'

'Yes.'

Sloth took a towel and went to the bathroom.

Tap said, 'Can I make a call?'

'Who to?'

'My mum.'

'Why?'

'Just to tell her I'm all right. Don't worry, I won't tell her I've been picked up by a strange man.'

Frank hesitated, then reached in his jacket and pulled out his phone, pressed the security code, then tossed it over.

'Frank,' called Sloth from the bathroom. 'There's no lock on your toilet door.'

'Afraid someone's going to burst in on you?'

'Try it on, and I'll mess you up.'

'Promises, promises.'

'Serious, Frank.'

Tap tried the number, but it went straight to voicemail. *'Hi. I'm on my luxury yacht in Barbados, darling. I can't pick up right now.'*

He left a message. 'Hi, Mum. I'm OK. How are you? Just want to know you're OK.'

'You all right?' said Frank.

'Just going to have a lie-down.'

'My phone.' Frank held out his hand.

'Oh. Right.' Tap handed it back.

In the small spare room, Tap opened the wardrobe. It was full of Frank's blue suits and beige coats. He ran his hands down a few jackets to see if there was anything left in the pockets, but there wasn't.

The bed had a single duvet. It felt so good to be warm, to be fed, to lie on something soft. He lay, closed his eyes, listened to the sound of the shower across the hallway.

He was already half asleep when Sloth came in, a towel wrapped around him.

'Shove over,' said Sloth.

'He said one of us could sleep on the floor.'

'Stuff that.'

And, smelling of shower gel and shampoo, Sloth lay beside him on the small bed.

Tap drifted in and out of sleep for an hour. In the front room, Frank had the TV on Netflix. His phone went a couple of times. The muffled noise entered snatched dreams. When he woke, Sloth had turned in his sleep, and his friend's arm lay over his chest, as if he was holding on to him.

Tap could smell the soap that lingered on Sloth's skin. He lay, not daring to move in case he woke Sloth or roused him that much that he would move away.

Over the last four days he had been scared, dirty and lost. Right now it felt good. The feeling of weight of the arm, the shine of his skin, the thin hair that curved with the shape of his muscle. This moment.

But when he looked up, he saw Frank was at the door, looking at them, a knowing smile on his face.

Tap glared at him.

'Just looking, Louise.'

The noise was enough to make Sloth turn to face the wall. Tap lay there a while, then got up and crept out of the room. Frank was sitting on the couch with a laptop and a cup of tea.

The flat looked half lived in. There were shelves at one end of the room, empty except for a sports award of some kind and a book about the Sistine Chapel. 'OK if I go for a shower then, Frank?'

'Don't leave the place in a mess like your lover boy. Keep the water off the floor.'

'Bog off, Frank. He's not my—'

'Really? Whatever you say.'

The shower wasn't like the one they had at home, a thin drizzle of water. This one, the water came out so hard it stung, but it felt good, pummelling all the sweat and dirt of the last four days out of him. Tap washed his hair and watched dark water swill down the plughole.

Afterwards he stood in front of the mirror, wiping it clean of condensation.

He needed a haircut for a start. Hair had grown on his face, too; not stubble exactly, just the kind of fluff he grew after a few days.

The young man who looked at him in the glass looked tired and scared, even after the nap. He opened the cupboard, looking for a razor, and, in amongst pill bottles and aftershave, found a plastic one. It hurt, scraping it across his face, and when he cleared the steam from the mirror a second time, he saw blood trickling into his mouth. He leaned forward to find the place where he'd cut himself.

A small flap of skin above his upper lip. He tore off a strip of toilet paper and held it against the cut. Red crept through the white.

He put his dirty clothes back on. Unlike Sloth, he didn't feel comfortable hanging out around Frank in just a towel.

★

Sloth had dressed too. He was sitting on a dining chair, watching the TV.

'Got any cigarettes, Frank?' asked Tap.

'Gives you cancer,' said Frank.

'Yeah. Got any cigarettes?'

No answer.

'Can you lend us a tenner to get some? We'll pay you back?'

Frank looked from one boy to the other. 'I hope you don't think I'm a mug.'

'Far from it, Frank,' Tap told him.

'You can pay me back,' said Frank. 'Any way you like.'

'In your dreams.'

'Are you even old enough to buy ciggies?'

'Course we are,' said Sloth. 'Otherwise you wouldn't have invited us back to your place, would you?'

He sat up slightly, pulled a wallet out from his back pocket and opened it. 'Don't get cheeky, lads, else I won't let you back in. Bet you like the wacky baccy, too, you two, don't you?'

Sloth burst out laughing. 'What you talking about?'

'You know, weed?'

'Wacky baccy? Nobody calls it that, Frank. Only social workers and lesbian vicars.'

'Tell you what. Get some cigarette papers. I don't mind a joint. I've got a bit of stuff stashed away.'

'You're trying to get us wavy? Get us all a bit stoned so you can have your wacky way with us? We're not like that, Frank.'

'You sure about that?'

'So much as touch us, and we'd cut you up, Frank.'

143

Frank held up his hands. 'Suit yourself, lads.' He opened his wallet and pulled out a ten-pound note.

'Is there a newspaper shop or something?'

'Nearest is the Co-op.'

Tap and Sloth exchanged a look.

'I tell a lie. There's a new Nisa just on the estate, just over by the Fastrack stop on Brunel Way. Don't go smoking them round here. I don't want you hanging around outside my door either. Lowers the tone.'

It was grey outside. A thin drizzle had started falling.

'Reckon he's a fag?' said Tap.

'Don't be a prannet, Tap. He's a raging paedo.'

They waited outside the shop for ten minutes, watching people come and go. An old guy walking a pair of Jack Russells ignored them. A couple of men from a building site, arms red from the sun, told them to get lost. Finally they spotted two young women coming towards them, arm in arm, laughing, one short and bleach-haired, the other ginger, towering over her.

'Oi, ladies,' called Sloth. 'Can I beg a favour? Will you get us some ciggies?'

'Ladies?' The blonde one made a joke of looking around her for them.

'Aw.' Ginger examined them. 'You boys too young to buy your own?'

'Bob along, boys. Kids ain't allowed to smoke.'

Ginger burst out laughing. 'Stunted that one's growth already.' She pointed at Sloth. 'What do we get out of it?'

'You can have one out the packet.'

'Each?' said Ginger, with a wink.

'Yeah. Go on.' Sloth gave them the ten-pound note. 'Get us a lighter as well, will you? And some Rizlas.'

'We're not going back there, are we? Thought you said he was a paedo.'

Sloth said, 'He's got some wacky baccy, bro. Besides. He's not exactly going to tell anyone about us, is he? We're his little secret. And if he tries anything on . . .'

Afterwards, they sat with the girls on the bench of the bus stop, smoking. The girls had four cans of lager in a blue plastic bag.

'You from round here?' said the short blonde one.

'Not really. What about you?'

'Just down the road. Work at the shopping centre. It's handy.'

'What's wrong with your lip?' the ginger one said, peering at Tap. 'It's bleeding.'

The cut had stuck to the cigarette and opened up again. 'Nothing. Just done it, shaving.'

'Shaving?' Sloth giggled. 'When do you ever need to shave?'

'Ah, God there. It's dribbling down your chin.' Ginger delved into her jacket pocket and pulled out a pack of tissues. Tap thought she was going to hand him one, but instead she leaned forward and gently dabbed it on his face, concentrating, tongue between teeth, like she was his mother or something.

'Sit still, little boy.' Oh so softly, she patted at the blood, all one-handed, holding her half-smoked cigarette out of the way with the other.

And, at the thought of his mother, whom he hadn't spoken to in days now, he couldn't bear the kindness of the gesture. He felt that huge black weight coming down on him again, pushing the air out of his body.

He stood up suddenly, tears pricking at his eyes, then flicked his cigarette out into the road. 'Let's go.'

'What's up?' said Sloth.

'I haven't finished. I missed a bit,' called Ginger.

'Come on, Slo. Let's frickin' go.'

Sloth stood too, puzzled. 'Where?'

'What about your change?' shouted the tall one.

'Weirdos.'

But Tap was already halfway to the corner and Sloth was trying to catch up with him. 'Where we going?'

'I want that frickin' smoke,' said Tap. A bit of weed would calm him down; stop him thinking so much.

'Bet he doesn't let us in.' Tap pressed the bell.

'Course he will,' said Sloth. 'He wants your arse.' But, as Tap leaned on it, the lock clicked and he almost fell inside.

Sloth was still laughing when Frank appeared at the top of the stairs. 'Quiet. The bloody neighbours.' Then, standing in his hallway, in his flat, he remembered something, 'Benjamin. Your dad phoned. He's coming to pick you up.'

Sloth and Tap stopped, stared at each other.

'My dad?'

'Yeah. He must have had my number on redial from when you called your mum.'

'You called your mum?' demanded Sloth.

'You were having a shower,' said Tap.

'I just told him I'd seen you wandering around. You looked hungry. Given you a bite to eat, nothing else. That's right, isn't it? Nothing else happened, did it, lads? I didn't do anything.'

'Benji don't have a father.' Sloth was shaking his head slowly.

'He said he was your dad.'

'On mum's phone?'

'When was this?'

''Bout twenty minutes ago.' Frank looked nervous now. 'Who was he then?'

Tap and Sloth exchanged a glance. 'Let's scarper,' said Sloth.

That was when the doorbell rang again.

TWENTY-ONE

In the middle of the room, sitting on a small oak stool, was a life-size sculpture of a naked woman.

She appeared to be made entirely of cardboard and adhesive tape, cut, stuck and carefully folded.

Considering the ordinariness of the materials she had been built from, the result was extraordinarily human, though strangely semi-transparent. The proportions of the woman were perfect. Light glittered off the many surfaces made by the tape. Her legs were crossed, one foot dangling above the floor, her bare head tilted slightly downwards.

And one arm was missing; her left.

'That's bloody Astrid Theroux,' said Ferriter.

'Astrid Miller, yes.'

'Mr Clough. What, exactly, are we looking at?'

'That's it, you see. I don't really know yet,' he said. 'That's why I wanted your help.'

The small bedroom doubled as Ross's art studio. A pale blind blocked sunlight from the window. A single mattress lay on the floor, covered in clothes. The lino floor was splashed with paint, the walls covered in sketches and pictures torn from magazines. Pasted to the walls were also dozens of newspaper cuttings about the severed arm. Instead Clough pointed to a series of charcoal drawings, carefully pinned up. One was of a cartoonish monkey with its arm in a jar, its eyes big and frightened.

'See?' he said.

The monkey trap, thought Cupidi. Place a nut in the jar; the monkey places its fist around it, but his greed means he won't let go of it, even though it means he can't pull himself free.

She rotated slowly about the room, taking in the drawings and the photographs while Ross stood, half nervous, half proud, in the doorway, like a child showing his mother a drawing he had done.

Sitting in the car in the wind-blown car park at the bottom of the block, Ferriter looked up at the building, towards the seventeenth floor and said, 'Bloody weirdo. Hundred per cent fits the picture, doesn't he?'

'Fits what picture?' Cupidi frowned. The moving clouds made it look like the tower above them was falling.

'Classic narcissist. Only got in touch with us because he needs us to acknowledge how brilliant he is.'

'If he's such a show-off, why was he reluctant to show us that room? Why didn't he let us see it straight away?'

'Drama, that's why. He wanted the big reveal.'

Cupidi said, 'You think he fits some sort of criminal profile, don't you?'

'I've read the psychology. Narcissist sociopath. The way he opened the door to us—'

'I've never found that calling people names, however fancy, ever helped me solve a case.'

'You got to admit, he was . . . creepy.'

'He's not a very good judge of other people, for sure,' said Cupidi. 'He's never going to be able to get that sculpture out of the flat, for a start. She won't fit out the door.'

'Don't joke, boss. The vilest thing I've ever seen in my life. It's like . . . some sex doll, except with an arm chopped off. At first I thought he'd actually wrapped someone up in Sellotape, swear to God.'

'Get his work rota for the Turner. Find out which days he was there.' Cupidi started the engine.

'Is that it? We're just leaving him?'

Cupidi looked at her watch. 'We're due at the Millers' house in three-quarters of an hour. I could leave you here if you like. You could do a bit of covert surveillance on Ross. It doesn't need two of us to go and see Astrid Miller.'

'No,' said Ferriter. 'You're OK.'

After twenty minutes on the road, Ferriter sat forward, so she'd be closer to the vanity mirror, and opened her handbag.

'Are you getting made up for Evert and Astrid?' asked Cupidi.

'I'm just more confident in the presence of women like that if I'm not looking like a sack of potatoes. Don't you feel like that, sometimes?'

'Should I?'

'That's not what I said.'

'Kind of.'

'No. You're just confident like you are.'

'Deftly done,' said Cupidi.

'I know.' Ferriter tugged at the fringe of her blonde bob. 'Seriously, though. You are crazy cool. When I'm your age, I wouldn't mind looking like you.'

Cupidi snorted.

'Actually, I was attempting to be sincere.'

They rose out of the flatland into the lush lanes of mid-Kent, hawthorn breaking through in the hedges they sped past.

'I was expecting something . . . I don't know . . . posher,' said Ferriter, disappointed.

Cupidi had done her research. Evert Miller had made his first millions in the 1990s from a series of price comparison websites, then diversified into online retailing and data marketing. Astrid Miller was his second wife; he had two children by his first. The divorce had been contested, apparently, and the children lived with their mother.

Long Hill, the Millers' estate, was not a single house, but a collection of ultra-modern buildings, made of wood, stone, steel, concrete and glass, some joined at angles with each other, others separate, but they were all of a piece. Above each structure, red-tiled triangles rose against the skyline like sails, attempting to echo the shape of Kent's oast-houses, the hop-drying towers that had once dotted the landscape. From a distance, it looked like some red-backed dragon had landed on the fields, its scaly spine raised skywards. Repeated motifs made each building feel part of a larger whole: round windows, flint-knapped walls, black

151

wood cladding. It looked expensive, but as millionaires' houses went, it was curiously unassuming, nestling into the shape of the hillside. Some surfaces were covered in solar panels, others grew vetches and stonecrops.

'Where's the front door?' asked Cupidi as she drove up a gravel driveway.

'Where the posh cars are.' Ferriter pointed. 'Course he's got a Tesla, hasn't he?'

A low red sports car was parked next to one of the bigger houses. Cupidi pulled up next to it, got out.

There seemed to be nobody around. The place was quiet.

'Remember,' said Cupidi. 'Watch yourself. We need to go gently. McAdam doesn't want us to go making the millionaires nervous.'

A black lead snaked from the red car across the gravel to a charging point, hidden by bushes. Ferriter peered inside the vehicle. When she stepped back, she saw she'd left smudges on the clean glass and set about polishing them with her sleeve.

Cupidi wandered away, down a pathway towards a second building, with a large glass wall. There seemed to be lights on inside. Ferriter followed her.

As they approached, they saw a young woman, sitting behind a glass desk, look up, surprised. Cupidi entered. 'Police,' she said.

'How did you get in?'

'We just drove up. There was no one around.'

The woman, dressed in a white silk blouse and black trousers, frowned.

'We've come about the Foundation,' Cupidi explained.

'Ms Gubenko is expecting you. She'll be with you very shortly. Please take a seat.'

'Ms Gubenko? I thought we were here to see Astrid Miller?' said Ferriter.

The young woman paused. 'I understood you were here to enquire about the business of the Foundation?'

'That's right.'

'Ms Gubenko is the Foundation administrator. She can answer any questions you have.'

'But Astrid Miller runs the Foundation?'

A smile. 'Of course. She and Evert. But it's Zoya Gubenko you'd need to ask about any details. Mr and Mrs Miller are very big picture.' She paused. 'Coffee?'

Cupidi accepted; Ferriter declined. 'Can I just have a hot water?'

'Naturally.' The woman disappeared.

There were two leather and steel armchairs; they sat.

'Aw,' said Cupidi her voice low. 'It looks like you're not going to see Astrid after all. She's too big picture.'

'Bloody gutted, actually,' complained Ferriter. 'Maybe I should have stayed watching Ross's flat instead. Did you see that woman's shoes? Those two-tone Oxfords. I've got the same ones.'

She picked up a copy of *Monocle*, flicked through it, put it down again.

The woman in two-tone Oxfords returned two minutes later carrying two white porcelain cups.

'What about Mr Miller? Is he here?' demanded Cupidi after she'd taken a mouthful.

'Yes,' said the woman, back at her desk, eyes fixed on her computer screen.

'Perhaps we could speak to him instead.'

The woman jerked her head back slightly, as if Cupidi had just said something inappropriate. 'I doubt it. He's busy. You can make an appointment.'

'So where is Mrs Miller?'

'Ms Miller,' she said, emphasising the title, 'is away.'

'Away where?'

The woman hesitated for a fraction of a second. 'As I said, I am not employed by Ms Miller. I work for Mr Miller. I'm sorry. I can't help you.'

'You are aware that we are involved in a murder investigation,' said Cupidi. 'Human remains were deliberately placed in property belonging to the Miller Foundation. We need to consider the possibility that someone has a particular grudge against Mr or *Ms* Miller. I had expected to speak to him.'

Ferriter frowned. The woman hesitated. 'I can ask. I have his diary. His schedule is very full.'

'Ours too.' Cupidi smiled back at her.

The woman's mobile rang. 'I'll send them through.' She looked up from her screen. 'Miss Gubenko is ready for you. Third on the left,' she said.

TWENTY-TWO

'Tell him we've gone,' hissed Sloth.

'Don't say we're here.' Tap rubbed the scab on his lip.

'Who is he?' asked Frank.

The boys looked at each other. 'Don't know.'

'What do you mean, you don't know? If that's not your dad, I need to know who that is ringing my front door bell.' Pacing the floor of his own apartment, Frank looked anxious too.

'We don't frickin' know, right? It's him we're running away from.'

Tap was thinking. *He was in my mum's house all this time.* Frank stopped by the entry phone, a small white handset that hung in his hallway next to the kitchen. 'You're running away from him?'

Again the buzzer sounded. Now Frank looked from the boys, to the phone, to the front window and back again, a triangle of indecision.

'Don't say we're here, please,' Tap pleaded. 'Please don't.'

The man was holding his finger on the bell now. A continuous *bzzzzzzz*.

Frank stepped forward, grasped the handset. 'Hello?'

'Hi.' The boys could hear the voice from the little loudspeaker, friendly and warm, like everything was perfectly normal. 'You had my boy there. And his mate. I've come to pick them up.'

'Yeah. Sorry.' Frank floundered.

'Say we went out to the shop,' Sloth hissed.

'They went out to the shop. They haven't come back.'

'I can wait.'

The three, Sloth, Tap and Frank, exchanged glances.

The buzzing stopped and now the silence was almost too loud.

They stood in Frank's flat, unsure what to do next.

'Is he just standing there?' said Tap. 'Can you see?'

Frank went over to the window at the end of the living room and tried to look down. 'Maybe he's gone.'

'No. He'll be out there somewhere.'

When Frank turned from the glass, there was something new in his eyes. When they'd met him, that morning on Ruby Tuesday Drive, and in the KFC, Frank had seemed cocky, superior, in control with his wallet full of cash. Now, Tap realised, he just looked scared. What was he so frightened of? Could he sense who this man was too?

'There another way we can sneak out?' asked Sloth.

'There's a back door, where the bins are. But you have to walk down the stairs to get there. If he's still at the front door, he'll see you through the glass.'

That's where he would be; waiting for them.

'Frank should call the po,' Tap told Sloth.

'The police? Really?' said Sloth.

'Honest. I don't give a crap any more. I just want to go home. I know we're in trouble but it can't be as bad as this. Call them.'

'What kind of trouble?' asked Frank.

Sloth turned to him. 'Yeah. Call the police. Tell them there's someone shady hanging around outside your flat. You think they're coming to rob you.'

Frank shook his head. 'No.'

'Why not? That'll scare him off for a minute, moment he sees their car. I promise you.'

This time veins rose on Frank's forehead. 'No.'

Sloth looked puzzled. 'What's wrong?'

'I can't call the police.'

Sloth's eyes widened. 'Oh Jesus. I get it. You're in trouble with the coppers, too. That's why you don't want to call them.' He laughed. 'That's superb. Absolutely bloody frickin' superb.'

Frank flopped down on the couch. Dust rose into the air, hanging in the sunlight. 'I just want you two out of here.'

'What happened to "Come on over to my flat?", Frank?'

'What are you in trouble for?' asked Sloth. 'Let me guess. Not hard, is it? Kiddy fiddler, is it?'

'I haven't done anything to you, have I?'

Sloth, standing next to the kitchen counter, back against the wall, slid down till he was sitting on the floor. 'Mind if I have a smoke?'

'Not in here. I don't like it.'

'Well I'm not going outside, that's for shizzle.'

A minute passed, and then another.

'How long are we going to wait?'

'Don't know.'

'What if he's gone?' said Frank. But his words were still in the air when the buzzer rang again.

'Tell him to go away,' urged Sloth.

Frank stood. Again he pressed the button. 'Hello?'

'Let me up,' the man's voice said. 'You know the police are after those boys, don't you? They killed a man. You're harbouring a pair of murderers.'

Frank looked at the boys.

'I can help. You don't want them in your apartment, I promise you. Let me come up. I'll have them off your hands in no time.'

Frank released the button, looked round at the boys. 'Is that true?'

'No,' Tap blurted. 'He's a liar. He's the one who's frickin' dangerous. He killed my uncle. We didn't kill anyone. Not on purpose.'

'Shut up, Tap,' said Sloth.

'Phone the police. Please. Think about it. Would we be begging you to call the cops if it weren't true?'

Again, Frank returned to the sofa, uncertain. The two boys watched him as he chewed on the skin on the edge of his thumb.

'You're useless, you know that? You have to do something.'

'Don't, Tap. He's scared. What are you so scared of, Frank?'

Frank shook his head. 'I'm a bloody idiot.'

'We're frightened too,' said Tap. 'It's why we were running away. He's going to kill us. He's psycho. Seriously.'

Sloth edged himself up from the floor. 'He killed Tap's uncle Mikey. That's what we were trying to get away from.'

Frank's eyes narrowed. He shook his head slowly, as if he didn't want to believe any of this. 'You're making this crap up.'

'It was on the TV. Just up the road. Last week. Man on the motorbike. Remember?'

Frank nodded. 'I saw that.'

'That was him. That was Tap's uncle.'

'What did your uncle do to him?'

'Nothing. That's the whole point. The man outside, he's psycho.'

'And he's after you? What the hell have you got me into?' he whined.

'Wasn't our fault. You're the one who picked us up. Why did you pick us up, first place, Frank?'

The bell rang again and this time kept ringing; a continual buzzing that filled the space around them. Frank put his fingers into his ears like he didn't want to hear any more.

'Now are you going to call the coppers?'

'If I ring the police, you got to get out of here, moment I do.'

'We can't get out of here till he's gone.'

'OK. Moment he's gone, you go, right?'

'Got to be sure he's vamoosed. Tell him. Tell him you're calling the cops. Maybe he'll go then.'

Frank stood, went to the intercom, pressed the button. 'Hello?'

There was a crackle. But no answer. Was that the sound of a man out there? Could they hear breathing, or was that just the noise of electronic circuitry?

'You still there?'

Just the same hiss.

'Are you still there?' He turned to the boys. 'Maybe he's gone.'

'Swear to God,' said Tap. 'He's hundred per cent still there. He doesn't give up.'

'You hear me? I'm ringing the police,' called Frank. 'Telling them there's someone suspicious outside my door.'

The intercom clicked. 'What those boys say about me?'

'I'm phoning the police,' Frank shouted, then put down the handset.

Silence.

Frank walked to the window, then flinched backwards. 'I can see him. He's still down there looking up. He's looking right at me. He's not moved.'

'Don't frickin' let him see you talking to us.'

'He knows you're here, boys. He's not stupid. If you say he is who he is, he'd go because he won't want the police here. Won't he? Why's he not moving?'

Tap could taste blood on his tongue. He realised he had scratched the scab off his lip again.

Sloth said, 'Because he doesn't believe you've called them.'

'Now you got to call them,' said Tap. 'Call them for real. He won't go unless he really knows they're coming. He needs to see the bloody cop car. Then he'll vamoose.'

'Will you get lost when he goes?'

Tap nodded. 'You don't want boys in your flat when the police are here. We get it. We understand, Frank. We'll scarper, moment he goes. Swear to God.'

Frank picked up his mobile, hesitated.

'Go on Frank.'

The boys listened. 'Police please.'

The bell rang again.

'Frank,' he said. 'Frank Khan.' He gave his address. 'There's a man outside trying to get into my house,' he said. 'He's making threats. He's ringing on my doorbell now. I think he wants to harm me.'

He hadn't mentioned them, hadn't given them away. The bell was like a kind of torture now. *Bzzzzzzzzzzz.*

'Hurry, please. Please. You can hear him, can't you? No. I don't know him. I'm scared.'

And then, just as he ended the call, the ringing stopped.

Nobody moved or talked, waiting for the doorbell to sound again.

After a while, Frank walked to the window, phone still in his hand and peered down. 'I can't see him. Do you think he's gone?' He looked round. Smiled suddenly like the old Frank, the one with whom they had sat in the KFC. 'Two minutes, and then you're out of here too.'

'I was just getting used to it here,' said Sloth.

'Get out.'

'Only joking. I'm happy to go, Frank. It's been real.'

But just as Sloth put his hand on the lock, a fist banged on the other side of the door.

'Shit.'

'Who is it?' called Frank.

Another bang. 'Open up.' The same voice that had come through the intercom.

Which was when Frank edged backwards into the kitchen and picked up the knife; one with a fat, curved blade and a small black handle.

161

TWENTY-THREE

In the corridor, Ferriter hissed, 'Oh my God. You tell me to watch myself, then you blurt out something about someone having a grudge against the Millers, even though we don't actually know that. Prize shit-stirring.'

'She was annoying me,' Cupidi replied.

'And there was I thinking McAdam had told us to go carefully.'

But before Cupidi could reply, they were already at another door. A woman in her thirties sat alone in another white room.

'I am sorry. An important call with N2N in Abu Dhabi. Terrific gallery. Do you know them? Please sit down.'

On the large canvas behind Zoya Gubenko's desk, a brown triangle occupied a space on a wash of light blue paint, so thickly applied that it had formed dribbles.

'You have coffee already, good. What can I help you with?' There were two chairs facing her, as if arranged in readiness. Cupidi sat; examined Gubenko. Like the previous woman, she too was thin and immaculately dressed. Her hair was short, dyed grey, and she wore a black suit and heels, with an orange chiffon scarf around her square shoulders. She spoke quickly, in perfect English, but with an accent; Eastern European or possibly Russian, Cupidi decided.

'A little background,' said Cupidi, taking out a notebook, 'on the Evert and Astrid Miller Foundation.'

'Naturally.' Gubenko beamed. 'The Foundation was established in 2011, initially as a straightforward investment fund with a mission to support emerging artists. There are many of these, you understand? The art market is very vibrant right now, but it does not always nurture new voices. There's always a tendency towards safe havens; it's all Rothko and de Kooning. Our strategy is to work with a very mixed portfolio. The value of investing in pieces by more established artists creates a platform for us to experiment with newer practitioners.'

She paused, as if waiting for questions from the audience. It was a speech she was used to delivering to investors and gallerists.

'As with all luxury goods, the art market is a healthy one right now, but within a year of starting the Foundation, Astrid Miller began to ask the question, healthy for whom? Is it healthy for the galleries? Yes, though obviously the internet is changing the gallery scene a great deal.'

'Obviously,' said Cupidi.

Gubenko paused, raised an eyebrow as if trying to discern whether Cupidi was being flippant or not, then continued. 'For the investor, things are extremely healthy right now. Don't be mistaken. You can make more money elsewhere, no doubt, on stocks

163

or property or whatever, but the art market is currently producing more than reasonable returns and people with money enjoy the world it connects them too. Entrepreneurs like Evert Miller are creative. Creative people like the company of artists. But Astrid and Evert Miller began to question whether the contemporary market was as healthy for the artist as it was for the investor. In terms of delivering profit, the greater investor return is often paradoxically realised by those newer artists. The art market benefits greatly from that. However, the artists, whose work is typically bought for next to nothing, usually see little of the money.'

Zoya Gubenko paused again, took her scarf between finger and thumb and rubbed it gently. Smiled. 'In 2012 Evert and Astrid Miller decided to change the model.' She said the phrase 'Evert and Astrid Miller' as if they were a single entity, a beautiful billionaire super-organism. 'Evert and Astrid Miller announced that the primary purpose of the Foundation was no longer profit. As Astrid says, the objective has become to nurture emerging artists by leveraging the existing machinery of the art market in their favour. When she buys a new artist's work, that artist becomes a co-investor in our art fund. She offers them shares in the fund so that, as the collective value rises, they are also rewarded. As a result she has become one of the figures the cutting-edge galleries seek out, and obviously artists much prefer to see their work come to a Foundation like ours. It has been phenomenally successful. Last year Mrs Miller was named one of the top one hundred influential people in the contemporary art world by both Artnet and *ArtReview*.'

Cupidi scribbled in her notebook. '*Ms* Miller,' she corrected, without looking up.

164

'Sorry?'

'Never mind.' Cupidi took a gulp from her coffee. It had gone cold during Zoya Gubenko's speech.

'So emerging artists actually make money not just from their own art, but from other works you've acquired. Like *Funerary Urn*.'

'Exactly. Though we have much more valuable pieces of art. We own several Koonses, a very good Luo Zhongli, a series by Cy Twombly.'

'But you share your profits with the newer artists?'

'And as a result, they seek us out. Unlike other art funds, we are all about transparency. It makes us extremely unpopular with the other funds, of course.' She smiled again.

'Really?' said Cupidi, looking up from her notebook. 'So you have made enemies?'

Gubenko paused. 'Obviously not in that way. Just within the art world.'

'You said you were extremely unpopular with other funds.'

'Only because we are getting more attention, perhaps.'

'Might they be trying to sabotage your reputation in some way?'

Gubenko laughed. 'Oh my gosh. What a thought. You are the police. Your job is to look for every bit of nastiness there is in the world. However, the art world is a very civilised one. It's true that we represent a threat to their business model. Effectively, our approach gives us a unique competitive advantage – new artists want to sell to us. But I doubt anyone in this world would want to risk their reputation in that way.'

'Tell me what you know about the movements of the artwork, prior to its installation in the Turner on April . . .'

'April fifth, yes. I was told that was what you needed. I have them here.'

She took a sheet of paper from in front of her and handed it to Cupidi. It was a list of dates and locations.

'This is where the piece has been since the Foundation purchased it.'

Cupidi scanned dates which went back five years. Ferriter pulled her chair forward towards the desk so she could see it too. The artwork had been in Spain, Beijing, Hong Kong and the UK.

She frowned and looked up at the administrator. 'Forensics seem to indicate that the arm has been in the jar for two to three weeks. There's no record of it being anywhere prior to arriving at the Turner.'

'That's because it was in storage. If it's not at a gallery, it would be at the facility.'

'Where?'

'The Foundation uses EastArt's services in East London. Many private investors do. It's of a very high standard and very secure indeed. They handle the transportation of the work as well. They're a very respectable company. Very discreet and very safe.'

'Can we have their details?' asked Ferriter.

'Of course.' She picked up her iPad and began scrolling through the contacts. 'But I assure you, nobody could have access to anything stored there, not without our permission.' Cupidi's phone buzzed. 'I have just sent the details to you,' Gubenko explained. The silence of the place reasserted itself. 'Will that be all?'

'So, just to be clear, nobody else has the authority to access the artworks?'

'Just Astrid herself. And Abir Stein.'

'Who is Mr Stein?'

'The Foundation's curator.'

'I'd like his contact details as well.'

She pursed her lips, picked up her tablet again. A second time, Cupidi's phone buzzed.

'You said three people had access to the EastArt store. Yourself, Astrid Miller and –' she glanced at the details that Gubenko had just messaged her – 'Mr Stein. Not Mr Miller?'

'No. Well, theoretically I suppose he could have. He represents the Foundation. But he is more interested in the structural and financial details of the trust than the artworks themselves.'

'That's Astrid Miller's role?'

Zoya Gubenko bristled slightly, but said, 'Yes.'

'Oh I see. It's your role. But she takes the credit?'

Gubenko glared at Cupidi. Ferriter intervened with a dazzling smile: 'We'd been expecting to see Ms Miller. Do you know where she is?'

'I'm terribly sorry. She's away. On business.'

'Will you be speaking to her today?'

'I don't know. She travels a lot. China, Africa. She is always on the lookout for new work.'

'And where is she now?'

'Brazil, possibly. Until she contacts me with a request for something, I rarely know. It can be quite frustrating at times.' A thin smile. 'But that is how she is.'

'We would like her details too.'

'I'll send her a message and ask her to contact you.'

Cupidi opened her mouth to object but, conscious of Ferriter's more emollient approach, just said, 'If you can let her know that this is extremely urgent. One more thing. Assuming that someone put the arm in the jar deliberately, could they have known in advance that it was going to be exhibited here in Kent?'

Gubenko paused, chewed uncomfortably on her lower lip. 'Possibly.'

'How?'

'In this case the artist's gallerist was a little over-excited when they learned the work was going to be included in the "In Memoriam" exhibition. They issued their own press release, even before the Turner had announced it. Not very good form.'

'So theoretically, anyone could have known that it was going to be there?'

'Unfortunately, yes.'

Cupidi stood, pushing back her chair.

Ferriter remained seated. 'What's it actually like, working with Astrid Miller?'

'She is a remarkable woman,' said Gubenko with a tight smile.

'Isn't she, though?'

But Gubenko was already at the glass door, holding it open for them.

At the reception desk, the woman looked up and said, 'Mr Miller can see you for a few minutes, if it's that important.'

Cupidi looked at Ferriter, a small smile on her face. 'Of course.'

'He's in the main house. Wait outside. He'll be there presently.'

'Bloody hell. It worked,' said Ferriter after they had stepped outside.

'Do as I say, not as I do, obviously.'

168

Back at the front door, Ferriter drooled over the red car again. 'I'd love something like that.'

'You're in the wrong career then.'

'Astrid's probably just really super-busy.' The door opened as Ferriter was talking. 'She does all this ultra-swanky charity millionairey stuff.'

They were both suddenly aware of a man in his early forties, dressed in a white Fair Isle jumper, standing at the door. 'Five minutes,' he said, looked them both up and down, and closed the door.

'Was that him?' asked Cupidi.

'Oh God. Do you think he heard me?' said Ferriter. 'I'd be so embarrassed.'

Leaning down towards the glass of the car's passenger window, Ferriter examined herself again. Normally, Cupidi would have laughed, except, today, she looked at the loose threads on the sleeve of her jacket and wished she had worn something a little smarter. Then reprimanded herself for such a ridiculous thought.

TWENTY-FOUR

When Frank yanked his front door open, knife in hand, there was no one behind it.

Cautiously, he emerged onto the landing, looked left and right. The shared space, with its nice peach-coloured walls, framed Constable prints and patterned carpet, was empty. Frank turned back to the two boys in his flat; they were staring past him, down the hallway.

'I think he's gone,' he said.

Tap was the first to think it. 'How did he get in in the first place?'

There was a second of silence before Frank said, 'I'll go and check.' He slipped the knife into his trouser pocket and turned again.

'He shouldn't go,' whispered Tap.

'Come back. Just wait for the coppers,' Sloth called after him.

But Frank had disappeared, out of view, leaving the flat's door wide open.

Tap said, 'Which way did Frank go?'

'Downstairs, I think. We should make a move.'

'No, Slo. He's still out there.'

They stood in the man's empty, soulless flat. The only way out would be to follow Frank down the stairs.

Sloth stepped forward into the small hallway.

'Where you going?'

Sloth turned. 'Nowhere. Stay calm, bro. Door's wide open. Going to shut the door, just in case.'

And before Sloth turned back to close the door, Tap saw the shadow move on the wall behind him. The look of horror on his face was enough to make Sloth stop and turn again to look at what Tap had seen.

The man who had chased them from Tap's house, who had followed them here, had not gone downstairs at all. He must have crept up to the next floor when Frank went down to look at him. Now he was silhouetted at Frank's doorway.

He wasn't particularly tall. An average-height man, dark-haired, brown-eyed, early forties, dressed in very ordinary high street clothes, plain brown shoes and leather gloves. No beard or moustache, eyebrows plain. No scars or tattoos, just a single small ring in one ear. Neither handsome nor conspicuously ugly. Even his face seemed unremarkable. There was no particular expression on it, no triumph at having finally found the boys.

Sloth lurched forward, grabbed the door to try and slam it, but the man stepped inside. He turned and closed the door behind him and walked calmly into the main space, the living-room kitchen. 'Tell me quick. The phone. The one you nicked.'

171

Tap found his voice. 'We gave it to my uncle. He brought it back to you.'

The man shook his head and talked slowly, as if the boys were simpletons. 'Not that one. You know the one I mean. The other one. The one you called me on. The one with the words on it.'

Tap said, 'You killed him, didn't you.'

The man approached. 'I want just the phone now.'

'What's them words about?' demanded Sloth. '*Tumour, paralysed, potential.* All that stuff?'

Another step closer. 'You gave me eleven words. I need twelve. Tell me the last word on the phone and you can go.'

'Swear it.'

'God's life,' answered the man.

But they didn't know the last word. The phone had died before Sloth could read it.

'*Survivor, analyst, battle,*' said Tap. 'Tell him where the phone is, Slo.' He stared at the man, wiping tears away from his eyes. When had he started crying?

'Phone or the last word. Give it to me now. It's best if you do that without any fuss,' the man said.

'It's not here. We can get it, though. Swear to God.'

'Where is it?'

'How come you're at my house?' Tap said. 'Did you do anything to my mum?' His eyes stung and his voice quavered, like a baby's.

The man stopped, put his head to one side slightly. The tiniest smile exposed a chipped front tooth, the first sign of anything individual about the man. 'Your mum?'

'My mum,' whispered Tap.

172

The two boys and this man, standing in a room, a metre apart.

'Get me the phone now or just tell me the bloody word and I'll let you know all about your mum.'

'No.' Sloth shook his head. 'Don't say nothing.'

'Frick sake. Let him have it, Slo.'

'Mikey gave him the other one. He still killed him, didn't he?'

'What was the last word?'

It was like they were in a puzzle and nobody had ever told them how it worked. *Nobody tells you the rules in this game. You got to work them out for yourself.*

'The word,' said the man again. Tap blurted, '*Aspiration.* That was the last word.'

For just a second, the man relaxed. Sloth was looking at Tap, eyebrows raised. 'Swear on our lives, man. That was it.'

Simple. They had made up a word.

How was he to know it wasn't true? Whatever strange game this was, he didn't know what the word was any more than they did. They could run away from this now. He would never know. But they could see him spelling the letters on his lips, counting them with the fingers of one hand.

'Lying.' The man's smile vanished. 'Ten letters. That's too long. You just made that up, you lying little bastards.'

He stepped forward, and in a swift movement grabbed Tap by the throat with one gloved hand and by his hair by the other. The hand around Tap's neck squeezed, digging into his carotids with finger and thumb; with his other hand he jerked Tap's head down, crushing his windpipe.

In a second, Tap was struggling to breathe, hands clutching at the gloves.

Sloth threw himself at the man, punching the side of his head. The man didn't seem to notice, but as Sloth drew his hand back again, he relaxed the grip on Tap's neck and the boy fell to the floor, panting.

'Shh!' The man raised his finger to his lips.

The doorknob rattled.

Frank called through the door. 'Boys?' The door muffled his voice, but they could still hear what he was saying perfectly clearly. 'He's gone. He got in at the back, but there's no sign of him. Swear to God.'

The man in front of them stopped, looked round.

Next, the sound of a key in the door. Frank was still talking. 'Now for pity's sake, you got to get out of here pronto before the police—'

The door swung open and Frank stood facing the three of them.

'What the—'

The boys saw the colour disappear from Frank's face.

Jerking into action too late, Frank reached into his trousers to pull out the knife he had hidden there before he'd gone out to the flat's landing.

But Frank wasn't good at this. He was just an ordinary man, unused to fighting. Grabbing the knife's handle, he tried to jerk it from his pocket, and instead caught it on a fold of cloth and lost his grip. The weapon spilled to the floor and spun on the laminate, coming to a halt with the blade pointing back towards him.

Frank seemed paralysed by the error and in that moment, the other man simply stepped forward, placed his boot on the knife and in a single movement scooped it up with his hand.

From there it was a fluid motion from floor to flesh. The

weapon that had been at Frank's feet a second ago was now thrusting upwards and before he had registered what was happening, it slid deep into Frank's stomach.

Pure bewilderment on Frank's face, as if wondering how things had come so swiftly to this.

Strange, thought Tap, in the lucidity of the moment, when action seems to slow to stillness, that Frank hadn't cried out, or screamed; he had just accepted the wound, as if it was his due.

Sloth edged closer to Tap.

At what point did Frank finally realise that his only option was to fight back? Knife still inside him, slicing his gut, he moved forward instead of back.

For the first time, the man was wrong-footed. He had leaned in to stab Frank; now his balance was off and he tottered back into the kitchen area.

Frank glanced up at Tap. 'Get out,' Frank whispered. 'Run.'

Tap was caught in the horror of it, too shocked to move. But Sloth came alive, grabbing his hoodie and tugging.

Leaving Frank alone with the killer, the two ran out through the door and down the stairs. At the bottom they paused. The back door was swinging open. Fresh air blew into the building. That must have been how he'd got in.

From far away came the sound of a siren.

'This way,' pleaded Sloth.

Tap hesitated, thinking of Frank. He stood no chance.

The siren was louder now.

They ran from the back door out into the sunshine, skirting their way around the flats. Soon they were running down the new pavements, feet thumping on tarmac.

As the police car came closer, they slowed, pulling their hoods lower over their faces.

'What's that about your mum?' asked Sloth.

They walked on, calm as they could. The coppers didn't look twice.

Later, sitting on the swings on a small kids' playground, smoking another cigarette, they heard sirens converging on the flat they had run from. They didn't talk much. As he put the fag to his lips, Tap saw the shaking in his own hand. However hard he tried, he couldn't stop it. The two boys sat in the children's play area, on its brightly painted equipment, both crying.

TWENTY-FIVE

Evert Miller emerged again, this time dressed in grey shorts and a white T-shirt that clung to a muscular frame. Two setters bounded out of the front door after him.

Ferriter squatted down and the dogs approached her.

'Is that all you have on your feet?'

Ferriter looked down. She was in kitten heels and tights.

'What am I supposed to have?'

'What size are you?'

'Six.'

Evert Miller disappeared back into the house, emerging with a pair of black wellington boots. Ferriter leaned against the police car bonnet, putting them on.

'Will they do?' he asked.

'They're huge on me,' she said, looking down and frowning.

'They're Astrid's. Eights.'

The frown disappeared. 'Astrid's boots?'

'I'm afraid it's the best I can do.' And he set off down the driveway, dogs trotting alongside.

'No, they're fine,' Ferriter said.

'Your house,' said Cupidi, making small talk. 'It's very . . . adventurous.'

'Thank you. I wanted something that could evolve, not a great big lump with a swimming pool and a garage. Though I have a swimming pool of sorts. I'll show you it, if you like.'

They passed a sculpture, a giant orange wire frame that made the shape of an open umbrella, as if drawn into the air. Cupidi paused to look at it and smiled.

'Astrid installed it there. A Michael Craig-Martin, I believe. It's the Foundation's, obviously. We have a few pieces here. Sculpture's so expensive to store, so why not have one or two of them here? There's an insurance cost here too, but I think it's a much better way, don't you?'

Cupidi wondered if he was trying to make her feel at ease in their company, or whether he was too rich to understand that a police sergeant was unlikely to have a garden like his, filled with rare sculptures.

They were disappearing down a track that followed a gentle slope downhill. Bright green clematis and honeysuckle tendrils swung in the air, anticipating something to wrap themselves around.

They walked quickly, almost jogging, as every second of his time was valuable.

Cupidi matched his pace. 'This is your home and your office?'

'I have other offices. But I prefer to work from here when I can. It keeps me sane. We wanted somewhere that was modular, that could change as we did.'

Behind them, Ferriter's wellingtons clopped unevenly against her calves as she tried to keep up. Evert Miller was a decade older than his wife, but fit and lean. 'You think this business with the arm is about a grudge against me, apparently.'

'To be clear, it's just one theory.' She pulled a notebook from the pocket of her trousers. 'Do you know of anyone who has a grudge against you?'

He stopped. 'You think concealing a severed arm at an art gallery might have been some message directed at me?'

Ferriter took the chance to stop, too, to scowl, lean down and rub her calves.

'At this stage we're struggling to understand what it was doing there, so we're exploring any avenue we can.'

'Of course there are people who don't like me. I am pretty rich, which causes a lot of resentment. This country can be a bitter place. And because of who I married, I have the media's attention, which is enough to make others resentful, but I don't know of anyone who'd resort to something quite so . . . strange.' He set off again. 'It is strange, isn't it?'

Cupidi picked up a stick and threw it across the meadow. The dogs bounded off together. 'They'll love you for that,' he said.

'You campaigned against Brexit.'

'Not campaigned, precisely. I added my name to letters.'

'You donated money.'

'Brexit was an act of vandalism. And I suppose saying that doesn't make you popular, especially here,' he said. 'But I can't see what that's got to do with a severed arm.'

'Nor me. Political campaigners these days are usually less cryptic in their messaging.'

He laughed, smiled at her. 'Yes. They are.'

'What about your wife?'

The smile vanished. 'What about her?'

'Anyone who might have a particular animus towards her.'

'No. Everybody loves Astrid, don't they?' He paused again. 'Do you seriously think there might be?'

Cupidi thought of Ross Clough. 'Again, I don't know.'

The dogs paused, sniffing at a badger's sett. 'Come,' he said, and they followed him again.

'Hold on a sec,' said Ferriter. 'I got something in my boot.'

Cupidi looked back. The constable was leaning one hand against a small alder, trying to shake something out of Astrid Miller's wellingtons with the other, one foot perched on top of the boot she was still wearing.

'Obviously I would ask her myself, Mr Miller, but she's not here.'

'True.'

'Do you know where she is?'

'Away working on some project,' said Evert Miller. 'She travels a lot.'

'In Brazil?'

'No. Yes. I'm not sure. Maybe.'

Cupidi paused. Evert carried on walking. 'When did you last speak to her, Mr Miller?'

'I don't mean to be difficult, but is that your business?'

'Yes,' she called after him. 'It is.'

He stopped now and turned back. He had reached the bottom

of the slope. A small stream trickled down the slight valley, fringed with dead daffodils, brown leaves flattened against the soil. 'She's a remarkable woman. She is incredibly passionate,' he said. 'Sometimes she goes off on a whim.'

The dogs whined, eager to move on.

Ferriter caught up with Cupidi. 'They're chafing like hell,' she whispered.

'I would very much like to speak to her,' Cupidi called.

'Did you tell Zoya what you needed? That's probably the best way.'

'Doesn't she call you?'

He looked away. 'Of course she does.' The dogs were splashing in the shallow water. 'Heel,' he shouted. 'But you haven't identified who the arm belongs to yet,' he continued.

'How do you know that?' she asked.

'I ask around,' he said vaguely. 'I know the police have no working theory yet about what's going on.'

'You're keeping tabs on this case?'

'I keep tabs on anything that affects my private life or my business life,' he said.

They walked on through a small stand of birches. The land opened out and they were suddenly standing in front of a large flat pool of water. It must have been created artificially, because there weren't any lakes around here – even small ones like this – but it looked entirely natural, except for a small wooden jetty with stainless steel steps that disappeared into the water.

Beyond the jetty was a small chalet, built in the same style as the rest of the houses, a glass door facing the pool of water, with a small patio, a metal fire pit and a barbecue.

181

'Swimming in fresh water is so much nicer, don't you think?'

'You swim here?' said Ferriter.

'I told you we had a swimming pool,' he said.

'It must be bloody freezing.'

'That's half the pleasure.'

Ferriter looked sceptical.

'I've been in here when there's been ice two inches thick on the top. There's nothing like it, I promise you. I can lend you a costume if you like.' He grinned, pointing to the chalet. 'We keep all sizes in the changing room over there.'

'Fortunately,' Ferriter answered, 'I'm on duty.'

'I have to ask, did you ever visit the EastArt facilities where the Foundation stores its work?' Cupidi asked.

Miller frowned. 'Why?'

'Because only you, your wife –' she looked down at her notebook – 'Zoya Gubenko and an Abir Stein have access to it. And in the timeline we have, it looks like the arm would have been placed into the artwork before it arrived at the Turner. Did you visit it at any time?'

'Honestly? I have never been there in my life. I have no reason to.'

'So the Foundation is in both of your names, but effectively your wife takes care of the art?'

He looked at his watch. 'Do you mind telling me why this is important?'

'It's probably not,' Cupidi said. 'But I have to ask.' They were heading back now.

'Astrid's not just one of these awful women who turn up for the cocktail receptions at Frieze and Miami Art Basel and buys

182

whatever's on trend. She visits studios all over the world. She goes to degree shows in London and New York to find new work. When she sees something she responds to she lights up. She insists we buy it. I wouldn't let her do it with our money if she wasn't so brilliant with it. You should see her.' He smiled.

'I would, but Zoya Gubenko seemed reluctant to pass on her number.'

'My wife is a very private person.'

'However, we do need to get in touch with her.'

'We made a decision at the start of our marriage that her life would be as private as possible.'

'Mr Miller. This isn't prurient interest. We have to assume that the victim may still be alive.'

For the first time he looked unsettled. 'You're serious?'

'So we don't want anything that slows down our investigation.'

'Of course,' he said. He considered for a second, then recited a number from memory.

Cupidi had to ask him to repeat it, so she could write it in her notebook. 'You own one of the properties on Dungeness?'

'You have been doing your research, haven't you?' For the first time there was an edge of irritation in his voice.

'I read it somewhere,' interrupted Ferriter. 'It's where Sergeant Cupidi here lives. Weird place.'

'Do you?' said Evert Miller, surprised.

'Yes. I do.'

'So few people actually stay there. Most of the houses seem to be empty all the time. Ours included, I'm afraid,' he said, as if looking at her afresh. 'It's Astrid's, really, not mine at all. We agreed, when we got married, that we would keep our finances separate.'

183

'I love it there.'

He examined her, as if with a new respect. 'I expect it takes a certain kind of person,' he said.

'Yes, it does.'

'Must be wonderful in bad weather.'

'Exactly,' she said.

'Since we built this house, we don't use the Dungeness place much. It's a bit neglected, I'm afraid.'

'Which one is it?' It was the sort of question you could ask about the shacks at Dungeness. No two were the same.

He smiled a little sheepishly. 'As you're aware, we try to protect what privacy we have. It's not really relevant, is it?'

They were back at the house. The PA who had given them coffee was standing by the front door with a folder.

Evert Miller put out his hand to shake. 'Good luck,' he said, keeping hold of Cupidi's hand. 'Thank you for your understanding. Maybe we'll meet one day at Dungeness.'

Ferriter was still metres away, struggling up the slope, hot and irritated.

Evert Miller walked to the black front door and threw it open. 'Towel,' he shouted.

'All that money,' said Ferriter, pulling the driver seat forwards and adjusting the mirror. 'I'd want to live somewhere much more glamorous.'

'I liked it.'

'He could afford a real swimming pool.'

It was Ferriter's turn to drive. 'I felt so stupid,' she said. 'Astrid Miller may be beautiful but she has feet like Krusty the Clown.'

'Where is she, though?'

'What do you mean?'

'Don't you think it kind of weird that nobody knew where she was? Her husband and the administrator of her company, neither of them could tell us. They were both evasive about when they'd last seen her, too.'

Ferriter reversed out of the parking space. 'He wasn't what I expected. A bit smarmy, ask me.'

'What do you mean?'

'I saw the way he was holding on to your hand. "Thank you for your understanding."' She took a hand off the steering wheel and moved a finger towards her mouth, as if she was going to poke it down her own throat.

'I didn't think he was that bad.'

'I saw how he was looking at you. It was, like, weirdly flirty.'

'Maybe he just fancied me,' said Cupidi.

'Oh come on. He's married to Astrid Theroux. The Astrid Theroux. A supermodel.'

'And your point is?' said Cupidi.

As Ferriter drove away down the narrow lane, Cupidi flicked through her notebook. She tried Astrid Miller's number first. It went straight to voicemail.

As she was hanging up another name appeared on her phone. PETER MOON. Cupidi swiped the screen.

'Two things,' Moon said as she placed the phone to her ear.

'What?'

'Number one. Something big's blown up. I've got to start on another case with DI Wray as SIO,' he said.

'Damn,' said Cupidi.

'Just come in. Attempted murder on one of those new estates just north of Dartford. A known paedophile. On the sex offenders register. Two assailants seen running out of his house, then a minute later the victim comes out and collapses on the front lawn from stab wounds. Chance he's not going to make it.'

The team was about to be stretched even thinner.

'And DI Wray says that Constable Ferriter's going to work with me on this one on witness statements. Will you let her know?'

'You're bloody kidding me.' She glanced across at Ferriter.

'This is a serious case, Alex. They suspect it might have been a vigilante thing, and we got a couple of other people on the register going apeshit about it, in case they're after them too.'

'Hold on. And our case that we're working on right now isn't serious?'

'You haven't even got a victim yet, have you?'

'Well, it's somebody's bloody arm. What's number two?' she asked Moon.

'Oh yeah. Sorry. Almost forgot.' As if he had already moved on to the new case. 'New pathology report on the arm.'

'Did you read it?'

Ferriter was on the main road now, heading back to base.

'You'd asked if it had been frozen? No obvious signs. You'd asked if there were any indications it had been stored for use by the Human Tissue Authority.'

She had wanted to know whether it was possible it had been a body part donated to science that someone had stolen.

Moon continued: 'No clear indication. No signs of preservative but unable to rule out refrigeration. If unrefrigerated . . .

blah blah blah . . . estimate the remains to be between twelve and twenty days old.'

'Gender?'

'DNA says male.'

'Was that Moon?' said Ferriter when the call had ended.

Cupidi nodded. The constable scowled.

'Apparently they're moving you to another case. There's been an attempted murder of a paedophile. DI Wray says you're to move on to work on witness statements. With Peter Moon.'

'Fuck sake,' muttered Ferriter.

'I know.'

Frowning, Ferriter opened her mouth to say something, but then closed it again.

Next Cupidi tried phoning the man whose name Zoya Gubenko had given her, Abir Stein. He wasn't picking up either. 'Mr Stein. This is Detective Sergeant Cupidi of the Kent Serious Crime Directorate . . .'

When she ended the call, she was conscious of Ferriter's silence.

'Jill?'

Ferriter said nothing.

'What's wrong? Don't say you're upset about being taken away from Astrid bloody Miller.'

Ferriter seemed to be wiping her eyes with the back of her sleeve.

'I'm the one being abandoned here,' protested Cupidi. 'This is a potential murder but nobody's taking it seriously.'

And then she realised that Ferriter didn't just have something in her eye.

'Oh shit.'

Blousy, perfect, undentable Jill Ferriter was crying as she drove the car.

'Bollocks. What did I say?'

A second time the young woman lifted her arm from the wheel, wiped her eyes with the sleeve of her shirt.

'Was I being a cow? I am sometimes. I don't mean it. I'm just a bit insensitive. Zoë tells me that all the time.'

Something was up. She tried to think what it could be. She remembered the night before when Ferriter had wanted to talk.

'Want to come to mine, for a bite after you're done? Talk about it? Spend the night with us?'

Ferriter shook her head.

'What about a drink, then, after we've clocked off? Tell me what's wrong?'

Ferriter rode for another mile before she said, cheeks still shiny and damp, 'Yeah. A drink would be good.'

PART TWO

On Margate Sands

TWENTY-SIX

They didn't speak again until they were back at the nick, shift over, Cupidi dropping the police car and swapping it for her ancient Nissan. 'Where do you want to go?'

'Somewhere there's no coppers.'

Cupidi drove to Folkestone, picking up a bottle of rosé and two plastic cups from a mini-market on the way, then parked up at the harbour.

'Fancy some chips?'

'Starving.'

They walked to the Stade and sat on the dockside, legs hanging above the water. Below them, small trawlers and day boats bobbed on the dark water.

'So. How is Zoë?' asked Ferriter.

Whatever it was, Ferriter would talk about it in her own time, figured Cupidi. 'Still strange,' she said.

'Good.'

'She has some new friends that she hangs out with, but she

won't tell me who they are. She sits in her room all day on the computer talking to them.'

'Like every other teenager.'

'Yeah. That's what's so strange.'

The sky on the eastern horizon was the deep blue of an early spring evening. 'She must be happy William South's back. She used to like him, didn't she?'

Cupidi didn't say that South had barely said a word since he'd been back at Dungeness; it was starting to bug her. She handed Ferriter two cups, opened the screw-top bottle and poured.

'It's your job to worry.'

'Yeah.' Cupidi smiled. 'And you? Should I be worrying about you?'

Ferriter took a mouthful from her cup, then took a breath. 'Thing is, what I want to say is . . . I can't work with Peter Moon.'

'OK.' Cupidi reached for a chip. They had gone cold but she ate it anyway. 'Why not?'

'Because I slept with him on Friday night.'

'Bully for you. Don't say I didn't warn you about sleeping with other officers. You know I've made that mistake.'

'You don't understand. I didn't mean to. I was drunk.' The constable took another gulp. 'Really drunk.'

As a divorced woman who had run out of London after an affair with a married man had gone bad, she was hardly qualified to offer advice on successful relationships. But as far as she knew, Ferriter had no close family to talk to; no siblings, no dad, and her mum had died a few years ago. 'I thought you'd just had a fling with him.'

'That was ages back. I used to fancy him stupid, but then

when I finally slept with him, it was over. Bang. Rose tint gone.'

Somewhere out on the black water, a pair of ducks started arguing. She would tell her to just get on with it. That's what she had done. Pretend it never happened.

'Top me up,' said Ferriter.

'Already?'

'I'm drinking for the both of us. You're driving.'

Cupidi poured. 'I can always catch a cab.' She took a sip from the wine; it was too sweet, but Ferriter didn't seem to mind.

'Last Friday night. Everybody on the team is feeling strung out with the workload, so we all go for a drink. You were there too, only you sneaked off.'

'You were pretty pissed when I left.'

'You're old. You can't keep up.'

'Try me,' said Cupidi. 'I just wanted to go home. I'm a single parent, you know.'

'Respect. I was raised by a single parent too and she never bothered coming home much.'

She had never talked about her mother, Cupidi realised. 'Did she work?'

'After a fashion.' Ferriter dropped a chip down into the water below. A herring gull scrabbled for it.

'What did she do?'

'She was . . . a kind of expert on criminal behaviour. Are you trying to change the subject?'

'Is that why you wanted to join the police?'

'That's not what we're talking about here, is it?'

'No. Just you never . . . Sorry. Carry on.'

Ferriter kicked her heels against the harbour wall below them. 'After you left the bar on Friday, we started doing drinking games. Jesus. Like we were adolescents or something. I spend the whole week looking after my body, wheatgrass smoothies and chia seeds. My body is a bogging temple. And then Friday night it's lager and vodka Red Bull chasers. I'm twenty-five years old on Friday and I'm still behaving like a big child.'

It was the top of the tide. The water beneath their feet looked deep and dark.

'I do remember talking to him. But I was talking to everybody. I'm like that. We were all there, weren't we? But by ten o'clock I was wrecked. We were in Cameo. I was feeling if I had one more unit I was going to deposit the contents of my stomach right there. So I stood up and said I had to go home. It's only, like, ten minutes' walk. And that's what I remember, mainly.'

Cupidi felt apprehensive, the way this was heading. She said, 'I should probably try and stop you here, shouldn't I?'

'Yep. But please don't though. I've thought a lot about this. And who I can tell. And there's just you.'

Cupidi said quietly, 'OK.'

'And then a million years later I'm waking up and my phone's going, to tell me someone has found a fuckin' arm, and I'm in bed and I'm naked and so's he. And I feel like a rat that's just eaten poison and . . . I'm sore.' She looked ahead, out to the harbour entrance. 'Obviously I know what happened. I just don't really remember it . . .'

'What about consent?'

Ferriter scowled. 'Don't remember.'

194

Cupidi put down her plastic cup, put her arms around the young woman and sat there for a minute.

'I'm not normally like this,' said the constable.

'I know.'

A dinghy with an outboard chugged slowly across the water, loaded with lobster pots.

And then the police officer in her kicked in. It was who she was, after all. 'You don't recall anything else after leaving for your flat?'

'Bits. You know. Maybe.'

'Do you remember having sex?'

Ferriter said nothing.

'Do you?'

'Not really.'

Cupidi reached in her bag for a tissue, but Ferriter had already found one of her own.

'I've got to ask this, Jill. You understand why, don't you? Did he rape you?'

Ferriter looked away. A little way down the quayside, a middle-aged man in a wetsuit was loading a kayak onto the roof-rack of a 4WD. Cupidi suspected he was aware of being watched by two women. The male of the species putting on a kind of display.

Ferriter said, 'It wasn't like that. No. I just don't remember. I'm not saying . . . I mean, I've interviewed the girls who've accused men of rape. Sometimes I've sat there saying to myself, "You're a lying cow."'

'That's what our job does to us.'

A third time, Ferriter held her cup out.

195

'If it was just any man who I'd picked up when I was drunk, I wouldn't give a toss. I would chalk it up to shit luck and alcohol. But I have to see him every day.'

Did Ferriter have any idea what she was doing, telling this to a senior officer? She must. If it was assault, it would be the end of Moon's career; possibly the end of Ferriter's too. She knew better than anybody that nobody liked a snitch who ended another copper's career. 'Did he rape you?'

'I know what rape is. I was steaming. I suppose it must have been more like I was too drunk to be bothered not to.'

'Did you consent to sex?'

'Don't be like that, Alex. I knew I shouldn't have started this.'

'Did you?'

'That's what I'm saying. I don't remember. I was drunk. It was just a shag, wasn't it? How pathetic is that?'

'Not if he took advantage of the fact you were drunk. That's a sexual assault.'

'It wasn't like that.'

'Wasn't it? Just because it might not meet evidentiary standards, that's what it sounds dangerously like to me.'

'Evidentiary standards? God's sake. Listen to yourself.'

'Sorry.'

'Don't you get it, Alex? I'm not even interested if it was a sexual assault or not,' she said, a little too loud. The man looked round, he had finished tightening the straps on his roof-rack and was tugging the sleeves off his wetsuit. He peeled the neoprene off his chest. He was muscled but darkly hairy.

'Oh for pity's sake,' muttered Cupidi, looking away from him.

'But I can't be in Moon's team. Not right now.'

Cupidi had somehow finished her small cup of wine. She felt like reaching out and pouring herself a little more. 'You know what you've just done, don't you?'

'Yes.'

'You have just told me, a superior officer, that you may have been assaulted by another officer.'

'And that's why I didn't ever, ever, ever want to tell you. I swear. Because I knew you'd be all like this.'

'All like what?'

'All official. But, thing is, I really don't want to work alongside him. I'll end up doing something really stupid. I just wanted you to help me, Alex.' She dropped another chip into the salt water. This time several gulls gathered to snap at it.

The water looked black now. 'You've just told me something and you know very well I have to act on it. It's not like I have a choice.'

Ferriter put a chip into tomato sauce and chewed on it. 'Yes you do. I've been thinking about it. I've told no one else about this,' she said. 'Swear to God. I don't really have anyone else to tell.'

'What we do isn't like any other job. If if there's even a hint he's a sexual predator I have to report him. All this shit we officers talk about us being on the victim's side,' said Cupidi bitterly. 'It's not true. You know that. When it comes to rape, if someone like you says what you've just said to me, you know what we do. We always protect our backs. We don't have any choice. Whether the victim likes it or not.'

'But no one else knows. I've gone over and over it in my head. I'm only telling you about this.'

197

'If it comes out later that I've done nothing about something like this I'd be disciplined. That would be my career over. Not just his. Or yours.'

'I promise. Million per cent. It won't.'

The man was finally covering his hairy chest with a black Ramones T-shirt. As his head popped through the neck he smiled at them, standing with the two empty neoprene arms of his wetsuit flapping at his side like a penguin.

Ferriter turned to her, fiercely. 'I don't want to be known forever as the copper who got drunk and was fucked by another policeman. The copper who wrecked another officer's career. It's not fair. I didn't want any of it.'

'It's not fair,' said Cupidi. 'But you've told me. I can't un-know it.' And Cupidi suddenly remembered saying the exact same phrase to her daughter, three days earlier when they were talking about William South. *I can't un-know it.*

'See, this wouldn't happen if we were, I don't know . . . chiropractors, or farmers,' Ferriter said. 'There wouldn't be these procedures. It's so stupid.' She drank from her cup again. 'See, I'm not a victim. I despise victims.'

'In our line of work, you're not supposed to say that.'

'Bollocks to that.' Behind the huge bulk of the Grand Burstin Hotel, the sun was red. The granite of the quay suddenly felt cold. 'So you're going to tell Professional Standards, aren't you? Wish I hadn't bloody told you now.'

The man meanwhile had packed up. There was no reason for him not to leave, but he lingered, checking his roof straps, walking round the car once, then leaning back against their side of the car, pretending to look at the scenery, though the

198

setting sun was in the opposite direction. Cupidi supposed he was waiting for them to offer him a drink. There were Peppa Pig stickers on the rear window of the kayaker's 4WD. He was a dad, a married man possibly too.

'No,' said Cupidi. 'You're OK.'

'What do you mean?'

'I'll try and work something out. I don't know what.' She would have to persuade McAdam that she needed to keep Ferriter on her team, though she was not sure how.

Ferriter put down her cup and put her arms around her boss. And as Ferriter held on to her, Cupidi was wondering if this would turn out to be the stupidest thing she'd ever said in her career. If word got out that she had concealed evidence about a potential assault on another officer, it could be her career, and her pension. Like Bill South, it would all be over. 'I can't promise anything, you know?'

'Sorry, boss,' said Ferriter. 'I've really fucked up. Such an idiot.'

'You're not to blame, Jill.'

'But I'm still an idiot.'

'Obviously.' She felt stiff now, from sitting down so long on the cold dock. She hoped that Ferriter was not expecting too much of her.

She felt drunk already. She would have to leave her car on the Stade overnight.

William South's shack was dark as the taxi passed.

Zoë had cooked something; it was sitting in a pot on the stove.

'What is it?'

'I'm not sure,' said Zoë. 'It has chickpeas in it. Want some?'

'I had chips already.'

'I bet you're just saying that.'

Cupidi tried to think of something funny back but she couldn't. Her daughter looked at her curiously. 'Bad day?'

'On the bright side, a multi-millionaire offered me a chance to swim in his pool.' She flopped down onto a kitchen chair. 'You seen anything of William South?' she asked.

Her daughter shook her head. 'You still waiting for him to come around and make up with you?'

'I'm just worried about him, that's all. He's being weird.'

For the first time, she noticed her daughter was wearing a jacket indoors despite the fact it was warm; a black faux-leather jacket she had picked up at a junk shop. 'Are you going out somewhere?'

Her daughter coloured. 'No. I was just cold. Are you sure you're OK?'

At the time, Cupidi didn't think anything more of it. 'Woman at work . . . offloaded on me.'

'Want to talk?'

'Maybe another time. What about you? Aren't you bored, hanging round here all day on your own? I could ask at the Fish Shack if they are looking for help?'

'Mum. I can't work there. I'm a vegan.'

Zoë scuttled upstairs to her room before her mum could offer any other helpful suggestions.

That night before bed, Cupidi looked out of her bedroom window. On dark nights the lights of the power station seemed even more lurid. Jill Ferriter would be alone at home. Still no light from William South's small house. He was in there though, she knew.

TWENTY-SEVEN

'I know DI Wray wants Jill Ferriter to start work on the paedo-phile attack,' Cupidi told DI McAdam, keeping her voice low, 'but I'd like to keep her with me for a couple more days.'

It was early on Wednesday morning. She had pulled her chair close to DI McAdam's so that no one would be able to listen in to their conversation. McAdam looked puzzled. 'Why?'

'Because I think we're getting somewhere.' From the other side of the room, Cupidi was conscious of Ferriter watching apprehensively.

McAdam frowned. 'An assault on a paedophile by a vigilante group is huge. Moon believes it's the start of something messy. We're going to need to get numbers onto it fast before it gets out of hand.'

'Right now, I need her too. We're on the point of making a breakthrough. I know it.'

McAdam frowned. Cupidi knew he trusted her; how far could she push that? 'Everybody thinks this is a Mickey Mouse case,' continued Cupidi. 'They're wrong. There's something in this. I know there is.'

McAdam picked up his phone and called DI Wray over.

'Can't you make the decision?'

'Not without consulting DI Wray.'

Damn, thought Cupidi. 'Just forty-eight hours. If we don't make a breakthrough by then . . .'

McAdam looked over at Moon, who was sitting on the edge of a desk at the far end of the room, still dressed in sweats. There was a gym at this building. Most mornings Moon took advantage of it.

Wray arrived, dodging his way round the desks, pink-shirted and full of *joie de vivre*. 'Good morning, Toby, good morning. To what do I owe . . . ?'

'Sergeant Cupidi here has asked if Constable Ferriter can stay helping her out on the Turner gallery investigation.'

Wray's smile grew. 'Not possible,' was all he said. 'Violent assault. All hands on deck.'

'In what way is the case I'm dealing with not a violent assault?' blurted Cupidi. 'You don't exactly lose an arm by accident.'

Wray turned to her, like a schoolteacher examining a pupil who had spoken out of turn. 'What I've been hearing is you hadn't made any significant progress on that. I'm still of the opinion it's just some medical student prank.'

'We've ruled that out,' said Cupidi curtly.

'Alex. I know you get very involved . . .' said McAdam.

Wray interrupted, wrinkling his small nose. 'Where's your evidence it's anything bigger?'

That was the point. Three days in and she still had no idea

of who the victim – if there was one – might be. Cupidi wasn't giving in that easily. 'That's why I need Constable Ferriter.'

'If we don't get on top of this paedo assault, we'll be looking at a right shitstorm media-wise, won't we, Toby?'

McAdam turned to Cupidi. 'I'm afraid I have to agree, Alex. It's a priority.'

Wray had known which buttons to press. McAdam was a good boss, but always too conscious of PR.

'Will that be all?' DI Wray was saying, rubbing his pudgy hands together.

Across the room, Cupidi caught the expression on Ferriter's face. Her eyebrows were raised in expectation. Cupidi had promised she would try to do something to keep her out of Peter Moon's way; she had failed.

'But I thought you said—'

'I tried. I promise. Wray is going to reorganise the teams at the morning meeting.'

Ferriter looked stung. 'Shit, shit, shit,' she said.

They stood in the downstairs ladies' toilet, each holding cups of bad coffee.

'Serve me right for being such an easy shag,' said Ferriter.

'Don't.'

'I'm just going to jack all this in. Transfer out to something easy like traffic or detention. I can't hack it here. Not with him. Makes me feel like a drunken slag.'

'Shut up, Jill. Not because of something stupid like this. You're good at this stuff.'

'I don't even remember if the sex was any good. Bet it wasn't.'

A uniformed superintendent emerged from the cubicle, looked at them, standing each with their paper cup in hand, and raised an eyebrow.

Cupidi gave her a thin smile. 'Morning, ma'am.'

'Oh Christ,' muttered Ferriter.

'Come on, Jill. We have an hour left. I'll keep chasing Astrid Miller and the Foundation's curator. You get on to EastArt. Get them to send any records they have about whoever signed in to access the Foundation's artworks in the last two months. If we turn up something before the meeting . . .'

'Seriously? Clutching at straws.'

'Most of my career.'

Upstairs Cupidi rang both numbers twice; left messages. Then she called Zoya Gubenko at the Foundation's office.

'No. Still nothing from Astrid,' said Gubenko. 'Not even email, no. Obviously I will pass on that you are keen to hear from her.'

'What about Abir Stein?'

'I've had a couple of emails from him. Just answering queries.'

'Tell me. How long is it since you've actually spoken to him?'

'Mr Stein? Maybe three weeks now.'

'Is that unusual?'

'I don't think so. As I said, he's answered emails. He works for other people too.'

'What about Astrid Miller?'

A pause. 'Maybe a week since I spoke to her.'

'She hasn't been home for a week?'

'I don't know. Maybe longer. But she hasn't been to the office. Or called.'

204

'Does she often just disappear?'

Gubenko dropped her voice. 'Yes, sometimes. But . . .'

'But what?'

'Usually she is in touch more regularly. It is kind of weird for her just to disappear like this. But she is her own person, you understand?'

'Are things between Mr and Mrs Miller OK?'

Zoya Gubenko didn't answer.

'Is there something going on in their relationship that we should know about?'

'No,' Gubenko said abruptly. 'Nothing like that. I must go now.'

Cupidi looked down at her watch. There were twenty minutes left until the morning meeting. Ferriter was nowhere to be seen.

Even if things weren't good between Evert and Astrid Miller, and she didn't know they weren't, that didn't necessarily mean anything, did it?

TWENTY-EIGHT

Ten minutes before the meeting, she looked around for Jill Ferriter, but she wasn't in the incident room.

Pulling out her phone, she texted her: **U OK? Where are you?**

McAdam appeared on time, clapping his hands. 'Come on, let's do this, folks.'

People gathered, arranging chairs into a semi-circle around the table as the meeting began.

If she hadn't made any progress on the Turner case, neither had the team dealing with the murder of Michael Dillman, the man found in the scrap yard. Forensics had turned up nothing on the gun that had killed him. There had been no shells left at the scene. The killer had worn flat-soled shoes that would be impossible to identify.

The best lead was still Dillman's motorbike, which had been spotted by number plate recognition software several times over a twenty-hour period following the murder; however, nothing had been seen of it since. Within a few days of a gang-related death there were usually whispers and rumours from informants. Even if it was nonsense, people liked the drama. This time, strangely, nothing.

'Maybe the killer was from out of town.'

'Possible.'

'Maybe it was something from his time inside, some grudge?'

'We've looked into that. But yeah . . .'

'This is weird, isn't it?' said Moon, from the back of the room.

'What do you mean?'

'Well, there's nothing to go on. Nothing that makes any sense.'

It was true, thought Cupidi. These days as a detective you were usually drowning in information, trying to prioritise what leads to follow. Weird that there was so little background noise about this killing. Even the team heading the investigation had lapsed into silence.

'Next,' said McAdam. 'Frank Khan. Attempted murder. Sergeant Moon?'

Moon stood and pushed through to the front. He started with a picture of the bloodstained doorstep of a block on a new estate.

Moon spoke. 'Mr Khan. Discovered outside his flat at Riverside Wharf by a neighbour shortly after he'd made a call to the police saying that he was worried about someone ringing his doorbell, behaving in a threatening manner. Stabbed by unknown assailant. He's currently in Darent Valley Hospital with multiple organ failure. He was interviewed at the scene of the crime by uniform, but he refused to say who'd attacked him. Uniform said he sounded scared. Another neighbour said they saw two young men running from the location but weren't able to identify them as they were wearing hoodies. We haven't been able to speak to the victim today because his condition has deteriorated.'

Moon continued. 'Turns out Frank Khan is known to us. Sexual offenders register. Used to be a piano teacher. Done for assaulting pupils. Served four years in Lewes Prison. Released a year ago under a Sexual Offender Prevention Order. So now we're wondering why he should be so shy about telling us who stabbed him. Pretty obvious that it's connected to his past. Former sexual assault victim maybe? Father of a child who he interfered with? Then last night it turns out that a group called England Rising published a list of six drug dealers and paedophiles with foreign-sounding names on their Facebook page just a couple of weeks ago. Khan was top of the list. It said they were watching them. This is looking more and more like a vigilante attack.'

'England Rising?'

'Far-right group, possibly affiliated to National Action. Their name started cropping up online last year after National Action were proscribed.'

Cupidi looked around the room. Where was Constable Ferriter? She was supposed to be here. She couldn't just disappear because she didn't want to be put onto Moon's team.

'Do we know who they are, the members of this far-right group?'

'There's about a dozen of them, we think. We have a couple of names based in Rochester. Trying to round them up now.'

Cupidi would be up next. It would not look good saying that she needed Ferriter on her team if the constable didn't even bother to turn up for the briefing. 'What about the description of the two assailants?' she asked.

'Only seen from behind by the same neighbour that found him. Both wearing grey hoodies.'

'Car?'

'He didn't see any.'

'Is it possible they're local to that area then? They knew who he was?'

'Don't know, yet. Someone must have recognised him, though.'

A constable piped up. 'Did the assailants attack him at the door, or in his flat?'

'Inside. From the blood pattern, it looks like he was stabbed in the kitchen or hallway.'

'Inside?'

'Sorry,' said Cupidi, 'but why would he let someone into his own flat if they were from some vigilante group?' People turned and looked at her.

'We don't know yet,' said Moon.

Cupidi was puzzled. 'How many people were on that list? On the England Rising list you talked about?'

'There were six names,' Moon said. 'Four were sex offenders, out on probation or on Prevention Orders, like Khan.'

'Have any of the others had any threats or attacks you know of?'

'We've been trying to get in touch with them, obviously. But no, as far as we know, none of them had been attacked yet. So at this stage, I'm looking for resources to profile any far-right sympathisers who might fit—'

Cupidi interrupted again. 'No sign of forced entry?'

A hesitation.

'These attackers were in his flat,' Cupidi said. 'Doesn't that suggest he invited them in? You said he refused to identify them? If they were England Rising, why did he invite them in?'

A young constable chipped in. 'Straight or gay? Those assaults he was done for, were they men or women?'

Moon paused. 'Just kids. They were boys.'

Someone else asked, 'Did you check what his contacts were on his phone? Had he arranged to hook up with anyone?'

'No. Not yet.' Moon looked less sure of himself now.

Another voice pitched in. 'Where would the attackers have escaped to if they were on foot? Can you show us a map?'

Leaning down, Moon fiddled with his laptop and brought up a Google map with a pin on it. When it arrived on the projector, Cupidi assumed he had made a mistake. It was exactly the same selection she'd been looking at on this same screen on Monday morning. Moon pointed to the pin. 'There. That's his house.'

'Hold on. Is this the same area as where the Co-op guard was killed last week?' she asked.

'Pretty much, yes. The shop was the other side of the A206 – just here.'

Cupidi sat thinking for a second.

'So they might have parked a little way off? Or had someone picking them up,' another constable was saying.

Cupidi raised her voice again. 'Anyone got the CCTV images of the two boys who were shoplifting?'

The chatter stopped.

'Why?'

'Because they were both wearing grey hoodies, weren't they?' she said.

There was a long pause as people considered this. Then someone broke the silence. 'Christ.'

'They were boys. Teenagers.'

Something seemed to shift in the room. Suddenly everyone was talking. 'What if he had been coming on to them?'

'That would explain why he wouldn't want to talk, why he was scared shitless. If they were teenage boys, he'd be going straight back inside.'

One of the constables had already logged into HOLMES and was searching through the files on that case.

'Got it,' she said, turning her screen round so that other people could see it.

'Jesus. You're right.'

The photo was fuzzy and it was hard to make out their features, beyond the fact that one of the boys was black, the other white. They both had their pale-coloured hoods up, half covering their faces.

'How old did the shop worker say she thought they were?'

'Sixteen, maybe seventeen.'

They all stood and crowded round the woman's screen, leaving Moon on his own at the front of the room.

'Explains why he'd be reluctant to identify them.'

'Where the hell are they, then? They're minors. They can't just disappear.'

Moon said, 'Maybe they were egging him on or trying to rob him.'

'They're kids, for God's sake,' complained another officer,

211

and Cupidi was grateful it didn't have to be her saying that. She thought of Zoë. They would be about the same age, probably as arrogant and vulnerable in equal measure.

'Lethal ones though, by the look of it.'

'What have we got, then? Rent boys committing a robbery?'

'Maybe self-defence. What if he was trying to assault them? He's got form, after all.'

'What about the man he said was ringing his bell?' Moon said.

Another copper said, 'Probably wasn't one. But he couldn't really call us and say, "Excuse me, I've just been stabbed by an under-age rent boy," could he?'

'Now you have something you can ask Mr Khan, when he wakes up,' McAdam said. 'Sounds like you need uniforms to help you look for the boys. Next. Alex? I think you said you were heading for a breakthrough?'

Cupidi looked around the room. No Ferriter. 'Right,' she said, standing. 'What we know is that the arm was placed into the ceramic jar between two to three weeks ago. We know that from forensics, and from the fact that CCTV confirms that the artwork remained untouched during its time at the gallery.'

'And?' McAdam said.

'Yesterday, we visited the Miller Foundation to confirm—'

The door at the back of the room swung open and Ferriter strode in, mouthing 'Sorry,' as Cupidi looked up.

Cupidi tried to remember what she had been saying. '. . . That the arm was stored at a unit called EastArt,' she continued. 'And we also know . . .'

What did they know?

The men and women all looked at her, expectantly.

'And we also know . . .'

Ferriter pushed her way to the front of the room. 'And we know that during that time frame only one person from the Evert and Astrid Miller Foundation visited the facility to inspect their artworks,' she said.

She reached the front of the room. 'EastArt is a secure storage service. It contains work worth millions and millions. Damien Hirst. Ai Weiwei. All of that stuff. And the Foundation has their own dedicated storage zone within that, rented from EastArt who happen to keep good records of everyone who visits and requests to inspect the art. I've just got off the phone to them and they emailed me this.' She reached into her folder and pulled out a single sheet of paper. 'It confirms that the only person who accessed the room that contained *Funerary Urn* was a bloke called Abir Stein,' said Ferriter, 'the Foundation's curator.'

Cupidi smiled at her, then took over. 'We have been trying to trace Abir Stein but have been unable to reach him. And it turns out that the Foundation have not spoken to him for about three weeks.'

'Why would he be involved in doing a thing like this?' asked McAdam.

'No idea,' said Cupidi. 'But the timing means he's the only person who had the opportunity to place the arm in the jar.'

The meeting broke up soon afterwards.

Cupidi caught up with McAdam and Wray by the door. 'Well?'

'Moon is the one who needs help,' said McAdam. 'He's wasted half a day already barking up the wrong tree.'

'Just give me Ferriter until we've tracked down Stein and brought him in. He's our main suspect.'

Wray sighed. 'OK. Just get it sorted.'

At her desk, Cupidi gave Ferriter's arm a squeeze. 'I thought you'd done a runner,' she said.

Moon was watching them from the other side of the big room.

Ferriter rolled her eyes. 'I know what you're doing, Alex. Forcing me to work for my freedom.'

'Call Zoya Gubenko. Get Stein's home address.'

As Ferriter sat down at one of the workstations, Cupidi left her and wandered over towards Moon.

'Thanks for your input just then.' Moon avoided looking her in the eye. She had shown him up in front of the rest of the team. 'It was very . . . useful.'

'Welcome.' Cupidi looked at Moon. For Ferriter's sake she had agreed to pretend she didn't know anything about what had happened between them. She hated the idea of pretending anything; she was never any good at it.

'You're looking for those lads, then?'

'Wish the CCTV from the shop was better, though. Been trying to see if Children's Services have any idea who they are.'

'They'll be local, I reckon.'

'Yeah.' He looked like a man who had had the wind knocked out of him.

'Ferriter's going to stay working with me for a day or two.' She watched his face.

'Yep,' he said quietly. 'Fair enough.'

She turned. Ferriter was holding up a bit of paper. She called across the room. 'Apart from those emails he sent to

Zoya Gubenko nobody's seen him for weeks. Complete radio silence. We got an address. He's in London. He's got a flat in the Barbican.'

Cupidi looked at her watch.

She could contact the Met and request someone go round to knock on his door, but that might take all day. Instead she looked up the Barbican Estate Office and made a call to them.

Within half an hour a man from the flat's management office was on the phone. 'Not answering, just like you said. Neighbour said he hasn't seen him for several weeks either.'

'You can't just take a look inside, obviously.'

'Nope,' said the man whose name was Erich. 'But I took a peek in his mail locker downstairs. Stuffed.'

'Smart thinking. So it looks like he hasn't been home in a while?'

'Confidentially, he's missed a service charge payment too.'

When she ended the call she spent a minute just staring at the empty surface of the desk. At last, a sense they were getting somewhere. Abir Stein hadn't just stopped answering the phone. It looked like he had vanished.

TWENTY-NINE

Cupidi and Ferriter parked in the car park beneath the great saw-toothed towers of the Barbican, then spent a while following the coloured lines that had been put down on the walkways in an attempt to make the huge estate navigable.

They found Cromwell Tower, then, standing outside the lobby at the base, the flat number and beside it the name 'Stein'. Unsurprisingly, there was no answer when they pressed the buzzer, so they called the Estate Office and the man who Cupidi had spoken to earlier, Erich, asked them, 'Have you got the warrant?'

'Yes.'

It took him five minutes to get there; a crisp young man, in shoes that shone. Cupidi handed him the envelope and he opened it and looked at it briefly. 'This way to Mr Stein's apartment then,' he said, pressing the button to summon the lift. It seemed to take an age. 'Sorry. One of the elevators is being serviced.'

The tower formed a triangle, each floor with three flats on it.

They knocked on the door of Stein's flat, number 383, called out, 'Police officers, Mr Stein. We have a warrant to enter your premises,' but as they had expected, there was no answer.

A middle-aged man emerged from 381, peering round his own door.

'Sorry. Not dressed yet,' he said with a smile, though it was late afternoon. 'I work from home.' He wore red slippers and green paisley pyjamas.

'Do you know Mr Stein, who lives here?'

'I spoke to someone at the estate office earlier who was asking about him. Was that you?' He addressed Erich. 'Is he OK?'

'Do you know where he is?' asked Cupidi.

'Like I said, I've not seen him for weeks. Sometimes he travels.'

Erich cautiously opened the door. 'Mr Stein?' he called.

The flat was empty, of course. Erich watched, frowning as Cupidi and Ferriter pulled on plastic gloves.

'Perhaps you can fetch Mr Stein's post for us?' said Cupidi.

The man hesitated, as if reluctant to leave them alone in a resident's apartment.

'When we spoke, you said the mailbox downstairs was full? Presumably you have some kind of pass key?'

'Right,' Erich said, hesitantly. He watched them peer inside into the hallway. 'I'll be going then.'

'Oh my God,' said Ferriter, mouth wide as she stepped down the hallway and into the living room. 'This place is bloody gorgeous.'

A polished dark wood floor bounced light up onto walls that were hung with art. Cupidi's father had loved contemporary art. She recognised what she thought was a Lucian Freud print; there

217

was another by Keith Haring, surrounded by other paintings and prints she didn't recognise. A couple of works by people you were likely to know were a subtle way of hinting at the value of the other pieces on display.

Ferriter stood in the middle of the room and turned, slowly. 'I so want to live here. This is so classy.'

Looking out towards the balcony was a spherical white sixties fibreglass chair, upholstered in orange. Beyond the balcony, the window looked out onto the strange geometries of the City's skyline; the Shard, the Gherkin and the Walkie-Talkie.

'It's like my dream place.'

Cupidi went to the kitchen, opened the fridge door, saw the litre of milk which had long turned sour, smelt the stench from a piece of fish and closed the door straight away. Cautiously she looked inside again, one hand at her nose, and began to examine the contents. The fish packet had a use-by date of early April.

'I can smell that from here,' called out Ferriter from the living room. The flat appeared to have been unoccupied for weeks. So where was Mr Stein?

Cupidi returned to the living room to find Ferriter sitting in the ball chair, spinning it round. 'Sorry. Had to try it. No sign of a phone anywhere. No wallet yet. No keys, neither. So do you reckon he's done a runner?'

'Check the bathroom. See what he's taken from there,' said Cupidi.

There was a delicate French Empire desk, a secretaire. Cupidi pushed back the dark wood of the lid, releasing the hint of old smells it had captured over years, tobacco, paper, and ink. Inside, to the right, there was a neat pile of headed paper: *Abir Stein: Curator, Art Dealer.*

An expensive pen. A watch. She pulled open the tiny drawers at the back. More pens, nibs, business cards, odd receipts, clips. A small neat wrap of cocaine. A collection of bank statements sat in the middle of the open desk. Were they waiting to be filed, or had someone gone through them recently? Cupidi noted the account number, then replaced them. And then, in the bottom drawer, lying on its own, a passport.

Cupidi picked it up and started flicking through it. A man in his late thirties. Not good-looking exactly, and surprisingly serious in his photograph. Thin lips and rather feminine eyes.

'His washbag is here,' called Ferriter.

The passport was full of stamps. In the last year alone he had visited Moscow, Abu Dhabi, Kuala Lumpur, Rio, Shanghai, St Petersburg, New York, Cape Town. But wherever he was now, he hadn't taken it with him. Nor, apparently, his toothbrush.

'We're going to need DNA,' she said. 'Toothbrush, razor. Bag them all.'

'Oh.' Ferriter's voice came across the hallway. 'Do you think he's . . .'

'It's a distinct possibility, yes.'

'But I thought you said that Zoya Gubenko had had a couple of emails from him?'

'How do we know they're actually from him?'

There was no landline in the flat, so no answerphone. Cupidi looked around. No laptop or mobile phone visible either. Had he taken them with him, wherever he'd gone? But if he had gone, it didn't look like Stein had intended to be away long. For the first time since being assigned to this case, she was beginning to feel a sense of vindication – the darkly guilty thrill of her work – because perhaps it wasn't just an arm now. He wasn't here. And he still wasn't answering his mobile phone.

'Check the bedroom,' called Cupidi. 'I'm going to talk to the neighbour.'

'It doesn't look good, does it?' said Ferriter, emerging from the bathroom with a handful of evidence bags. She dropped them onto the table and then sat in the white chair again. Like an adolescent on a playground ride, she pushed with her feet against the dark wood floor and spun around one last time.

'Bedroom,' ordered Cupidi.

Reluctantly, Ferriter extracted herself from the chair.

Cupidi went back out and knocked on 381's door again. He seemed to take an age opening the door. 'Sorry. Lock's jiggered. Been meaning to do something.'

This time he was in jeans and a pale jumper. 'Thought I better finally face the day,' the man said. He was a writer, he explained. 'Don't normally get dressed till after the sun goes down.'

His flat was messier; his living room looked south, towards St Paul's. In the middle sat a huge desk, an iMac struggling for space in amongst piles of papers, manuscripts and books. An elderly Yorkie slumbered on a chair.

She asked for his name, and when he gave it, Cupidi half wondered if she recognised it from the covers of one of those books her mother read.

'A couple of people have rung my bell asking if I'd seen him. It's annoying but the flats are organised so you can tell which numbers the neighbours are. I'm 381, he was 383, next number up is 391 so it's pretty obvious that I'm on the same landing as him.'

'What kind of people?'

'Foreigners, by the sound of it. Abir moved in very cosmopolitan circles.'

'From where?'

'I don't know. There were always some Russians, I think. All sorts. When he's here he always has quite a few visitors.'

'What sort of visitors?'

'Always well-heeled. He was clearly rich himself. Friends. Business. Both, really. He knows a lot of very powerful people.'

'Lovers?'

'No. He was pretty asexual, I think. One guy . . .' He tailed off.

'What?'

'Before he went I saw one fellow coming out of the flat. Like, early in the morning. Seven o'clock or something. Which was weird, because I always thought of Abir as very self-contained. Maybe just a friend staying over. I don't know. Sorry. I'm not a very good witness.'

'Can you describe the man?'

'Jesus . . . Sort of medium. Sort of . . . I can't actually remember.'

'Light complexion. Dark?'

The man tugged at his ear. 'Honestly? I couldn't tell you. It was the time of day I noticed, that's all. He didn't say hello or anything. Just kind of turned his back and headed for the lift.'

Cupidi's mobile rang. She saw it was the caretaker and excused herself. 'Funny thing,' Erich was saying. 'But somebody's emptied Mr Stein's mailbox.'

221

'What?'

'It was full earlier when I checked, I promise you, but . . .'

She was about to ask how that could have happened when she thought she heard someone shouting. 'Quiet,' she snapped.

The man, watching her silently, looked bewildered.

It came again, clearer this time. 'Help!'

Ferriter's voice. Cupidi ran back down the hallway and tried to yank the door open, but it wouldn't give.

'Sorry. Lock,' said the man. 'Jiggered. Let me.'

'Police. Help!'

Twisting the lock, tugging the handle uselessly, Cupidi pressed her eye up to the peephole in the door in time to see that Stein's door was wide open. And a shadow moving rapidly across the landing floor.

THIRTY

The man in 381's hands replaced hers on the lock and handle, pushing her aside.

'There,' he said, opening the door.

'Jill?' yelled Cupidi.

Just as she approached the door opposite, Ferriter staggered out, a line of blood streaking down the left side of her face, dripping onto her pale shirt. Jesus.

'He was in there, all the bloody time.'

'What?'

'Sorry, boss. He was hiding in the bedroom. Jumped me. I let him get away.'

Cupidi looked round. 'Where is he now?'

Ferriter looked a little dazed but she was standing. The wound looked superficial. Cupidi spun around, thinking, looking, taking in details. 'Description,' she shouted. 'What does he look like?'

'Didn't see him. He got me from behind. Knocked me over.

Hit my head on the bedstead. Bastard.' She raised her hand to the cut and winced.

Cupidi was thinking fast. A triangular lobby; four doors, three lifts. The man had said one of the elevators wasn't working. All three were stationary. One was at the tenth floor, the other two appeared to be at the ground floor. They were at the thirty-eighth floor, four floors below the top of the building.

Where would someone have run to?

The writer emerged from his flat, took one look at Ferriter and said, 'Oh my God. What's going on?'

Cupidi ignored him. To escape, you would not go up, would you? Nor would a fugitive wait for an elevator to arrive; it could take too long. That shadow she had seen crossing the floor.

Ferriter was thinking exactly the same thing. 'The stairs,' she said.

They both pushed open the door to the stairs and leaned over the metal banister to peer down a triangular concrete stairwell.

The view was stomach-churningly precipitous, a repetitive pattern of monochrome greys that seemed to continue downwards for the entire height of the building. Cupidi listened, heard nothing, tried to look for motion among the shadows, saw none.

Quick. Think.

Thirty-eight floors would take an age to run down. After a few floors – when he was sure he had put a safe distance between himself and anyone who could be chasing him – wouldn't he have stopped, re-entered the landing area and called a lift? That would be the fastest way to get out of the building, surely?

Cupidi returned to the landing where the neighbour was still

224

standing. Her eyes flicked back up to the indicator lights above the lift. Sure enough, one of the two on the ground floor had started to move upwards. Only two of the shafts were working. Either someone had called one from the lobby and was now travelling up, or the attacker himself was trying to descend.

Ferriter reappeared from the stairwell too.

'Do you need a sticking plaster?' the neighbour asked.

Cupidi dodged past him and pressed the call button too. The elevator on the tenth floor was still stationary – somebody holding the door open? – but the other was now rising fast. Because she had called the lift, it would pass whoever called it and travel here first and then descend back down. As long as the lift on the tenth floor remained stationary.

It seemed to take so long to arrive, but finally the doors pinged open. The compartment was empty as Cupidi stepped in. Ferriter followed her. 'He called the lift?'

'Think so.'

'So whatever floor this stops on . . .'

'Maybe.'

The lift sped down three floors and then slowed rapidly. It was stopping at the thirty-third floor. Just about as far as a man could have run in the few moments that had passed.

'Ready?'

They pressed themselves back on either side of the doors to try and make the most of the element of surprise.

The doors slid open. Lit from behind, they made out the shadow of a figure standing at the door. Cupidi held her breath, ready to spring.

★

225

It was a woman who stepped into the lift, elderly, wearing large white-framed sunglasses and holding a yellow wicker bag, the type you might take to the beach on a day out.

The woman looked at the bloodied constable, then at Cupidi; her red-lipsticked mouth opened wide in shock.

'Did you call the lift?' Cupidi demanded.

'Sorry?'

'Was it you who pressed the call button?'

'Obviously,' she whispered.

'Damn,' said Cupidi, holding the lift door open, then turned to Ferriter. 'I'll go on to the bottom. You do the stairs.'

Ferriter ran straight out of the lift and was pulling open the door to the emergency stairs when the lift doors slid closed.

'What are you doing?' asked the woman, as the lift started to descend again.

'Did any man pass you while you were waiting?'

'He didn't pass me.'

'Sorry?'

'The man. He was waiting with me. Just now.'

Cupidi's eyes widened. 'Where did he go?'

'Just before the lift arrived, he left. I think he must have forgotten something.'

Damn. He had figured out what Cupidi was trying to do, and run for it. Maybe he'd waited and called the other lift? Or returned upstairs? But if she took this lift to the bottom, it would at least mean that she would be at the ground floor before him.

But the lift slowed again and stopped on the third floor, not at the ground floor. The elderly woman got out. Before she realised what was happening, the lift started to rise again.

Damn, damn, damn. Cupidi cursed her stupidity. She had assumed the woman had been going down to the lobby, but nobody had ever pressed that button and now the lift was rising again, fast. She was wasting valuable time trying to make it to the doors of the building.

This time it stopped at the eighth floor.

A woman stood in the doorway with two young children, girls with identical coloured ribbons in their hair. 'It's my turn to press the button, Mummy.'

'No, it's my turn. She did it last time.'

Cupidi barged her way past them and pressed the CLOSE button, then the LOBBY one. Both girls burst into tears.

The girls were still crying when the lift finally reached the lobby, the mother still glaring at Cupidi as she tried to calm them.

'Naughty lady.'

'Yes. She is.'

Cupidi was scanning the lobby. Everything seemed surprisingly quiet and normal. The carpet under her feet was soft. The high ceiling seemed to mute the complaining children's voices.

'Tell her off, Mummy.'

'I've a mind to.'

Shit. She had lost him. Then, through the glass doors, Cupidi spied a young woman, sitting on the ground, surrounded by bags of shopping, oranges spilling out around her over the walkway.

Cupidi pushed out of the doors and sprinted towards the woman, who was by now standing up and trying to collect her spilled fruit.

'What happened?' Cupidi demanded.

227

'Stupid man. Ran into me,' she muttered. 'Didn't even apologise.'

He must have waited for the other lift instead, beating Cupidi to the ground floor. 'Where did he go?'

She pointed down the highwalk that headed south. The centre had been designed with a bewildering network of walkways connecting the buildings. She could continue south or continue west towards the Barbican Centre.

Which route would he choose? To the west? The arts centre would be crowded. It would be easier to lose yourself there.

Or would he go for the quieter route, with less chance of there being witnesses?

Pausing, trying to decide which way to go, she didn't hear anything.

And then she was flying sideways. He must have been behind the circular concrete pillar, right behind her all the time.

His shove unbalanced her before she could offer any resistance, toppling her forwards towards the edge of the walkway.

She grabbed the concrete edge, but he had the momentum. Dropping his hands to her thighs, he lifted her and in that second she realised that he was trying to pitch her face-forward over the walkway wall to the solid ground below.

Somebody screamed. It might have been her.

Her hands had managed to grab the rough edge of the wall, but her head was already way out over the drop. Her belly scraped against rough concrete. Two floors below, a gaggle of startled passers-by looked up as he tried to lift her legs so the weight of her own body would pull her over the wall to her death.

Unable to let go with her hands, which were the only thing that prevented her from plummeting, she kicked blindly, as viciously as she could at her attacker, preventing him from getting a proper grip.

Blood rushed to her head as her legs tipped further, and though her scissoring limbs were preventing him from getting a decent hold, she couldn't manage to swing back to safety either.

Her shoes hit flesh and he grunted. And a second time; this time it had felt like his head. Having failed to tip her over with the rush of his first assault, the width of the walkway wall meant that he was now struggling to lever her weight over it.

Below, nobody seemed to move. They were paralysed by in-action. They just gaped up, open-mouthed, silent.

'Police!' A shout. Ferriter's voice.

And then, as suddenly as he had attacked her, she realised he had gone, leaving her waving her legs in empty air.

By the time she had manoeuvred herself back onto the safety of the walkway, gasping for breath, there was no sign of him in any of the three directions he could have run. It was as if he had never been there.

She slumped down, turned, sat back against the cool concrete wall, feeling her heart thumping hard in her chest as Ferriter ran towards her, chasing the attacker.

THIRTY-ONE

'Jesus,' said Ferriter. 'That must sting.'

'Brutalism,' said Cupidi, and then laughed at her own joke.

Ferriter looked at her, puzzled, then back at the mirror and her own wound.

They were in the Estate Office bathroom. Cupidi had taken off her T-shirt and was dabbing the cuts on her stomach with cotton wool.

'Did you see him at all?' asked Cupidi.

'I was too far away. No idea which way he went. This place is a nightmare. Think this will scar?' said Ferriter, peering at her split eyebrow.

Cupidi looked up at Ferriter's face. 'I don't think so.'

'Wouldn't mind if it did. Badge of honour.'

'Seriously?'

'What? You think I just spend all my time trying to keep pretty?'

Cupidi said, 'I was looking down and seeing people looking

back at me and thinking, they're going to watch me fall. And I was thinking, "Bastards." They're just going to stand there and watch my skull crack open on the pavement.'

'I don't get why he even tried to kill you. Why didn't he just run for it? That's seriously psycho.'

Cupidi winced as she dabbed the longest red scrape with cotton wool.

'He left me alone,' Ferriter thought aloud, 'but he deliberately waited and tried to kill you. Why? Because he thought you'd clocked him.'

That made sense, Cupidi realised.

'He thinks you can identify him? Can you?'

'No. He was never in sight. But he didn't know that for sure.' Cupidi looked at herself in the mirror, the scratch on her pale belly. 'Maybe he thinks I may have seen him running from the flat.'

'But why would he be bothered?'

'Because he thinks we'll be able to identify him.'

'Christ,' said Ferriter. 'What if it's someone we've already met?'

Cupidi nodded. A Metropolitan Police forensics team would search the flat now it was a crime scene, but the neighbour had said that Stein had many visitors so it was unlikely that they would turn up anything that would help find out who the attacker had been. The CCTV might be more productive. Erich was in the office, recovering the footage recorded in each of the two working lifts.

'So he was there, in the flat, all the time we were searching?' Ferriter demanded.

'Must have been. I think he must have a key. He's been letting himself in.'

'Was he waiting for Abir Stein to come back?'

'Frankly, I don't think Abir Stein is ever going to come back,' said Cupidi, gingerly pulling down her shirt again. 'From the food in the fridge, it looks like he's been missing since the end of March.'

'We've got him on record as visiting the EastArt storage unit at the start of April.'

'Assuming it was him.'

'Bloody hell.'

'I know.' She turned and looked at Ferriter; saw the blood on her pale shirt. 'Look at us,' she said.

'Like out of some horror movie.'

But when, after a few minutes, Erich found the CCTV footage of the man getting in at the thirtieth floor, it turned out to be useless. He showed it to them on a screen in the building's security centre. The man had deliberately entered the lift walking backwards into it, the back of his head to the camera.

'He must have been using the lift to get to the flat, though,' said Erich. 'There must be more footage of him.'

Erich replayed the footage. A dark shape, cautiously stepping backwards.

'I bet he does that every time,' said Cupidi. She looked at the video playing forwards, then backwards, then forwards again, the man stepping in and out without ever showing who he was. 'This is someone who knew exactly what he was doing.'

★

'We're getting somewhere,' said Ferriter as she drove the car back to Kent. 'Aren't we? Else that guy wouldn't have tried to kill you.'

'You're happy about that, are you?'

'Yes, boss.'

It was true. In the passenger seat as they drove towards the M20, Cupidi had been making a mental list of everything she had figured out that day. In a few hours they had learned more than they had struggled with in the last four days.

One. Abir Stein was not just not answering his phone. He was definitely missing, if not dead.

Two. Zoya Gubenko had said he had answered a couple of emails. If he was missing or dead, someone had presumably been answering on his behalf.

Three. Another man had been visiting his flat.

Four. That man was willing to kill. He had attempted to kill Cupidi, at least, presumably because he was worried that she would recognise him.

Five. So did that mean Cupidi had already met him, as Ferriter had suggested? Or just that he was someone she was likely to come across during the course of the investigation?

Six. Whoever he was, he wasn't stupid. He knew how to protect his identity. He was a man who walked into lifts backwards.

Seven. Abir Stein had disappeared not long before someone had signed into East Art using his name.

This churn of the sudden possibilities wasn't just a puzzle to be unravelled. Cupidi felt it physically; a kind of anxious thrill, buzzing in the pit of her stomach.

And eight. This had not been some prank. All along, she had been right.

'Have a word in private?' asked Peter Moon.

Cupidi looked up warily from her desk where she was writing her notes.

'What's up with Jill?' asked Peter Moon, his voice low, so as not to be overheard by the others in the incident room.

'I don't know what you mean,' Cupidi answered, evasively.

'She has a bloody great sticking plaster on her forehead. Hadn't you noticed?'

'Oh. That.' Relieved, Cupidi explained the day's events in London.

'Jesus. Is she OK?'

'She says it's just a cut.'

Moon frowned. Then he dug in his pocket, pulled out his phone and said, 'Seen Facebook?' He navigated until he'd found what he wanted, then held up his phone screen: *Serve the pervert right. Who are we coming for next?* Above a picture of Frank Khan.

She peered at the small rectangle. 'What's that?'

'England Rising's only gone and claimed responsibility for the stabbing of Frank Khan. Thought you might be interested. I just got a call from the Communications Team who wanted to know what was going on. Apparently the national press are onto it already.'

Cupidi frowned, staring at the screen. Had she been completely wrong at this morning's meeting? 'Do you think it's genuine?'

'Well, it might, be, mightn't it?' said Moon.

'Or are they just trying to get publicity?'

'You tell me. You're the one who said it couldn't have been them.'

Cupidi digested the information. What if it had been an extremist group, after all?

'You wanted to know why he had opened the door to his attacker. What if he didn't? What if the two boys did? What if they were just bait?'

'What do you mean, bait?'

'Paedo hunters. They're vigilantes, aren't they? They use entrapment to catch paedos all the time, don't they? Pretend to be little girls online and that stuff. I reckon they put the two boys up to it so they could get access to Khan.'

He reached towards her and retrieved his phone.

'Yeah. But they wouldn't use actual children, would they? That would undermine the point.'

'These people are nut jobs, Alex. Extremists.'

She frowned. 'Have you been able to interview Frank Khan yet?' she asked.

'Only for a couple of minutes. He's conscious, but he's still pretty weak. Hooked up to all kinds of stuff. It was touch and go last night apparently.'

'And did you ask why he'd made the call to the police?'

'Course.'

'And?'

'He said he didn't know who it was, but said someone kept ringing on his bell so he got scared.'

'He didn't say he thought it was some vigilante?'

'Well, obviously he wouldn't, if it had been a trap. Because

235

it would be like he was admitting there had been teenage boys in his flat.'

'You still think it's a vigilante attack, don't you?'

'I'm not ruling it out, Alex. That's what I'm saying. Open mind. I just think we were a bit hasty this morning, given this.' He held up his phone again.

'What about door-to-doors? Did they see a man?'

Moon shook his head. 'Interviewed all the neighbours. Couple of people say they saw the lads, but no one that says they saw the man yet. Why would they? Middle of the day. Weekday. Not a great time for witnesses. And people will always notice teenage boys. They're not so likely to notice anyone else.'

That much was true, Cupidi thought.

'One report of a young Afro-Caribbean lad nicking a sleeping bag from a garage off Central Road, not far from Frank Khan's flat, but that's all. I chased it up but it didn't go anywhere.'

'Frank Khan said nothing at all about the boys?'

'Course he didn't. If he pulls through, he's going down,' said Moon. 'I'm going to make sure of it.'

'But if Khan's not going to talk, then it's even more important we find the two boys.'

Moon nodded.

Ten minutes later, he appeared at her desk again with a brown envelope and whispered, 'I'm organising a collection. Buy Jill some flowers on behalf of the whole team.'

'I was injured as well, you know. You buying me flowers too?'

'Were you?'

'Want me to show you?' She put her hand at the bottom of her shirt, as if preparing to lift it.

236

'No,' he said. 'You're all right.'

'Word to the wise,' said Cupidi, looking him in the eye again. 'Forget the flowers. Jill Ferriter wouldn't like it. I know for a fact she doesn't like being seen as a victim, you see. Whatever the situation.'

This time, the slightest flicker of confusion in his gaze before he looked away.

'Wouldn't mind chocolates myself, though,' she called as he returned to his desk on the far side of the room.

When she turned back to her screen there was an email notification from a police officer whose name she didn't recognise: a Constable Devon King. Cupidi had earlier left a message for the Metropolitan Police's Art and Antiques Unit. Had they come across an Abir Stein? Now here was a reply and a phone number.

Cupidi called back.

'Abir Stein. Yes, we'd come across him.' From the noise in the background, Devon King was somewhere busy; computer keyboards clacked around him.

Cupidi sat up, interested. 'Does that mean he was involved in something shady?'

'Not necessarily. He had various clients who were on our radar for one reason or another. It doesn't necessarily mean anything. We had a long list of people we were keeping any eye on, just in case.'

'In case of what?'

'Do you know much about the fine art market? The high-end market can be like the Wild West, only politer.'

'And is Abir Stein a goodie or a baddie?'

'That's what we never found out. The difficulty a unit like ours has – used to have . . .'

'Used to?'

'The unit was disbanded months ago. It takes a lot of work to uncover art fraud and it's difficult to prove. Sometimes results don't come right away just because you want them to. So we were moved to other, more productive duties. No chance of it being funded after Grenfell.' The scale of the police investigation into the London fire had sucked resources dry across the force. 'I just get the occasional message forwarded on still. When I saw the name Abir Stein, I thought it might be worth calling back. But no. There is no Arts and Antiquities Unit any more.'

'Bugger.'

'We're much more efficient now, obviously,' said Devon King drily.

'So why was Abir Stein on your radar?'

'In the art market, buyers and sellers are notoriously shy. They're often wealthy, well-known people who don't like having their name in the papers. But it's just accepted in that world. You can buy a painting for ten million dollars and not even know who you're buying it from. Can you imagine any other business in which that's OK?'

'The art market is a trade in things that have no price,' said Cupidi.

'Yes. Exactly.'

'My dad used to say that.' As a child, Cupidi's father had loved taking her to galleries. He could stand still for twenty minutes in front of a piece of work, just contemplating it, saying nothing at all. It had driven her mother mad.

'It's very well put,' said the constable. 'Nobody can say what the real value of a work of art is. The price is simply what people pay for it. And in these times, that can be pretty much anything. They're just symbols. Like Bitcoins.'

'Except Bitcoins have no meaning.'

'You're deep for a Wednesday afternoon.'

'Apologies.'

'I like it. Excuse me. I'm going outside. I might lose you. Phone me back if the call drops.' Cupidi heard him standing, moving away from the noise of a police office. 'So as far as we know, we have no sensible way of telling what a piece of art ought to sell for, whether someone's overvaluing it or undervaluing it.'

'So it could be a fraudster's paradise?'

'That's why I bloody loved working there. I was gutted when they wound it up. It's a fascinating world.' He was outside now. Traffic hummed around him. 'It's not just the value. The buyers and sellers are anyone from the great and the good to out-and-out bloody gangsters. Nobody wants to be seen buying and selling stuff. If you're a billionaire, why would you want people to know your business? So people hide their identity. Even crack dealers know who their sources are, for God's sake. It's the least transparent industry in the world. Abir Stein brokers big deals between people, companies, art institutions, whoever. That's what he lives off. He came to our attention a year ago selling a Rothko.'

'He had a Rothko? They're worth millions.'

'That's the point. It was in his name on the sale papers but that set bells ringing, because he's not rich enough to own a Rothko. Turned out to really belong to some investment fund and he was just handling the paperwork.'

'Not the Evert and Astrid Miller Foundation, by any chance?'

'No. This was some Russian guy who keeps all his funds tucked away in the Cayman Islands. That who you're looking into, Astrid Miller?'

'I'm not sure,' said Cupidi.

The flick of a lighter. The constable was a smoker; that's why he had gone outside. 'I never heard a word against Astrid Miller, have to say.'

'But Abir Stein?'

'Put it this way.' The sound of a breath as he sucked smoke. 'He was involved in some grey areas. It's big business, you know.'

'Nice for money laundering too.'

'Exactly, because it's hard to prove who's selling what. It's not just that people don't want to give their real names. Nobody wants to actually say what they bought such-and-such a piece of work for. The trail can be pretty obscure, to say the least. And if you do get paperwork, who's to say it's real? How do you actually check? Just because you've got a receipt for ten mill, doesn't mean that's what has changed hands.'

'Thing is, I think Abir Stein's gone missing.'

'Oh.' Another pull on the cigarette. 'That is interesting.'

'Did you ever get the idea he could be in over his head on something?'

'In that kind of world, anything is possible. Have you got a look at his bank statements?'

'I'm getting them. I'm looking for someone who can make sense of them. My boss will want someone from our force, but . . . is there anyone you'd recommend?'

'Yes. I know the exact person.'

240

'You?'

A laugh. 'It's what I did on the unit, chase all those little numbers. I find them much prettier than all the pictures, to be honest.'

'I'll see what I can do. Trouble is, my boss is kind of obsessed by numbers too.'

'Aren't they all? Send it along though. I would love to do some of that stuff again. I'll do what I can. Just between you and me. Can't promise anything.'

She thanked him.

'Something else,' he said. 'I'll give you a name. George Gilchrist. They were friends. Close friends. He's an art dealer. Old-school guy. Talk to him.'

Afterwards, she locked herself in a cubicle in the bathroom and lifted her shirt. Around the scratches on her stomach, her skin was yellowing from the bruises. Colleagues had made assumptions about this case; that it had been something frivolous, something that was beneath their talents. At least she was sure, now, that she had been right all along. This was something dangerous, dark, and much bigger than an arm in a jar.

THIRTY-TWO

Cupidi sat watching the late news, got up, peered through the window, sat down again, tried to listen to a discussion about gross domestic product, gave up, and went upstairs to knock on her daughter's door.

Her daughter was in bed, playing on her phone. Cupidi sat down on the bed and ran her hand through her daughter's short hair as she focused on the game. Eventually Zoë gave up, put the device down.

'What did you do today?'

Zoë shrugged. 'Not much.'

'It's spring. Isn't this when you get all excited about the new birds coming over?'

'Kind of.'

Cupidi looked at her daughter, puzzled. There was so much she didn't understand about the girl. 'Wasn't it this time last year you were all giddy about the poopoo?'

'Hoopoe,' huffed Zoë, pulling her mother's hand off her head.

'I knew that.'

'I don't feel like it, that's all.'

Every time she thought she had begun to understand her own daughter, Zoë seemed to elude her. Birds had been the one thing in her life that seemed to make her daughter genuinely happy.

Cupidi shuffled closer to her daughter; as she leaned against her arm, Zoë flinched.

'What's wrong?'

'Nothing.'

Cupidi reached out to touch her. Her daughter pulled back.

'Have you hurt your arm?'

'No.'

She put her hand on the sleeve of her daughter's shirt. Zoë pulled away. 'Let me see.'

'You'll go mad,' Zoë said.

'What's wrong?'

'Nothing's wrong, Mum. Nothing at all.' Angrily she pulled her shirt over her head. 'That's all.'

Cupidi stared at the fresh tattoo on her daughter's arm, red skin raised around dark blue ink.

'You're seventeen. That's not legal.'

'I was wondering how you'd react,' said Zoë. 'Typically, you're seeing this as a law-and-order issue first of all.'

That's why she had been wearing a jacket indoors last night. 'Who did this?'

Zoë pulled her shirt back down. 'Why would I tell you? You'd only go and arrest him.'

'I would. You're right. There are perfectly rational reasons why you're not allowed to tattoo seventeen-year-olds. Is it infected?'

'No. It's fine. Just a bit sore.'

She had never imagined it, her daughter wanting a tattoo. 'Oh, Zoë. I wish . . . I wish . . . you'd talked to me about it.'

'You'd have only tried to stop me.'

'Of course I would.' How much other stuff was Zoë doing these days that she didn't want to talk to her mother about because she knew her mother wouldn't approve? 'What if . . . when you're older . . .'

'What if I change my mind?'

Stupid question, Cupidi chided herself, feeling an unexpected kind of grief. Her daughter's perfect body, that she had given birth to, raised, fed, kept warm, tucked in at night, was no longer hers at all. Her daughter had claimed ownership of it.

'What is it, anyway?'

A circle with arrows through the middle.

'Just a tattoo, that's all. You can't do anything about it.'

'I know I can't.' Cupidi paused, closed her eyes, opened them again. 'I was just wondering if I should get one too.'

Zoë laughed. 'That's ridiculous.'

'Is it?' She pulled up the sleeve of her T-shirt. 'I think it could look pretty good.'

Zoë's laughter was less certain now. 'You're just trying to put me off having another one, aren't you?' She reached out to hug her mother. This time it was Cupidi who winced.

'What?'

'My own tattoo.' She lifted her shirt and showed the grazes on her stomach. New colours were emerging beneath her skin.

Zoë's mouth fell open. 'What happened?'

'Just stupid work stuff.'

'Mum!'

'You should see the other guy.'

Unfortunately she hadn't seen the other guy at all.

They sat on the bed, holding each other for a couple of minutes. Then Zoë picked up her phone again and it seemed there was no more to be said.

Downstairs, she called the number given to her by Devon King.

'Good evening. George Gilchrist here.' The voice was elderly, very English, distinctly patrician.

Cupidi explained who she was, that she was looking for any information about Abir Stein.

'Oh God. Have you found him?'

Cupidi was surprised by his reaction. 'Why do you say "found him"?'

'Well, he's just disappeared, hasn't he? I haven't heard a snippet from him in weeks.'

Gilchrist was an art dealer. 'Retired,' explained Gilchrist. 'I just keep my hand in here and there. Stein was my protégé. A wonderful young man. Absolutely brilliant radar for new work. Furniture, painting, sculpture. He has such an eye. The pupil surpasses the master.'

'If you think he's disappeared, can you think of any reason why?'

'Oh please. We handle valuable objects. I heard about a book collector recently who was killed for owning an original edition of *Wind in the Willows*. Wasn't that awful?'

'You think he might have been killed because of an artwork he handled?'

245

'The kind of people we deal with say they are interested in art. I've always said most of them are just interested in money.'

Zoë started playing music upstairs. Cupidi closed the living-room door to shut out the noise. 'Had he seemed worried about anything recently?'

'That's the thing. These last two or three years he definitely aged. Something was eating away at him, but whenever I asked about it he just changed the subject. Started talking about the latest absurdity at Miami Art Basel or something. Abir was always very controlled. He hated the idea that anybody might not see him doing well, but I was sure there was something wrong. I asked him all the time. Whether it was his health or his business I never knew. He was the kind of man you never saw drunk, if you know what I mean?'

'Not a copper, then.'

Gilchrist laughed. 'But I'm serious. Half an hour in his company and you could end up loving any piece of work he talked about. He was so enthusiastic and knowledgeable. And entirely self-taught when I met him, too. Of course, I hope I added to his knowledge but really, most of it was there when I first met him. Immigrant parents. He was full of ambition.'

'You said most of the people you deal with are interested in money. Did that apply to Mr Stein?'

'Of course it did. To a degree. He came from nothing, you know. Absolutely nothing. His father was a taxi driver. But he hid it rather well, I think.'

Downstairs, Cupidi looked up on her computer the symbol she had seen on her daughter's arm. A circle with three arrows in it.

It was a political symbol from the 1930s, created by Germans militantly opposed to Nazism and Communism. More recently it had been adopted by anti-fascist protest groups.

Her daughter was a passionate girl. She had always liked that. It reminded her of herself at that age, of her mother even more. When Zoë had been detained in London at the anti-fascist demonstration last year, Cupidi had tried to talk to her daughter about politics. Her daughter had just shouted at her. 'You wouldn't understand. You're a police officer. Your job is to maintain the status quo. I hate the status quo.'

Cupidi switched off her computer, put her head in her hands. It had been a long day. She should go to bed. Light still shone from under her daughter's door. In her own bedroom, she lifted her shirt up and stared at herself in the mirror for a minute. The bruises seemed to be darkening as she looked at them. Then she turned to the window, looking over the hump of shingle to William South's bungalow bathed in nuclear electric light.

She pulled the shirt back down again, reached in the cupboard and took out a woollen jumper.

Arum Cottage, alone on the stones, apart from all the other houses.

There was still a light on somewhere in the shack's living room. She knocked on the door. 'It's me, Bill,' she said.

Silence. The nuclear power station was venting hot air. It sounded like a distant kettle boiling.

'I'm not going till you answer the door.'

When he finally opened, she could smell the whisky on his breath, even a pace away.

'I wanted to ask you something, Bill.'

He swayed slightly. 'What?'

'Some rich people called the Millers have a place down here. You were the community copper. Do you know which one it is?'

'Was the community copper,' he said.

Cupidi waited, standing in the dim pool of light from his shack. 'Please, Bill. Less of the self-pity. It's a murder case.'

'Your favourites.'

'Don't, Bill. It's important, that's all I mean.'

It had been a murder case when they had first met; an investigation which ended with one murderer dead, and William South going to prison for something he'd done a long time ago.

He stood, looking at her for a long time.

'And I'm worried about Zoë,' she said finally.

He grunted. 'When weren't you?'

'Maybe you could take her birdwatching again, like you used to?'

'That was when she was a girl. She's grown out of that now.'

'It would do you good, too. You're cooped up in this place, on your own.'

'I kind of got used to being cooped up,' he said.

She wanted to sit with him and talk to him about Zoë, and how she worried she'd become caught up in activism, but he hadn't invited her in. 'Let us know if you need anything, Bill, will you? I'm worried about you, that's all.'

'If I show you the house, will you stop worrying?'

'Of course not.'

Reaching behind the door, he grabbed a donkey jacket. He

didn't bother to lock his door, walking ahead of her towards the beach.

'Do you have a torch?'

'Never carry one. In a place like this, torches don't help you.'

She thought about what he meant and realised it was true. When it was dark everywhere, torches only showed what was in their beam and made the darkness thicker.

The oldest houses on the beach were a row of Victorian railway carriages, lined up on the shingle by the old quarry workers. At the head of the line had been an old First Class coach, to which other structures had been tacked on like barnacles on a rock. An artist lived there, selling canvases to the tourists who came in the summer and at weekends. To the north, a few of the other original carriages remained. Through neglect or misfortune, some had disappeared and been replaced by other ramshackle structures. At both ends of the line, and on the empty space behind the track that led to the lighthouses, others had added new makeshift buildings.

In recent years, the rich had bought them, one by one. Some had been lovingly restored, some given to architects to reimagine. One entire carriage had been preserved inside a new modernist rectangle made of wood and glass. The results appeared in glossy magazines. But the Millers' cabin was not one of them. It turned out to be one of the least conspicuous, one Cupidi had barely noticed before, an old carriage that had been rebuilt over time, extended by wooden additions on all sides.

'She's had it for years. They're never there.'

They walked towards the building.

'Though this is new,' he said, pointing to a tiny outhouse

tacked onto the side. 'So they must have been around. I don't remember seeing her here for years though.'

A wind was blowing at the wave crests, making pale lines in the darkness.

'I'm glad you're back though,' Cupidi said.

'And I'm showing you which house the Millers live in,' he said.

She turned towards him. 'Don't indulge yourself thinking that I feel guilty. I don't. I was doing my job, that's all. I did what I had to do.'

He turned his back on her and seemed to be about to head back home when he stopped. 'Look,' he said.

She didn't realise what he was saying at first because it was hard to see. From behind heavy drawn curtains that covered the seaward windows, a thin strip of light seeped out. Someone was in the Millers' cabin.

The front door was at the rear of the building, facing the road. William South standing behind her, she pressed the button on an intercom and heard a buzzing from within the wooden house. From here, the house looked completely dark.

She listened for footsteps.

Nobody came to answer the door.

'It's late,' said South. 'Only an idiot would open a door to you, this time of night.'

Undeterred, Cupidi pressed the button a second time.

After a short wait, she walked back round, to the seaward side of the house. The glow that had crept through the gap between curtain and floor was no longer showing.

Had it just been a security light, on a timer? There was no car parked outside the building, so if someone was in there, how had they got there?

South was still waiting at the front of the bungalow when she returned.

'Well?'

'I think someone's in there. They're just ignoring me.'

'Don't blame them,' said South.

Cupidi laughed. 'Let's go,' she said.

He turned and headed back towards Arum Cottage. She followed, a few paces behind. When he reached his porch he paused, waiting for him to turn so she could thank him, but he simply opened the door and went straight inside.

As she stood, wondering whether to knock on the door again, the brief silhouette of a bat passed the light. Then a second.

Then the bulb was turned off. So she headed back home.

Zoë's room was dark. Cupidi lay in bed, thinking, her bedroom window wide open, listening to crickets, owls and the distant crunch of the waves.

THIRTY-THREE

Cupidi knocked on her daughter's door before leaving the house the next morning.

On the other side of the door, Zoë groaned. 'What?'

'I'm about to leave for work. Can I come in?'

She opened the door. Zoë's head was peeping out from under a single sheet. For a teenager, she kept her room surprisingly neat. There were still her careful drawings of birds everywhere round the walls, paper a little yellow now, her clothes on the chair, neatly folded. 'What?'

'You heard of a group called England Rising?'

Zoë sat up a little more, suspicious. 'Why are you asking me that?'

'Because of your tattoo.'

Zoë rolled her eyes. 'I bet you looked the symbol up, didn't you?'

Cupidi sat down on her daughter's bed. 'Obviously if I'm going to get one the same, I need to know what it means.'

'You're not even funny, Mum.'

'So I figure you'll know about neo-Nazi groups. What about England Rising?'

'They're not funny either,' said Zoë.

'Do you know anything about them?'

Zoë sat up in her bed. 'Are you involved in that case on the news? About the guy being stabbed?'

'It was on the news?'

Zoë was suddenly more interested. 'All over Facebook, Snapchat and everything. There's sick people saying "Good for them", because the police do nothing about paedophiles. Did they do it?'

'Do you know about them?'

'You want to know?'

'I do. Yes.'

'They're another front group for National Action, that's what people say. When the government banned them after that MP got stabbed, all these other groups suddenly appeared, like Scottish Dawn, NS131 and England Rising, saying the same old poison. England Rising have been posting a lot of nasty stuff online in the last few months. Either they're copying National Action or they're basically the same people. Things like this are great for them. They want to be seen as champions of the people. Other neo-Nazis have done it in America, posted videos on humiliating gay people and calling people child abusers.'

'Where do you know all this stuff from?'

'Friends, you know. Websites. Chat.'

'Is this what you do all day?'

Her daughter looked away and said, 'You know what these people want, don't you? They would throw everyone who isn't white and straight out of this country. They hate Jews, they hate Muslims. They hate everybody. They see their job as being to goad more stupid people into action – like the bloke who killed the MP. Don't they terrify you?'

Her little girl. The thin, gawky one who picked at her food. The one who used to draw careful pictures of birds.

There had been an Afghan refugee girl Zoë had tried to help two years ago. Zoë had tried to befriend her, to teach her English. Their worlds turned out to be too different. The girl had lived with such extreme violence all her life, seen and experienced things she couldn't put into words – at least, not words she could share with a teenager brought up here in England. The things you witnessed built a wall around you; she knew that. Zoë herself hadn't seen it that way; she just thought the girl never really trusted her because her mother was a police officer. After a while, Zoë had stopped going to visit her.

Cupidi thought for a while. 'This lot don't appear to have posted a video of the attack. Do you think that means they're claiming responsibility for something they didn't do?'

'Either they're too stupid to press the on button on the camera, or it wasn't them at all.'

'So someone might have seen what they put on Facebook and gone out to punish this man?'

'This is what they want. And now loads of people will be thinking, "Well maybe they're not neo-Nazi nut jobs after all. Maybe they're on our side. Because the police aren't."'

'Is that what you think? The police aren't on your side?'

A moment's hesitation. 'Course not, Mum. But it actually doesn't matter what I think, does it?' Zoë nudged her mother off the bed and stood up, still in the same greying Harry Potter pyjamas she'd been wearing all week.

She wandered to the bathroom and came back with her tooth-brush in her hand and said, 'You spend your whole time looking for people who break the laws. That's what you're all about. I understand. William South. He broke the law. He has to go to prison. But what if these people end up making the law? That's what they want. They want to get everyone so scared they'll make legislation that punishes migrants, punishes queers, punishes people who don't go to work. Some of that's already happening, now. What will you do then, Mum?'

Cupidi watched her daughter, all fire and anger.

Zoë said, 'Go on then. I know you're thinking it. You're going to say everything I say is rubbish, aren't you? You're going to patronise me now, aren't you?'

'All I was going to say is that's the longest conversation I've had with you in the last six months.' And she leaned forward and kissed her daughter on the forehead. 'I have to go. Are you going to be all right?'

'Never,' her daughter hugged her back. 'It's all your fault.'

'That's what I'm here for. One thing. One theory is that Eng-land Rising may have used two teenagers as bait, to attract the paedophile. Does that sound plausible?'

'Course. They're not exactly following legal process in the first place, are they?'

'What if one of the teenagers was black?'

Zoë snorted. 'No way, then. That bunch are hardcore racial purists. Even if a black kid was stupid enough to join them, they wouldn't want him anyway.'

'You sure?'

Zoë was about to answer, but Cupidi's phone was ringing. 'What?'

'Ross Clough,' said Ferriter. 'He's just been taken in.'

'What?'

'He was caught trespassing just now at the Millers' house at Long Hill. Apparently carrying a weapon.'

'Jesus. Have they charged him with anything?'

'Not yet. He's at Canterbury nick.'

Cupidi was already on her way down the stairs, rifling through her bag to find her car keys.

THIRTY-FOUR

Canterbury Police Station was very 1970s, all brick cladding and white-framed glass windows.

'He had a knife. Jesus. I knew it,' said Ferriter. 'I bloody knew it.'

There was no space in the main car park, so they drove around for another ten minutes looking for somewhere to leave the car. Ross Clough was being held in the custody suite.

'So what's the plan?' she asked as they walked down the long corridor that ran past the locker rooms. 'He'll just say he was there researching some art project or some bollocks like that.'

Cupidi stopped and thought. 'Let him say that, then. On paper he's done nothing wrong except for trespass on private land.'

'With a weapon?'

They hadn't put Ross in a cell; he was sitting on a bench near the desk. He smiled when he saw them. 'It's you.'

'Want a cup of tea or something?' a constable asked them.

'You're OK,' said Cupidi. 'I was told Mr Clough was carrying weapons. What were they?'

'Knives. He had them in a bag.'

'Knives?'

They took Clough to an interview room, a pale, windowless cubicle, with a plain table and plain chairs. Spaces like this made Cupidi want to be outdoors, away from this. She recited, 'You do not have to say anything . . .'

'They already said that,' he said.

'Well in that case you won't mind if I say it again then.'

'Knock yourself out.'

'So,' said Cupidi when she had finished. 'What were you doing at the Millers', Ross?'

'Research.'

She looked at him. There was nothing hostile about his gaze; it was more one of aloof amusement. 'What kind of research, Ross?'

'Very interesting research. For my sculpture.'

'Right. The one of Astrid Miller with an arm chopped off?' said Ferriter drily.

'I think it's going to be a series.' Ross Clough sat back in his chair, swept hair out of his eyes. 'Do you have a pen and paper?'

Ferriter left the room and returned with a single sheet of paper and a biro. Clough took them, laying the paper in front of him on the table.

'Why did you take knives?'

'Because they're my tools.'

'What do you use the knives for, Ross?'

'For cutting things, obviously. I'm a sculptor. Among other things. They're box cutters, for God's sake. Not daggers.'

'What exactly were you hoping to find out, Ross?'

'If I knew, then I wouldn't have had to go there. That may be how a police inquiry works, but it's not how an artistic enquiry progresses. I've been thinking about that arm. Freud says that any limb is a representation of the penis.'

'I beg your pardon?' said Ferriter.

'A penis. You know about them?' He smiled. He picked up the pen and, instead of taking notes, started to draw. 'You are investigators. I am too. You investigate what you can see. Art is a form of investigation that goes behind what you can see.'

Cupidi peered at his pad. He was drawing a human arm, like the ones they had seen on the walls of his flat in Margate.

'I tried looking you up on the internet, Mr Clough,' said Ferriter. 'I was expecting to find some information about you online, but know what? I didn't find much. You're not actually a very successful artist, are you?'

Cupidi admired her use of the word 'actually'. For the first time Clough looked rattled. 'It depends what you mean by successful,' he said.

'An artist whose work people give a stuff about,' said Ferriter.

'Opportunity in the art world is not evenly distributed,' said Clough.

'Oh, I see,' Ferriter continued. 'You're angry about the artists who have made it?'

'No. Not really. If they're good, why should I mind? If they're not, good luck to them.'

'Angry about the people who stop you from making it, then?'

Maybe there she had hit a nerve; the muscles around his mouth tightened. 'I came from a disadvantaged family,' said Clough. 'My

259

father was a builder. He did not want me to go to art school. It's a closed world. You have to have the right connections.'

'So you resent people who do have the right connections, like Astrid Miller?'

'I have a great admiration for people like her, as a matter of fact.'

'So you make naked sculptures of her?' asked Ferriter.

'I was thinking of making one of you,' he said, looking at her for a reaction.

'You had a knife.'

'Several.'

'Why did you have them?'

'It's where I keep them. In my pack.' He looked up. 'Otherwise they'd get lost.'

'You know what it looks like, don't you? We call it "going equipped".'

He laughed. 'What, "equipped to make an artwork"?'

Ferriter took out a sheet of paper from her pocket and looked at it. 'April the second. A Monday. You weren't on the rota at the Turner. Where were you?'

2 April: the day someone signed in as Abir Stein at EastArt.

'I had Mondays off. On account of working the weekend.'

'What did you do?' asked Ferriter.

'I don't really know. Why is it important?'

'Do you keep a diary?'

'Normally I'd be working in my studio, but it was a low point. I couldn't work out what to do. I was really stuck. Until this came along, I was in a bit of a hole. This case. Our case. We're working on it together.' He smiled at them some more.

'Our case?'

'Yes. As in the case we are all interested in right now.'

First time round in interviews, you just got them to give their version. You weren't trying to pick it apart yet. That would come later. But you had to make the most of it. Second time around, you might not have the same chances. They would always be more cautious, more guarded, especially if you had charged them by then.

'Do you know a man called Abir Stein?'

'Spoke to him. Never met. On the phone. Actually he was a bit pissed off I had his number.'

'Why?'

'See, I kind of nicked it. It was on the paperwork when the "In Memoriam" exhibition was in planning. Couldn't believe it. It seemed like it was meant. So I just copied it down. He's really famous, you know.'

He leaned forward and started to draw on the paper Ferriter had brought.

'You realise it's an offence taking somebody's private number from the workplace like that?'

'You peeked around my flat without asking. I saw you do it. You didn't think I noticed, did you? I could probably complain about that,' he said.

Cupidi said, 'Be my guest.'

'But you have to be a bit cheeky, don't you, if you want to find out what's under the surface? I was just doing that. You're the same.' Clough looked up at Ferriter, then down at the page again. 'I called him up and asked if I could show him some of my work. But he wasn't very receptive.'

261

Ferriter leaned forward. 'He turned you down.'

'It's like a closed circle sometimes. It's so incestuous.'

'What is?'

'The art world, of course.' He paused, looked up again at her. 'The sticking plaster suits you. The Japanese have this idea of beauty in imperfection. The beautiful wound.'

Ferriter ignored him. 'What did Abir Stein say?'

'He asked how I got his number. I told him. I'm always honest. I was hoping he'd see how committed I was, but he was just angry.'

'How did that make you feel?'

'Sad, obviously. Very sad.'

'And were you angry yourself?'

'He's supposed to be interested in art. But I'm used to it. I've had a lot of rejection. I've sent stuff to all the big people in art. Hans-Ulrich Obrist, Larry Gagosian, Sadie Coles – you know of these people?'

Cupidi shook her head.

'One time, I doorstepped Iwan and Manuela Wirth at their gallery in Somerset. Hauser and Wirth? I had made sculptures of both of them, but they didn't even look. You've never even heard of it?'

'Did you ever go to Stein's address?'

Clough shook his head. 'I couldn't find out where he lived. Do you think it's his arm, then? The one we found in the gallery.'

Cupidi looked at Ferriter, then back at Clough. 'Why do you say that?'

He didn't look up from his drawing. 'Because you're interested in him. Because he's been very, very quiet these last few weeks.

Suspicious, no? I've tried calling his number but it goes straight to voicemail. Can I go now? I haven't actually done anything wrong, have I?'

'Stalking. Trespass.'

'Are you going to charge me?' There was little concern in his voice. If anything, he sounded like he wouldn't mind it at all.

'What would you like us to charge you with?' asked Ferriter.

Scritch-scritch-scritch went the biro on the paper as he hatched shade on the side of Ferriter's face. He had drawn her looking across the table at him, sticking plaster over one eye.

When they said Clough could go, Cupidi was about to lead him out to the front office when he stopped and said, 'What about my bag?'

'Right you are,' said the custody officer. He returned from the locker with a black canvas backpack and was about to hand it to Clough when Ferriter took it.

'I'll take that,' she said.

Ross hesitated. 'Why?'

'There are knives in it. We're hardly going to hand it to you in here.' Ferriter put on gloves, took the bag and, watched by Clough, emptied it onto the custody desk. Pens, two black notebooks and a water bottle fell out, some masking tape rolled off the table onto the floor, followed by two artists' scalpels, the blades tucked into wine corks.

She picked up the knives first, pulled the cork off one and examined the blade. She looked up at Clough, but he didn't seem concerned. Then she opened the notebooks.

'They're private,' said Clough loudly.

She turned a page.

'I don't want you to do that.'

And then another page. 'Bloody hell,' she said.

It was another drawing of her, done in biro, just like the one in the interview room. Ferriter's face, lips slightly parted, a slight smile on her face.

'Are you actually allowed to do that? It's my personal notebook. I don't show that to anyone.'

Cupidi took him by the arm. 'We'll return the bag to you at the entrance to the station.'

When Ferriter brought the bag out two minutes later he grabbed it off her, unzipped it and peered inside. 'Did you take anything?'

'No, sir. Of course not.'

He delved around, then looked up, still frowning.

Back in their car, Ferriter took out her phone and started flicking through it.

Cupidi said, 'It wasn't him who assaulted us. He doesn't have the physique.'

'You'd have broken him in two if he'd had a go. Wishful thinking.'

'You don't like him much, do you?'

'No.'

'We need to get CCTV from EastArt, though.'

'Jesus,' said Ferriter, still staring at her phone. 'He drew a picture of you too. It's creepy. Take a look. You look pretty good. I look like some porn star. It's revolting. Is my mouth that big?'

The photograph on her phone was of a page from Clough's

small sketch pad; the whole sheet was densely covered in notes and angular, scratchy ink drawings, like the ones they had seen on the walls of his studio in the flat in Arlington House.

'He's written something too. What does it say? Pinch out,' said Cupidi.

Ferriter peered in towards the screen. 'Oh, the little bastard.' She held up the device. Under Ferriter's face was the word 'stupid'. 'That little weirdo,' complained Ferriter. 'Who does he think he is?'

Cupidi took the phone to look more closely at the drawing of herself. 'You're just stupid. I'm a pervert apparently,' said Cupidi. Under the sketch, the word 'pervert'.

'I'll wring his neck. He's an arrogant little git.'

'You photographed every page?' said Cupidi, scrolling through her photo folder.

Five pages were given over to a timeline. The day he had first noticed a smell in the art gallery was on a section labelled 'Day One'. There were all sorts of other scribbles on the page. 'Missing girl aged five or six. Man said "Like meat, horrible".' There were dozens of other notes too, but many too small to read.

Cupidi peered at the screen. 'Listen to this. "Young police-woman. Very sexy. Wearing Jo Malone perfume but breath smells of stale alcohol".'

'Oh my God. I do wear Jo Malone.'

'And your breath?'

'It was last Saturday.'

She read again: '*Gods and auspicious animals*. That was what was written on the plinth of the artwork, wasn't it? He noticed all this stuff. I want to get this blown up.'

She held up the phone. In amongst it all was a small drawing of a middle-aged man. Ross's style was simple. He used a few lines of ink, hatching carefully for shading. The face looked familiar to Cupidi but she couldn't place it.

That afternoon she called up Devon King, the constable who had been with the Met's Art and Antiquities Unit. 'I've emailed you all the transactions we can find on Abir Stein's account. Will you have time to look at them?'

'These things can take weeks to go through, you know.'

'By Saturday, then?'

'It's easier if you know what you're looking for.'

'Big suspicious chunks of money. I want to know about what's going to and from the Foundation from his account.'

'You think this is about a deal that's gone wrong?'

'Honestly? I don't know.'

'I can't promise anything.'

Ferriter was standing by her desk, holding her phone again. 'Look.' She held up the biro drawing of the man that Cupidi had thought she recognised. 'That's Abir Stein, isn't it? Clough told us he hadn't met him.'

She was right. That's who it was.

'It's a drawing,' said Cupidi cautiously. 'It doesn't prove anything.'

But there was that feeling in her stomach again. The sense of getting close to something dark.

THIRTY-FIVE

'Oh my God,' said Ferriter. 'This is it?'

'Yes.'

She had done her lipstick two minutes ago. 'Oh my God. I mean . . .' Ferriter leaned her head to one side, quizzically.

'What?'

Ferriter and Cupidi were standing on the Dungeness shingle in front of Astrid Miller's small shack, by the old front door. A humble-looking wooden shack a little to the north of the old lighthouse, covered in thick layers of paint that had been chipped and repainted over the years.

Ferriter looked gutted. 'I just mean . . . it's not what I expected. I mean, he's a multi-squillionaire. She could afford one of those really cool ones with the big glass windows and the hot tubs. But I suppose she was never into that kind of superficial stuff.'

'Go on,' said Cupidi. 'Ring the bell.'

'She was always deeper than that. Political, you know? Not

shy about telling journalists what she thought. You sure she's in there?'

'Someone was last night.' Cupidi stepped up and pressed the bell. Nobody answered. 'At least, I thought so.'

'Maybe we should leave it.'

Cupidi walked round to the other side of the cottage, the side that faced the sea, and tried to remember how the fabric had hung in the big window. Had that gentle fold of material been like that last night? Or was it just a trick of the light that made her think it was different?

She rapped on the glass with her knuckle. Again, nothing.

Heading back to the front of the house, she paused at the side. There was that new lock-up built on the side. Though it was bolted, there was no padlock. Cupidi drew back the bolt and looked inside, and saw it was a store for the property's green bin. Beyond it, an old door which must lead into the old cottage. The collection around here was on Mondays. She opened the bin and peered in. Neatly wrapped, three small bags. She leaned in and pulled one out. Through the thin black plastic she could see the rubbish it contained: an empty box of fishfingers, a milk carton, cardboard toilet paper tubes. Nothing particularly out of the ordinary. She poked a hole in the bag to read the use-by date on the milk carton. *20 April*. It was fresh. She dropped the rubbish back inside the bin and bolted the door again.

She pulled out her mobile, found Astrid Miller's phone number and called it. The moment it started to ring, she pressed her head against the walls of the summer house.

Clearly, unmistakably, a tiny tremble shook the wood. The vibration stopped as soon as the message kicked in.

She texted: **Hi Astrid. I know you're in there. I am a police officer. I just need to talk about Abir Stein.**

She went to the glass door at the front, knocked and waited.

A hand pulled back the curtain, revealing a woman dressed in a polka-dot shirt and a pair of khaki trousers, looking back at Cupidi and Ferriter.

'It's bloody her,' whispered Ferriter. 'Oh my bloody God.'

Behind her, the wooden room was painted bright, vibrant yellow. An open book sat on a black table in front of a white sofa that looked like it had been slept on, a bright red woollen blanket lying rumpled near it. A bookshelf was full of large books, some with scraps of paper poking out of the pages. On the floor lay lines of flints taken from the beach. The pale white and brown stones were arranged in long curving patterns that snaked into curls and circles, as if they belonged to some strange ritual.

'Go away,' the woman called through the glass, hands on slightly cocked hips. There was always something a little absurd about seeing famous people in ordinary places; like hearing an English word suddenly spoken in the middle of a foreigner's conversation.

'We need to talk.' Cupidi held up her police warrant card.

She squinted. 'Did Evert send you?'

'No.'

She put the key into the door and turned it, pushed the door open. 'You don't look like coppers.'

'Thanks,' said Ferriter, with a giggle.

Even un-made-up, with her hair messed, older than she was in the photos, Astrid Miller was unmistakably beautiful. Straight-backed, broad-shouldered, fine-boned, she stood looking defiantly back at them. 'It's about the arm, then, is it?'

'I left messages on your phone. You've not been answering them.'

Astrid Miller took a step backwards. 'I'm on a digital detox. I'm here for privacy, so I'd appreciate if you have something to say, please say it. Tell me, did you find out whose arm it was?'

'Not yet. Do you have anything you want to tell us about it?'

The woman looked surprised. 'Why on earth would I?'

'Or any theories about how an arm got into an artwork of yours?'

'Of course not. I mean, the whole thing is nuts, isn't it?'

'May we come in?'

Astrid Miller breathed in, then out, and took a step backwards. Cupidi moved cautiously into the room, stepping over a line of the stones. 'To be honest, we're struggling to understand it ourselves.'

Astrid laughed darkly. 'Please don't look to me for help. Right now, I have my own concerns.'

'Which are . . . ?'

'. . . none of your business.'

'But you must have wondered why someone put an arm in something you owned.'

'Of course I have. But I don't know why. I really don't.' She looked at Cupidi warily.

'I talked to your husband. He said he doesn't know where you are.'

She laughed again, more hollowly this time. 'Did he really? Well, it wouldn't have been hard for him to find out. Well, would it? After all, you could find me. He knows exactly where I am. You'd do better asking why he doesn't want you to talk to me.'

'Why would he want that?'

Astrid sat down on the big white couch, leaving them standing, Ferriter a pace behind Cupidi, unusually silent. 'You met Evert, didn't you?'

'Yes.'

'Well? Didn't you spot it?'

'Spot what?'

'That he is a total control freak. Everybody knows that.'

Cupidi thought back to the brief time she had spent in Evert's company. How much of his charm had been a facade? 'There's something wrong with your marriage?'

'I sincerely hope that's not what you're here to talk about.'

'I'm just trying to find out why somebody put an arm in an artwork that belongs to your foundation.'

'And so am I.'

Cupidi looked around the room at the lines of stones and tried to see some kind of logic in them.

'Those are just stones.' Miller seemed to have read her thoughts. 'I've been keeping myself to myself in the day. At night I wander on the beach. *Pick up Anything at Your Feet*. Do you know that?'

'Sorry?'

She leaned down and picked up a flint. 'It was an artwork in the sixties by a man called Ben Vautier. He was part of Fluxus, with Yoko Ono. The work was just an instruction. I find it comforting. *Pick up Anything at Your Feet*. Round here it's just stones. So . . . I pick them up, you see?' Astrid held the stone and smiled. 'I just come here to be on my own, to think. To refresh myself. To be honest with myself.'

'And have you come to any conclusions?'

'We do have enemies, obviously, Evert and I. Evert thought at first it was an attempt to undermine the credibility of our fund.'

'Did he? He didn't mention that to me.'

'Because mentioning it to you would be tantamount to admitting it might be true.'

'How much have you invested in it?'

She turned one corner of her mouth into a smile; the other stayed where it was. 'Evert wouldn't want me to tell you that.'

'A lot?'

'As long as you don't need to liquidate assets in a hurry, art is a good place to leave your spare cash. Evert is a very, very rich man. He likes to be tax-efficient.'

'So if the reputation of the fund was to drop, you could lose a great deal of money?'

'Buckets,' she said.

'So what if someone is trying to undermine its value?'

'Well, that would be interesting, wouldn't it? The value of that piece might rise, through notoriety, obviously, but it does our reputation no good, and the overall value of the fund would take a hit. It hasn't though, yet, I promise you. The opposite, in fact.'

'Does Evert have many enemies?'

'Oh, please. What do you think?'

'I asked him about that. He gave the impression that he hadn't thought a great deal about it.'

This time a small laugh bubbled out of Astrid. 'Of course he did. He would hate you to think he was obsessed by that kind of thing. Men like Evert don't like to show weakness.'

'So you think it's possible that this is something done to attack the art fund?'

'Obviously it's possible.'

Cupidi looked around the shack. 'So you come here a lot?' she asked.

'I don't like to advertise my presence here. It's surprisingly easy to remain anonymous in Dungeness. The people who've always been round here respect each other's privacy. The new people, the ones with all the money . . . they are barely here anyway, so they don't know who else is here.'

She didn't have any problem calling other people 'the ones with all the money', Cupidi noticed.

'I've had this place for years. From back when they were cheap and only a few artists were interested. Before I met Evert. When we married, I insisted it stayed in my name. It was part of our prenuptial agreement.'

'If the fund is an investment vehicle for your husband, what's in it for you?'

'You're very direct, aren't you? The frustrating thing about being a rich man's wife is that people immediately assume you have no brain of your own. I hadn't expected that. All this was a world I was interested in before I met Evert. I resent the idea that it's my plaything.'

'That's not what I meant,' said Cupidi.

'It sounded very much like what you meant.'

'If someone did want to somehow lower the value of the art fund, why would they be doing it?' asked Cupidi.

Astrid rubbed the back of her neck, rolled her head around as if she was stiff. She took a minute answering. 'The better question to ask would be, if someone wanted to lower the value of our art fund, would they do it like that? I'd estimate the potential sale price of *Funerary Urn* has probably doubled since it started appearing in national newspapers. If anything, we're ahead on this at the moment, though that might change, I suppose, if they do something else to attack us. Do you mind closing the door? I really don't like people knowing when I'm here.'

Ferriter, who'd been standing with a grin on her face through most of the conversation, sprang into action.

'The value has increased. I should regard you as a suspect then,' said Cupidi.

Astrid smiled. 'I expect you already do. That's how you work, isn't it?' She stretched her arms, then relaxed again. 'You live here, don't you?'

'How did you know?'

'I recognise you. You have a girl. A teenager. She used to be out here on the beach all the time.'

Cupidi was unsettled by this; she had never seen Astrid before in her life, and she was supposed to be the observant one. Astrid must have picked up on that, because she smiled again and said, 'See? Most people don't like it when their privacy is invaded. Why should I be any different, just because of who I am? We're all the same, us women.'

'Yes,' said Ferriter.

'Do you know where Abir Stein is?' Cupidi asked.

Astrid looked up sharply. 'No. Do you?'

Cupidi shook her head. 'He doesn't appear to have been in his flat for several weeks.'

'I know. I've been trying to call him.'

'Has he emailed you? Zoya Gubenko says he's replied to her on a couple of occasions.'

She frowned. 'Has he? I've had nothing at all from him.'

'He seems to have left his flat in a hurry.'

'You've been to his place?'

'We searched it yesterday. His passport was there, but he wasn't.'

Astrid chewed on her lip. 'I was in touch with him pretty much on a weekly basis until about three weeks ago but I've not managed to reach him since then.'

'Why didn't you tell anyone?'

'On one level, it's not that unusual for him to disappear for a while. He has fingers in pies. It's not just us he works for.'

'What kind of pies?'

Astrid Miller looked at her sharply. 'What do you mean?'

'Do you trust him?'

'The art world is full of gossip and backbiting, much like fashion. I know a bit about them both. If you go around asking, you'll hear a lot about Abbie. But you'll never meet a more knowledgeable, passionate man.' She turned her head away; picked a book off the shelf and started leafing through the pages. 'You know what? If he hadn't agreed to work with us, this art fund would never have been as important as it turned out to be. I've been involved in art most of my life, and I thought I knew a lot. He's taught me so much, though.'

'Did you ever meet the other people he works for?'

'Of course I did.'

'Do you think he could have got himself mixed up in some-thing . . . serious?'

275

'Yes. Obviously. Art is about honesty, but it's also about money because of people like us – the patrons. And money is never about honesty. But if he has got mixed up in something like that, it would only be because of his passion. Abir Stein is not . . .' She tailed off.

'Is not what?'

'Whatever you hear, Abir Stein is an honourable man. He cares about truth too much. That's why he is so good at under-standing art. Good art is about honesty.'

'Is it?'

'The British think it's all a scam. That artists are laughing behind our backs, getting one over on them. You hear it in the sneer of the reviewers. But they're wrong. Artists are truth-tellers. It's what attracts me to it.'

She dropped from the sofa into a kneeling position and started gathering up the stones, one by one, putting them in a fresh pile.

'You have no idea where Mr Stein is?'

'No.'

'Does that worry you? Because it's starting to worry me.'

On her hands and knees, she followed a line of the pebbles, picking them up. 'Of course it worries me.'

She thought about what the constable from the Met's Art Unit had told her. As far as she had been concerned, Abir Stein was almost certainly handling other people's money.

Astrid Miller sat back down on the sofa. 'You think it's his arm?'

'I can't be sure. Yet.'

There was a tremble to her voice when she said, 'I sincerely hope you're wrong.'

'Do you know anyone who had a key to his flat?'

'No. Why?'

Cupidi ignored the question. 'I need to get an idea of how the Foundation works, and what his role was in it.'

She sighed. 'Sometimes I would find work – or come across an artist. Sometimes it would be Abir. Abbie was better at discovering pieces by established practitioners that might become valuable. My interest was always more in emerging artists.'

'What about your husband?'

'He isn't interested in that side. He's just the money man.'

'So once you'd find an artist, Evert would do the deal?'

'With Abir, yes. Evert doesn't have a clue how to talk to gallerists, still less the artists themselves. It's not his world. But together, Abir and Evert take care of that. I was less interested in the money, except, of course, for the fact that we were able to return some of it to our artists. If we made a profit, they got it back.'

Ferriter finally spoke. 'Excuse me. I was wondering, have you heard of an artist called Ross Clough?'

She looked at Ferriter as if she had forgotten she was there, then thought for a while. 'No. Is he new?'

'No. He's quite young. He's not established. He lives in Margate and—'

'Oh, God. If it's who I think it is . . . Kind of pale. Tall-ish. Not a real artist. A bit full of himself.'

Ferriter nodded. 'Yes.'

'Talks with a smile on his face, like he knows something?'

Ferriter's laugh was high-pitched. 'Oh God. That's him, exactly.'

She addressed Ferriter directly. 'He's a stalker,' she said. 'He stalked me, as a matter of fact.'

Ferriter looked at Cupidi. Her face said: *See? Told you so.*

277

THIRTY-SIX

'He drew nude pictures of me. He sent them to me via email.'

'Creep,' said Ferriter.

'Yes. After I'd turned him down – as an artist, obviously. As a way of trying to attract my attention, it's the artistic equivalent of a dick pic. He also does awful sculptures. Contemporary tape-art and mixed materials . . . he's a quasi Thomas Hirschhorn rip-off.'

Ferriter looked baffled.

'Hard to explain. Hirschhorn's very good, very influential. Creates these hyper-saturated installations that are like accretions of his research. He works collaboratively with local communities. This guy doorstepped me once. Came to our house at Long Hill with photographs of his work to try and persuade me to buy it.'

Again, Cupidi and Ferriter exchanged a glance.

'He's been there before?'

'What? Why?'

Ferriter said, 'He was there this morning. Your security man found him on the premises.'

'Really? Mulligan found him on our land?' She looked unsettled.

'It must happen to you loads and loads. Artists wanting to show you their stuff . . .'

'Never, actually,' Astrid Miller answered. 'Real artists understand the system. That's not how it works. Really. That freak literally turned up out of the blue.'

Cupidi interrupted. 'But you agreed to meet him?'

'I'm a sucker for artists, in case you haven't noticed. I don't want to miss anyone who might have something to say. He had gone to the effort of finding me. So yes, I gave him a little time. He came to our office with his portfolio and took out all these photographs of his work. Screeds of it. I had to tell him to leave. It was rubbish.' Astrid Miller's mouth dropped. 'Is he involved in this?'

'Again. We can't say.' But Cupidi made a mental note; Clough had not mentioned that he had been to the Millers' estate previously.

'Oh God. It would make sense. He was such a misogynist. He seemed utterly self-obsessed, convinced of his own worth. People like that are of no interest to me.'

'I thought all artists were self-obsessed and convinced of their own worth,' said Ferriter, trying to make a joke.

'How very English of you.'

'No. I like art. I love it.' Ferriter looked stung.

'I'm being mean. And a total snob.' She smiled at Ferriter for the first time. 'And if there's anything I hate, it's art snobs.'

'Me too,' said Ferriter.

Cupidi interrupted again. 'You gave him the time of day, though?'

'Of course. You can't hurry these things. You have to be patient and try and understand them. To allow it to speak to you. But really, his work has nothing to say except ego, ego, ego. He has a crippling sense of male entitlement.'

'Yeah,' said Ferriter.

'Are you done? I'm very tired. I usually sleep now. I don't want to be rude . . .'

'Will you be at Dungeness for long?' Cupidi asked.

'Is this the police telling me I need to stay in touch?'

At the open door, back to the wide beach, Ferriter paused and said, 'One thing I meant to say . . .'

Astrid Miller frowned. She had said she was tired. She wanted these people out of her space now. 'What?'

'Just . . .' Jill Ferriter coloured a little. 'I really wanted to say . . . thanks.'

'What for?'

'All that stuff you used to say about women being whoever they wanted to and not giving a crap, you know. When you were a model. In interviews.'

'I was young and very gobby.'

'When I was growing up . . . I had it pretty rough when I was younger. It meant a lot to me.'

The frown turned into a soft smile. 'Really?'

'Me and loads of girls. Yeah. Big fan.'

Cupidi stood between them, looking from one to the other, feeling that she was somehow in the way. 'Did you get to where you wanted?' asked the millionaire.

'Still going through some serious bloody crap now.' Ferriter's smile was thin and brittle.

'Me too.' Astrid Miller's face softened. 'Is there a man involved?'

'Not like that, but yeah. Kind of. And whatever you're going through . . . I just want you to know that you helped me through a lot, you know?'

'The main thing is that you should never let them stop you doing whatever it is you want to do,' said Astrid Miller. 'Fuck them all. That's what I used to say.' She looked directly at Cupidi. 'Still do as a matter of fact.'

Outside, Ferriter cupped her hands over her mouth and said, 'God I am so embarrassed. Did I make an absolute gold-plated tit of myself?'

'Gold-plated. It was kind of sweet though.'

'When I stopped at the door, I was just going to ask her for a selfie, but I couldn't. I bottled it. So I just sort of blurted that other stuff instead. I can feel myself blushing now. It was like I was at confessional. You can probably see the glow for miles.'

'Better than a selfie,' said Cupidi.

Ferriter frowned. 'A selfie would have been brilliant. Nobody's ever going to believe me when I tell them I was with her. For like, ages. Want me to drop you home?'

'No. It's not far.'

'When Astrid Theroux was twenty-five she was on magazine covers all around the world. She was being photographed by Mario Testino and Rankin. Bet she didn't get drunk in a shit wine bar in Ashford and end up in bed with a loser who lives with his mother. You'll come out with us, won't you, on my birthday tomorrow? Stop me doing something stupid again.'

Cupidi took her time walking back home.

Astrid Miller, Ferriter's idol, had charmed Ferriter, but she had been lying. She had been avoiding them. Her phone had been on, for all the talk of a digital detox. Because the Millers' marriage was in trouble? Possibly. Evert had gone out of his way to conceal that too. It wasn't just Evert Miller who liked to be in control; Astrid was the same.

The spring air had gone cold. Out at sea, a fog bank was forming out over the Channel, blocking the horizon. The greyness seemed to suck the spring light out of the sky. She took the long route home, along the steep bank of stones that dropped towards the sea.

The fog-horn started just as she was drifting off to sleep; a low blast, repeated three times every minute. She had always found sleep impossible when the horn was sounding. It made such a lonely sound out here on the edge of the land. She lay awake, unable to sleep, but also unable to think clearly about what it was that was bothering her. When she last looked at the clock it was six in the morning.

Next thing, Cupidi's daughter was shaking her. 'Mum!' When she opened her eyes, Zoë was beside her bed, holding her mobile phone.

'I'm awake,' she mumbled.

'Your phone has been going off.'

'What's the time?'

'Gone eight.'

She groaned, took the phone and looked at it. A London number.

'Sergeant Cupidi?' It was the pathology laboratory. 'Well,' said the voice. 'At least we know who that arm belonged to now.' She knew immediately what they were going to say.

'Tell me.'

It was now, finally, a conventional murder inquiry, with a real victim.

THIRTY-SEVEN

The arm was definitely Abir Stein's. This morning's email had brought more news. Crime Scene Investigators had found traces of blood throughout Abir Stein's flat. Somebody had cleaned the place well, but you could always find it. There had been traces in the piping too, in the U-bend beneath the bath in which, almost certainly, Stein had been dismembered.

Though she was late, Cupidi paused on the way to work, parking by Astrid Miller's cottage. It looked deserted just as it had before. She got out, rang the bell, knocked on the door. There was no answer, so she walked round to the seaward side and banged on the window.

'Astrid. It's me. Alex Cupidi. I need to talk. I've had some bad news.'

Still no answer.

'Astrid. This is important.'

She tugged on the back door. It was locked.

She opened the side lean-to again and pulled out the bin.

Behind it was an old kitchen door. The frame was old, the lock was loose.

'Astrid?'

She leaned against the door and it gave way easily.

'Astrid. It's just—'

The air was filled with loud noise.

'Shit.'

She had triggered an alarm, a ululating electronic squeal that pulsed so hard that her ears hurt. Hands clamped against the side of her head, she went to inspect the alarm box.

It was just inside the front door. She took the number of the company that operated it and made her way outside the building. It seemed only marginally quieter there.

'Shit, shit, shit.'

A man emerged from a nearby cabin, looking towards her, concerned.

'It's OK. Police,' she shouted, above the noise.

The man didn't budge, stood looking at her, still suspicious. She stepped far enough away to be able to make a call without her voice being drowned out and called the alarm firm.

'There's a response vehicle already on its way,' someone told her.

'How long will it take?'

'He'll be with you in forty minutes. We have to ask you to remain on the site until the vehicle arrives.'

'Forty minutes? I have to be at work.'

The man apologised. Ended the call.

The alarm was deafening. Pretty much anyone who still lived on the beach had come by, some faces Cupidi recognised, some openly hostile about the day's peace being destroyed. When it stopped after twenty minutes, the silence it left seemed at first huge, until the quiet crackle of sea on the stones reasserted itself. Eventually a Prius pulled up next to her old Micra. A man in his forties got out, looked her up and down. 'You the one that triggered the alarm?' he said.

She got up off the front step of the shack, where she had been sitting.

'Name?'

'Detective Sergeant Alexandra Cupidi.'

The man raised his eyebrows.

'I was asked to remain on the premises till you arrived and secured the building, and being a good public citizen, I did.'

The man looked sceptical. He was fit-looking, the kind of man who spent time in a gym, but not out of vanity. 'What were you doing, breaking in, as a good public citizen?'

'I'm a police officer. I was trying to contact the owner. Can I go now? I'm due at work.'

'Did you have a warrant to enter the premises?'

'No. I did not.'

'Oh dear,' said the man. 'You are supposed to have the paper-work to do that sort of thing. I know. I was a police officer myself.'

'Of course you were.'

'Don't look like that, love.' He smiled. 'I was like you once. You're looking at your future.'

'Don't be bitter.'

'On my wages? Why would I be bitter?'

'You work for the Millers?'

285

'I'm their head of security.' He pulled out a card. She looked at it. Allan Mulligan.

'What force were you with?'

'Same one as you. Kent's finest. Don't recognise you though.'

'I'm still sort of new round here,' said Cupidi.

'What did you want with Astrid?'

Cupidi was cautious about what she wanted to share. 'I'm a neighbour. I was looking in on her. Do you know where she is?'

He shook his head. 'Even if I did, which I don't, why would I tell you?'

'Did you just drive from Long Hill?'

'What of it?'

'Couldn't you just get some local security firm to handle it? There are plenty of them.'

'You wouldn't have the pleasure of my company if we did.' Mulligan smiled. 'I'll obviously need to report this. Mr Miller values his privacy.'

'So all this is Mr Miller's doing? I thought this was Astrid Miller's place. Or does he want to keep a special eye on her?'

He went to his boot, opened it and pulled out some tools. 'You wouldn't really expect me to answer that, would you, Sergeant?'

'Where is she then? Astrid Miller?'

'Haven't the foggiest,' he said.

'She was here last night. I came to see her, then she seems to have vanished. I specifically asked her to stay in touch with me.'

'I'll pass on your request.'

'Of course you will. Is everything all right between Astrid Miller and her husband?'

He stood with a hammer in one hand. 'I'll be telling Mr Miller you were asking personal questions too.'

Great, thought Cupidi, smiling, unwilling to give Allan Mulligan the pleasure of knowing how much that would annoy her boss. Though being a former policeman, he probably knew that already.

'Happy birthday, Jill,' said Peter Moon, holding out a card and a bunch of supermarket daffodils.

'Oh shit.' Cupidi had meant to pick something up on the way in.

'Drink still on tonight?' asked Moon brightly.

Ferriter looked at him. 'Maybe. I might not bother.'

'But it's your birthday.'

'Exactly,' said Ferriter grimly.

'Oh, come on,' chided Moon. 'Celebrate good times.'

He looked from Cupidi to Ferriter and back again. 'It's like, every time I come close you two are in this huddle.' They were both staring at Ferriter's computer screen. 'What are you looking at?'

Ferriter had pulled up the photos she had taken of the drawings in Ross Clough's notebooks.

'Oh, whoever stabbed Frank Khan,' said Cupidi, 'if it's those two lads involved, it's not England Rising. Think about it. One of them's black for a start.'

'How do you figure that?' asked Ferriter.

'Turns out I know an expert on far-right groups.'

'It was just a line of enquiry,' said Moon defensively. He leaned in closer to Ferriter's screen, spotted the drawing of her.

'Hey! That's you. You're way better-looking than that, though, Jill.'

Cupidi could feel Ferriter tense.

'What's that written underneath?'

Ferriter pressed the sleep button. The screen went black before he could read the word 'stupid'.

'Right. So. See you down the wine bar later, Jill.'

'Mm.'

'What happened to "fuck them all"?' said Cupidi, when Moon was far enough away.

Ferriter chewed on her lip and, after a minute said, 'Know what? I'm bloody fine. And I'm not stupid.'

'Course you're not,' said Cupidi.

'Whatever this creep says,' she said, bringing up the photo of Ross Clough's drawing once more, 'he's the one who's stupid.'

Cupidi looked at the photos again. The scrawl of the word under her name.

She now examined the sketch closely. 'Maybe he's not so stupid after all.'

'What?'

'Ross may be weird, but he's recording everything he sees, everything that he hears.'

'What?'

'You said the whole monkey-fist thing was stupid, yes? That's why he wrote "stupid". Because you'd called him stupid, not the other way around.'

'You never called him a pervert though.'

Cupidi thought for a minute. 'I said he was potentially guilty of perverting the course of justice.'

Ferriter looked at the photo. 'How do you remember all that?'

'That's what we're supposed to do, Constable. Notice things. Remember them.'

'I barely noticed that Laughing Boy was in my bloody bed last week . . .'

'Enough. Stop beating yourself up.'

Cupidi clicked the mouse, looking at the screen shots of the pages of Ross Clough's notebooks, looking forwards, backwards and forwards again. She noticed the drawing of the man she thought she had recognised. She zoomed in as close as she could before the small drawing started to pixillate.

From the other side of the room, Moon called, 'Teenage boy. Afro-Caribbean. Spotted on Joyce Green Lane. That's just by Central Road again. On his own. Anyone spare to come with me?'

'I don't want to be that person. The woman who gets drunk and gets taken advantage off,' Ferriter was saying. Cupidi looked at her.

'Anyone?' called Moon.

'I mean, I was drunk so it was my fault too.'

'You know that's not true.'

She smiled thinly. 'Fuck him. You know what? Happy bloody birthday to me. What Astrid Miller said. Fuck them all.' She stood and called out. 'I'll go with you, Sarge.'

Simultaneously, Cupidi and Moon said, 'You sure?'

But she was already on her way out of the door, her face hard.

Now Ferriter had left, a big birthday card dropped onto Cupidi's desk with a post-it note on it: *You're the last to sign it. Don't forget to bring it along to the party tonight xxx*. Cupidi pulled it out of the envelope. On the front it read 'AGE IS JUST A NUMBER'; inside 'IN YOUR CASE A PRETTY BLOODY BIG ONE'. And dozens of handwritten messages: 'Go girl xxx'. 'We love you Ferret x'. 'Don't get too pissed tonite LOL, gorgeous xxxx'.

She realised someone was standing behind her and shoved it hastily back under the mat and turned.

'Only me,' said McAdam. 'And I've already signed it.' He stood, arms behind his back, awkwardly official. 'We've just received a complaint from Evert Miller's lawyer about you, Alex.'

'*Quelle surprise.*'

'Apparently Ross Clough isn't the only person who has been trespassing on his property. Is that true?'

'I just knocked on the door of Astrid Miller's bungalow and it kind of opened.'

'So it is true.'

'It was just a nudge.'

'So you were on his property?'

'Her property. Yes, but—'

'Without a warrant.' A statement, not a question.

'It was just a simple mistake. You know how he knew I was there? Evert Miller has had his own private security man keeping watch over her, a man called Allan Mulligan. Used to be on the force here. Did you know him?'

McAdam sat on the edge of her desk. 'Mulligan? Yes. Retired about five years ago. Is that what he's doing now?'

'You think he's still in touch with other officers here?'

'Of course he would be.'

'I think he's feeding back details of our case to Evert Miller somehow. He says he's keeping tabs on us.'

She handed him the pathology report on Abir Stein's arm. 'We've got to get forensics down to their art storage facility. From what we know of the timeline, it's where the arm must have been placed into the jar. Whoever put it there signed in as Abir Stein. But CCTV from EastArt shows a man with the usual complement of arms, so we know it can't have been him.'

McAdam's eyes were scanning the report. 'Do you see his face? The man on the CCTV?'

'Of course not. He knows what he's doing, this man. Whoever it was who signed in wore a wide-brimmed hat. Like a homburg. We'll need permission to access the EastArt archive. We need to get a forensic team in there. Because I'm pretty sure whoever put the arm in there is the person who killed Stein. And from his modus operandi, the person who attacked me and Ferriter too. You coming tonight, sir? Jill's birthday?'

'I should, shouldn't I?' He looked up. 'Why is Miller that interested?'

'Exactly,' she said, digging out car keys and standing.

THIRTY-EIGHT

The sky was darkening by the time she arrived in Margate.

Ross Clough was at home. He opened the door, looking surprised. 'You sure you want to come in?' he said.

'I want another look at your room,' she said.

'Finally. A fan,' he said archly. 'It means so much to me. Where's your delicious companion?'

'She has other work.'

'Shame.'

Pulling her phone from her pocket she swiped the screen until she reached a photo of a page from Ross Clough's notebook. 'Who is this a drawing of?'

'That's my notebook.'

'Correct.'

'You photographed that without my permission.'

'Who is it?'

Ross squinted at the screen. 'You know who it is. Abir Stein.'

'But you told us you had never met him.'

'It's a drawing.'

'I'm aware of that.'

'I could have copied it from a photograph.'

'Did you?'

'What do you think?'

Without being asked, she sat down on an armchair. 'Astrid Miller said she saw nothing in your work apart from a desperation to be adored.'

Ross Clough flinched. It was as if her words had been solid and had struck him in the face. 'She clearly knows nothing at all about real art.'

'She said your work was all ego and no substance.'

'She said that?' He looked stung.

'Did you meet Abir Stein?'

'The art establishment closes ranks. If you're on the outside you're never going to get in by the usual means. You have to find other ways to make it. I've figured it out now. You need powerful people on your side. No. I never met Abir Stein. He wouldn't meet me. Doubtless Astrid Miller had poisoned my reputation already.'

'You never told us you'd been to the Millers' estate before.'

'Yes. It didn't go as well as I hoped, obviously.'

'But you went back for more.'

'Because this is my big break. This time I'm really getting somewhere. I've figured out how to do it, to get people on your side. I'm making an exhibition. I was thinking of calling it "Abir Stein's Right Arm". It is the right arm, isn't it?'

The path lab results had only arrived this morning. It hadn't been made public yet.

'Oh come on,' he said. 'I figured that out ages ago. I even told you about it. He hasn't been seen for weeks.'

She said, 'Your notebooks are interesting.'

He looked surprised. 'Really?'

'You've been following the case, haven't you?'

'This is the one that's going to make them notice, finally. Nobody's ever done an artwork like this.'

'You've been recording it all. That's why you went to Long Hill. You were just teasing us. You wouldn't have minded if we had arrested you at all, would you? It might even add a bit of notoriety to your artwork.'

'All publicity is good publicity.'

'I want to look at everything you've done.'

He looked at her for a while. 'If I help you, will you help me?'

'That's not really how it works, Ross.'

When she stepped into the small room, Astrid was still there, one-armed.

'You like to see her mutilated, like that?'

'She's one of these super-rich people who run the art world,' he said as she looked at the sculpture. 'They have great power. Their taste dominates everywhere. Everybody sucks up to them. We need to see a total revolution in the art world.'

'Because she didn't like your work?'

'Very funny. She didn't understand it. How could she? She lives in her nice, pretty little world where everything is perfect. Or so she thinks.'

'What do you mean by that?'

'Oh. Her and her perfect relationship with her perfect million-aire husband. It's not exactly perfect, is it?'

'How do you know?'

'Oh please,' he said. 'That's obvious too, isn't it?'

'You said you were confident that this time you were getting somewhere. Why's that?'

'Because this is good art.'

'But you said that wasn't enough. You needed powerful people on your side. Which powerful people?'

He smiled. 'I just have a hunch, that's all.'

'About what?'

'That powerful people are going to be a little more interested in investing in me.'

'Why?'

'That's not really how it works, is it, Sergeant?' he mocked.

'Do you mind if I take photographs?'

'You're actually asking this time?' He waved his arms around the room. 'Go ahead. Document. Document.'

Cupidi stared hard at the walls. What was it Astrid Miller had said? You have to take time to let the work speak to you.

The number of biro notes and sketches had increased since she had last looked. He had added a drawing of the Millers' house, made when he had been trespassing there, presumably. There was a naked woman too, crudely drawn. There was something lecherous about the lines, like the kind of masturbatory sketch you would find on the wall of a men's toilet. The drawings verged on the fantastical. And there was another of Abir Stein, this time the full body, naked, one-armed. Clough had drawn red blood flowing from the stump.

She photographed the room carefully. He didn't seem to mind.

'Why don't you stay for a drink? My landlord has sherry. He thinks I don't know where it is.'

'No thanks.'

He had also taken pins and red wool and made lines linking items to each other, as if in a kind of imitation of the fake murder boards they always had in TV crime shows. A track of the wool ended at the new sketch of Abir Stein.

He had put two sheets from a calendar on the wall. From various dates, lines of red wool ran, heading towards more drawings or newspaper clippings.

She followed each one. One led to a fuzzy drawing. She peered at it. There was something familiar about it, but she wasn't sure what it was. Two dark outlines, hunched.

She moved closer, photographed it.

And then the penny dropped. The two boys who had been present at the attempted murder of Frank Khan. The picture was of the CCTV photograph from the Co-op that Moon had shown them in the incident room: the obscure outline of two hoodies. Her skin prickled. It had nothing to do with her investigation, or his, surely?

She held her phone up to the drawing, pressed the red button.

'This one. Why is it here?' she asked.

'You tell me,' he said, smirking.

'If you know something that you're not telling me . . .'

'It's there because it is. Haven't you noticed?'

'What?'

'The connection.'

She shook her head slowly. 'What connection?'

'The dates. That was the day we discovered the arm. Two

296

boys rob a supermarket. The guard tries to catch them and gets killed in a road accident.'

She stared, trying to understand. 'But there's no link between the two incidents.'

'On one level, obviously not. But for me, there is a connection. My job as an artist is to see what it is.'

She looked around and the penny dropped. Everything was here. Like some fanatical religious convert who saw significance everywhere, for Ross, everything was connected. That was what this artwork was all about. How he saw himself as the centre of everything that had happened. By treating him as a suspect, they fed that ego.

He must have been trawling the local papers ever since the discovery of the arm.

'This one, see. I went there last week and drew that.'

Another biro drawing of what looked like piles of junk.

'I don't understand,' Cupidi said. 'You went where?'

'Where that drug dealer was shot,' said Ross. 'It was in the news. It's an amazing place. Old crap everywhere. Bits of cars piled up. It's like Armageddon.'

'You went there because . . .'

He waved his arms. 'Because it's all part of this.'

'And why do you think that is linked?'

'Because that man was shot on the Friday. The day before we found the arm.'

'Right. Because it happened the day before?'

'Yes,' he said, missing the scepticism in her voice.

Signal and noise; it was always her job to distinguish between the two. Ross seemed incapable of knowing what was signal

297

and what was noise. To him, they were twins, impossible to tell apart. What was that quote? *On Margate Sands. I can connect nothing with nothing.* Ross Clough connected everything with everything . . .

She took another photograph and turned, smiled. 'Thank you,' she said.

A red herring. Just random incidences.

'You're quite good-looking too. You know that?'

Cupidi didn't answer.

'For someone your age.'

Get out of this place, she told herself. She had wasted too much time here already. She was going to be late and she had promised to be at the wine bar. Two boys. Runaways, but what were they running away from? Go and have a drink with your colleagues. Friday night. Forget the trouble of the world.

The wine bar on Hythe Road was loud with the hubbub of chatter and music. However bad the local pubs were, Cupidi preferred them to the wine bars whose attempts to achieve cosmopolitanism seemed desperate.

Cupidi squeezed her way through to the table Ferriter was on and eventually found a free stool to sit on next to her. The constable had returned home and changed. She was wearing a short dress and a little lopsided smile. 'Where were you? You were supposed to be here to stop me getting drunk?'

'I missed that window of opportunity.'

'Long gone. Champagne?' she said, lifting a bottle from a bucket on the table in front of her.

'Get you.'

'People keep buying it.'

'Peter Moon got you one?'

'I made him fetch the most expensive. Fuck them all.'

Cupidi looked across the room. Moon was standing, leaning over one of the civilian staff, one arm against the wall that she was pinned against. A young data analyst whose name Cupidi didn't remember.

'You and Moon have any luck finding that lad?'

'By the time we got there he was long gone.'

'Well done, though. You did it. You worked alongside him.'

'Look at him, will you,' Ferriter said darkly. 'Cock.'

'Leave it alone for tonight, Jill. It's your birthday.'

'How was Clough?'

'He was . . . harmless. That's what he is. Harmless. I'm pretty sure we can cross him off our list.'

Ferriter made a face. 'Don't give me that.' She was looking at Peter Moon as she said the words. 'Go on. Have a glass.'

'I'm driving. And looking after you.'

'Oh go on. Catch a taxi back. Being sober in this lot is like being the only fully dressed person in a nudist camp.'

'I'm here to make sure you don't do anything you're going to regret.'

'I'm going to do nothing I regret.' Ferriter shot Cupidi a fierce look, then stood up abruptly and shouted, 'I bloody love this tune,' and began singing along to Justin Timberlake, pumping her arms out.

Another woman constable stood, too, and started to dance. A few people whooped and cheered.

'Go, birthday girl.'

'She's on a mission,' said a woman.

'She drink much before I got here?'

'We started back in the office.'

Arms raised, Jill Ferriter tossed her head from side to side, flicking hair across her face. Nobody danced in wine bars, but it was Ferriter's day, so they let her, and the staff had to put up with it because most of the crowd were police.

'You all right, Alex?' DI McAdam had the end of a pint of bitter in his hand. He would only be drinking to make the other officers feel comfortable. 'Tomorrow morning. Nine o'clock. EastArt. Somebody will let you in. There will be a forensics officer there. I took the opportunity to apologise to Evert Miller but assured him that you weren't trying to spy on his private life. He seemed to accept that. I also warned him that trying to spy on operational details of a case was not legal.'

'Thank you, sir. Appreciated.'

A power ballad came on and still Ferriter gyrated, even if there was not much rhythm to the tune. The other woman who'd been dancing with her drifted away and people turned their backs, leaving Ferriter on her own.

Wiping her mouth with a tissue, Cupidi picked up her untouched wine glass and walked over to Peter Moon. She asked, 'How's it going with the Michael Dillman murder?'

He looked round. 'What made you think of that?'

'Just something I'd seen.'

The young woman he'd been explaining something to took her chance. 'Just going to the loo,' she said.

'Well?' Cupidi said.

'Nothing. We've interviewed everyone with gang connections.

300

All of them swear blind they know nothing about it. But they would, wouldn't they?'

'You think they do know something about it?'

'You would have thought, wouldn't you? He was a little scumbag who stepped on someone's toes. We may never find out whose. That's what happens, in these parts.'

He was looking past her, already scanning the room for someone else to talk to.

'What about the two boys?'

'Drove around for an hour this afternoon. They've gone to ground again. Know how many kids around that age are in contact with social services in this area?'

She turned her back to watch Ferriter, who was swinging her hips from side to side now, head back, laughing. 'Turn the music up. It's my birthday.' As she spoke the words, Ferriter careered into a table, spilling drinks. 'Oops.'

She would give her five more minutes, then take her home.

Cupidi stepped outside onto the street. It was a cool evening. A group of people from Ashford nick were there, holding cigarettes. Cupidi stood close and breathed in the loose smoke.

'Any of you work with a man called Allan Mulligan?' she asked.

'Yeah.'

'See anything of him these days?'

'He's around. Comes out for a drink sometimes. Likes to talk about the old days.'

'He ever ask about what you're up to now?'

'Course. Can't be a copper all those years and not be interested.'

Through the glass, they all watched Ferriter dancing.

'She's a good girl,' said one of the older coppers. 'Nothing wrong with letting go, time to time. I used to know her mum.'

There were a few tuts.

'Didn't we all?' said another.

'Jill's mother?' Cupidi asked.

The coppers nodded. 'Don't say you heard it from us.'

'Why not?'

'Her mum was all right,' said one of the older men. 'Not like the young ones today. Just used to like a drink a bit.'

'And that.'

'She died, didn't she?'

'Yes. Few years back now. She just keeled over on the street.'

''Mazing really when you think of it, having a daughter like that.'

'There's nothing wrong with Jill Ferriter,' said Cupidi, defensively.

The man forced a cigarette into the outdoor ashtray to put it out. 'That's what I mean. Considering we all knew her mother.'

'Jill said her mother was an expert in criminal behaviour,' Cupidi said.

Everybody laughed hard at that. 'She's not wrong.' One of the coppers was crying, wiping tears from his eyes, he found it so funny.

'She wasn't in the police, then?'

Everybody still finding everything she said hilarious. 'Known to police, not in them.'

Two years on, she could still feel an outsider here. Cupidi looked back inside at the young policewoman, dancing. Even drunk she looked cool, so very sure of herself.

302

One of the older coppers, a constable, leaned closer to her. 'Her mother was a sex worker. Young Jill was in and out of care, everything. You didn't hear it from us, though. She got through a lot.'

Cupidi peered through the closed folding glass doors at her colleague. 'She always seems so perfect.'

'Yep. She is. Everyone's got a lot of respect for young Jill.'

The girl growing up, wanting to be Astrid Theroux; the woman disgusted at herself for having drunken sex with a policeman.

'She joined the police despite knowing that you all knew . . .'

'Yep.'

Cupidi had joined the police because both of her parents had been coppers; Ferriter had joined in spite of hers. How come she had never figured that out?

And then there was a cake with sparklers being walked across the room by one of the waitresses. 'We better go inside,' said Cupidi. Hesitantly at first, people were blundering into the tune of 'Happy Birthday' in several keys, gradually coming together as one by the time they sang Jill's name.

Ferriter leaned forward and puffed ineffectually at the candles. 'I'm so fucking old,' she said.

'And we got a card. Where's the card? Alex? Didn't you have the card?'

Shit. She had left it on her desk. 'One minute. I'll be back. Make sure she doesn't do anything daft.'

It was only five minutes to the nick and back. What could go wrong in that time?

★

She picked up a pen and wrote, '*Jill Ferriter. You are crazy cool xx*' then put the card in the envelope and walked into the darkness.

She could see the blue lights reflected in the shop windows before she even turned the corner.

'Oh shit.' She broke into a run.

A police car parked outside the wine bar; everyone out on the street around it. An officer was holding a bandage to Peter Moon's face. There was blood on his shirt.

'What happened?' she demanded, panting as she arrived, still clutching the unopened card.

'She punched him in the face, didn't she?'

And now an ambulance pulling up. A paramedic jumping down from the cab. Peter Moon was saying, 'I'm fine. It's nothing.'

'Who?'

'Jill. She just went batshit.'

'How's Peter?' someone was asking.

'Where is she?'

'She stormed off home.'

'He'll live.'

The party was over. People were drifting home.

'Going to have to report it, aren't they?' someone was saying.

She walked back to her car clutching the big pink envelope. As she buckled her seatbelt her phone buzzed. A text message: **Fuck them all**.

PART THREE

The Rattle of the Bones

THIRTY-NINE

At first Tap thought the shaking was just nerves. Frank had been stabbed, after all. To see the knife rise so smoothly into the depths of a man's body; to see the blood creep into the white of his shirt . . .

Tap felt so old. When he'd been younger, thirteen, fourteen, he'd seen a guy stuck with a knife. It had meant nothing to him back then. Now he was seventeen, it made him sick. Literally sick. He felt so cold. Everything was wrong. His whole body was starting to hurt; his eyeballs and his fingernails, everything. Walking from the flat, back towards their secret HQ, had felt like he was dragging a pallet of bricks behind him. The joints in his legs ached, Sloth pulling him on as he glanced over his shoulder for coppers.

Tumour. Paralysed.

Stumbling across the rough ground of the marsh was such an effort he felt like just lying on the damp earth and sleeping. And when he finally lay down, back in their hut by the old fireworks factory, teeth chattering, Sloth laid his hand on his head. 'You're burning up, bro.'

'Feel bloody freezing. He stabbed him in the gut, bro.'

'Frank may have been a creep but . . .'

'He tried to save us, Slo. Told us to run. Jesus. I'm scared, Slo. Why didn't you just tell him where we left the phone?'

'Your uncle Mikey gave him the other one and he still killed him. Weird stuff happening, bro.'

'Real scared.'

There was something curiously comforting about being back in their secret place. 'Don't be afraid, Tap. I'll mess that frickin' guy up if we see him again. Guy won't stand a chance.'

Playground threats, thought Tap.

'Comfy?' Sloth looked at him, anxiously.

'Kind of. OK if I rest a bit?'

'Want me to read you a bedtime story?'

'Bog off.'

'I'll keep a lookout, mate. Scout around.'

Sloth disappeared; Tap lay on the hard ground, trembling, drifting in and out of sleep.

At one point he thought he heard voices; men laughing. Was it the same day or the next? He wasn't sure. He wasn't sure either whether he had dreamed them, or whether it was the noise of fishermen from the riverbank. It was so flat around here, sound travelled. What was far away sounded close. There was a big old guy they'd seen a couple of times, tramping up the path by the creek.

Next time he woke, he tried to open his eyes, but couldn't.

They were crusted in weird gunk. He prised them apart, blinking in brightness, looking for Sloth.

How long had he been gone? Hours? It was impossible to tell.

It was practically dark when Sloth returned. 'Get in that.'

He threw something dark at Tap. Tap tried to focus on it, to ask what it was, but his throat had swollen. His neck felt huge. Sloth was untying his trainers, gently tugging them from his feet.

'Jesus. Your socks,' he complained. 'They're bad.'

Then he was yanking whatever he had brought back with him over Tap's trousers. A sleeping bag, Tap realised. Right then, it felt like luxury. Where had he got that from? Nicked it, most certainly. Where from?

There were jumpers and shirts too; they smelt fresh and clean. Must have been filched from someone's washing line. He bundled them up and lifted Tap's head, wedged them underneath.

When he woke it was morning. He tugged crust from his eyelids and tried to focus.

'Eat this.' Sloth was holding out a chocolate digestive. Where had he got that?

'Not hungry.' His voice croaked.

'You got to eat something, bro.' Sloth lifted a water bottle to his lips and he drank. The water soothed his aching throat.

'What's that about your mum?' asked Sloth. He had asked the question now several times, Tap realised. 'You were talking about her in your sleep.'

'He was at my house, the man. That's how he found Frank. I called her, left a message. He'll have done last-number-redial. Frank told him where he lived.'

'Shit. So what about your mum?'

And whether it was because he was ill, he didn't know, but something inside him started to break. His chest was suddenly so heavy he could barely breathe.

'Tap?'

'Sorry, mate. I'll be OK in a sec.' He lifted his forearm and wiped his eyes.

Sloth pushed Tap's trainers to one side, making space on the concrete floor. He lay down alongside him and put his arm across Tap's heaving frame. It only made Tap's crying worse.

'It's OK,' Sloth said quietly. 'It's OK.'

'What if she's dead? He must have been in our house. That's how he found us.'

Sloth tightened his arm around him.

'We're going to go back there, soon as you're better. Promise. And we'll get him. We'll mess him up good. You and me, bro.'

They lay together on the hard floor as the evening darkened again. It must have been low tide on the big river. He had got used to the pulse of life here, the times when the mud was exposed and the birds landed to feed. The noises they made were primitive and sorrowful.

FORTY

The Saturday after her birthday was always going to be a day off for Ferriter. Cupidi was grateful for it now. Chances were, Ferriter would be facing a misconduct hearing. If Peter Moon added a formal complaint to that, there was the danger that people would start to ask why Ferriter had punched him on the nose. Ferriter's brilliant career with Serious Crime would be over.

Cupidi drove alone to London and emerged out of the Black-wall Tunnel onto the dusty dual carriageway that led up to Victoria Park.

The cafe by the boating lake was full of families with young children running and screaming. When Zoë had been four or five, she had brought her to places like this. Other parents had told her, 'You have to remember this time. It goes so quickly.'

When they had said that, Cupidi had felt guilty; she had longed to be able to hold a decent conversation with her child. And now there were days when she couldn't have any conversation at all.

'Alexandra Cupidi?' said a voice.

She looked round. 'Devon?'

He was tall and good-looking, dressed in running gear with a small backpack over one shoulder and, holding on to his hand, a serious-looking boy of about five who clutched a *Star Wars* lightsaber. 'This is my son, Malik.'

Malik nodded warily.

She stood, but he still towered over her. 'Coffee?' she said. 'Something for Malik?'

'Just water please.'

Malik said, 'I want juice.'

'Please,' scolded Devon.

Cupidi returned with a plastic bottle and a carton. 'You live near here?'

'All my life. Council flat up there.' He pointed to the north edge of the park. 'Imagine how popular I was when I told them I was joining the force. We still live up there with my mum.'

While Malik sat at the small table sucking at the juice straw, Devon put his backpack down on the ground and pulled out a typewritten sheet.

'Is that what you have?'

'Not much,' he said. 'But two things stand out. Over the last twelve months alone, the Foundation paid approximately six million into Abir Stein's account.'

Cupidi whistled.

'Just over four of that was shelled out to galleries and art dealers, right? Perfectly bona fide, that looks like.'

'So this is the account he used to purchase artworks for the Foundation?'

'Apparently so. So the first thing I would want to see is the paperwork from the Foundation. On paper, how much do they think they're spending on the art from the galleries?'

'I thought you said . . .'

'What these accounts show is how much the gallery actually received. But it doesn't tell you how much Abir Stein tells the Foundation they're going for.'

'I'm sorry. I don't understand what you're saying.'

'Because I said about four million had gone out to galleries and dealers. The remaining two million was paid out of this account to another that belongs to a company called River Deep. What's going on gets clearer once you drill down into each transaction. On the eighteenth of December, 2018, the Foundation pays £867,000 into Stein's account, see?' Devon pointed to a column on his sheet, then moved his finger down the page. 'Third of January, 2019, £653,000 is paid to PPLAR. That's a gallery in Rio. All fine and good. And the same day, £214,000 is deposited into River Deep.'

'The exact difference between what the Foundation paid and the gallery paid. Is that Stein's commission?'

'That would be a bloody substantial commission.'

Malik paused from sucking at his juice and frowned at his father. 'You shouldn't say "bloody".'

'Sorry, mate,' apologised Devon. 'You're absolutely right.'

'So he's skimming money off the top?'

'I can't say for sure, but that's what it looks like to me. To River Deep. Kind of a deliberate joke name. Muddy Waters. Because River Deep are registered in St Lucia.'

'Not for the sunshine, I suppose,' said Cupidi.

'My great-grandmother was from there, as it happens.'

'Was she a banker?'

Devon's laugh was high-pitched and loud. 'I wish. She was a nurse.'

'So he set up River Deep to squirrel the money away?'

'I tried to find out a little about River Deep, but there's not much there. People who choose places like St Lucia do so because there's a lot of corporate secrecy allowed there. On paper they have a single named officer, a director called Ernesto Baines, but if he's even real he probably doesn't even know what his name is being used for. River Deep is a shell company, designed to conceal the beneficial owner.'

'Which is Abir Stein?'

'Honestly? Hard to know for sure. To me it looks like what's been going on here is a simple transfer-pricing scam. Charge one price, declare another. It would not be the first time this has happened in the art market, believe me. Stein may be the beneficiary but you'll only find out when you discover who's taking out the cash at the other end. That would be the harder part to track down. Presumably they're taking cash out of St Lucia, but that's easier said than done. I can see how they're putting it in, but there's no trace of how they'd be taking it out.'

'Could he have been doing backhander deals with the galleries?'

'Unlikely. The Foundation has bought from all sorts of sources. No chance of them all being in on it, I'd say, but each transaction comes with a sum set aside for River Deep. I bet Stein will be making a tidy sum from it, even if it's just commission.'

'Not any more. He's dead.'

314

'Oh.'

A girl on a pink bike lost control, falling sideways onto the thin mud at the edge of the lake. As she stood, she let out an enormous wail. Malik looked up from his juice, concerned, as the girl's mother ran from a nearby table to comfort her.

'This is just twelve months' data,' said Devon. 'How long has the Foundation been running?'

'Five years.'

'If they're taking two million a year out of that, that would be a hell of a lot of money. Like I said, what you'll need is to get the paperwork from the Foundation, but I guess Stein's been invoicing them for one sum and paying the galleries another.'

'And nobody noticed?'

'It's a business that relies on trust, and I presume the Foundation trusted him. Though by the sound of it, somebody didn't.'

Cupidi thought for a while, looking at the serious little boy at the table next to her. He finished his juice. 'I want to go home now.'

'As you see, I have to go,' said the policeman.

'Thank you so much.'

'Like I said, I enjoy it.'

Standing, she shook Devon's hand with a kind of awkward formality, and then, with greater solemnity, Malik's, and watched the two of them walk away together across the park.

From there, Cupidi drove south, to the big grey cube of a warehouse in East London; the Crime Scene Investigator was already there, waiting at the reception; a young man, heavy for his age, who sweated at his armpits, even though the day was cool.

'We have to wait for the representative of the Foundation to arrive,' Cupidi explained.

The coffee they were offered was surprisingly good.

'You any idea where the rest of the body is yet?' asked the officer. 'Not going to be in here, is it?'

'It would be nice if it was, wouldn't it? There's CCTV of our suspect, carrying a holdall. He must have had the arm in there, but you'd have to be ambitious to bring a whole body in here.'

'So where do you think it is?'

'We don't know.'

Cupidi picked up her handbag and pulled out an envelope. There were three images. A man in a long overcoat with a large hat, with a dark canvas holdall in one hand, walking across the tarmac outside the facility and two fuzzier photographs of the same man inside the building. Only on one of the screenshots was the bottom of his face visible.

'A homburg, not a hoodie,' said Cupidi, thinking of the two boys.

'What?'

'By keeping his head fixed on the floor in front of him, the man effectively used the hat to obscure any sight of his face. He must have parked on the road outside or caught the train. There's an overground station just beyond the gates –' she pointed to the east – 'so we've no number plate to go on.'

'It's a funny thing to do.'

'Isn't it? He was sending someone a message, but I have no idea what the message was, or who he was sending it to.'

They both looked round as Zoya Gubenko swept into the

316

room in a plain pale turquoise dress and white heels. 'Shall we get this done?' the woman said tetchily. 'It's my day off.'

'Whereas as public servants, we don't get days off, obviously,' muttered the CSI. Cupidi decided she liked him after all.

She watched the security man check her details. The man who had impersonated Abir Stein would have gone through the same process, though the man on the desk was making a show of doing it with particular care today.

Entering the heart of the facility, their footsteps resounded as they were led down grey metal-walled corridors, turning a corner, mounting a staircase, until they reached the Foundation's private vault.

'It's all climate-controlled in here to one degree Celsius,' explained the young man from EastArt.

'And nobody has been to this room since the visit of Abir Stein at the start of April?' asked Cupidi.

'Not according to our manifest. Nothing has left or entered the room.'

He unlocked the door with a key and pushed it open. Like the corridors, the room was a uniform grey. Paintings were stored on rows of wire racks that slid out on runners. Sculptures and other objects were crated and arranged around the room. The CSI was putting on gloves, stepping into the protective suit.

'Do you see anything unusual?' Cupidi asked Gubenko as they peered around the door frame.

Gubenko looked into the private vault. 'No.'

'Where would the jar have been kept?'

'With the other pieces. There.' She pointed to the corner

317

where several large wooden boxes were stacked, each carefully labelled.

The CSI was already at work, spraying the floor with some chemical.

'I'll leave you to it then,' Cupidi said.

'How long's he going to take?' asked Gubenko pulling out her phone.

'Long enough for you and I to have a chat.'

Gubenko turned to Cupidi. 'What would you want to talk to me about?'

Cupidi strode ahead, not waiting for Gubenko to follow her.

'Can't you tell me now?' she called.

'I think it would be better to converse in private, don't you?'

'What do you mean?' she said, less certainly, trotting to catch up.

Cupidi had a rough idea of the geography around here from when she'd been a copper in London. After standing in this enclosed box, she hankered for open space.

Gubenko caught up with her at the lobby. 'I have a lunch appointment. In Pimlico.'

'This way,' said Cupidi, heading outside. A few hundred metres away she could see a concrete bridge. That would be the River Lea, she guessed, the old waterway that flowed through East London to the Thames. Gubenko caught up with her again.

'How long has Evert Miller's marriage been in trouble?'

Gubenko stopped walking. 'What?' she said.

Cupidi turned to look at her, repeated the question.

'Where on earth did you get that one from?'

Cupidi said, 'How long?'

318

'I can't believe I'm hearing this from a policewoman. You'll understand that there are always rumours that swirl around Evert and Astrid. But it's a lie, obviously.'

Cupidi turned and walked on. She could let it simmer. Ross Clough had come back from Long Hill full of himself. He had seen something there, she was sure. Only a guess though.

'And anyway, what on earth has this got to do with your investigation?'

'I was hoping you would tell me.'

'I don't really believe you're asking that kind of rubbish. I am going to inform Mr Miller.'

'Call him now,' said Cupidi. 'Go on.' A bluff, but she was tired of pussyfooting around these people. Cupidi watched the woman put her hand into her bag, feel for her phone, but she didn't pull it out.

'OK then. Walk with me for a while.' The bridge was just ahead of them now. She waited while Zoya Gubenko caught up with her again. 'I was hoping we might cooperate with each other,' said Cupidi.

'I am here, aren't I?'

'Your employer's marriage is in trouble. It's natural you would want to keep that secret . . .'

'What? And if I don't speak to you, you'll go to the papers. Is that how you're threatening me?'

Cupidi's smile widened. 'Well, I hadn't been planning to, but it's a thought. I had rather hoped you would talk to me of your own free will because a man has been killed.'

Gubenko said quietly, 'I am loyal to my employer.'

'I'm sure you are. But I have a job to do. All I need is

information.' Cupidi found the concrete steps that led down to the path that ran alongside the east side of the river. A pair of swans were tucked under the bridge, digging at weed.

'This way,' she said, descending.

'I am not happy discussing the private affairs of the Miller family,' said Gubenko.

Cupidi looked out on the water.

'I'm a police officer investigating a serious crime. If you genuinely want to stop this blowing up into something toxic, you should talk to me now. I'm really not your enemy.'

Fresh green reeds were poking above dark mud and plastic rubbish. A fisherman shifted his rod so they could walk past.

'Astrid's gone, hasn't she?' said Cupidi. 'They've split up.'

'No comment.'

'Is Evert having an affair?'

'I'm not discussing this.'

'Talk to me, Zoya. I need your help.'

'I don't see what any of this has to do with Abir Stein.'

'Abir Stein is almost certainly dead. I'm trying to understand why someone killed him. Right now, everything is relevant.'

Gubenko's eyes widened. 'Stein is dead? Oh my God. That is awful.'

'Were things particularly bad between Astrid and Evert?'

'Back when I started work with them, three or four years ago, I always assumed he set up the Foundation to try and keep her interested in him. He's a good man, you know.'

'It was his idea?'

'Yes.'

320

A flash of blue passed along the opposite bank. 'A kingfisher,' said Cupidi.

'What?'

Cupidi looked to see where the creature had gone, flashing on up the river, but it had disappeared from sight. She shook her head slowly. 'Sorry. My daughter is mad about birds.'

'He wanted to give Astrid something to do. That's how it started. She had been used to working as a model and then when she married him all that tailed off. But she thought she knew about contemporary art,' Gubenko said, a little contemptuously. 'So he bought her a toy.'

'The Foundation is a plaything?'

'Don't get me wrong. It's a serious business now, with a substantial value and an excellent inventory. But at the start Astrid just purchased whatever she liked. She paid a fortune for some Paul McCarthys at the top of the market and they weren't even very good ones. It was a mess. She didn't really know what she was doing. But then Abir Stein came on board, and they advertised for an administrator. And ta-da! Here I am. We have bought some very good work over the last few years.'

'And Abir Stein handled that?'

'He is the broker. He buys the artworks on our behalf. That's why we employed him.'

'Who hired him?'

'Evert found him through colleagues. He wanted someone who would offer a practical balance to Astrid's passions. Astrid had no experience of the art world, you understand. She doesn't even have a basic-level degree or anything,' she said, as if such qualifications were essential. 'She relied on him very heavily. Sometimes you could hear her parroting a piece of his wisdom about an artist or a movement. Whenever she says anything about art, it's almost always straight from Stein's lips. Or mine, of course.'

Cupidi nodded, thought for a while.

'When the Foundation makes an investment, who authorises the financial transfer?'

'Evert and I. Everything has to be countersigned.'

'Not Astrid?'

'No. She has a position of director of the Foundation, but it is non-executive.'

'Why not?'

'I don't know. Maybe he didn't trust her. You heard about his first wife? She took him to the cleaners.'

'I think the phrase you mean is, "She demanded an equitable share of assets".'

Gubenko snorted. 'Mr Miller is naturally cautious now, put it that way.'

'If they were to divorce, who would control the Foundation?'

'Evert, undoubtedly. It's well known that after his first marriage, he was careful to create a prenuptial agreement that meant his assets would remain his. And effectively the Foundation is his asset. She just works for it. Are we going far? I should let my friends know I'm going to be late for lunch.'

'You don't like Astrid Miller, do you?'

'I don't dislike her. She's just pretty high maintenance. She thinks she knows best about everything. She pretended she's not interested in her own celebrity, but she uses it whenever she needs to. She came into this business a complete novice. Five years on, she thinks she's Peggy Guggenheim.'

322

Cupidi wondered if she was going to explain who Peggy Guggenheim was, but she didn't. 'What does River Deep mean to you?'

'It's a song, isn't it?'

'You've never heard Abir Stein, Astrid or Evert Miller mention it?'

'No. Can we go back?' They turned and started retracing their steps.

'Ross Clough, an artist from Margate, was found trespassing at Long Hill last week. Did you see him?'

'Creep,' she said. 'Yes. Mulligan discovered him lurking around the public footpath. He had been spying on us.'

'On you?'

'Not me, obviously. On Evert.'

She walked in silence back to the steps to the road, thinking about Ross Clough, and then of the two young boys in his sketch. Where were they? They seemed to have completely disappeared again. They made her feel anxious; as if she had failed them in some way.

What was clearer was that Evert Miller had control of the finances of the Foundation and he had deliberately brought Abir Stein on board.

Back at the art store, the CSI was sitting in reception, having finished packing up his equipment. 'Anything?' Cupidi asked. He was sitting, computer on his lap, eating a packet of sweets.

'As it happens, yes,' he said, chewing slowly. 'Something. Come here and take a look. I don't know what to make of it.'

And he moved to one side, so that Cupidi could sit next to him. A photo. A single pale comma-shaped bug. It took Cupidi a second to see that it was a maggot.

FORTY-ONE

The fever got worse that day, not better. Tap was thirsty, but his throat stung every time he swallowed.

Sloth said, 'I should call an ambulance. I don't think you got to give a name or anything.'

It hurt Tap to shake his head. If they went to a hospital, they would fetch the police. 'You should go. Go home to your mum.'

'He knows where I live too, remember.'

'You should go. She'll be worried,' said Tap. 'What if she's in danger too?' He wasn't sure which parts were in his dreams and which were real. He closed his eyes again.

At some point, the big river beside them rose, lifted him gently and floated him out, under the big bridge that stretched across the wide water, past the marshland and out to a calm grey sea.

Then the water turned colder and he began to shiver, and he felt himself sliding beneath it, the weight covering him.

★

When he woke later, his eyes were again gummed shut; he was used to it now. He heard Sloth shuffling about at the entrance to the hut.

'The thing is, I been meaning to tell you something, bro. I think my mother may be dead,' he whispered.

Sloth said nothing. There was the sound of the fire being stoked, so he carried on. 'I think the phone man may have killed her. Stabbed her that day we fell down Ninety-Nine Steps.'

He heard the flick of a lighter.

'Say something then, bro.'

'Your mother is dead.'

But that was not Sloth's voice.

Shocked, Tap managed to tug one eye open. It wasn't Sloth he had been talking to. He gasped for breath.

Silhouetted against the light, the shape of a strange man, much bigger than Sloth.

He tried to scream but he couldn't.

This had all the quality of the dream he had just been having, but this time he knew it wasn't.

Eyes wide now, he adjusted to the brightness of the spring day.

The man was sitting on a large blue box, just at the doorway, smoking a cigarette.

'Sloth,' Tap gasped, trying to shout.

No answer. Sloth wasn't there. He scrabbled back on his elbows away from the man.

'He's not here,' said the man. 'You're alone.'

And then, as Tap's eyes adjusted to the light, he came into focus.

★

325

Tap looked at him. Blinked.

It was not Phone Man. This one was old, his face dark with dirt, and he watched Tap struggling to sit up with little expression on his face.

'Where's my friend?' Tap asked, his heart still thumping. His voice sounded as old as the man he was looking at.

The man shrugged. *Don't know.*

'This is our place,' Tap croaked. 'Our hut. Our fire. Go away. Bog off.'

The man snorted; took another pull on his toothpick-thin cigarette. Tap watched the paper curl as it turned to ash, then fall to the ground.

'Your hut.' The man snorted. 'Your bloody fire,' he said. As if owning a fire was a ridiculous idea.

'When my mate comes back, he'll mess you up,' Tap muttered.

Dropping the remains of the cigarette into the fire, the man stood up. As he did so, Tap realised he was huge, six-foot something, hands the size of plates. Upright, Tap saw he was wearing an old, tattered work jacket and beneath it dark olive waders that came up above his belly, into which he had tucked a greasy woollen sweater. He looked like he'd been dredged out of the river.

'Like to see him try.' The man turned, picked up a piece of an old wooden pallet and added it to the fire. 'Our fire,' he said again, laughing, moved his blue box a couple of inches back as the flames grew hotter, then sat down again on it.

Tap raised himself slowly. His head swam from the effort. He had to stand and go and find Sloth.

'Sit down,' said the man.

Tap glared at him, legs trembling. He did not feel safe with this stranger invading their space. As he tried to step out of the sleeping bag, his foot caught and he stumbled, banging his arm on the brick wall. With the pain came prickles of sweat.

'Down,' the man said again, this time impatiently.

Slumping back to his spot on the concrete, Tap wished the old man would go away. The effort of trying to stand had exhausted him. Behind his eyes, a sharp pain grew. Sloth would be disappointed in him for not protecting their HQ.

The man reached inside his coat and pulled out a small tin. Carefully, he set about making more cigarettes, dropping tobacco, licking papers and rolling them with the fingers and thumb of a single hand.

Tap would have asked for one, but the sight of his filthy nails and the string of spittle that stretched from paper to lip whenever he licked one made his stomach churn.

He turned his head to one side, and when he turned back it was dark. He was alone. He must have fallen asleep somehow.

The fire was still burning though. He could feel the heat warming his feet.

FORTY-TWO

It was Saturday afternoon when Cupidi made it to the hospital in Dartford.

There was a cafe in the huge glass reception area. She bought herself a coffee and a chocolate bar and sat on a hard plastic chair for a minute, thinking. Around her, visitors mingled with patients in pyjamas.

She pulled out her phone to switch it off. There was a text from Jill Ferriter: **Sorry. Please call me.**

She would do it in a minute, she decided. Putting her phone back into her pocket she drank her coffee, then stood and walked to the lift.

The nurse on intensive care looked at his notes. 'Mr Khan's condition deteriorated last night. He has septicaemia. The knife he was stabbed with may not have been clean.'

Outside, relatives waited with drawn faces, clutching undrunk cups of tea. A boy in a green Incredible Hulk suit lay on the floor, bored.

'OK to go in?' she asked.

'He's on a lot of painkillers. You might not get much out of him right now.'

Cupidi went in to the side room. She had seen many dead bodies in her life and Khan didn't look that different. His head was propped on a pillow and his eyes stared at the ceiling. They didn't move when she entered the room, so she leaned over him, into his field of vision.

'Who are you?' he whispered.

'Police.'

His eyes were sunken, dark-ringed. 'Good. Because they're killing me in here,' he said, his voice paper-thin.

'I've come about the boys.'

He blinked slowly.

'I want to find the boys,' she said. 'The ones who were in your flat.'

He gave his head the tiniest slow shake. 'No boys in my flat.'

'I know you're lying.'

He blew spittle from his lips. It bubbled and burst as he tried to turn his head away.

'Tell me something. Were they scared?'

'Yes.'

'The man who stabbed you. What if he was trying to kill them, not you?'

He closed his eyes.

'That's what was happening, wasn't it?'

The tiniest nod. That was why the boys had not been found, she thought. They didn't want to be, because they were running away from something.

'What was he like, this man?'

'Didn't get a chance. To see him.'

'Listen, Frank. I need to find those two boys. If he was trying to kill them, they might still be in danger. You have to tell me where you met them.'

'Seriously?' His lips turned upwards, but Cupidi wasn't sure whether it was a smile or a spasm of pain. 'So you can bang me up?' She leaned in close. His voice seemed to be composed of faint notes heard from a long way off.

She looked round, found a chair, sat and watched him breathing. Each breath seemed to take an age.

'I won't lie. None of this is going to go well for you, Frank. But I think they're in big trouble,' she said. 'Don't you?'

He hissed slowly. It took her a second to realise that he had said yes.

'So you do give a shit, don't you, Frank? If he gets to them before we do, it'll be bad. Why does he want to kill them, Frank?'

He said nothing; his eyes were shut. The grey vertical blinds on the window were closed. She stood and pulled two of the fabric slats apart and looked out.

From here you could see the massive span of the Queen Elizabeth II Bridge, crossing the Thames.

'I've got a daughter. She's seventeen,' she said. 'About the same age as those boys, maybe. It's such a dangerous time. You don't know what you are yet. There are bad people out there. You know that only too well, Frank. It could go either way.'

Outside, the ward was hushed. Two nurses whipered behind a curtain.

'I love my daughter. But it's so hard to be there, halfway

between being a child and an adult. We go all soft about small children, but I think the really vulnerable ones are the teenagers. Easy for people to pick on, aren't they?'

He seemed to be asleep now, or at least, was pretending to be.

'I've spent years locking up killers,' she said. 'Some people seem to become immune to it, but all that time I've found the idea of killing repugnant. It still wakes me up at night, you know? It has done all my life.'

An orderly appeared, looked around the door. 'Oh. I'll come back in a minute.' The door closed.

Cupidi spoke again. 'There are people who want to kill you, Frank, aren't there? How must that make you feel?'

No reaction. Not even a flicker.

'But the harder I think about it, I don't think that guy who stabbed you was one of them. I think you were just in the way. We've got a chance to help those kids. You and me, Frank. I really need to know where they are.'

The man beneath the sheets didn't stir. A machine at his bedside whirred. A small cog twisted on his drip.

She watched Frank for a while. And then his eyes opened. And he whispered something.

The noise of the hospital seemed to grow louder.

She leaned closer. 'What did you say, Frank?'

'Twelve words,' he said. 'They only had eleven.'

'What are you trying to say, Frank? Where are they?'

'*Paralysed . . . Potential.*'

She took out a notebook.

'Ruby,' he said.

'I don't understand.'

331

'Ruby Tuesday.'

'Ruby Tuesday? Like the song?'

His eyes closed again and this time his mouth fell open. Cupidi fetched the nurse who she had spoken to a few minutes earlier. 'Is he OK?'

'It's just the morphine,' she said. 'Makes you hallucinate. He's a pretty sick man.'

Outside the ward she switched the phone back on. It buzzed instantly.

She caught the lift down with a teenage girl and her parents; the girl had no hair. The parents were smiling, joking, like parents of sick children did.

It would be from Ferriter.

Please! Call me. It's important. To do with Zoë.

FORTY-THREE

'What was his name?' demanded Tap. 'The man who was here? Scared the balls right off me.'

Sloth's face was visible in the firelight, eyes glittering red. 'Asked him, but he wouldn't say. Here, have another spoonful.'

Tap opened his mouth and Sloth spooned the tomato soup from the lid of the thermos. Tap's throat stung, but he managed to force it down. It tasted magical.

Standing just inside the hut, there was an old tartan shopping trolley like the ones old women pushed around. According to Sloth, who had carefully taken everything out, then put it back in again, it contained a loaf of bread, a packet of digestives, a lump of cheese, two bottles of water, a bag of sweets and half a dozen eggs.

It had been there in the hut when Tap had woken. The man with the blue box was a fisherman. He had come every day to fish on the creek, the other side of the big fence. The first few days he had paid the boys no attention. Only when Sloth had left Tap alone had he approached the shelter.

'You left me alone. Where did you go?' asked Tap.

'To try and get food. Think the po saw me. Got freaked and hid.'

'The police?'

'Yeah. So it took me forever to get back here and I was, like, panicking.'

'Tosser,' said Tap. The soup was good. He could feel its warmth reaching his arms and legs, as if it was flowing directly into them. 'Don't have to worry 'bout me.'

'Why not? You're shit without me.'

'Bog off.'

'Anyway. Got back in the night and this man was in the shed with you. Stinky old feller. I thought he was robbing you. I was screaming at him and everything. He just ignored me, and then I saw what he was doing. No jokes, bro. He was looking after you. Put a blanket over you, fetched more wood for the fire. Everything.'

'Almost shit myself when I woke up and found him here,' said Tap. 'No lie.'

'Smell like you did, anyway.'

'Bog off.'

'He buggered off and two hours later he's back with this shopping trolley. Want it back he said. Pick it up in the morning along with his thermos.'

'Reckon he's poisoned it?'

'Don't fricking care.' Sloth poked a stick through a slice of white bread, then held it over the fire. His first attempt caught alight, but the next one he skewered toasted all over, if unevenly. Placing it on his lap, he broke off a bit of cheese and crumbled it onto the top. 'Delicious, man,' he said when he'd finished it. 'Best thing I ever tasted. Maybe Mum's right. I should be a chef.'

The soup had made Tap feel better too. He sat up and watched the fire.

'Why'd he do it?' said Tap, looking at the trolley full of food. 'I don't get it.'

'Nor me, bro,' said Sloth. 'Mysteries of the universe. Want a wine gum?'

Tap sucked on it slowly. The sugar calmed his throat. Evening starlight pulsed through the rising heat from the embers.

The next morning, Sloth lay sound asleep, thumb in his mouth.

Tap stood, held up an imaginary camera and took a photograph. Days now without a phone. It was weird. He looked into the corner of the shed, where they had buried the stolen phone. There was just a hole there now. Someone had taken it, he guessed. Maybe the old man. Good riddance.

His fever had gone. Ravenous, he dipped into the trolley while Sloth slept on. He ate two slices of bread on their own, washed down with water. A third he folded in two, placing half a dozen wine gums inside. After he'd laid the sleeping bag over Sloth, he ventured out into the marsh.

The tramp was there again, a hundred metres away. He sat on the other side of the wire fence on his blue box, rod out across the muddy water.

'Caught anything?'

'Never do.'

The sun was warm. Bugs buzzed around the fresh grass. 'Thanks for the food,' Tap said.

The man didn't even turn. 'You're welcome,' he said. Tap was about to return to the HQ when the old man said, 'Word of warning. Council security was down this morning looking round the place. They're little bastards. They don't want anyone squatting it. They'll be back again later. Better bugger off out of here, if I was you.'

Tap said, 'We ain't scared.'

'Didn't say you were.'

A sluggish current rippled the black water. 'We were going anyway,' Tap said.

And he looked around at the big sky. It was time to leave, he thought. It was time to get things sorted out.

FORTY-FOUR

When Cupidi arrived at the Majestic Shine Car Wash she couldn't see her daughter among the crowd, but two Immigration Enforcement vans parked on the opposite side of the road confirmed that she was in the right place.

Ferriter had given her the address of the car wash, just on the outskirts of Ashford. As she approached she could she that the immigration officers were standing in a line at the edge of the gate to the industrial unit. A group of young people, mostly dressed in black, blocked their way. Some uniformed coppers were standing close by, dressed in high-visibility jackets and tactical vests. A press photographer Cupidi recognised from one of the local papers was calmly photographing the scene.

'You got here fast.' She turned towards the voice. Jill Ferriter was wearing dark glasses.

'Is Zoë in there?'

'That's her. Beside the big bloke with the stupid hair.'

Cupidi squinted. It took her a second to recognise her, among all the line of misfits and activists, next to the man with dread-locks. There were about a dozen of them. Women with shaved heads, or dyed hair. One man wore dungarees. Another man had a 'V for Vendetta' mask. A middle-aged woman stood with a sign that read #*noborders*.

'You OK?' she asked Ferriter.

'Bit fragile. Bit embarrassed.'

'Bit hungover?'

'I don't regret hitting him, you understand?'

'Too well,' said Cupidi. She nodded towards her daughter and her friends. 'How did they get here?'

'Apparently they take it in shifts to wait outside the Immi-gration Enforcement depot in Folkestone. They just follow the Immigration vans round all day on motorbikes and cars. Try and get in the way of the raids.'

That's what her daughter had been doing that she hadn't wanted to tell her about, she realised.

'How did you find out she was here?'

'Pal in uniform spotted her. Sent me a pic. "Is that DS Cupidi's kid?" I told him it wasn't, obviously.'

'How long have they been here?'

'Almost forty minutes. They're obstructing the Immigration people from entering the premises.'

'So they're going to charge them?'

'Any minute. You want me to get her out of there before it kicks off?'

'You're a police officer. You can't do that.'

'Come on. I'm probably going to be suspended anyway on

Monday, when Peter Moon puts a complaint in about me. I think my career is pretty much up a creek, isn't it?'

Cupidi didn't answer because it was true; the one friend she had made in her two years on Serious Crime in Kent would be disciplined as a result of the complaint. If she didn't lose her job, she would almost certainly be moved off the murder unit. She reached out to squeeze Ferriter's hand, but Ferriter pulled away. 'Don't,' she said.

Another police car arrived, disgorging officers. What would have been a quick job picking up an undocumented worker had turned into a public event. Immigration officers had clearly decided this was beyond their powers, so they had had to call in uniforms, which had given time for the press to arrive. Everything the demonstrators wanted, presumably.

Whether the person – or persons – the officers were seeking were still in there was doubtful, too.

'I'll get her out of there then,' said Ferriter.

'No. This is my responsibility. I'll go,' she said, walking towards the gates of the car wash.

The protesters had linked arms.

The line of immigration officers looked bored, tired and exasperated. Turning as she approached, a senior officer said, 'Please stay away, madam.'

At times like this, like it or not, you had to identify yourself. She dug out her card and held it up.

'What is a DS doing here?' he asked, suspicious. 'Is there something I should know?'

'Nope,' she said. 'Nothing you should know at all.' She

waved at her daughter. Zoë didn't notice. She called her name out loud.

Zoë looked up, her expression changing rapidly from shock to embarrassment, then to a glare of resentment.

'That your mother?' she heard the boy in dreadlocks next to her say.

Cupidi approached.

'What the hell are you doing here, Mum?'

'Came to get my car cleaned. You OK?'

'Of course I am. Why wouldn't I be?'

'And do you know who you're trying to protect here?'

'Don't tell me they're terrorists or something, Mum,' said Zoë. 'They're just people. Like us.'

The police who had been asked to attend were talking to the Senior Immigration Enforcement Officer. Sensing that something was about to happen, some of the demonstrators started chanting, 'Refugees are welcome here.'

A woman enforcement officer muttered resentfully, 'They're not even refugees.'

Cupidi asked her daughter, 'Do you know what's going to happen to you?'

Zoë was pleading now. 'Go away, Mum. This is none of your business.'

The immigration officers shuffled, impatient, annoyed at how they were being cast in the role of bad people.

'Are you going to stop me? Because I'm breaking the law? Is that it?'

'Of course I'm not.'

Zoë looked puzzled, for a second, almost disappointed.

A sergeant Cupidi didn't recognise pushed himself forward. 'You're this girl's mother, I heard.'

Cupidi turned to him, a soft-faced-looking man in his forties. 'Yes.'

He looked relieved. The man led her out of earshot of the demonstrators and the Immigration Force team. 'Listen. Will you help get her and her mates out of the way? We don't want to end up pulling them all in. The whole thing is just a massive waste of time. Wouldn't be surprised if the migrants they're looking to remove are already halfway to London anyway.'

Cupidi turned back and looked at her daughter. She was such a small wisp of a girl in amongst all the burly demonstrators. She expected other parents cried when their children picked up awards at school; Zoë had never been that kind of girl, or she that kind of mother, but something of that feeling flooded into her now. All these men around her in those bulky tactical vests that made them look huge and intimidating. She had worried about Zoë, a shy, slight, difficult girl who struggled to find her place in the world. Now she was standing in a line of strange misfits and troublemakers, but looking like she would try to hold back the approaching line of police officers all on her own. She felt proud.

'Have a word, will you?' the police sergeant was saying.

'Nope,' she told him. 'I won't do that.'

'What do you mean, no? You want her to get pulled in?'

The police were already moving in and Cupidi found herself being pushed backwards away from her. The protesters were shouting as the press cameraman pushed his way into the melee.

*

341

Cupidi waited with Ferriter back at the station. They sat on a bench out front, where members of the public normally waited.

The arresting officer had announced they would release Zoë without charge almost immediately because she was a minor, but that still took an hour.

'About last night. I'm so sorry,' said Ferriter.

'I'll bet you are.'

'Honest to God, it's not what I had planned. But when I was there, in that bar and he came up and asked for a birthday kiss, it kind of . . .'

'Is he filing an assault charge?'

'He said he's going to talk to McAdam on Monday and then lodge a formal complaint.'

'Are you going to tell McAdam why you hit him?'

'Of course not. I can't, can I?'

Not if she didn't want the truth about what had happened the week before to come out. Not if she didn't want to endanger Cupidi's career.

'So I expect they'll suspend me on Monday.'

'Yes,' said Cupidi. 'I expect they will.'

'I only ever wanted to do this job,' she said. 'I was never sure about it at first, but when you joined up I thought, that's what I want to do. Be like you. Messed that up, didn't I?'

Somewhere, on the other side of a closed door, an officer was whistling an irritatingly chirpy tune. 'It's not Monday yet,' said Cupidi.

'Broke it, I think. His nose.'

'You could have at least waited till I was back.'

Saturday evening. The station was already busy.

'I come from a long line of fuck-ups. I thought I was different. I wasn't going to be like that.'

'You're not a fuck-up,' said Cupidi.

A constable finally led Zoë out to the front desk. He looked at Jill Ferriter with a kind of hostility that made Cupidi think that word had probably got around. By now, anyone who hadn't been at the wine bar last night had heard about what had happened there. None of them knew why she'd taken a swing at Peter Moon but they'd probably already made up their minds about her.

Zoë looked tired and dirty. There was a smudge on her cheek and a tear in her trousers. 'If you think I'm going to apologise,' she said, 'I'm not.'

'Shouldn't be hanging around with people like that, darling. They're trouble,' Ferriter said, opening her arms for a hug.

Zoë ignored her. Instead she went to her mother. 'Are you angry with me?'

Cupidi kissed her daughter on the forehead. 'More hungry than angry. You?'

'I'm bloody starving,' said Ferriter.

'She meant me,' Zoë objected. 'So you don't think I'm stupid for doing it?'

Cupidi held her daughter and squeezed her. 'No. Not at all. You believe in a principle, you should stand up for it.'

Zoë wriggled out of her grasp. 'So if you agree with me, that it's important, you should have joined us. That would have made a real statement.'

Cupidi was exasperated. 'I'm a police officer. I was on duty. I just can't do that.'

343

'My point exactly,' said Zoë, and led the way out of the police station.

In spite of everything, Ferriter found the energy to laugh.

They ate an Indian takeaway on a blanket on the beach at Dungeness. It was chilly still, but Cupidi kept a box of old rugs and jumpers in a box just inside the front door for occasions like this.

Zoë picked at her food for a while and then went back to the house. Ferriter had said she didn't want wine, but when Cupidi opened a bottle, she had a glass. 'It's like . . . I got until Monday morning and then I'll be off, won't I?'

'Yes.'

'I really wanted to do this case. For Astrid Miller. I keep thinking, what have we missed? And it's too late now. Monday morning, it'll all be over.'

'Well. You've still got tomorrow.'

'Very funny.'

'I went to see Frank Khan this afternoon.'

'In hospital? Why?'

'A hunch. I was thinking about those boys, the ones involved in the assault. Ross Clough has this weird kind of theory that they were connected to our case somehow. I can't get them out of my head.'

'Teenagers.'

'Yes. It's that. We've been getting nowhere with this, so I was thinking – and you'll say this is nuts – but what if Clough saw a connection that we were missing, because we always see things logically?'

'Speak for yourself. I can't string thoughts together in any order right now.'

A big ship was out on the horizon, white light blazing, working slowly from west to east. 'There's nothing to connect the boys to the disappearance of Abir Stein apart from the fact that the day they first turn up on our radar is the same one the arm was discovered.'

In darkness, Ferriter poured herself another glass of wine.

'We've got twenty-four hours. Some time on Monday morning, you're going to be suspended.'

'I know.' Ferriter nodded.

'Twenty-four hours. Desperate measures. I asked Frank Khan where he found the boys. First he said something about twelve words. Then he said something like "Ruby Tuesday". It's a song.'

'Is it?'

'You never heard it? I forget. You're just a baby, really.'

'I'm twenty-bloody-five.' Like it was the end of the world.

Cupidi told her about the visit to EastArt and her meeting with Devon King and the company River Deep.

'So this is all about money?'

'I think so.'

'If Abir Stein was taking cash off the top, do you think Evert Miller was the man responsible for killing him?' Ferriter asked. 'And maybe Astrid knows something about that and that's why she's being so weird?'

Cupidi shivered, pulled a rug more tightly around herself. The cold was good, though. It sharpened her senses. 'Why would Evert then put evidence in his own artwork? It makes the trail lead straight back to him. That wouldn't make any sense.'

345

Ferriter had her phone out and was scanning YouTube. 'Is this the song?'

Cupidi listened. Her mother had an old 45 of it somewhere. She would have seen the Rolling Stones playing it, probably, back in the sixties. She had been that kind of teenager, escaping to the city to find herself. Now the tune sounded quaint and stilted, the ancient sound of a young band trying to prove themselves in groovy London.

When the song had ended, Ferriter said, 'I quite like that.' She began tapping the phone with both thumbs. 'Let's assume you're not insane. Ruby Tuesday. It's a women's clothes shop in the shopping centre in Dartford. Jesus. What would the boys be doing there? Buying frocks?'

Cupidi frowned. 'I don't know. Are they open tomorrow?'

But Ferriter was still looking at her phone. 'No. Hold on.' She scrolled down the search results. 'Bloody hell. That's weird.'

'What?'

'Ruby Tuesday Drive. Look.' She held her screen up, pinched out on Google maps. 'It's a place. Those new builds north of the town. Look.'

Ruby Tuesday Drive. Barely a quarter of a mile from Frank Khan's flat. Less than half a mile from where the Co-op guard had been killed. Cupidi shivered again, but this time it was not because of the cold.

FORTY-FIVE

When they reached the Ninety-Nine Steps they paused.

After a week out in the open, out on the mudland by the Thames, the town seemed crazy busy to Tap, with cars coming at them, and people crowding the pavements. They were twitchy, nervous and unwashed.

Tap was still weak. 'I need to rest.'

The woods by the houses seemed bigger and greener than they had when they had last been here, running away from the phone man.

'Let's wait here for a bit,' he said. 'Think of the plan.'

They ducked under the railing at the top of the steps and sat in the copse, among the discarded sweet wrappers.

'Only one way to stop this.'

A boy of about six, with purple shorts and a red T-shirt burst into the undergrowth. The park was full of kids mucking about while their mums sat on the benches. A gang of them were playing hide-and-seek.

His eyes went wide when he saw the two older boys crouching in the darkness.

'Go away,' said Sloth.

The boy hesitated, unwilling to give up the perfect hiding place.

'Bog off,' hissed Sloth, raising a hand.

The boy jolted backwards, falling back out into the sunshine.

'How?' asked Tap. 'He shot Mikey. And he stabbed Frank.'

'Don't know yet,' said Sloth.

The noise of the town seemed so loud. Tap had liked it out on the marsh, just the two of them and the sound of the birds. 'My mum's sister killed herself by drinking drain cleaner.'

Some girls were chanting, '*I went to the barbershop, to get my hair cut off . . .*'

Sloth frowned.

'*Cut it long, cut it short, cut it with a knife and fork . . .*'

'You can't just make him drink poison. You'd have to pour it down his throat, wouldn't you?'

'Suppose. What about electrocution? Put wires on the door handle.'

'How do you actually do that? We can't even steal a phone without cocking it up.'

'Don't know.'

'Don't know, don't know.'

'Shut up.'

'*He snipped with his scissors, he slipped with his shears, he cut out my eyeballs and both my ears.*'

'Petrol. Burn your house down,' said Sloth.

'It's my house,' protested Tap.

'What if we use the phone as a trap?'

'Frickin' hell, Slo. You still got it, you dick?'

It was Sloth who'd dug it up, after all.

'If we got it, he'll come to us. That's all I know.'

'And kill us like he killed Mikey.'

Stupid, dirty and useless, that's what they both were. The kind of boys for whom nothing would ever go right.

Dressed in a filthy blue nylon housecoat, Annie Lee was in her kitchen, scrubbing a pan.

'Almost had a heart attack. What you doing sneaking up on me?' She was that deaf they had made it over her back fence, up to the open back door without her even noticing.

Tap grinned. They were standing in Annie Lee's back garden. When he was a kid, he'd played here all the time, but recently she had let the place go. Brambles had overtaken her rose beds. The new grass was poking through last year's dead leaves and a broken dining chair lay in pieces under her kitchen window. 'Your mum was asking after you,' she said.

'Was she?' asked Tap, cautiously.

'Just once. Saw her out on the street. Maybe a week ago. Don't think she's been too well.'

But she was alive. Something lightened in Tap. If that was true, anything could happen.

Tap said, 'Drinking?'

'She can't help it, Tap. She tries.'

'I know.'

'That new man doesn't help.'

Tap glanced back at Sloth again. 'What new man, Annie Lee?'

'Don't like him at all. He doesn't talk. He's a bugger. He's not good for her. I seen him turn up with the bottles. She must 'a fell over and banged herself a bit, I think. Black eyes.'

'Brown jacket?' Tap said. 'Got a little earring?'

'Only ever seen him at night. I can't sleep. I'm up with my bladder. He's sneaking in there.'

Tap pictured the man slapping his mother; her falling down. Anger grew inside him. He thought of the house, just a few doors away, wanting to go there now. But Sloth asked, 'Got anything to eat, Annie Lee? We're starving.'

She pursed her lips disapprovingly. 'What's wrong with your mum, Benjamin? Don't she want you any more?'

'Please, Annie Lee,' Tap said. 'Going to die of starvation if we stand out here any longer.'

She grunted. 'Come on then.'

Annie Lee's was the first house they had been inside since they had run out of Frank's place, leaving him dying on the floor. When they closed the back door behind them, the house felt strangely solid and comforting.

More or less opposite Tap's house were two double garages, set back a bit from the road, with a little space between them that created narrow alleys in which the boys could hide, peeking round at the house.

Saturday night and they were stuck in an alleyway, crunching discarded McDonald boxes underfoot.

'Had enough of all this,' said Tap. A proper meal and the news about his mother had given him new energy. Time to end this.

In the darkening evening, they could see that there was one

upstairs light on in Tap's house but that didn't mean anything. His mum always left it on.

'What if we sneaked round the back?' suggested Sloth. 'Took a look?'

Tap shook his head. 'Look. It's a spike. Get him through the heart.' In the undergrowth, he had found an iron pole, sharp at one end. Must have been an old fence, or a park railing. He lifted it, hesitated.

'Scared?' said Sloth.

'You saw what he did to Frank. We've got to have a plan.'

'If it was my mum, I'd be straight in there.'

Tap smacked Sloth on the head. 'You ain't even talked to your mum for a week. You're frightened of her.'

Sloth laughed. 'Yeah. Right.'

''K off. We got to do this right.'

At around eight, a bunch of fifteen-year-old girls emerged from number nine in full make-up, arguing. One of them was a girl who'd had a crush on Tap when she was ten. Tap ducked back out into the shadow. If she saw him she'd want to come and say hello or, worse, shout out his name and ask what they were doing hiding there, looking like a couple of rough sleepers.

'Trouble,' muttered Sloth.

'They're all right,' said Tap.

'Serious. Them girls are trouble. Slags.'

'You don't like girls anyway,' said Tap.

'What you frickin' mean, bro?'

Tap didn't answer.

'Bollocks, man. What you mean? You're telling me I'm scared of my mum, next minute talking shit about me and girls.'

351

'Just saying.'

'I'm going to smash your mouth in. Seriously.'

'Shh, you idiot,' said Tap. 'They'll hear us.'

'You're the one who's never had a girlfriend. You're the weirdo. I've had millions.'

Tap giggled. 'Yeah. Like who?'

'Plenty, bro.'

'Pfff.'

''K you, Tap.' Sloth swung an arm, catching Tap on the side of the face. Tap's head jerked back and banged against the pebble-dashed wall of the garage.

'What you do that for?' he asked, shocked.

'Just shut your face, OK?'

Tap rubbed the back of his head to see if there was blood but there wasn't any. 'You need to smoke something, bro. You're crazy. Me, I ain't ever going to be bothered with girls.' He was looking his friend in the eye, remembering the afternoon at Frank's, when Sloth had lain with his arm around him. Sloth looked away.

Tap peered out into the road. It was quiet again, now the girls had disappeared. As he looked left, towards his house, the street lights came on, making the evening suddenly feel darker.

'I looked after you when you were sick. I did that because I'm nice, not because . . .'

'Please, bro,' Tap pleaded. 'Leave it.'

'You're frickin' strange, bro,' muttered Sloth behind him in the darkness.

'I just said I'm not interested in girls. That's all.'

'I don't deal with that.'

Tap turned back. 'Forget it. '

And then Sloth was grabbing his hoodie, face contorted, one hand on each arm, and shaking him.

'Let go of me. What's wrong with you?'

But Sloth kept on pushing him and pulling him back and forward, harder and harder.

'Ow. That frickin' hurts, man.'

'Is that what you've been thinking about all this time?'

'What? Let go of me, man.'

'You've always been faggy, Tap.'

'Jesus. Calm down. We're mates, aren't we?'

'I saved your life last week. I bloody turned up on my bike and saved your life.'

'I didn't say nothing, bro.'

Sloth started to kick out. The first time, he hit Tap on the shin, the second, right on the kneecap. Furious now, Tap fought back, slapping Sloth hard on the ear. In retaliation, Sloth shoved him backwards.

Tap fell into the grass and rubbish. Looking up, he said, 'We're supposed to be mates, Slo. We're supposed to be getting the phone man.'

'Your mum's fine. Didn't you hear Annie Lee? Your mum's been looking after him. All that shit about how he killed her.'

'What about Uncle Mikey?'

'Your uncle. Not mine.'

'What about Frank? You saw what he did.'

'Frank was a paedo. You like a bit of that, Tap, do you?'

'I didn't mean it about the girls, bro. Honest.'

'You're the one who should be worried about girls. You homo.'

The last he saw of Sloth was him disappearing off into the darkness, leaving him lying in the dog shit and rubbish.

He woke shivering. It was still dark, but he had no idea of the time. The fever was back and his head hurt, but there was a lump in his chest too, a heaviness too big to lift. The kind of sadness that felt so big, as thick and cold as the big river.

Stupid Tap. Opening his stupid idiot mouth. Getting a meal in him had made him feel confident that things were going to work out. But they never were. Everything had been fine until he had tried to get Sloth to talk about things, trying to make them more real. But they weren't real. They would never be. He was a freak and he was alone and nothing would ever be right. He cried for a while, worrying that someone would hear, unable to stop himself, more alone than ever.

When he raised his head, the pain worsened and he felt sick. He thought an alarm must be going off somewhere, the noise was so loud. Placing palms against the rough wall, he lifted himself, swaying slightly as the world whirled around him. The ringing, he realised, was in his own head.

He sucked in air and steadied himself, then walked out of the alleyway into the open.

Ahead, the sky was already brightening. It would be morning soon. The light was still on at his house.

He went to the front door, iron spike in his hand.

Didn't care any more about anything.

Pressed the bell and held his finger on it while it played the two-note chime, over and over. And when the shadow appeared behind the glass of the uPVC door he saw right away that it was larger than his mum's would have been.

FORTY-SIX

Sunday morning, Cupidi was woken at eight by the sound of someone moving downstairs. She found Jill Ferriter in her shirt and knickers, poking through a box of herbal teas Cupidi's mother had left there. She had stayed over. 'Couldn't sleep. Everything going whoosh in my head. You think those boys live round there? Ruby Tuesday?'

'Maybe,' Cupidi said.

Ferriter picked out a bag. 'I was thinking. Let's go there.'

'Now?'

'You and me. Why not?'

'Because it's, like, Sunday morning.'

Cupidi smiled. It was something, to see Ferriter looking eager.

'I may never get another chance.'

'I suppose we might,' said Cupidi. 'Your last day on the case.'

'Don't.'

'Of course you realise if we go we should call Peter Moon? Let him know.'

356

'Oh for pity's sake. Why?'

Cupidi looked out of the kitchen window. A spring dew and low sunlight were making the world out there shine. The sea kale that sprouted between the stones took on a deep blue green. 'Because he was working on it. Trying to look for them. We have information he needs to know. Whatever you think of him as a man, he's always been a good copper.' Ferriter's smile vanished. Cupidi poured coffee beans into a grinder. 'He's doing his job. Besides, if it's him who finds them it'll look good and he might not be so hard on you when he talks to McAdam.'

'I hate him, you know.'

'Well aware.'

She looked out of the window. 'Oh great. Now I have to make him look good, don't I?'

'Yes. You do.'

Cupidi pressed the button on the grinder. For the next minute the kitchen was filled with noise. When it finished, Ferriter spoke again. 'Bollocks. You call him. I'm not going to.'

Then both of them looked round. Zoë was standing at the door.

Cupidi watched as Jill wrapped her arms around her daughter and kissed her forehead. 'Sorry I called your friends trouble. Your mum told me off.'

'Some of my best friends are trouble,' said Cupidi.

'Blah blah,' said Ferriter.

Zoë folded herself into Ferriter and yawned.

Cupidi hesitated before knocking on William South's door. He was in there; she knew he was.

357

His curtains were open. He was awake. 'Let me in, Bill. Please.' She kept knocking until he opened up.

He looked older when he didn't shave. The grey hair had turned to a beard that hid the bottom half of his face.

'I want your help.'

He paused, looked at her, lips pressed together hard.

'Let's go inside, Bill.'

He had been a neat man when he was still a copper. A man whose kitchen surfaces had been spotless and whose windows had shone. Cupidi had hoovered the week before; already there were new cobwebs in the corners of his room.

'Mind if I make tea?'

She went to the kitchen and started opening the cupboards.

'Leave me alone, Alex. I'll be OK in a while.'

'You've been home a week and you've barely emerged from your house.'

'What's it to you? I'm just finding my way.'

'I'm not here about you, Bill. It's about Zoë. I want you to look after her for me. I have to go out today.'

'Work?'

'Yes.'

'That murder?'

Even if they'd kicked him off the force he would always be a copper.

'Two boys. Pretty much Zoë's age, I think. If I'm right they're in real trouble.'

He chewed on his lip.

'It's a hangover, Bill. You'll live.'

'I'm not ready, that's all. I'm not well.'

'All I want you to do is go to my house. Keep an eye. She was caught up in a bit of trouble yesterday. Maybe go and look at some birds. It would do you good. Just be there for Zoë again. Please, Bill.'

He turned his back on her and started clearing dirty plates off the dining table.

'Or you can sit here and be miserable for the rest of your life.'

He didn't answer. She was halfway back to the Signals Cottages when she heard the shout behind her.

'Wait.'

She looked up while he caught up with her. Overhead, jet trails criss-crossed a blue sky.

'Are you sure it's a good idea? Convicted murderer as childcare?' Zoë was sitting on the couch, still in her pyjamas, eating a bowl of Cheerios and watching *Friends* on the TV.

'Kindest man I ever met.'

'Did you speak to Moon?' asked Ferriter.

'He's going to see us there at eleven.'

Outside, Ferriter checked her watch. 'We'll be there long before then. Give us a chance to look around. What did he sound like?'

Cupidi opened the door to her car. 'Pissed off with you, for a start.' Her car, as always, was filthy inside. There were chocolate wrappers on the dashboard and mud in the footwell from where she hadn't changed her boots after walking. The unmarked car they'd swap it for when they reached town would be cleaner, at least.

★

Another long drive from the south coast of the county, up towards the northern edge, alongside the wide Thames estuary. Sunday morning and the roads had been clear. They started ringing the bells the moment they got there. The street was mostly maisonettes and flats. Many weren't even occupied.

'Two lads. Sixteen to eighteen years old. One Afro-Caribbean, one white? Wearing hoodies.'

'Nope. No idea. What've they done?' Nobody had seen them; nobody had a clue where they were.

They widened the search to Binnie Road, but there, too, the houses seemed mostly empty.

'Where's Moon? He's late.'

'I wouldn't mind one of these houses,' said Ferriter.

'Really?' Small modern estates, each with a tiny individual parking space outside the front door.

'Maybe a fresh start. Go into sales or something.'

'Shut up, Jill.'

An old man was walking towards them slowly; he was huge, six foot or more, dragging a blue fishing box.

'Wasting our time here,' said Ferriter sadly. 'Maybe it was the clothes shop, after all. Or maybe he was just on so much morphine he was talking gibberish. I'm hungry. We haven't even had a proper breakfast yet.'

The next door they approached had a notice below the bell: *No Hawkers*.

'What's a hawker?' asked Ferriter. 'Sounds like something out of Dickens.'

As Ferriter pressed the button, Cupidi turned her head towards the passing man. 'Excuse me, sir . . .' And she described the boys for the twentieth time.

'Left yesterday,' he said.

Ferriter turned her head.

'They was camping out there for a few days.' He pointed to the other side of the road.

Cupidi tensed, stepped towards the man. 'The two boys? You're sure? Where?'

Ferriter was excusing herself now, trying to get away from a conversation with the resident.

'Can you show us?' asked Cupidi. Ferriter was by her side now. Already there was something different about her. She stood a little straighter; her eyes were brighter.

The elderly fisherman led them to the fence and pointed to a derelict shed about a hundred metres away.

'They were squatting there?'

'Didn't do anyone any harm,' said the man. 'One of them was sick.'

'Sick?'

'Had the flu or something. They holed up. Nobody bothered them.'

Opposite them a sign on the fence read: *Coming Soon. Luxury Apartments.*

'How did they get in there?'

'There's a path – back there.'

Cupidi walked further along the road and there, sure enough, a straight path cut across the marshland towards the river.

'Come on,' she called to Ferriter.

'Oh Jesus. I never have the shoes.'

Cupidi left the tarmac footpath and started walking across the uneven ground towards the shed.

The sun was high now. An asymmetrical 'V' of geese flew over her head.

'Hold up.' Holding her arms above her head, Ferriter was picking her way through brambles hung with black bags of dog shit.

Looking back at her, Cupidi caught sight of the huge bridge crossing the Thames.

The boys had left their rubbish behind in the disused shed. A sleeping bag. The cigarette butts, an empty wine bottle, a pie wrapper and another from a packet of biscuits. Cupidi squatted, picked up discarded cellophane, read the wrapper. 'Co-op. Look. It was them. Here.'

'They were hiding, weren't they?'

Cupidi looked at the derelict land around them. 'Seems like it.' In the corner of the shed someone had been digging through loose earth. She poked the sand with a stick, but there was nothing there. 'Look,' said Ferriter. Freshly scratched into brick at the back of the small enclosure: *Sloth. Ben-G aka TAP.*

As Cupidi was photographing the graffiti, her phone rang. She stood and answered it.

'Where are you? You said you'd be in Ruby Tuesday Drive.' The voice hostile.

'He's here,' Cupidi told Ferriter.

'Shit.'

'Come on.'

'Right now, I'd rather stay here hiding, like them boys,' said Ferriter.

They walked back the way they'd come. Moon was leaning against the bonnet of his Skoda, unsmiling. There was a white bandage across the bridge of his nose. 'Well?'

'Good morning, Peter. Sorry to hear about . . .' said Cupidi.

'It's Sunday. I could be at home in bed. Recovering.'

'How's the . . . ?' Cupidi pointed at his nose.

'It's broken.'

Ferriter made no attempt to apologise.

'What's this about?' he asked.

'We have a significant lead on the two boys from Frank Khan's flat.'

'Yeah?' Cupidi could see he was nervous in Ferriter's company, but he was interested now.

'I know there's stuff between you and Jill. Today, we're just working, all right?' Cupidi crossed her arms.

Moon looked from one to the other, trying to make up his mind whether he believed her or not.

'Your two lads were here. The ones from Frank Khan's flat.'

'OK. How do you know?'

'I asked Khan where he'd picked them up. He said around here.'

'Why didn't he tell me that?'

Ferriter muttered something dark.

Cupidi held out her phone. 'They were staying over there.' She pointed to the outhouse in the distance, beyond the fence. 'A gentleman just ID'd them. I think those are their names.'

Moon peered into the screen, mouthed the names, and then said, 'Oh hell.'

'What?'

Moon looked from one to the other. 'In that case, I'm pretty sure I know who one of them is.'

FORTY-SEVEN

At the door was the man they had robbed, the man they had seen stab Frank. The same plain round face, the same jeans and brown jacket he had been wearing the day they had stolen his briefcase. The same earring. With a roar, Tap ran at him with the spike.

The shock on the man's face was only fleeting. He just stepped back and swept his left forearm in front of his chest, deflecting the iron pole, then grabbing on to it with his right arm.

Tap tumbled in, fell to the floor; the man swung his body round and stamped his foot on the small of his back, blowing the wind out of him and pinning him to the ground. As Tap twisted his head round to struggle free, he saw the man standing above him, pole raised, spike down, ready to impale him.

'Don't. Fucking. Move.'

The man leaned down, feeling Tap's jeans pockets with his free hand, then his hoodie, looking for something. The phone, obviously. When he'd confirmed they were empty, he released him, closed the front door.

'Where's my mum?'

'In bed.'

'Let me see her.'

The man jerked the spike down at him and Tap flinched.

When he opened his eyes, the spike was just above his throat. 'Why did you come back?' the man demanded.

'Nowhere else to go.'

The man leaned down again, grabbed him by his hood and pulled him to his feet.

'Upstairs,' he said.

His mother's bedroom door was open; she was lying on the bed, covers on the floor. Her pale pink duvet was grubby, stained, and peppered with cigarette ash. The bruises on her cheek and arm were dark, fading to green. An empty bottle of supermarket vodka sat on the table next to her, beside a smaller bottle of sleeping pills.

'What have you done?' said Tap.

'She gets lonely and she likes a drink, that's all. I've been keeping her company while you're away.'

She was breathing slowly, chest rising and falling.

'You've been hitting her?'

'She's a drunk. Sometimes she falls down.'

'You've been buying it for her?' said Tap.

The man ignored the question. 'So where is it?'

The phone, obviously. 'Haven't got it. Threw it away.'

'Where?'

'Days ago. In a creek. Up near the river. Chucked it in the mud,' he lied.

Responding to the voices, Tap's mum mumbled something

in her sleep and rolled over in bed, grabbing the duvet as she turned.

'I don't believe you. You're stupid, but not that stupid.'

'Swear to God, man. It was only a shitty little phone.'

It wasn't even fast, the way the man turned, reached out and grabbed him by the hair and, in the same movement, slammed Tap's forehead against the wall. There was a flash of red light inside Tap's head.

And again.

His ears were full of ringing noise. 'I promise,' Tap pleaded. 'We threw it. What good is it to us?' Slam. Back against the plaster, but this time his head slipped from the grip, and when he looked up again, the man was still holding a handful of his hair.

'You're a lying little prick.'

It took Tap a second to realise he was free, but too dizzy to move. His legs seemed to be stuck in mud. He tried to walk, but stumbled forward into the man's feet.

The man kicked him, leaving him face down, breathing dust from the old brown carpet.

He should get up. He should run away. He should start screaming. But he didn't. Instead he lay crying.

'It was the phone I called you on. You kept it. You said you could get it, last time.'

'Yeah. But lost it. Swear to frickin' God.'

'Don't. Lie.' Another kick into the small of his back. 'Your pal says you had it.'

If they hadn't stolen the man's phones, none of this would have happened. But if they hadn't, he wouldn't have spent that time running away. How pathetic a life it was, he realised, that

367

that was the best time he'd ever had. Two weeks with Sloth, together. Scared, hungry and sick, but finally alive, finally breaking through the greyness of it all.

He heard the sound of drawers being yanked open in his mum's room, saw clothes being tugged out onto the floor.

The man returned with a belt. He moved with such simple, purposeful motions, grabbing Tap's right arm, then his left, strapping them together behind his back. Then white searing pain in his arms and shoulders as the man pulled him up by the wrists that had been secured behind his back. Just as the scream emerged, the man's other hand clamped over his mouth.

'Shh,' said the man calmly.

The hand that had yanked him up set him briefly on his feet, then easily lifted him off the ground.

He carried the unstruggling boy into the bathroom and laid him face up in the white enamel bath, then switched on a tap.

The water was cold. It soaked the back of his trainers, then his trousers as it inched its way up. It rose slowly to his chest, chilling him. The man sat there, saying nothing. It seemed to take an age to fill the bath, but when the water reached Tap's chin, the man leaned across and turned off the tap.

Sitting on the toilet, seat closed, the man pulled out a phone and began texting.

'What's on the phone? The one we nicked?'

'My future.'

'How?'

'Shut up.'

'*Survivor. Analyst. Battle.* All that.'

'It was never just a phone. It's a bloody key, that's what it is.'

'What do you mean, a key?'

'Where is it? That's all you got to tell me.'

'Why? 'Cause you'll kill me anyway.'

'Quiet.' The man tapped his knees, as if he was waiting for something. And he was. A few seconds later, the handset rang.

'Calm. It's me. Control yourself,' he was telling someone on the other end of the call. 'Take breaths. That's better.'

Not long now.

'No, I haven't found it yet.' He lowered his voice. 'But I've got one of the boys here. I'll get it out of him and then we can be finished with this.'

The man listened.

'Don't you talk to me like that. What happens to him is your fault, not mine. You started all this, remember. I'm just clearing up your mess.'

Tap realised that the man didn't care what he heard, which meant he was probably going to kill him.

'I'm going to need a car. You have to come here.'

Life was very easy to give up on; strange how much of a fuss some people made about it.

'I don't care. You have to do as I say or I'll tell them where the rest of the body is and you're in deeper shit than I ever was. I'll give you an address. Pick me up here. Don't write it down, just remember it.'

And he took an envelope from his pocket. It was a letter from the council. URGENT: DO NOT IGNORE THIS. His mother had piles of letters like that. He must have found it on the doormat downstairs. The man read out the address printed on the front, repeated it.

'When? Now. Quick as you can. Drive here, then wait outside. When I'm finished here, we can go and fetch your key and then we never have to see each other again.'

Who was he talking to? Tap didn't understand anything. There had been a couple of good weeks and now it was all gone. What a shit little life.

The man looked up. Grabbed a hand towel off the rail and threw it into the water Tap was lying in.

'Where's your friend, Benjamin? The boy called Joseph?'

'What?'

The man repeated the question. 'Don't piss me about. Your mum told me about your pal. You and him. Besties,' said the man. 'He was the other one who stole the phone, wasn't he?' He held up the black handset again. 'He's got it, hasn't he?'

Tap didn't answer. He had been cold when he had entered the house, now icy water was making him shiver.

'Where is he?'

'Don't know, buddy.'

'I'm not your buddy,' the man said. 'Where is Joseph?'

'Don't know.'

'What's his number?'

Tap turned his head away, towards the side of the bath.

The man lifted the towel, sopping wet and laid it methodically across Tap's head, arranging it on his face.

The effect was immediate. Tap sucked air, but there was none. He panicked. The wetness of the cloth was suffocating him. He thrashed from side to side trying to loosen the towel, but the more he moved, the more the fabric clung to his face. It was surprising how quickly terror gripped him. All thought left him. Even the banging on the side of the bath seemed alien, as if it was someone else's limbs thrashing.

The desperation for breath was inseparable from pure fear.

Then the man lifted the towel and he could breathe again, gulping air.

Such a simple motion, lifting the cloth; the difference between life and painful death.

'Where is he?' A plain question.

'Don't know,' he panted. 'Don't frickin' know.'

He would never tell him even if he did. The man lifted the towel again ready to drop it on his face.

'Al? Is that you?'

They looked round. Tap's mum had woken and was calling from the bedroom. He dropped the wet towel back onto Tap's face so he couldn't cry out.

This time he tried his best to control his panic. The man's name was Al. Or at least that was the name he had given his mother.

'Go back to bed,' shouted Al.

'I need the bathroom. Urgent.'

As the oxygen left his blood, he began to lose control, thrashing from side to side, trying to shift the wet cloth from his nose and mouth where it blocked all breath. Mum was outside the door. 'What's that noise?' his mother called.

The man seemed to be counting seconds, as if he knew how

long you could last without oxygen.

After another age, he placed a finger in front of his mouth – *Don't make a noise* – then removed the cloth.

Tap gasped.

'What are you doing in there?'

'Want me to come out there and deal with you?'

'I need the toilet.'

'Go away. I'll be out in a minute.'

There was a banging on the door.

'I'll hurt you if you don't go away,' said Al.

There was a weeping sound. Then: 'Wet myself.'

The man turned back to Tap. He held up his phone. 'Call your friend. Tell him to come here.'

Tap shook his head.

This time he tried to fill his lungs before the wet towel covered his face but no breath was big enough. He lay still, not breathing, for as long as he could but there was no way of stopping his body using up the oxygen. Slowly it slipped away.

Lying still, trying not to panic, watching the man's lips mouth each second as it passed, counting along in his head. When the count reached sixty-five his lungs exploded in pain. He lost control of himself again. The movements were animal, coming from no rational place within him, a monolith of fear that blocked out all thought.

How long did it go on this time? He didn't know. It seemed like an age.

He was aware that he was about to lose all sense of himself, to disappear completely, to black out. It felt as if the room around him had vanished and a calmness crept over him. He was dying. It was over.

And then, again, he was breathing.

'Tell me where he is.'

At first he couldn't answer. It was all he could do to fill his lungs with air.

'Tell me.'

'Rather die,' whispered Tap.

The man frowned. 'You don't understand. I have nothing left to lose,' he said.

'Nor me,' said Tap.

The man seemed to consider this for at least a minute. 'OK,' he said eventually. 'I won't kill you. I'll kill your mother. And you'll watch.'

'You wouldn't,' said Tap.

But the man had left the room and, with his hands tied behind him, however hard he struggled, Tap couldn't raise his body from the bath.

FORTY-EIGHT

They stood on the neat new tarmac of Ruby Tuesday Drive, just across the road from the scrubland of Dartford Marshes.

'Five days ago, this woman called up the police to say her son had gone missing,' said Peter Moon. 'She didn't seem that worried because he'd bunked off before. He was a black guy, seventeen years old. I went to her house . . . showed her the photo of the two boys from the Co-op CCTV and asked if she recognised either of them. She took one look at it and shook her head. "That's not him," she said. "Definitely not." But on the missing persons form they ask for nicknames too, don't they? I remember his was Sloth. Couldn't forget that. Had a laugh about it.'

'Two names. Two boys,' said Cupidi. She looked at her phone screen: *Sloth. Ben-G aka TAP.*

Ferriter was piecing it together too. 'His mother didn't want to say it was him, because she knew that if you were showing her CCTV stills, he was in trouble for something.'

374

Moon nodded. 'Trying to protect him. I never thought.'

Cupidi said, 'Do you have her address?'

He opened the car door and pulled out a notebook. Cupidi looked over his shoulder as he leafed through the pages. His handwriting was tiny, but extremely neat. He held out his pad towards Cupidi, called out the address and Ferriter looked the place up on her phone. It was not far.

'See you there in fifteen minutes.'

He hesitated. 'I can do it on my own, you know.' Cupidi knew what he was thinking. He wasn't sure he wanted to work with a copper he was probably going to make an official complaint about in the morning.

'Yes. You can. Completely your call.'

He got into his car and looked at them both warily before starting the engine.

'Why not let him get on with it? It's his case,' said Ferriter. 'We've done our good deed for the day.'

Cupidi hesitated.

'You still think it's connected, don't you? Just because of what Clough said.'

'He's a teenage boy. We think somebody tried to kill him. May still be trying. It's our job.'

'Yeah. But you still think it's connected, don't you?'

'No,' said Cupidi, defensively. 'Not necessarily.'

Felicia Watt stood on her doorstep and said, 'My son Joseph is not here.'

'This is his picture, though, isn't it?' Moon was showing her something, holding it close to her face.

'He's not here.'

'Could you please answer the question, Mrs Watt? Do you think this could be your son in the picture?'

Cupidi could hear the woman repeating, 'I would prefer not to answer anything at all,' as she walked from the car.

On Cupidi's approach, Felicia Watt said, 'Oh my God. Now there are more of you. How come there weren't this many when I first said my son was missing?' She wore a silver charm bracelet around her fat wrist; Cupidi watched a letter 'J' glint in the sunshine.

'Alex Cupidi. I'm Detective Sergeant Moon's colleague, and this is Constable Jill Ferriter. What if we talked inside for a moment?'

'I really don't think so. Today is my day off. I was resting.'

A next-door neighbour – a bulky man with a cut under one eye and grease on his T-shirt – looked up from under the bonnet of a Peugeot. 'They bothering you, Mrs W?'

'We just need five minutes, Mrs Watt,' said Moon. 'Your son may be in some danger.'

Mrs Watt sighed.

Her house was spotlessly clean. The three officers stood around a shining wooden coffee table in a small living room lined with silver-patterned wallpaper.

'We believe that your son and another boy may be witnesses to a serious assault, Mrs Watt,' said Moon. Felicia Watt's face had been expressionless up to now, but Cupidi could see fear there now.

'Whatever trouble you think they're in, that's not important. But we do need to find him for his own safety,' said Cupidi.

'How long is it since you saw your son, Mrs Watt?' Moon asked.

She sat heavily in an armchair, took out an asthma inhaler, and pumped twice into her mouth.

'Last night. He was here.'

Cupidi exchanged a glance with Moon.

'About ten or eleven. His new trainers, the ones he begged me for. They cost me over eighty pounds and they are totally ruined. I think he has been living on the streets. I screamed at him so loud. I told him to tell me what kind of mischief he'd been up to but he wouldn't say.'

She pressed her lips tight together, as if holding back the emotion, looked down at the shine of the coffee table, a woman too proud to cry in front of three coppers.

'I was thinking he was on drugs or something. He smokes marijuana in his room sometimes. I tell him I'll skin him alive if I catch him at it, but he's stronger than me now.'

She looked sideways, out of the window. Through the thick nylon nets, Cupidi could see the silhouette of Mrs Watt's neighbour, backlit by the morning sunshine, standing on the concrete in front of the house, trying to see what was going on inside.

'He had a shower. I gave him some chicken. He ate it like he had eaten nothing for the whole week. Then I sent him to his room. When I got up this morning, he was gone. No note. Nothing.'

She looked back at Cupidi, again her lips pressed tight. Moon opened his mouth to ask a question, but before he could, she spoke again. 'I swear to God, I don't know where he's gone. On Jesus Christ's name.'

There was a moment's silence. Ferriter leaned down towards

her and asked, 'This is important, Mrs Watt. Did he say anything about what he's been doing in the last few days?'

At first Mrs Watt didn't answer. 'He didn't talk. I asked him. He was angry about something. I could tell. You know how boys are. They store it all inside them. I asked him but he wouldn't tell me anything at all. He just went upstairs and closed his bedroom door tight. I knocked but he asked me to leave him alone.'

Cupidi glanced upwards at the ceiling.

'Don't even think about it,' said Mrs Watt. 'I've invited you into my house, but I wouldn't let you in there. Not without his permission.'

'What about his friend. In this photo?' Moon held it up again. However grainy the image, it was clearly two boys, one about a foot taller than the other.

She frowned. 'Benjamin? He's no good. If something bad has happened, it will be Benjamin's fault. I'm single. My husband is gone. I do what I can, but it is not easy with a boy.'

'Did Joseph pack a bag or anything?'

She shook her head. 'I don't know.'

The strong desire to protect her own child; Cupidi understood that.

Cupidi squatted down in front of her and said, 'We think he may be in serious danger, Mrs Watt. We're trying to help him, I promise. Cross my heart. If you don't want us to look in his room, will you do it? Any clue. Anything that's missing. Anything that he left behind that might tell us where he is.'

Felicia Watt chewed on the inside of her lip for a while, looking Cupidi straight in the eye.

'You're not just saying that to make me . . .'

378

'No. I'm not saying that. I don't know what kind of danger he is in, but I do think the threat is very real. I think he's been running away for good reason. Trying to hide.'

'I am not giving up on my boy, Sergeant. I'm not turning him in.'

'I know. You're trying to help him. We are, too. I promise. I have a girl the same age.'

'Wait here,' she said, pushing herself out of the chair. At the door, she hesitated. 'Don't touch a single thing. OK?'

Nobody spoke until she had left the room and they could hear her moving around upstairs.

'You really think he's in that kind of danger?' asked Moon after a minute.

The stairs creaked. They listened in silence.

Mrs Watt appeared at the door again, pausing this time to scrutinise each of them in turn, as if she suspected them of rifling through her drawers.

'He left this,' she said eventually, producing a small black phone from behind her back and holding it up. The make was Alcatel; one of those you could buy anywhere for ten pounds. They only did voice and text; which is why the kind of people who used them liked them.

The expression on the mother's face was one of resignation; as if she knew as well as the police did that a phone like that was probably not a good sign.

'Is that his?'

'He has this place. In his cupboard, behind his shoes. He thinks I don't know about it. But.'

Cupidi was already digging into her shoulder bag for something to put it in.

'I've not seen it before,' Mrs Watt said. 'It wasn't there before. I looked when he was gone the first time. If it is his, I didn't buy it for him.'

Cupidi held out the clear plastic evidence bag for her to drop it in. The woman looked pained, as if she believed she had somehow betrayed her own child. 'What about his friend? Benjamin. Where does he live?'

While Ferriter was writing down the address, Cupidi examined the phone. There was dirt in the keys that looked like earth. She pressed the ON button through the polythene of the bag. The screen stayed dead. The battery was flat. She was about to put it in her bag when she noticed something scratched into the plastic casing. She held it up to the light.

Clearly visible, scored into the plastic: *2767*52.*

FORTY-NINE

Five minutes later, the man returned to the bathroom and lifted Tap out of the cold water.

He stood him on his feet, water cascading off him, into his shoes and out onto the bathroom floor, hands still tied behind his back.

The man nudged him forward.

Stupid idea, stealing phones, Tap thought. It had just been the thrill of it; him and Sloth against the world, daring each other, getting in deeper and deeper. And now Sloth hated him and everything had gone to shit. He had not snitched on him. But now his mother's life was in danger and he was going to have to choose between them.

They crossed the landing and entered his mother's bedroom. It was dark, curtains drawn.

'Benji?' His mother was lying in bed in a mess of pink sheets, eyes bleary.

The man called Al gave him a push, shoving him towards his mother.

'What are you doing here, Benj?' Her voice was slurry. She was having trouble forming words.

'I came back for you, Mum.'

'I'm so bloody stupid, Benj. What a mess I'm in.' There was exhaustion in her voice.

His hands were tied. How could he take Al on with no hands?

'Time for your medicine,' Al told his mother.

He had pushed Tap to the foot of her bed and was standing between him and the door.

'What medicine?'

'I brought you some pills.'

'Don't want any pills,' she said, like a small child.

In his gloved hand, he held something up. Even in the dim light Tap could see it, small, round, light blue. Poison, thought Tap. Before Al could leave the doorway to approach his mother's bed, Tap knew he would have to take his chance. He was exhausted, worn out from the near drownings, but he had to try.

With a roar, he lowered his head and ran towards the doorway. Holding the pill, Al only had one hand to fend him off with, and no time to prepare himself for the force of the teenager hitting him. And Tap had got his trajectory right. Al collapsed backwards, slamming into the wall at the top of the stairs.

As he tried to steady himself, Tap jerked his head up, hitting Al under the chin with such force he heard his teeth smash together. He heard him groan, sliding down to the floor.

Tap kicked him straight in the mouth then turned to go down the stairs. His right foot hit the first step, but something snagged his left leg. Arms still bound, he had no way to catch himself.

And then he was falling, twisting for long enough to see Al's hand extended. He had put out his hand and simply tripped him. Nothing would ever go right.

Head first, he sailed downwards, crashing into the floor at the bottom of the stairs.

The man gathered him up, tossed him onto the bed near his mother. She was sound asleep already, as if she was dead drunk.

'Do you love your mum?' asked Al.

'Yeah.' Automatic answer and automatically true, despite everything.

'Well, she's going to die, probably very soon. Know what Fentanyl is? Doesn't matter if you don't. It's a drug. I've given her it now. It'll stop her breathing soon. The only way you can save her is tell me where the phone is. You've got minutes.'

He looked at his mother. She was on her back, eyes closed, the breath already coming very slowly.

'I don't know.' He tried to answer as urgently as he could.

'Your friend then. The one who drove the scooter.' The man looked desperate now. There was blood on his chin, and his mouth looked swollen, from when Tap's head had hit him, or maybe his foot.

Tap shook his head.

'I don't know where it is. I don't frickin' know where it is.' His mother or Sloth? How could he choose? But he couldn't betray one to save the other either. He was useless.

The man dug into his pocket and pulled out a small plastic bag with two more blue pills in it.

'You little shitters have ruined my life,' the man said. He took out one pill. 'You're next,' he said.

The man took his phone out again, texted a message. Put it back in his pocket, then jumped as the house phone rang loudly. It felt good to see fear on the man's face at the unexpected noise. He was desperate too, it seemed.

Tap watched his mother's chest, looking for signs of it rising and falling. He should have saved her, but he had messed everything up again.

The phone stopped ringing. The voicemail kicked in. '*Hi. I'm on my luxury yacht in Barbados, darling. I can't pick up right now.*'

His mother's voice, but she wasn't speaking.

FIFTY

'We can charge it up, though, can't we?' Ferriter was looking at the small black device that looked more like a children's toy than a real phone.

'Oughtn't we to leave it for the tech people?' Moon said.

They stood in the street outside Felicia Watt's house. The neighbour who had been outside fixing his car stood with a dirty cloth in his hand, his eye still on them.

'Risk to life,' said Ferriter, fingering the device through the polythene. 'What if it has numbers on it that we could use now? That's our priority.'

'You're right. Go on then,' said Cupidi.

'Only, I haven't got a USB. Only got an iPhone charger.' Ferriter looked at Moon.

'My car then.' His Skoda was parked a few doors down. Sitting in the driver's seat, he took the bag from Ferriter, held it in one hand, the lead in the other.

'Just poke a hole in the plastic,' urged Ferriter.

He stuck the USB cable into the bottom of the phone. The screen remained blank. 'It's probably been flat for a while. It can take up to half an hour.'

'Obviously,' muttered Ferriter.

They lapsed into awkward silence. Minutes passed. Occasionally Moon raised a hand to his nose, touched it gingerly.

When Ferriter prodded the phone again, Moon chided, 'Leave it alone.'

And then, as it lay between the two front seats, the screen lit.

'Two, seven, six, seven. That's got to be the lock code,' said Ferriter.

'OK.' He thumbed the full code in; she was right.

'Last numbers dialled,' Ferriter urged him. 'Here. Give me it.'

'I know,' protested Moon. 'I'm doing it.' They sat in the car park while he prodded at the keys. 'Got it.' Then: 'Write them down. One incoming call . . .'

'What about text messages?'

'Give me a chance. Jesus. Take down this number. It's local.'

He read out the number. Cupidi called it straight away on her own phone. It went to voicemail: '*Hi. I'm on my luxury yacht in Barbados, darling. I can't pick up right now.*' Cupid rang off after the beep. 'Not in.'

'One message too. Jesus.' Moon held it up for them to see: *U win I will pay u half ££ if you promise to leave me alone.*

All three looked at each other. 'What the hell's that?'

'What number is it from?'

He read the digits aloud. Cupidi was already dialling the number into her own phone.

'Jesus bloody Christ,' she shouted.

'What?'

Sometimes everything about an investigation changes in a second.

Even before she tried to call it, her iPhone had recognised it. It was one she had called before.

'Whose number is that?'

She looked up, startled. 'It's . . . Astrid Miller's.' She held up her phone so the others could see. 'I had the number off Evert Miller. I know it's hers. The one I texted her on.'

'Must be a mistake . . .' said Ferriter. 'That's impossible. I mean.' She checked one phone, then the other. Identical. 'Bloody hell.'

All three looked at each other. 'What is Astrid Miller texting that lad for? What is she saying about paying him?'

'Definitely that number,' said Moon, still examining the screen on the phone in the plastic bag.

All three of them, dumbfounded, trying to work out what this meant.

'When was it sent?'

'A week ago Friday. What's a rent boy like him talking to Astrid Miller for?'

'Who says he's a rent boy?' protested Ferriter.

Cupidi pressed the CALL button on her own phone. It was unfathomable. Two separate cases – the dismembered arm, the stabbing of a paedophile – had just been joined by an unlikely thread. The fog of the last week seemed to have blown away, but despite that, there was still no shape to what Cupidi could see.

Astrid Miller didn't answer. Her call went to voicemail too.

'*I'm not available. If it's important, leave me a message.*' Her voice, though, unmistakably. The millionaire Astrid Miller's details on the shoplifter Joseph Watt's phone. But why? It made no sense at all.

Cupidi had seen the boys as victims, but the phone made out they were blackmailers who had some hold over her. She dialled home.

'What are you doing?' asked Ferriter.

'We need to find Astrid Miller right now. I think she's in some kind of trouble.'

No answer from her home, so she tried Zoë's mobile. 'Where are you?' she asked when she answered.

There was the whip of wind in the background. 'Burrowes Pit,' Zoë said. 'When are you home?'

Burrowes Pit. One of the huge gravel scrapes that had filled with water at the centre of the shingle banks. 'You're bird-watching?'

'Birding.' She never liked it when her mother called it 'bird-watching'. In spite of the drama of the moment, she found herself smiling.

'I need you to get an urgent message to Bill South.'

'He's here. With me. At Burrowes Pit.'

'He is?' Another surprise.

'Yes. He came by this morning. Said you'd told him to look after me. I'm seventeen, Mum.' Despite the attempt at resentment in her daughter's voice, Cupidi could also hear a happiness too. She had grown up; but she was still the same girl who looked for birds, too. 'I'll pass him my phone, OK?'

'Love you.'

'Shut up.'

Then another voice, hesitant. 'Yes?'

'You're outside, Bill. With Zoë. Thank you.'

A grunt of acknowledgement.

'Anything good?'

'Supposed to be some Egyptian geese around, but we haven't seen them. What did you want?' Grumpy, truculent.

'You're birding. How does it feel?'

'All right, I suppose.'

'A favour. Can you go and check on Astrid Miller's cottage? It's urgent.'

'Why?'

'I need to talk to her and I haven't time to get back myself . . .'

'Astrid Miller's not there.'

'What?'

'After you asked about her, I've been keeping an eye on the place.'

'I thought you were just sitting at home feeling sorry for yourself.'

'Bit of that, too, yes. She came back there this morning in a red sports car, stopped at the cottage.' Inside, still a copper, still observant. 'Saw her driving away up the Dungeness Road a couple of hours ago.'

'Did you get the registration number?'

'Give me a break, Alex,' he said.

Moon was saying, 'What now?'

'The other boy,' said Ferriter. 'One of us should check on him.'

Moon looked from one to the other. 'Yes,' he said. 'Fair play. I'll go.'

'We should probably come with you,' said Cupidi.

He looked at Ferriter.

'I'll be fine on my own, thank you very much.'

'Suit yourself,' said Ferriter.

Cupidi hesitated, wondering if she should insist, but the atmosphere between the two of them was so bad, she decided to leave it; besides, there was other work to do. The last they saw of Moon was when he dropped them back at Cupidi's car.

'Astrid Miller,' she said, as he drove away. 'Come on. I think we need to put a stick into the beehive.'

'What do you mean?'

Cupidi drove in silence. Astrid Miller was connected somehow to the two shoplifters. None of this made sense. Cupidi remembered Ross Clough's wall of drawings. Just because, like a zealot seeing visions, Clough saw a pattern where others saw nothing, that didn't mean there wasn't one.

FIFTY-ONE

A bright shaft of sunlight fell, stinging Tap's eyes.

The man called Al had lifted a corner of the curtains and was peering out. 'I can see you,' he said. 'Give me a wave. That's good.'

He seemed to be speaking on the phone to someone on the street outside.

'Wait there. I'm almost done. I need to tidy up here. Fifteen minutes. Good girl.'

Tap lay on the bed, trussed for slaughter.

'Mum.' His voice was just a whisper.

'Mum.'

The man's lip had been bleeding. He approached the bed. 'Last chance. You have one minute to tell me where the phone is. If you call the ambulance you might be able to save her.'

The man leaned down. 'I can't hear you.'

'Loser.'

The man slapped him. 'Your mother is dying. She'll be dead

391

very soon. If you're lucky, you can call an ambulance for her and they'll give her something before her heart stops beating. But you have to tell me.'

The man was pretending that Tap could save her but whatever he said, he would kill them both anyway. He was sure of that now. The only good thing Tap could do was to save Sloth by dying without telling the man anything.

'I had a good time.'

'What are you saying?'

'One week. I had a really good time. I was sick. I was hungry and dirty. But, you know what? I had a really good time.'

The man seemed momentarily confused, like an actor being fed the wrong lines. 'What you on about?'

Sunrise. Exceed. Purpose. 'Nothing much.'

'Last chance. You know what happens if you don't tell me, do you?'

'Same as if I do tell you. You killed Mikey, didn't you.'

'Who?'

'Uncle Mikey. He told you it was us who stole your phones, didn't he? You killed him anyway.'

'You shouldn't have nicked the phone.'

'No. Shouldn't.' Tap was crying now.

One hand shot out and pressed on Tap's throat, choking him. 'If you don't give me that phone, you have literally destroyed millions of pounds. Up in fucking smoke. It's that you should be crying about.' There was a quiet fury in the man's voice. 'You worthless little shitters. Making everything around you worthless too.'

The man straightened, walked a little way across the room,

and turned his mother's bedside radio on. It was tuned to BBC Radio 2. Worst music in the world. Katy Perry. His mum loved it though. He hoped she could hear the song still.

The man knelt down again by Tap's side. Something shone in his hands.

Tap's heart jolted. That's how he would die.

He had watched execution videos. All the boys had. He had never understood how the victims seemed to accept their fate, allowed themselves to be killed in such a way. And yet now it was his turn, he had no struggle in him at all. It seemed inevitable.

Mum lay beside him on the bed. She was still. There was foam on her lips.

But he didn't use the knife. 'Here you go. Open wide.'

The round pill was a pretty pale blue. Holding it in one hand, he grabbed Tap's hair and tugged his head backwards. Tap clamped his mouth shut.

'It's OK. It's not a bad way to go,' said the man. 'Better than you deserve. They pay good money for this kind of stuff out there. It's your lucky day. Open wide.'

The hand with the pill, concealed in the glove, clamped over his nose again.

Tap lasted as long as he could, but a finger probed in his mouth, released a pill, then the palm clamped tight again across his lips.

'Swallow.'

Tap shook his head, not because he thought he could win, just because it was the only power he had left. Instantly the chemical was bitter on his gum.

'It doesn't matter if you don't swallow. You'll be absorbing it already.'

He was right. His mouth was already coated with the bitter taste. He felt a dizziness. Was it that strong?

Tap was trying to spit saliva onto Al's gloved palm, but the man was still holding it tight against his mouth, and it was hard to eject any liquid. A warm white blanket was already wrapping itself around him.

Nobody would be that surprised, his mother overdosing. She had been a substance user for years. It would be in the papers: Mother and Son Die in Drug Tragedy. The kind of thing that happened, round here.

He had to hold on as long as he could. The man seemed in no hurry either. He turned him over and sawed through the belt, threw it away. It wouldn't look like an overdose if he was tied up. That's what the knife had been for. Then the man produced another pill.

And then there was a banging on a door somewhere far away.

The man swore as he dropped the second pill, watched it bounce away under his mum's bed.

A door handle rattled.

The thumping again, louder, then it stopped.

'Open up,' shouted a voice.

The man knelt by him, his hand clamped still to stop Tap from saying anything.

'Police officer!'

Police? Tap sucked air in through his nose to try and shout. 'Mmm.'

The man pressed harder against his face to prevent any sound escaping. Tap tasted blood in his mouth.

Another yell. 'Anyone there?'

Tap struggled harder. The man reached for the bread knife he had cut the belt with, allowing him to twist away in the bed. He fell to the floor with a loud thump.

The man's face betrayed fear.

Tap kicked out one last time, catching a mannequin that stood by the side of the bed, covered in glad rags. It crashed to the floor.

Would the police have heard it? The man fumbled in his brown jacket for his phone, pulled it out again.

'You still there?' he whispered. 'How many police are there? Where are they?'

Whatever the answer, the man looked puzzled.

The sound of a window breaking somewhere. They were coming in.

Unsure of himself, the man loosened his grip.

Tap spat, then tried shouting, 'Here. I'm up here.' But his voice was weak.

The man smacked him hard, moved round the bottom of the bed, towards the door, scrambling to find a place to hide.

'Up here,' Tap said woozily.

He turned his head to see a look of confusion on the man's face, as they heard the noise of someone climbing the stairs.

FIFTY-TWO

'You don't want to ring Evert Miller first?' Ferriter said.

'No. I don't.'

From the lane, Long Hill looked deserted.

'Aren't we going in?'

'Ross Clough said there was a public footpath. I want to see where he walked.'

'Why?'

'Because it's a nice day.'

'Really,' said Ferriter. 'You're serious?'

Something else from Ross Clough's drawings was starting to make sense now, too. If she remembered rightly, the public path by which Clough had got into the estate lay a little to the north of the lane that served as an entrance to it. Parking the car by the main gate, she walked back down the road a little way until she came to a small gap in the hedge.

A dead elder branch had been laid across the entrance, as if it had fallen there, but there was no elder tree nearby. Someone must have placed it there deliberately to disguise the path. At her feet in the undergrowth was a sawn stump. She guessed it had once been the post that had held the sign to the footpath.

The rich liked privacy.

'This way,' she said.

'God. Not again.'

Cupidi pulled back the branch and moved down the path.

As she passed under the tree, Cupidi noticed the small wireless security camera, mounted on the trunk. She paused, gave it a small smile and a wave.

The woods were little more than a copse, hiding the estate from the lane. On the far side the land opened out into gently rolling open country, rich with wild flowers.

'Wait for me,' said Ferriter.

The countryside was so quiet around here. No surprise, perhaps. It was a hot Sunday.

The path was barely visible. Discouraging ramblers had worked. Another, newer woodland lay ahead. From behind it they heard the sound of gently lapping water.

The public footpath merged with one that looked more familiar, this one newly cut back. They entered another copse. Damselflies hung in the air, iridescent in the sunshine. There was a buzz in the grass around them, and again, from a distance, they heard the gentle splash.

As they rounded the corner, they could see Evert Miller's head above the water. Zoya Gubenko, lying glamorously on a sunbed in nothing but a pair of white shorts, was the first to hear them. She sat up, squinting, making no attempt to cover herself.

'Evert,' she said, warning him.

Turning in the water, Evert Miller looked, then frowned. 'What are you doing here?'

'You invited me for a swim, remember?'

'It's Sunday. I hope you're on overtime.'

He turned again, swimming a casual breast stroke towards the opposite edge of the pool where the cabanas were. Cupidi wondered if he was naked, but not for long. When he reached shallow water he found his feet, and his buttocks emerged from the water.

'Where's Allan?' Zoya Gubenko asked. Allan Mulligan, the security man, Cupidi guessed. He was supposed to be here, protecting them from intruders.

'I don't know,' said Evert Miller.

'You should sack him,' Gubenko said. 'He's become so unreliable recently.' She stood, handed Miller a light brown towel as he emerged. He turned, using the towel on his hair but leaving the rest of his body uncovered. His land, his rules.

'This is nice,' said Cupidi.

'Fancy it? Or your lovely friend.'

'Creep,' muttered Ferriter.

'Looks bloody cold to me,' said Cupidi.

'It is. That's what's so invigorating.'

Finally he lowered the towel, wrapped it around himself.

'To what do I owe?'

'Your wife.' She looked at Gubenko. 'I need to contact her urgently.'

'Why?' He pressed the towel against his groin, as if drying it. Patting his genitals in front of them seemed to be intended to communicate some kind of mastery of the situation.

398

'I can't say. But it's urgent.'

Another security man arrived, heavy-footed in boots, hot in his uniform, down the path from the houses.

'Sorry, Mr Miller. Didn't see them getting in.'

Only now there was staff present did Zoya Gubenko wrap the towel around her breasts. 'Where's Mr Mulligan?' she demanded.

'Said he had an emergency at home.'

'My wife, for reasons that may be becoming obvious to understand, is not speaking to me,' said Evert Miller.

'Because you're having an affair with her assistant, presumably.'

'Our relationship has always been an open one,' said Miller.

Ferriter snorted.

'So you have no idea where she is?'

'No.'

'That's what you told me last time. You knew where she was all the time. When I last saw her, she appeared to be scared of something.'

'You saw her? When?'

'Last week.'

'Where?'

Cupidi hesitated. 'At her cottage in Dungeness. You knew that.'

'No. I didn't. I swear.'

For a second, Cupidi was confused. Allan Mulligan had certainly known she was there. But Evert Miller hadn't? 'You didn't?'

'Why would I lie?'

Zoya Gubenko turned her back and pulled a white T-shirt over her head, then turned back to face them.

399

'She hasn't been answering phone or email. I don't know where she is.'

But Allan Mulligan had? Sweat prickled on the back of Cupidi's neck. She felt suddenly overdressed in the heat of the spring day. 'Has she behaved like this before?' she asked.

'Actually, no. Not like this. She's disappeared, but never for this long.'

'You don't seem particularly concerned about her.'

For the first time, Miller looked unsettled. 'Of course I'm bloody concerned about her,' he said.

'Yeah, right,' whispered Ferriter.

'We think she may be in some . . . danger. We'll need her car registration number.' They needed to find her, but she did not want to be found. Why? 'Have you ever heard of a seven-teen-year-old boy called Joseph Watt?'

'I think it's time you left,' said Evert Miller.

'Have you?'

'No. I haven't.'

'When you hired Abir Stein, were you aware he had been involved in money laundering?'

Miller frowned. 'I want you off my property now. I'm going to contact my lawyer. I'd advise you that any further communication must now go through the proper channels.'

'I need the car registration. I'm serious. Your wife may be in serious danger.' Someone was blackmailing her and it was connected somehow to the missing boys, the stabbing of Frank Khan, and the death of Abir Stein.

'My lawyer will be in touch. Get the hell out,' said Miller.

They had no choice. They walked the way they came, branches swatting on their faces.

'How did you know that was going on – that he was shagging that woman?'

'I didn't. But it fits now. Ross Clough had hinted he was about to find a major backer. He'd figured out the affair before we did and I think he's blackmailing Evert Miller into supporting his artwork.'

Cupidi tried calling Moon as they made their way back through the hot grass. 'Funny,' she said. 'Moon's not picking up.'

'Because he hates us.'

Just as they were getting back into the car, a text arrived. It was from Zoya Gubenko's number.

When Cupidi opened it, it contained some numbers and letters. A vehicle registration.

Then a second message came through from Gubenko: **Pls don't tell Evert I sent this.**

'Interesting,' said Cupidi.

She called Moon again. It rang a while, then went to voicemail.

'Maybe he's driving.'

She tried again. Then called the incident room.

'I've got a vehicle registration number. Can you check ANPR and get back to me with where it was last seen?'

A fourth time she called Moon, but there was still no answer.

'What an arse that man is,' Ferriter said. 'I can't believe she ever married him. He's going to kick up a stink, isn't he?'

'Yes.'

'Well, now you're in the shit tomorrow morning too. He's going to make a complaint about you, I'll bet.'

★

The day was the hottest so far; humid, too. Cupidi pulled over at a lay-by off the A2.

'Why are you stopping?'

Cupidi pointed at the ice-cream van, parked ahead. She wasn't the only one who had thought of it. There was a queue of half a dozen people.

Ferriter wrinkled her nose. 'Don't like ice creams. They use pig skin, you know, as thickening agent.'

'Yum,' said Cupidi.

Ferriter's phone went. She picked it up, listened. Her mouth opened wide. 'You're shitting me,' she said.

'What?' demanded Cupidi.

Ferriter ended the call. 'Incident room said they've just had a ping from Astrid Miller's car on ANPR. Fifteen minutes ago. And bloody guess where it is?'

'Just tell me.'

'Camera on Overy Liberty in Dartford.'

'I don't understand.'

'That's like . . . two hundred metres from where Moon was headed just now. Literally.'

'Why would she . . . ?'

'No bloody idea. But it's too much of a bloody coincidence now. First one of the boys has her number, and now she's there.'

'Call Moon.'

Ice cream was out. Cupidi checked her watch, switched on blue lights and put the car into gear, pulling out into traffic and ramming her foot onto the accelerator. They were still half an hour away at least, even with the siren going.

402

'Peter. Pick up. If you're at the lad's house, look out for a . . . What is it?'

'Red Tesla.'

'Get back to me. Please let me know you got this, Peter, OK?'

Cars parted ahead of them on the dual carriageway.

'Get some uniforms to that house,' Cupidi said. 'Then get back to the incident room and let us know the first sign that car moves again.'

While Cupidi roared northwards, Ferriter tried calling again.

FIFTY-THREE

Instead of a policeman standing in the doorway, lit by the light from the landing, there was a boy. And the boy spoke: 'Tap?'

'Sloth?'

'What you doin', bro?'

'Where's the cops?' Tap whispered.

Sloth, beautiful Sloth, stood there, a big grin on his face. 'Ain't no cops, bro. Just me. I thought that man might still be here. Thought I'd come and mess him up, y'know. Like we said.'

And then the smile vanished from Sloth's face as he took in the room and realised something was wrong.

'Run,' said Tap, but his voice was too weak.

'What . . . ?'

'Run.'

Everything else seemed to slow except the man, who pulled the door back, stepped forward and grabbed him, knife against his throat, hand over his mouth.

Sloth stood, utterly bewildered, suddenly terrified.

Tap fighting so hard to stay awake. The knife so tight against Sloth's throat that the blood started to drip down his white T-shirt.

'Where's the phone?'

'Don't tell him, bro,' whispered Tap.

It was quiet for a few seconds. And then came the sound of a car pulling up outside.

The man holding Sloth tensed, tightened his grip on him.

A man rattling the front door. 'Hello? Police.'

Real police, this time. You could tell. The man was panicking now. He could let go of Sloth and try and run for it, but Sloth would cry out.

'Hello?'

With a single movement, keeping his hand over Sloth's mouth, he plunged the knife into his neck. Sloth's eyes widened in fear and pain.

Tap could only watch, horrified. He was conscious of a noise coming from somewhere and it took a second to realise that it was from his own mouth.

When the man removed the knife, blood spurted onto the linen.

'Police. I'm coming up.'

Sloth fell face first onto the bed.

Moon noticed the red Tesla, parked a few metres away from the house. What was a car that tasty doing around here anyway? There was a woman in it, who looked away as he pulled up outside the house, phone buzzing in his pocket.

Funny. The curtains were all drawn, upstairs and down.

Getting out, he took out the handset. Missed calls from Ferriter, this time. An apology? Like that was going to happen. It was like walking on eggshells, working with some women.

He was going to have to call her back, though. His hand hovered over the button on his phone, but he stopped. Looked at his feet. Glass on the ground. Something was seriously wrong here.

A pane in the front door at the address he had been given had been smashed, and recently. There were shards on the doormat.

The door had been opened. He put two and two together. Someone had broken the door, put their hand inside and let themselves in. Nudging it, it swung back.

'Hello?' he called into the house. 'Police.'

At first, it seemed to be quiet.

'Hello?'

He was about to go back to his car and call it in, get some uniforms down here, when, from above, he heard the sound of someone sobbing. He listened. There was a deep sadness in the crying, a quality that was impossible not to be affected by. A weariness too. The noise sounded almost animal-like.

'Police. I'm coming up,' he said. And he started up the stairs, taking them two at a time. For some reason, though, he felt unusually apprehensive. There was a stab vest in the boot of the car, he remembered. He should be wearing it, shouldn't he?

But he carried on upwards, towards the sound of pain and distress.

PART FOUR

Fear Death by Water

FIFTY-FOUR

The road was strangely quiet. No pedestrians, no cars moving. No sign of the Tesla either.

'Bollocks,' said Cupidi. 'I was sure she'd be here, for some reason.'

After the dash to get here, it seemed to be an anticlimax, arriving. She spotted a marked police car on the corner and ran across to it.

'We were told to come here and look for a red Tesla. Waste of time,' said a constable, looking up from his notebook. 'No sign of anything like that.'

'Have you seen Sergeant Moon of Serious Crime anywhere?'

'Who?' said the constable.

Ferriter looked around. 'That's Moon's car there, isn't it?'

Moon's car was parked on the pavement in front of a house, but he was nowhere to be seen, and when Cupidi looked at the number on the front door, she realised that was the address they had been given by Joseph's mother.

Something was very wrong. There was broken glass on the front step. The door was open, too, just a couple of inches. She noticed the small jagged hole where someone had reached inside to twist the lock. Cupidi's heart accelerated. She stepped into the house and smelt the oddly familiar scent, like wet rust, only more cloying, more sweet; she felt her pulse beat in her ears.

'Jill,' she shouted. 'Get the constables in here. Now.'

The living room looked ordinary, untidy. Pizza boxes and empty cans.

Then a small noise from upstairs. The shifting of a foot. There was someone up there.

'Jill?' But she would be in the car across the road, on the radio.

Cupidi climbed the stairs, alert, looking around, moving towards where she imagined the noise had come from.

On the landing floor, just by the bedroom door, a belt. She looked at it, puzzled for a second. The buckle was still done up, but the leather had been cut.

Reaching the top of the landing she looked to her right, into a bedroom.

Beyond the doorway, the carpet changed from dirty pink to a deeper colour, one that seemed to shine in the electric light.

It was the blood she had smelt when she entered the house. She took another step forward.

'Police,' she called.

Then another step, pushing back the half-open door; it knocked against something soft.

There was someone behind the door. Cautious, she put her

410

eye to the hinge and looked through the crack between the door and the jamb.

But there was no one there, was there? So what was stopping the door from opening fully? Then, looking down, she saw a dark shape on the floor below her, legs splayed out. Someone was sitting against the wall by the door.

Heart thumping, she took a step into the room, her foot landing on the wet carpet. Blood rose from the nylon pile around her shoe as her weight pressed down.

Then she was in the room.

She stopped. In front of her on the bed were three people. One boy was being cradled by another; the one lying still, his dark hoodie shining with the same wetness, must be Joseph. She guessed he must be the boy from the CCTV still. He looked in a bad way. Joseph was being held by another boy who was quietly crying. The white boy from the same picture.

Also on the bed, a woman in a ridiculous pink nightdress, eyes half open, spittle and foam on her lips, her skin paper white.

It was a small room. The bed took up most of the space. She stepped backwards, back into a blood pool, and pushed the door back to discover who was behind the door.

'Oh Christ! No.'

Peter Moon slumped, not moving, eyes closed. Some blood still trickled from a wound in his chest. The rest of it lay around him.

Hands trembling, Cupidi took out her phone. 999.

You had to think quickly, times like this. She may have seen some bad crime scenes in her time, but nothing as brutal as this, with so many dead or wounded.

As the call connected, she looked around, pushing the horror away. First duty was always preserve life, but with only one pair of hands, which one do you try to save? The crying white boy looked healthiest, though there was something strange about the way he was behaving, as if he had barely registered her arrival in the room. Was it shock, or something else?

To her right, Moon was silent, unconscious. So was the woman.

The fourth person, Joseph, was slowly oozing blood from a wound in his neck but his eyes were still fluttering.

'Hello . . . Which service do you—'

She interrupted, identified herself, her location. 'Ambulance. Multiple serious injuries. Four victims. Two stabbings, bleeding out. Not sure about the others. Hurry.'

She pulled a pillow from the bed and tore off the pillowcase, scrunching the material up into a tight wad.

'Hold it against the wound,' she told the white boy. She noticed all his clothes were soaking wet.

He looked at her dimly. There was the strangest smile on his face. It unnerved her.

The boy was having trouble understanding her, but she took his hand, shoved the pillowcase into it and pressed it hard against the gash in the other lad's neck. 'Here,' she said, looking into his dark pupils. 'Hold it tight here. You can save his life if you press hard. Do you understand?'

The wet-cheeked boy nodded slowly, still smiling, and held the cloth on the wound as she had told him to.

Then she turned to Moon. He was sitting against a wall, eyes shut. Like the woman's, his face was white. It was a deep wound. He had lost copious amounts of blood.

Where was Ferriter? What was taking her so long?

'Jill. I need help up here,' she called out.

Cupidi was squatting down now, trying to feel Moon's pulse, but there was nothing at all. Or could there be? Was there some faint flutter beneath the skin or was that just her imagination?

'Jill. Christ sake. Upstairs, now!'

But no answer.

She stilled her own breathing to try and feel again for a pulse. Above the bed, a framed picture of a pink rabbit holding a sign: *Pink is always an option.*

There was no pulse. He was dead, or very close to it.

'Jill?'

Someone was moving up the stairs now. She dropped Moon's wrist and, as it flopped onto his wet lap, straightened, looking around for a weapon. The knife they had been stabbed with was nowhere to be seen.

Instead, she bunched her fingers into a fist.

FIFTY-FIVE

'Boss?'

She breathed again, unclenched her fist. 'That you, Jill?'

Ferriter was standing on the landing outside the half-closed door. 'Coming in.'

'Warn you, it's a real mess in here, Jill.'

The door pushed open. Ferriter looked around, eyes wide.

'Ambulance is on its way.'

'Peter,' Ferriter whispered, and dropped to her knees in the blood.

'No pulse,' said Cupidi.

Ferriter burst into tears. Shock affected everyone differently, but this was a man she had slept with, whatever the circumstances.

'Lay him down flat,' said Ferriter.

Together, Ferriter at his head, Cupidi at his feet, they laid the sergeant down onto the bloody floor.

Ferriter leaned across him and started chest compressions with one hand, the other pressed against the wound. Cupidi stepped past her, towards the half-conscious boy.

'You're doing so well. Let me take over. I'll take care of him now.' Cupidi replaced his hand with hers on the nylon pillowcase.

Slowly the boy nodded.

'Did you do this?'

He shook his head.

'Your friend?'

Again, the shake.

She pressed her hand down on the pillowcase.

'Have you taken drugs?'

The boy nodded slowly, still with that strange smile on his face.

'Don't close your eyes. Stay awake. Please.'

But nothing she could say could persuade him to keep his eyes open. He had held on for as long as he could, pressing the cloth to his friend's bleeding wound, but now he was gone.

The small road outside the house was crammed full of vehicles flashing blue light on the walls of all the buildings around, on the faces of the crowd that had gathered.

Cupidi and Ferriter stood in bare feet as the dead and wounded were moved from the house to the waiting ambulances. Their shoes had been abandoned; they were ruined, soaked in Moon's blood. Upstairs, they had worked on him for what seemed like an age, but without any response.

'It's my fault.'

'None of this is your fault.'

415

'He wouldn't be here on his own except for me. We could have gone with him. I'm such a stupid cow.'

Cupidi took the younger woman by the shoulders and looked at her. 'This is not the time, Jill. Look at me.'

People worked around them. Neighbours had opened windows and were staring at the activity in their small street. More vehicles were arriving, lights flashing.

'What's going on?' people called out. 'We live here. We have a right to know.'

'There was a murderer here,' Cupidi told Ferriter quietly and calmly. She was still in shock. 'He's getting away. We have to think fast. We came here looking for Astrid Miller. If she was here, she's gone.'

'It's not her, though? Did this?'

'No. A man did this. I think it's the one who stabbed Khan. But if she was here . . . she might be in danger too.' She released Ferriter, leaving bloody hand-prints on both sides of her jacket.

'Her car,' said Ferriter.

They scrambled past the throng of coppers who were waiting to be told what to do, towards their car on the other side of the street, closing the door against the growing wailing of sirens.

Cupidi phoned the incident room. Sunday, half staffed, and a full-on emergency operation underway. It took an age for anybody to pick up. 'That car you were keeping tabs on with ANPR? . . . Yes. Astrid Miller's. Can you see if it's triggered any cameras in the last –' Cupidi checked her watch – 'thirty minutes?'

'What's going on out there? Phones are going crazy here. McAdam's on his way in. Heard there's been a major incident in Dartford? Is it true about Peter?'

'Yes.'

'Jesus. Dead?'

'I don't know. They've taken him to hospital.'

'Oh, Jesus Christ.'

She ended the call. She didn't have time to think about that. Focus on the task.

Ferriter had found some hand wipes and was trying to clean Moon's blood from her hands and her knees, tugging at her skin, breathing heavily as she did so. The incident room called almost immediately. She listened then hung up.

'There are two pings from the vehicle, both within the last thirty minutes. First one was on the M20 at junction nine. Second in Ashford town centre. You think the murderer is in that car?'

'Christ. She's driving him, isn't she?' said Ferriter. 'You think she's a hostage?'

'Or he's stolen the Tesla.'

'Sergeant Cupidi?' A sergeant was rapping on the window. 'Gold wants to know if you think the person who killed Moon is in the vehicle.'

Gold command would be running everything now. Cupidi said, 'Yes. I do.' She realised their one advantage: the killer would probably have no idea that they had connected him to Astrid Miller through the phone. He would feel safe in Miller's car, far away from this scene of crime.

'Is Jill OK?'

'Bit shaken up.'

'Ashford? You think he's aiming for the train?' asked Ferriter, coming to. From Ashford International you could head to the Continent.

417

Cupidi was thinking: but why drive all the way to Ashford to catch a train? There was a station in Dartford.

Then she had a thought. 'Oh Jesus.'

'What?'

'I don't think he's heading for the station at all.'

While Ferriter watched, puzzled, Cupidi called her daughter. 'What are you doing?'

'Where are you?' Cupidi asked, when Zoë answered.

'On the beach. It's warm. There's a cloud like a dolphin.' Cupidi could hear the sound of waves crunching somewhere close. It all sounded so normal. She was grateful for it and her beautiful, strange girl.

'Where's Bill?'

'He's here.'

'Still with you?'

'It's like he thinks he's my dad or something.' Zoë laughed.

'I need to speak to him.'

'I don't know if he wants to speak to you,' her daughter mocked.

'Please. It's important.'

Her daughter sounded less certain of herself. 'You sound funny.'

'Something has been going on here. It'll be on the news, but I'm fine.'

Her daughter handed over the phone.

'What?' he said, guardedly.

'I want to ask you a favour.'

The man stayed silent.

'Where are you, exactly, Bill?'

'On the beach. Just east of the old Coastguard Lookout. Why?'

Cupidi pictured it in her head. The Coastguard Lookout was a tall redbrick building from the 1950s with a window that looked out to the Channel. Another luxury home now, of course. It lay a little to the north of the power station, but was almost at the end of the line of cottages that stretched along the beach. 'Can you see Astrid Miller's place from where you are?'

'No. I need to be further up.' She could hear him moving, the shingle crunching up the beach. 'Let me get there.'

'Is there a car outside?'

'Wait . . .' He walked on. 'No. No car. Why do you want to know?'

Disappointment kicked in, but it had only been a hunch. 'There's been an incident. The man I've been looking for all along. He stabbed a policeman. They think he's not going to make it. I had a hunch the attacker may be trying to get to Astrid Miller's cottage. Definitely no red car outside?'

'No. No car there at all. Anyone I know?'

'Maybe you worked with him. Peter Moon?'

'We were together for a while when he first joined up. Bit green, but not a bad cop.'

'I'm sorry.'

'How did it happen?'

'He stumbled into the wrong place at the wrong time. We think he may have been trying to save a child's life.'

There was a silence. Then he said, 'Right.'

'Look after Zoë, won't you?'

She ended the call, glad she had been mistaken. She didn't

want the murderer to be anywhere around her home or her daughter. Or around William South.

'They'll need to take statements from us,' Cupidi told Ferriter. 'Afterwards, come and stay at mine. You shouldn't be alone tonight. You can have a shower.'

Ferriter dropped her head and started to cry. Wiping her wet cheek with her hand, she left a pink smear of Moon's blood there.

'You said he was trying to save the kids.'

'I think he was. I don't know.'

Cupidi put her hands round the constable again and hugged her, and was conscious of a buzzing in her lap. Someone was trying to call.

'Everyone can see me,' Ferriter complained as she cried. It was true. Concerned coppers and nosey neighbours were peering into the car at them.

'It doesn't matter,' said Cupidi. And she held her until the crying subsided. When she looked down at her phone she saw the missed call, the red name on her screen. Her daughter.

She called her back. 'Hello?'

Zoë spoke. 'A car just drove up to the cottage. Just after you talked to him. Bill said you'd want to know. There was a man and a woman. They got out. Some sports car thing.'

A man and a woman in a sports car.

'Red?'

'Yes.'

It was them. Oh Christ. 'Where's Bill?'

'He's gone to look. He said he'd phone you back in a bit.'

Cupidi's stomach lurched. 'How far away are you?'

'You want me to call him? William!' She shouted his name across the beach.

'No!' screamed Cupidi into the phone. 'Don't.'

Zoë sounded scared now. 'What is it, Mum? What's happened?'

'Can you attract his attention somehow? Without following him? Don't go near the place. Promise. But if Bill looks your way, beckon him back. Please.'

'What's wrong? I can see him there now.'

Cupidi held the phone away from her ear and wound down the window. She shouted, 'The killer's at Dungeness. Tell Gold.'

'Oh Jesus.' Beside her, Ferriter tensed.

'Who's at Dungeness?' Zoë was saying on her handset.

'Go home now, Zoë. Quick as you can. Go home and lock the door.'

'Mum. What's wrong?'

'For once, do as I say. Please, love. Please. Go home, quietly and quickly, and when you're there, call me to tell me you're safe.'

'Safe from what, Mum? What about Bill? He's at that cottage with the red car now. I can see him. Why do I have to go home, Mum?'

'Go home.'

The white boy was being taken out of the house now on a stretcher. Curious locals were filming it all on their smartphones.

'But Bill's there. He's looking at the car now.'

Oh Jesus. William South, thought Cupidi.

FIFTY-SIX

A uniformed policeman drove Cupidi and Ferriter all the way back to Dungeness at high speed, blue lights flashing.

'What's wrong with you, boss?' said Ferriter.

'I think I'm finally starting to figure it out.'

They sat in the back, side by side, watching the traffic part for them. 'What out?' asked Ferriter.

'Everything.'

'What you mean?'

'Why did she go to West View Road? She went there on her own. To pick him up.'

Ferriter sat for a while, then said, 'Because he's got some kind of hold over her. *U win I will pay u* – that was a message from her to the attacker, not to the boys.'

'That's right.'

Ferriter was silent for a long time before saying, 'Oh shit. The arm.'

'I think so.'

She frowned. 'He was using the arm to blackmail her?'

'I don't know. But that's why it was there. A signal she would understand.'

Ferriter put her head in her hands. 'Oh Jesus. No. So she knew Abir Stein was dead all along?'

'That's the only way it makes sense to me.'

'She was there with us, saying she didn't know where he was. She lied?'

They leaned forward in their seats, listening for any news of what was happening at Dungeness. There were so many messages on the radio it was hard to figure out what was going on. It was obvious that a huge operation was unfolding. They were calling in units from neighbouring counties now. As they approached the tip of the south coast, the scale of it was becoming clear. Cupidi stared out of the window. The coastline was alive with blue lights. There were dozens of police cars parking up along the Lydd road. A helicopter hovered, blowing green reeds flat.

They bumped down the track towards the lighthouses, to find Astrid Miller's cottage surrounded by police vehicles. The Tesla was parked at the back, by the French window facing the sea, where it couldn't be seen from the main road. Uniformed police teemed around the place. Their car wheels crunched on the dry stones and came to a halt.

'Oh Christ. I told her to go home . . .'

Astrid Miller was sitting on the back step of her cottage, with her arm around Zoë, who looked paler than usual.

Cupidi ran towards her, bare feet on the hard ground.

'She's OK,' said Astrid, looking up with a smile. 'Your daughter is an amazing girl.'

'Yes, she is,' said Cupidi. 'Now step away from her, please.'

Astrid released her, shocked.

Zoë stood and flung her arms round her mother. 'Why are they all sitting around, Mum? He's got Bill,' she said.

'What?'

'The man. He's got Bill.'

'I'm sorry,' said Astrid, standing too. 'I couldn't help it. He's insane.'

'Who's insane?'

An officer was talking into his lapel. 'No sign of either of them here.'

'Because he's not here,' shouted Zoë. 'They ran that way. I told you over and over.'

The radio crackled. 'Confirm suspect and hostage not on site.'

'Who?' said Cupidi, struggling to understand what had happened. 'Hostage?'

'Allan, of course,' said Astrid.

Cupidi blinked. 'Allan Mulligan? Your security man?'

The constable interjected. 'Woman here said the man, Allan Mulligan, attempted to take her hostage.'

'That's right,' said Astrid. 'He killed Abir. It was him. He was on the run from the police but he thought he'd be safe here. When he heard the sirens he took a knife, tried to make a break for it.' She stopped. 'Have either of you got a cigarette? I'm supposed to have given up . . .'

'Go on.'

'He just grabbed me and ordered me to come with him. I'm

424

sorry. This sounds so crazy. He threatened me with the knife. I had no choice. And then when I got outside there was this man there—'

'Bill,' interrupted Zoë, still clinging on to her mother.

'Were you there too?' Cupidi said.

Zoë nodded.

'But I told you to go home. I told you.' Cupidi realised she was shouting.

Zoë released her. 'Bill was in danger. I could tell. You said I was to go home and lock the door. That meant he was walking towards something awful, so I went to warn him, but just as I was getting close, that man came out with this woman –' she nodded towards Astrid Miller – 'and he had a knife. And she started screaming at us that she was a hostage. It was scary, Mum. But Bill was so calm. He stepped forward and told the man he should trade places with her.'

Her daughter had been that close to the killer. Cupidi had just been with the two boys who were Zoë's age; she had no idea whether they would live or not.

'The man . . . He persuaded Allan to take him instead of me,' Astrid explained. 'He seemed to know Allan.'

They were in the police together, Cupidi realised.

'I mean . . . I would have gone. But he was amazing. He's a total hero. He saved my life, I think.'

'Bill recognised him,' said Zoë. 'Called him by name. He told him how he knew it round here, every inch of it. He was so calm and cool. He said he knew where to disappear. And the man knew Bill had been convicted of murder. I think that made the man trust him.'

It would make sense, thought Cupidi. A man with no knowledge of this area wouldn't stand a chance.

'Bill told me, "Don't worry." It was strange . . .'

Ferriter interrupted, pushing through the uniforms to confront her hero. 'You. What did he have on you?'

Astrid Miller blanched. 'I don't know what you mean?'

Ferriter's hands and face were still flecked with Moon's blood. She looked wild. 'We have seen the text you sent him. You were giving him money. You drove him here in your car. You went to meet him in West View Road.'

'Not now, Jill. This is not the time.'

'He was armed. I had no choice.'

'Don't give me that,' said Ferriter, shaking. Her voice rose to a shout. 'Don't you, of all people, give me that shit.'

Cupidi moved in to address the millionaire before Ferriter could say more. 'Astrid Miller. You do not have to say anything, but it may harm your defence . . .'

Astrid Miller looked aghast. 'This is wrong. You're making a mistake. You don't understand.'

'Today . . .' Ferriter faced up to her, nose to nose. 'Today has been the worst day of my fucking life. You have no idea how much I understand.'

Cupidi took Ferriter by the arm and pulled her gently away. 'You need to step back, Constable Ferriter. You need to calm down. You're contaminated with evidence from the last scene. We need to let someone else take her in.'

When she'd finished cautioning Astrid Miller, Cupidi ordered a constable to detain her.

'You do actually know who she is, don't you?' the constable said.

'Oh yes. We know who she bloody is,' said Ferriter.

'Mum?' said Zoë. 'Where are your shoes, Mum? We need to go and look for Bill.'

'You're making a huge mistake,' Miller was saying.

Another constable stepped forward and said, 'There's a full search going on. All the marshes and ponds up to the Lydd road. Never seen anything like it. Every spare copper in three counties is headed here.'

The three of them walked slowly down the road, back to their house, past William South's empty bungalow, Cupidi and Ferriter picking their way cautiously in their bare feet.

'You should be looking for him,' complained Zoë.

'It doesn't work like that, love. There are experts out there.' Cupidi heard the car behind them first, looked round, and recognised the unmarked Audi coming towards her.

'Here we go,' she said.

McAdam pulled up alongside them. 'Did I get that right? You've just detained Astrid Miller?' He stared at Ferriter: blood on her skin and clothes, toes poking through holes in her tights.

'She knew Abir Stein was dead all along,' said Cupidi.

'Christ. Sure you've enough to justify it?'

'Oh yes. Any news on Moon?'

'Nothing so far.'

'What about the boys?'

'The one who was stabbed is stable. The paramedics got to him before he'd lost too much blood. The other is OK. He'd

427

been given some drug. His mother was dead at the scene, though. This man, who did this . . . he's out there?'

'Alan Mulligan,' said Cupidi.

'What?'

'The man who did this. It's Mulligan.'

The blood left McAdam's face. 'Oh Christ. So he's been pumping our officers for intelligence all along? He's been following every step.'

Cupidi nodded.

'How easy would it be to get away?' How easy would it be to get away?'

'Depends how well you know the land.'

DI McAdam scanned the flat horizon. 'And he's with Bill South?'

Beyond the southern tip of the promontory where they stood lay twelve square miles of uninterrupted scrubland extending in a quadrant from the north to the west. Some of it was deep lakes; old gravel pits that had flooded with water. Wartime bunkers dotted the land. A haze of low trees blocked the long view, interrupted by the electricity pylons that marched away to the higher ground beyond the marshes. It was a land made to get lost in.

FIFTY-SEVEN

Ferriter volunteered to cook. She had showered and was wearing a plain khaki shirt of Zoë's. 'I just need something to do, to keep my mind off it.'

When Ferriter complained about Cupidi's knives being blunt, the place went quiet for a minute, and all you could hear was the sound of the police helicopter overhead. It was dark outside now, a beam of light sweeping across the broad flatland.

Mulligan was ex-police, but before that, it turned out he had been in the army. Even without South's knowledge, he would know how to hide in a landscape like this.

'Bloody noise,' Ferriter said. 'Is there a radio?'

Zoë switched on some pop music.

When the meal was served, Cupidi sat at the head of the table trying to eat, but she wasn't hungry. When she looked up, nobody else was either.

Ferriter gave up on her plate and started looking at her phone.

'They've got an army team in, apparently, to help with the search. Think like he does, I expect.'

'He could be anywhere,' said Zoë. 'There are so many places.'

According to the local news, they had begun checking the empty properties along the shoreline to eliminate them, while strengthening a perimeter from the Dungeness Road in the north, to Jury's Gap Road in the west: around fifteen square miles.

'He'll head for cover,' said Zoë.

Cupidi turned to her. 'What cover?'

'The only real cover there is. All the scrubland up by the reserve and to the east.'

'Is that where you would hide?'

'That's the bird reserve,' Zoë said, frowning. 'That's too obvious. What about the sunken woods?'

Years ago they had dug shingle from a rough circle of land, exposing thin soil. Sallows and a few birches had taken root, growing into a small tangled woodland, stunted by the wind that buffeted the flatland. It would be a good place to hide, but only for a while. If he was there, it was small enough to throw a cordon around.

'But he said the strangest thing as he was going. I was trying to tell you.'

Cupidi and Ferriter looked at each other.

'What did he say, love?'

'He said, "Don't worry. I'll be long."'

'He meant "I *won't* be long".'

'That's what it sounded like. But it wasn't. He said, "I'll be long." It was kind of sad, the way he said it. Like he was going away again. But he said it looking right at me.'

'Do you think it might have been a hint?'

430

'I don't know.'

The music on the radio paused, the news came on.

'*Police are hunting a man who stabbed a twenty-nine-year-old policeman . . .*'

'Bloody hell.'

'*. . . A woman was also found dead in the house. The sergeant and another teenage boy are in intensive care.*'

'Switch it off,' snapped Ferriter.

Zoë's mouth had formed an 'O'.

Cupidi looked at her. 'What?'

Zoë jumped up from the table, flapping her arms up and down. 'Oh my God! I'm so stupid. Long Pits. That's what he was trying to tell me.'

'Where?' said Ferriter.

'Long Pits. We've got to go there. I wasted all that time. He's been waiting for us but I was too thick to get it.'

'You're sure?'

'Yes. "I'll be long." Not "I won't be long", or "I'll be back". *I'll – be – long.*'

Long Pits. From the south, where they were, where the operations control centre was based, you wouldn't even know it was there. From this angle, even if you could see the three-quarter-mile long scrape in the shingle, it looked small and insignificant.

Cupidi stood. 'Wait here with Jill,' she said, putting on a nylon jacket. 'And lock the door behind me.'

She ran the whole way from the cottages to the control centre. The helicopter was far to the west, beyond the power station, making slow methodical passes over the shooting ranges.

431

As she passed the Britannia Inn, a pair of soldiers stopped her, shining a torch into her eyes.

'Police.' Cupidi held up her ID.

She ran on, past the line of shacks. What if he's already outside the cordon? He would be waiting for the right time. Round here, best chance is to hunker down. The moment you're out in the open, you're easier to spot. But it was dark now. He'd want to use the cover to make a break for it.

They had set up floodlights around the incident unit; a white Mercedes van, with orange and yellow fluorescent markings on the side.

'Cupidi, isn't it?' said the Bronze commander. The harsh light shone off the inspector pips on his shoulder.

'I know where he was headed.'

He frowned. 'How?'

She explained.

'South is an ex-con,' he said.

'But he's a good man,' said Cupidi. The commander nodded towards the van and they both stepped inside. One side of the vehicle was loaded with communication gear; on the other was an Ordnance Survey map, pinned at each corner, covered in crayon marks, which divided it into makeshift zones. A circle had been drawn around the bird reserve.

Cupidi pointed towards the blue line of water on the map. 'Here,' she said. On paper it just looked like bare land; the trees that surrounded the water weren't even shown. But Cupidi knew it. She had been there with Zoë many times, waiting while her daughter patiently counted grebes, or whatever she was looking

432

at at the time. The water was fringed with dense clumps of willow and alder.

The senior policeman pointed to the bird reserve to the west, where the more obvious cover was. 'This is where we've been concentrating our search. That's where the army advisors told us he'd head if he wanted to stand a chance of getting past us.'

'But Bill took him here,' Cupidi said, putting her finger on the map.

'Your daughter reckons? And she's how old?'

'Seventeen.' She saw the flicker of doubt in the man's face. 'But she knows this place. And she knows Bill. They used to go everywhere together. She's sure he was trying to tell her where he would hide.'

She could see the commander looking at where she was pointing. The pits ran up to the Lydd road. Mulligan would be waiting for a chance to break out there, she guessed. If Zoë was right, South would have expected them to follow him there hours ago. Had they left it too late?

'The chances are that the police cars were already visible along the road, so he'll have gone to ground here on this bank.' She pointed at the west side of the body of water. 'About there, I reckon.'

'You know it?'

She nodded.

'You're sure? You understand that with a search site this big, the perimeters are hard to watch? If we pull people off other areas, there's a risk he'll get away.'

'Yes.' And she realised with a start as she spoke that this was true: she trusted Zoë. 'But that's where he is.'

433

The radio crackled. 'Sector H, clear.'

A constable leaned past them, took a pen and put an 'X' through one of the zones on the map.

The inspector picked up a handset. 'Blue Team. We're going to try something different.'

FIFTY-EIGHT

In the thickening darkness, they drove in a dirty grey Land Rover over the shingle, Cupidi thinking what Zoë would have to say about them tearing the land apart. She would be torn between saving South, or the terns and plovers whose chick-filled nests they might be destroying.

Cupidi pointed just as the helicopter appeared overhead, shining its beam onto the darker line of stunted willows. They grew thickly here. It was an ideal place to hide. 'Just along there,' she said.

Other vehicles, less suited to the land, were arriving too, now, scrambling over the uneven ground, sumps scraping as they bounced.

If Mulligan was there, thought Cupidi, he would know that he was trapped. How would he react? South used to walk here all the time and had the advantage of knowing the land, but had spent two years in prison cells. The time had weakened him. Allan Mulligan was stocky, muscular and fit. They had both been

435

coppers, and could both handle themselves, but she didn't think much of the odds if it came to a one-on-one fight.

Men and women were piling out of vehicles now, forming a line.

'Stay here,' said the commander. 'Don't move, OK?'

Like Ferriter, she had come from a place where murders had been committed. If this ended up being a second crime scene, they would want as little forensic cross-contamination as possible. She pushed the thought of what that might mean out of her head, wound down a window and watched the officers huddle, discuss tactics, break up into groups, spreading out on both sides of the long thin water.

The air was cut by the helicopter blades above them. Its engine noise roared. It was dark now, and a thin drizzle had started to fall. She watched the torchlight swinging into the thick black branches, shining on the dark water.

The teams were working from north to south, from where the lakes met the Lydd road, back towards the Land Rover, slowly combing the thick vegetation. Another line of officers were stationed in a line that ran south of the lake in case Mulligan made a dash in that direction. It was like a shoot, Cupidi realised, with beaters driving birds towards the guns.

She waited, wishing she could be out there too, but the commander had told her to wait, so she waited. It was a steady, methodical search. After maybe forty minutes, sitting alone, her phone rang; it was Ferriter.

She was crying. 'He's dead,' she said.

'Oh. Jesus.'

The call had come through from the hospital five minutes earlier. Peter Moon had been pronounced dead.

436

'It's because of me,' Ferriter wailed.

'No,' said Cupidi. 'No.'

'I just feel it's my fault. I didn't even like him.'

A policeman killed. Word would be spreading now out there too, passing from copper to copper, and with it, a sense of anger and indignation. It was inevitable in this kind of work, when you shared so much, working in the face of public contempt and resentment, this collective sense that somehow the murder of an officer weighed even more heavily than the killing of a civilian.

'If anything, it was my fault,' said Cupidi. 'I should have figured it all out so much earlier.'

'Any sign of Mulligan?'

'No.'

They were closing in on the south end of the lake. Resources had been concentrated here because of what she had said – of what Zoë had said.

A sliver of doubt; what if they had been wrong? What if they had pulled coppers from another part of the operation and that had allowed the man who had killed Peter Moon to escape?

Not just Peter Moon. Had he killed Abir Stein too? The boy's mother? Almost certainly her. Cupidi felt sick.

The torch beams swept the land, coming so close now, dazzling her. They made the darkness around her blacker.

Ferriter, still on the phone, said, 'Zoë wants a word.'

Looking into the blackness she remembered, with a start, what South had once told her. *In a place like this, torches don't help you.* She sat up and peered, not into the light but beneath it, holding up a hand to shield herself from the beams, trying to look into the blackness and discern shapes.

'Mum?' Her daughter's voice. 'Are you all right?'

'Sorry. I'm fine. I'm just watching. They haven't found him yet.' She heard the sound of a radio in the background, chattering news. 'Tell me something. Do you know where Bill used to come when he was here? Did he have a hide here?'

'He never used hides. He'd just head for somewhere in amongst the osiers, close to the water.'

'Which side of the lake?'

'Any side. Depended on the weather.'

The torches were getting closer.

'I'll call you later.'

'I love you, Mum.'

'I have to go.'

A roosting duck, disturbed by the men and women prodding sticks at the undergrowth, blurted out across the water, quacking loudly. At any second she expected the shouts to go up, the lamps all to shine on the fugitive. But they didn't. The slow, methodical progression of officers across the uneven ground continued. And then beaters were in line with the Land Rover, moving past, and the commander was at the window and the helicopter was moving far away out towards Lydd.

'Wild goose chase,' he said, quietly but tersely, as if not wanting to criticise her to her face for directing the operation to this small part of the landscape. 'We'll drive you back.'

'Do you think he's got past you?'

'We're putting roadblocks further out now.'

Zoë had been wrong. She felt crushed on her behalf; guilty, too. If Mulligan had slipped away, it would be her fault.

'I'll walk. I'd like to.'

He shook his head. 'Operation still in progress. Don't want you alone out here.'

She looked around. 'I'll walk back with those officers then,' she said, pointing towards a small group who were trudging back towards the control centre.

'Suit yourself,' he said and started the engine.

She waited a minute, until the rear lights were jumping across the uneven land, then turned the other way, walking back to the Long Pits.

She had sat here, amazed at the young girl's concentration, sitting so still on the bank, peering through the reeds.

The landscape was empty now. Where only a few minutes ago there had been a bustle of activity there was now stillness, save for the call of the odd bird and the soft patter of the drizzle on the water.

The blackness of the edges of the water was deep, rendering its world shapeless and sinister. The Pits were about three-quarters of a mile long, from top to bottom.

She walked up the western edge of the pit for about ten minutes until she reached the grassy bank that separated the two fingers of water. Water ran off her nylon waterproof, soaking her canvas trousers. She began to shiver slightly.

From the middle of this causeway you had a view of the entire lake. To the south a good-size moon was trying to show through the rain clouds. Its dim light shone onto the water, pale against the black that ringed it.

She squatted down on her haunches and put her head in her hands, exhausted, grateful for the quiet. It had been an awful

439

day, the worst she could ever remember on the job, full of blood and tension. People had died. She had sent William South to prison; now she wondered if she had done something much worse. She pictured his body lying somewhere in this stony land.

She had been so sure.

At first she thought the sound of lapping was made by some creature. An otter perhaps?

But when she turned and looked behind her at the north lake where the water was darker, she saw the dark shapes forming out of the water, the shapes of two men rising, and the sucking of mud underfoot.

She crouched down low behind the fishing station. The two men were emerging from the water onto the east bank of the northern lake. She felt in her pocket for her mobile phone. Turning her back to hide the light of the screen, she texted hurriedly to Ferriter: **Get help found him big pits urgent**. Then she set off sprinting towards the edge of the water where she guessed they would emerge.

At first, as she approached, it looked like the men were having trouble climbing up the bank, falling, sliding back, trying to get up. The water would be bitterly cold still at this time of year. How long had they been hiding in it?

A louder splash and she realised they weren't just trying to get out, they were fighting, waist deep, attempting to land blows on each other. The last time she had seen Mulligan he had been armed with a knife, the weapon he would have been using to keep South silent.

By the time she reached the bank closest to them, there was

only one man standing. She was not sure who it was, but something shone briefly in the moonlight. She was sure she had seen the glint of Mulligan's knife.

Stripping off her jacket, she shallow-dived into the water. She was used to swimming in cold seas around here, but the ache in her bones was instantaneous, blowing the breath out of her. Gasping for air, her head emerged from the water and she looked around. Where there had been a man, there was no one.

Shit. She looked from left to right. Where had Mulligan gone?

And then he burst out of the water close by, silhouetted, knife in hand. From his mouth came a loud, raw groan.

And then a second head emerged, more slowly, bobbing up to the surface.

She didn't have time to check on South. Mulligan was coming at her, knife in hand.

FIFTY-NINE

She dived to the left to avoid the knife, into shallow water, thick with reed, knowing that when she surfaced again, Mulligan would still be above her.

But she was a strong swimmer. She pushed back, rose two metres away, tried to find her feet, then discovered that the bottom had disappeared. She sank for a second, pulled by the weight of her clothes, bobbed up again in open water, coughing. When she spun round to look, she saw Mulligan's black shape between herself and the bank, coming towards her fast.

Somehow she had to keep him here until help arrived.

If help arrived.

He took another step forward, then another, each time descending a little lower into the water. Out here, knife below the surface, she wouldn't be able to see it coming.

Taking one more step he slid, cried loudly, caught out by the sudden incline. This was her chance. She dived under again.

Below the surface, it was impenetrably black. She could only guess where she was heading. She swam low, feeling stones scraping against her jeans. Her left leg seemed sluggish. Was it cramp? Could she be sure she was even swimming in a straight line?

She slowed as the water became shallower, tried to orientate herself, hoping that she was close to the bank behind him.

He had killed Peter Moon. He had tried to kill her at the Barbican. She swivelled slowly in the water, feet now touching the bottom.

And sprang up, arms wide, hoping desperately that she had estimated her position correctly.

Her weight bellyflopped into empty water.

She had miscalculated. Worse, she had given him the upper hand, falling right at his feet.

Her head crashing onto the stones, she flailed for his legs, found one and, just as he thrust down with the blade, yanked the leg sideways.

This time she was luckier. His footing slipped. She felt his weight shift. She jumped up a second time and as she did so, her head slammed again against something hard – his back this time, she realised. She had pitched him forwards into the water.

She struggled up, but by the time she wiped her eyes, he was there, in front of her, arms extended, the knife in one hand.

'Give yourself up, Allan.' Her voice sounded thin and tired.

Instead, he lunged towards her.

She tried to step away but her foot was caught in reeds. She tumbled backwards, and when she came up, spluttering, he was there above her, suddenly silhouetted.

Brain fogged with cold, squinting into the glare, it took a beat for her to realise that they were surrounded by dazzling light and noise.

She tensed for the blow but he, too, seemed confused by the sudden arrival of the helicopter above them. It gave her the time she needed to roll sideways, and away.

Amongst the noise of the rotors, the sound of shouting: 'Armed police.'

She stood slowly. Officers were jumping from the bank, arms extended to help her, to drag her out. In the brightness, she could now see South, on all fours on the grass, vomiting.

Shaking away the helping hands, she dropped down beside him, panting, as someone fetched blankets and stretchers.

'Obviously I'd weakened him first,' said South, wiping his mouth.

'Shut up.' For the first time she noticed a dark streak of blood running down her left leg. He must have caught her with the blade. In the cold she hadn't even felt it.

'What is it with you arresting bloody coppers, anyway?' muttered South.

In spite of it all, she laughed. She turned to look. Mulligan was knee deep in water, illuminated from all sides. Armed officers were shouting at him to raise his arms.

South came home from the hospital that night. Zoë made him soup and they sat at his table in Arum Cottage.

'We sat in the water for ten minutes, maybe more, while the search came past, just our noses above the water. I thought I was going to die,' he said. 'He held the knife to my throat and it was shaking so badly I thought I was going to be salami.'

It was lentil soup. Zoë had watched, trying not to look disappointed as South had piled salt into it. He held the cellar awkwardly, hands bandaged from the defensive wounds on his palms.

'After the searchers had gone, we sat on the bank trying to get warm. He was ready to make it out onto the road. And then he saw someone on the causeway and he dragged me back in. He knew he didn't need me any more, so I guessed he was going to try and kill me there. I had to get him first. But I was too cold. I tried, but I couldn't.'

'Mulligan went with you because you were a convicted killer,' said Cupidi quietly.

'As it turns out, yes. A criminal record has some uses.'

The news was full of the arrest of Astrid Miller on a charge of conspiracy to commit murder. That morning they woke to film crews from all over the world, camped along Coast Drive. There were photographs of Astrid in all the papers; the same ones Ferriter had collected as a teenager. Her expensive lawyers were claiming she was a victim.

At work, Cupidi phoned Devon.

'The phone the boys stole off Mulligan had probably been modified,' he said. 'It contained a text file that you could only get at if you knew the key code.'

'We think it was Abir Stein's phone,' Cupidi told him. 'When they searched Astrid Miller's bungalow yesterday, they found an identical one. When they repeated the keystrokes, it turned out it has twelve more words on it too.'

'It's a word-seed,' said Devon.

'A what?'

'A twenty-four-word private key. Almost certainly. Separately, the words on each phone were useless. Together they would unlock a currency wallet.'

'I have no idea what you're talking about.'

'Crypto-currencies. Getting the money into an offshore bank is easy, but getting it out again without leaving a trail for financial investigators is harder. I'm guessing here, but I'm pretty sure this is about getting the money out of St Lucia.' She could hear Devon lighting a cigarette. 'It probably worked like this. They employ an intermediary to buy into a crypto-currency such as Bitcoins, using River Deep's cash. That cash is stored in a wallet that can only be accessed via a twenty-four-word key. The twenty-four-word key generates your 256-bit private keys.'

'Still no idea . . .'

'The twenty-four words are basically what get you access to a big pile of Bitcoins. Without them, the money doesn't exist. It's the only way to get hold of it. The intermediary – I'm still guessing here, but I bet I'm right – divides the twenty-four-word key into two twelve-word phrases and stores each on a simple phone. It's easy enough to take two cheap phones out of a country. They don't look like millions of pounds, but that's what they are.'

'So two people were stealing money from the Foundation, paying it into a separate account, and taking it out of the tax haven as Bitcoins.'

'Pretty much,' said Devon.

'And neither knows what the other twelve words are,' Cupidi ventured. 'So what the phones tell us is that it's two people who don't trust each other. Neither knows the other's half of the key.'

'Guess so.'

'But something happens, and two chancers on mopeds steal one of the phones off Allan Mulligan. And suddenly, without the phone, there are no millions. They vanish into thin air.'

'Exactly.'

'So what happened to Abir Stein?'

'Not my department,' said Devon.

Allan Mulligan said nothing. The angry, bitter glares of officers at a man who had been one of their own were met by dull impassivity.

'No comment.'

He had nothing to gain by talking, after all. An ex-copper who had killed a former colleague, he would go down for a long time anyway. Why did he care?

When Cupidi interviewed Astrid Miller, she was the opposite. 'I can explain everything,' she said.

'Go on then.' *Just let them talk*, ran the mantra. Sooner or later they will dig a hole for themselves.

So she talked. Allan Mulligan had a crush on her, she explained. When she had discovered that Evert was sleeping with Zoya Gubenko, she had felt hurt and rejected. Mulligan had comforted her and they had ended up in bed together. A terrible mistake. From a single liaison, he had become obsessed by her, fantasised an entire life together and become furious when he heard that, should she leave Evert, she would not be entitled to a share of his fortune because of their prenuptial agreement.

'He was jealous of everyone around me. He is a monster. Abbie Stein was terrified of him.'

Cupidi raised her eyebrows. 'You think Allan Mulligan killed Abir Stein?'

'Well, hold on,' she said. 'We don't actually know that Abbie is dead, do we? I mean, you haven't even found a body.'

'What do you know about River Deep?'

'Never heard of it,' she answered crisply.

Cupidi pushed a photograph of a simple phone across the desk. 'Can you explain this? We found it in a safe in your shack.'

'That was not mine. Abbie gave it to me for safe keeping,' she said.

'He did? What was so special about it?'

'I have absolutely no idea at all. But he seemed very worried about it.'

Another sheet of paper, this time a photograph of the other phone's screen. On it, the message: **U win I will pay u half ££ if you promise to leave me alone.**

'You sent that message?'

'Of course.'

'Why did you send that text to Allan Mulligan?'

She looked shocked. 'I most certainly didn't.'

'It was on the phone the lads stole off him. It was sent by you.'

She smiled. 'But it wasn't Mulligan's phone at all, was it? It was Stein's. You know that. I was sending Abir a message, obviously, not Mulligan. I didn't even know he had it. Me and

448

Abbie had argued about money, that's all. We did sometimes,' she said.

'Smooth,' said DI McAdam in the corridor outside the interview room.

'Very,' said Cupidi. 'She's denying everything. But that message had to be for Mulligan, not Stein. Why else was she outside the house while Mulligan was killing Peter? She was in it with Mulligan.'

'Oh, I believe you. But that's not what matters, is it?'

They had applied to keep her in custody for another twelve hours. Astrid Miller's lawyer was demanding they release her immediately on bail, threatening the police with legal action.

Joseph Watt was sitting up in his hospital bed, his mother at his side. 'I hear you're taking in Benjamin,' Cupidi said.

'He has nowhere else to go,' Mrs Watt explained. 'It's my duty as a Christian.'

'That's good of you.'

'He's my son's friend. I will never forget that he saved his life. Course, he almost got him killed, too.'

It was true. In spite of the drugs that he had been given by Allan Mulligan, Tap had kept Sloth alive by staunching the bleeding while they waited for the ambulances to arrive.

'It's not going to be easy. They're both hooligans. Benjamin says he wants to go to art school. Can you imagine?'

'I shouldn't be telling you this yet, but we found your son on CCTV. Him and Benjamin.'

Sloth sat up a little more. 'At the Co-op we robbed?'

'I am so ashamed of my son, Sergeant.'

'No,' Cupidi said. 'On Spital Street, outside the Royal Victoria Hotel. They tried to steal a woman's phone. We're going to charge them both with attempted robbery.'

'I'll murder you,' said Mrs Watt.

Cupidi looked at the boy. 'It would save a lot of police time.'

Mrs Watt smiled for the first time. Cupidi turned to Sloth. 'That's what happened, isn't it? You stole Allan Mulligan's phone. The same day as you were outside the Royal Victoria. Where was that?'

'Phones,' said Joseph. 'Nasty little one and the iPhone. You going to charge us for that?'

'You probably want to talk to a lawyer about that before we take it any further.'

'That's why he killed my uncle Mikey, isn't it?' said Benjamin. 'Because we gave him the wrong thing to take back. It was the other one he wanted.'

'No, bro,' said Joseph, gently. 'Wasn't our fault really. He'd have killed him anyway, wouldn't he? He had been a copper, hadn't he? Bet your uncle Mikey recognised him in the first place. Didn't want anyone to be able to identify him.'

'Still our fault.'

Joseph was probably right, but again, she couldn't comment. She tried to imagine what it had been like for the two boys, out on the edge of Dartford Marsh, not knowing why they were being chased.

'Any sign of mischief and Benjamin is gone. He can look after himself.'

'Are they keeping Joseph in much longer?'

'Long as they like,' his mother said. 'Keep him out of trouble.'

★

Ferriter had not come back to work. She was on sick leave. The doctor had prescribed antidepressants, but Ferriter refused to take them. Cupidi missed her.

On the second day, McAdam approached Cupidi's desk with a copy of that morning's paper in his hand: 'Did Abir Stein Fake His Own Death?' A one-armed man resembling Abir Stein had apparently been spotted in St Lucia.

'You don't actually believe it, do you?' said Cupidi. 'That story came straight from Astrid's lawyers. The rich can run rings around the truth.'

McAdam looked anxious. If nothing changed, they would have to release Astrid Miller later that morning. The press were outside the building, waiting for her to emerge. She would make a statement to the press. It was like the old days, when everyone wanted to know what Astrid Theroux said.

'They're burying Peter Moon next Wednesday,' McAdam said. 'His mother has asked me to speak at the service. Jill Ferriter knew him well, didn't she? Do you think I should call her at home, ask her for input?'

'Definitely not.'

He looked down. 'You're right. Still too raw.' It was time to go. 'You ready for this?'

She picked up her notebook, nodded slowly, stood.

She and McAdam walked in silence down the stairs to the inter-view room. Officers watched them as they passed, giving little nods of encouragement. Once there, they only spoke to identify themselves for the record, then Cupidi stared at Mulligan for a long time until he finally broke her gaze and looked away to the

451

red blinking light of the video camera above their heads. She had had time to think about this; about what she would say to him.

'There are a lot of people outside that door who'd like to be where I am now,' she said finally. 'You should hear the things they say they would like to do to you if they had the chance.'

His lawyer, a middle-aged man with frameless specs, shuffled in his seat.

'It's all talk,' she said.

Not a flicker from Mulligan.

'Because they're police officers. Good people. They don't do stuff like that.'

Just a little blink of the eyes that time.

'What was Astrid Miller like in bed?'

That seemed to work. He took his eyes off the video camera and stared at her, as if trying to understand what she was trying to do.

'She talks a lot. She has been telling us she had sex with you.'

He frowned.

Cupidi laughed. 'No. To be honest, I couldn't see it, either. Not with you. You're not exactly supermodel material.'

'Funny,' he said, finally.

'She's saying a lot of things that probably aren't true. Doesn't that make you angry?'

He lapsed back into silence.

'You know that when we find his body, she'll say you killed Abir Stein, don't you?'

Scrit, scrit, scrit. The lawyer made a note on his yellow pad.

'When did Evert Miller ask you to start spying on his wife?'

Nothing.

'That's when it all began, wasn't it? All that time, watching her. Figuring out what she was up to. You're a copper, after all, somewhere underneath.'

She had spent the morning poring over his police records. He had been the kind of copper who got sent on gender sensitivity training courses, but other than that, old-school, diligent.

'I read you were a pretty good one. Once.'

He smiled. 'Better than you lot of nancies, poncing around worrying about your pensions.'

She smiled back. 'Doesn't look like it to me. You're sitting there, and I'm sitting here. Go on then, prove it.'

'I know what you're trying to do.'

'Astrid Miller is running rings around us. And we can't do anything about it. Prove you're better than us. Think about what it would be like if you were sitting on this side of the table. Go on.'

The lawyer frowned.

'Prove that you figured out what she was up to with Abir Stein all along. That you're not some mindless thug. You're a clever man.' If she had meant that to sound flattering, it hadn't.

But he had lapsed back into silence.

They waited another few minutes. Perhaps she had overplayed her hand. She had thought she could use his arrogance against him, make him think like a copper again, but he didn't care at all.

She was conscious of McAdam checking his watch. They would be out of time. 'We need to go,' he said.

'No,' Mulligan said. 'Wait.'

They paused.

'You're right. I figured it out. What she and Abir Stein were up to. Evert Miller hated his wife. But he wouldn't let her go. He was jealous of her.'

It had started the previous year, he said. At Evert Miller's request, he had been reporting on what his wife did every day. Mulligan had even put a GPS tracker on her car. A few weeks ago, he had followed her to Cromwell Tower. He drove there, loitered behind the walkway pillars.

Usually she was only there for half an hour or so, doing business. That time, she stayed late. Some time around midnight, he saw her emerge running from the lobby, looking pale. There was blood on her dress.

Evert Miller cared about his reputation most of all. Mulligan was there to protect it. If something bad had happened, it would be his job to deal with it. So, before she could reach her car, he confronted her.

She was shocked at first; wanted to know why he was there. Then she told him there had been a fight. She claimed Stein had tried to sexually assault her. She had fought back. She was not sure what she had done. So he went to find out.

Upstairs in the flat he found Stein dead on the living-room floor. He had his doubts about the story even then; Stein had not been the kind of man who assaulted people. Besides, he had been killed by a blow from behind.

'Did she say why she killed him?' Cupidi asked.

'No, but it's not hard to guess. Stein wasn't built for that kind of thing. I think he wanted out. I remember thinking he'd looked rough for a while, as if something was bugging him. Maybe he wanted to confess to Evert that he'd been stealing his money for years.'

Mulligan told Astrid they would have to go to the police. She pleaded with him not to. Instead, she offered him money to help her.

'I was greedy,' said Mulligan. 'I took it.'

'You got rid of the body for her.'

'At the bottom of Evert's swimming lake. Wrapped up tight and weighted. Easiest place I could find,' he said. 'Most of the remains, anyway. I kept something back.'

'Why?'

'Why do you think? As a kind of special pension plan of my own.'

Cupidi looked up at the camera. Someone would be watching. They would be sending a team there now.

The next day, said Mulligan, Astrid had called him again. She wanted him to go to Stein's flat and look for something. A phone. Nobody knew Stein was dead, so there was no risk involved, but could he go to Stein's apartment, let himself in, and bring it back for her? Again, he asked for more money. Astrid agreed. It took several nights' work to find the phone. Stein had hidden it in a jar of rice in his kitchen. Taped to it was the unlock code and instructions about how to retrieve a file hidden on the device.

But when he got back to Long Hill, he refused to hand the phone over. A third time she offered him yet more money: this time a million pounds. That's when he became convinced the phone was worth a great deal more than that.

So he asked for more; the whole story. He wanted to know how much he could walk away with. And when she didn't tell him, he thought of a plan. 'I knew she'd freak out if the arm was in something that could let people link it back to her. And I was right.'

455

It had been simple enough. He told her that Abir Stein's arm was concealed in one of the Foundation's artworks, one of the many that had been loaned out. It would be discovered soon, and then it would be easy to trace it back to her. If she cut him in on the deal, he would tell her which piece of work the arm was in so she could think of some excuse to recall it before the arm was discovered. He had calculated that it would take a few days before the smell became too bad, but he had not factored in the over-heated gallery room at the Turner. But for now, his plot worked. Panicked, she told him the whole story. Nine million pounds, extracted deal by deal from the Foundation, sitting somewhere in the blockchain, encoded as data. He demanded half.

'She gave in,' said Cupidi. 'But that was the day you lost the phone.'

'And my luck ran out. What are the odds the person who brings back my bag knows exactly who I am?'

Cupidi took a photograph of Michael Dillman from her envelope and put it in front of him. 'So you killed him.'

'Stupid. I panicked. I crossed a line. After that, there was no going back.'

'We never found the gun. What did you do with it?'

'Slung it in the Thames. It's a big river. I'm not stupid. I was a copper.'

She stared at him for a while, thinking of William South. 'Make sure to tell that last bit to the lads in prison too. They might be interested.'

He winced.

After the boys had stolen the phone, he had spent days in Abir

Stein's apartment in the Barbican, searching for a copy of the missing words, checking his email and post to see if Stein had left a duplicate of the list anywhere, looking for any clue about how to retrieve the money from the blockchain. He couldn't believe that nine million pounds could just disappear. Until one day the police turned up there.

'And all the time, I was trying to find the boys.'

'They were terrified.'

Next, she pulled out a picture of the dead security guard from the Co-op. 'You can't put that on me,' he said. 'Not my fault.'

Then she pulled out the picture of Tap's mother. And finally a picture of Peter Moon. She had chosen a picture from his passing-out parade. A young man in uniform, buttons shining. Mulligan's face hardened again.

It was May when they buried Peter Moon in Bybrook Cemetery. Funerals for the young always draw a bigger crowd. Every copper on the force that Cupidi knew was there, and more besides. The chapel was so full, people had to stand outside.

Standing by the coffin, McAdam said, 'He was young and ambitious. He went up to the room where he almost certainly knew a murderer might be, to save the lives of others. That is a remarkable act of a remarkable man. He knew the risk. He represents the finest among us.'

Many cried. Moon had been an only child. His mother, a small woman, stared at the crowd who'd gathered, bewildered by the event.

Afterwards they went to the local, and sat under the gentle curve of its oak eaves for drinks and sandwiches.

Ferriter was all in black. 'Did you see today's papers?' she asked.

'I've given up on them.'

'Astrid Miller's lawyers are laying out another sob story. How Evert Miller was an abusive husband.'

'What do you expect?' said Cupidi. 'It's not about whether she's going down now. It's about how long she's going down for.'

Astrid Miller's version was changing daily, as new details emerged. She had admitted using the art fund to siphon away her husband's money. The money had been rightfully hers, she said. Now she was attempting to blame the conspiracy on Stein.

'Evil cow,' said Ferriter.

'Yes.'

'I loved her. I genuinely did. Oh God,' exclaimed Ferriter. 'Oh shit. Help me, Alex.'

Mrs Moon was approaching, a glass of something dark in her hand. She looked a little drunk.

'You're Jill Ferriter, aren't you?'

'I'm very sorry for your loss. Peter was a . . .' Ferriter hesitated.

'He was a good policeman,' said Cupidi.

'Yes. He was,' said his mother. 'He talked about you a lot, Jill. He was in love with you, I think.'

Afterwards, Ferriter sat in the car and howled again. 'What was I supposed to say? "He had sex with me when I didn't want it"?'

'No. You weren't.'

'I feel so bad.'

'It's not you,' said Cupidi. 'He made those decisions himself. Every single one of them. The good ones and the bad.'

But nothing she could say could console the constable.

★

458

The summer passed. They let Frank Khan out of hospital, but he went straight back inside for breaking his Sexual Offender Prevention Order by inviting boys back to his flat.

Cupidi kept busy. She took days off, going for long walks and cycle rides. Her mother, Helen, came down to stay with a boyfriend who had been in some 1970s rock band and who did yoga naked every morning on the ridge that surrounded the houses, where all the neighbours could see him.

The opening of Ross Clough's exhibition was held the following autumn at a disused shop in the middle of the Old Town in Margate. It was called 'The Murder of Abir Stein'. Cupidi had found an invitation on her desk. A note: *I really hope you can come! I have some very special guests of honour.*

Ferriter had been hauled up in front of professional standards over being drunk and assaulting another officer. She had received a formal warning, but nothing more. Moon had never made his formal complaint. Did she want to come to the exhibition, Cupidi asked?

'Oh Jesus, no. I don't want to come. I think I'd end up killing him. You're not actually going, are you?' Ferriter had said.

They parked next to the old roller coaster and walked down to the Old Town.

Ross Clough had waited until the trials of Allan Mulligan and Astrid Miller were completed before announcing his exhibition.

The small shop was packed when they got there. The glass had steamed up because it was so full inside. People holding wine and cigarettes had spilled out onto the streets.

Their names were on a list at the door. The sculpture of Astrid

Miller sat in the middle of the room. Cupidi wondered how he had managed to get it out of the small room. He had made another one of a grotesque monkey, arm stuck in a jar.

The walls were full of drawings joined by lines of red wool. The picture of the two boys, the Long Hill estate, herself, Abir Stein and a new one of Jill Ferriter. 'He's such a letch. My boobs are never that big,' said Ferriter.

Clough had added more. On one wall was pinned a huge composite drawing of Dartford Marsh where the boys had hidden; there was also a portrait of Benjamin's mother, another murder victim.

'*Artist Ross Clough's action research project "The Murder of Abir Stein" is the only artwork which has been pivotal in solving a crime,*' Ferriter read from the catalogue. 'What bollocks.'

'It's true. He did help us form connections.'

'I hate this,' said Ferriter. 'It's all voyeurism. Aw, Christ. Look,' she said.

In a dark corner, brightened by a single spotlight, was a picture of Peter Moon. It had been copied from the *Kent Messenger*. A picture of him as a boy in a football team, taken from his bedroom wall.

'Are you all right?'

'No.' She was drinking orange juice, avoiding alcohol. 'I'm bloody not.'

Cupidi squeezed her hand.

When Ross Clough spotted them, he was delighted. 'I'm so glad you came. You are looking absolutely beautiful.' He leaned forward to kiss Ferriter on the cheek, like they did in the art world.

'Fuck off,' said Ferriter, recoiling.

'Where did you get the money for all this?' Cupidi gestured around the room.

'I have a sponsor.'

'Is that what you call it? You got the money of Evert, didn't you? In return for not telling the world about Zoya Gubenko.'

'It's a confidential arrangement,' he said. 'I can't discuss it, obviously. I'm expecting a journalist from *The Times*. I'm hoping you could speak to him. Some people from *ARTnews* too.' He stood up on his toes, scanning the room, as if concerned that they might already be here.

'I'm not sure that would be appropriate.'

'Just a few words,' said Clough.

'I'll give him a few words,' muttered Ferriter.

'Wait. Some people I want you to meet.'

'Who?'

'My guests of honour.'

He took them both by the arm and pulled them over to a corner where the two boys were standing with Joseph's mother, Felicia Watt.

'Well, there.'

'Hiya,' mumbled Sloth, shy in this unfamiliar environment.

'Keeping out of trouble?' asked Cupidi. 'They gave you community service, I heard.'

'Mum won't even let me have wine. I'm eighteen now. I should be able to do what I want.'

Tap re-appeared, clutching a plastic cup. His had red wine in it. Sloth scowled. 'He's got some, Mum.'

Cupidi laughed. 'What do you think? Of the art.'

'Total rubbish,' said Sloth. 'Tap's pretending he understands it. He's started at bloody art school now. Tap did a picture for the exhibition. You should see it.'

'Really?'

'It's way cleverer than anything Ross has done,' said Sloth. 'That's why he stuck it in this corner. He's ashamed at how much better Tap's stuff is. He's such a knob.'

'Correct,' said Ferriter.

The pencil drawing was framed. A small sign next to it said it was called *Mum*.

'I didn't know you could draw,' said Cupidi.

'See?' Sloth stood in front of it, pointing. 'That's me. Only not as good-looking as real life. He's real good though, isn't he?'

It was a picture of the bedroom in which Tap's mother had died. In the drawing, his mother wasn't dead, though; she was kneeling behind her son on the bed, just where Cupidi had been when she had been trying to persuade the drugged boy to staunch the flowing wound on his friend's neck. Tap was sitting up, cradling Sloth as the wound on his neck bled.

'I think it's a little disturbing, but he did it for his counsellor. So maybe it helps him,' Sloth's mother said.

'I think it's dead good,' said Sloth.

'So do I.' Cupidi leaned into it. The tenderness with which he held his friend.

'I kept dreaming about what happened,' said Tap. 'Because my mum was there that day. Swear to God. She had died, but she was there with me. She wouldn't leave me. I heard her telling me what to do. She told me to hold a pillow on you to stop you dying, mate. She was there with me all the time. Just like what

462

I drew. And when I was weak she helped me. She said, "Don't close your eyes. Stay awake." I felt like it was my fault she died, but she was there with me, helping me.'

Cupidi said nothing. She had noticed Ferriter's reddening eyes.

'Don't get weird again,' Sloth muttered to Tap.

'I mean, it's very good,' said Clough, seeing the press of people around it. It seemed to be attracting more attention than his own work. 'In a naive way.'

Behind his back, Sloth curled his fingers round into a circle, flexed his wrist up and down. *Tosser.* Cupidi laughed out loud.

'Tap's got a boyfriend at art school now, you know,' he said to Cupidi. 'Don't tell my mum. She'd go mental.'

'How do you feel about that?'

Sloth shrugged. 'We're still besties.'

'I'm glad. You went through a lot together.'

'Yeah. Did, didn't we?'

The crowd was thinning out. Ross Clough looked disappointed. Nobody stayed long at these events. The journalist from *The Times* had not appeared, nor the people from *ART-news.*

'It doesn't matter,' Clough said. He was drunk and looked angry. He was still on the outside, looking in.

Later, Cupidi strolled down the harbour arm with Ferriter, past the neon sign that read *I Never Stopped Loving You.*

'How's Bill?' Ferriter asked.

'Still pretty dark, but he's getting there. He's started training with an ecology company. He counts bats at night. He's obsessed with badgers.'

'Badgers? Are you serious? Actually, I wouldn't mind something like that,' said Ferriter. 'Something where all this doesn't matter.'

'Same.'

'Liar.' Ferriter punched her arm. 'You'd be lost without this.'

Cupidi quickened her pace, leaving the younger woman behind.

Only that morning she had left her desk to find an empty stall in the bathroom, locking herself in. She had been in it more often than she wanted to admit to herself, in recent weeks, on the days when she could still feel Peter Moon's cold blood soaking through the knees on her jeans. Behind the door, she would close her eyes and dig her nails into her palms and wonder how long she could keep doing this.

THANKS

Thanks to Brian Ogilvie, Lisa Cutts (several times), Rebecca Bradley (again, several times), Graham Bartlett and Michaela Crimmin for advice, Karolina Sutton and, as always, to Jane McMorrow. And, again as always, to the awesome foursome: Roz Brody, Mike Holmes, Jann King and CJ Sansom.